T0354668

BOLSHEVIK LEGACY

BOLSHEVIK LEGACY

The Intrasyn Conspiracy

CANAH BUNDY

PARTRIDGE
A Penguin Random House Company

To order additional copies of this book, contact
Partridge India
000 800 10062 62
orders.india@partridgepublishing.com

www.partridgepublishing.com/india

Comments from Critics
& Eminent Authors

'Reads well'- by Arthur C Clarke the author of 2001 A Space
Odyssey

Prologue

Yorbachev looked out of the window from his office, the afternoon sun was bright and he could see children playing in the park across the street. He turned towards the door as he heard footsteps approaching. He was expecting Pushkin, it was the 11th of March 1985.

Pushkin walked in smiling, there were others seated around in the room, Zhirnovsky, Albakin, Sorovsky and Yeltsin.

He walked towards Yorbachev, held out his hand, 'Congratulations Secretary, you are the first General Secretary of the Communist Party to have been elected after the revolution.'

There was a buzz in the room as the others went around shaking the hand of Yorbachev.

It was time to celebrate, Pushkin poured out the drinks and the men around helped themselves to a glass. They raised their glasses in a toast and downed it, refilled their glasses and took their places around the table. Yorbachev was waiting for them, to plan for their date with destiny, the 30th of October 2017, the centenary of the Bolshevik Revolution. They had a lot to do to achieve their dream, to realise their legacy, The Bolshevik Legacy.

International Trading Syndicate would be formed as a legitimate trading organisation headquartered at Muhu in Estonia, with the members present as the founding members. The organisation would generate money, large amounts of money, by any means.

They spent the rest of the day working on their plan and arrived at a consensus, they would set in motion a movement which would build an opposition in Russia headed by Yeltsin, later they would stage manage the sacking of Yeltsin and work towards the election of Yeltsin as the President of Russia. Soviet troops would be withdrawn from Afghanistan to pave the way for increased American influence, a strategy through which the Americans would be bogged down in Afghanistan for decades. The Rouble would be devalued and private ownership of businesses and property allowed. Privatisation would enable influx of American and European funds, and would eventually increase the strength of their communist brethren, the DSP in USA and the PES in Europe. As a reformed Party, all political prisoners and dissidents would be released and steps would be taken to allow the Berlin wall to be pulled down, when the opportunity arose, and without showing any weakness.

This would be achieved by the end of 1991. Once accomplished, Yorbachev would resign as President of the USSR, declare the office as extinct and cede all powers to Yeltsin the President of Russia.

Yorbachev and Pushkin would focus on the larger agenda of Intrasyn, one of which was the infiltration of Intrasyn personnel in key positions of Russia, Ukraine and Belarus.

Intrasyn would have a covert arm, staffed with men who owed them allegiance drawn from the KGB and the armed forces. Incumbents in key positions would be eliminated, if they were not Intrasyn men, and replaced. By the year 2004, Intrasyn would control all policy, and the armed forces and intelligence services in Russia, Ukraine and Belarus.

Intrasyn would grow as an international conglomerate and control world trade in nuclear materials, petroleum products and commodities, starting with Russia. They would engineer this with the influence they had in Russia, Ukraine and Belarus and the war chest created by Intrasyn.

To achieve world dominance, they would re-draw the borders of Russia and Europe, rebuild the Communist Party of USA and unseat the Republicans from the White House. Olamide a comrade in the American establishment, had been identified, he had been moulded by David Frank Marshall, and would be their choice to lead the Democratic party in the future. Sorovsky would provide funds for Olamide's election to the US Senate and later for the U S Presidency.

The stage was set for The Intrasyn Conspiracy.

Chapter 1

Date: 25th August 1999. Place: Moscow. Time: 3 pm

Mogrovsky was a Colonel in the Russian army, now assigned to special duties in the Otryady Militsii Osobennogo, also known as the OMON, or the 'Black Berets' an arm of the Interior Ministry. He had been a brilliant soldier and had served time in Afghanistan. He was particularly loyal to Boris Grachev, the first Deputy Interior Minister.

Mogrovsky studied the latest report received on Siberia. The report highlighted the state of Tyumen; that in spite of producing 70 per cent of Russia's oil and gas, it had the lowest standard of living in Russia.

Mogrovsky was interrupted as the red light lit up on his desk, which signalled that his secretary had received an important document. He pressed the intercom button.

'A dispatch from ministry sir', his secretary said. 'Bring it in right away', he said, putting aside the report. She came in with the envelope and handed it to Mogrovsky. The envelope had a red border, signifying it had come from a senior Kremlin official. He looked at the top right hand corner, sat upright when he realised whom it had come from, tore open the envelope and hastily pulled out the two sheets of paper.

'Comrades, this is a critical hour for our motherland and our people. A great danger looms over us, the policy of reform at the initiative of our leaders as a means to ensure our freedom and development is in danger. It is being undermined by those who are unwilling to move down the path of progress…… those that must be sacrificed for the greater good of the country'.

Mogrovsky read the rest of the note and turned his attention to the paper enclosed with the note. As he read it, he felt the familiar thump in his chest. The paper was authorisation by the group, each member had signed.

Grachev had briefed Mogrovsky a couple of months earlier on what was expected of him. He was to await the location and authorisation, which he now held. He burnt the notes, as instructed after reading the note twice.

'Cerkessk', said Mogrovsky aloud, he had heard of the discontent that was being voiced there. He walked across the room to his filing cabinet and picked out the file on Cerkessk.

Chapter 2

Date: 29th August 1999 Place: Moscow
Time: 10.30 am

The village of Cerkessk was situated in a valley in the Krasnodar region, across the hillock, on the right bank of the Kuban. The village was in the lower reaches of the Adygeja Mountains, surrounded by hills and dense forests. The population was small with only about four hundred inhabitants. Their primary occupation was farming. The village was known for its political influence and its pro-communist stance. It was vehement in its criticism of 'Glasnost'. The village was known to have many active supporters in the Soviet Politburo, who foresaw the breakup of communism as the beginning of US imperialistic dominance. A sizeable number of pro-communist Politburo members had in fact originated from Cerkessk.

Mogrovsky spent an hour reading, focussing on the politics of the region and indeed of the village. Many ideas had originated from Cerkessk, which had had a profound influence in Russia's politics. He thought about it long and hard. The problem was similar in every aspect to Riga, with one exception, the region and indeed the village was politically more volatile.

He buzzed for his secretary.

She walked in, 'Yes sir?'

'I want to see Bukovsky', he said.

'Yes sir, I'll send word'.

3

He thought for a moment, Bukovsky would have a long way to travel. 'Make it Monday, next week', he confirmed.

Major Bukovsky was tall and heavily built, with close set eyes, a narrow forehead and a square heavy jaw. He had a knife scar along the right cheek which gave his face a very cruel appearance. The scar was the result of an encounter with a group of afghan soldiers. Major Bukovsky was the only man who had walked out of that fight alive. An ex-KGB officer, he had moved to the OMON at the behest of Mogrovsky. He was a loner and had no family or friends, his companion was a black Doberman.

Bukovsky was known to be ruthless, with no feelings, which was perfect for the task Colonel Morgovsky had set for him, Bukovsky owed him total allegiance. Bukovsky was known among his OMON colleagues as the 'Executioner'.

Mogrovsky's office was in an apartment block in an obscure neighbourhood of Moscow. The OMON did not exactly publicise its presence. All OMON personnel drove unmarked cars. To the common man on the street, the OMON was just another government establishment.

It was eleven in the morning when Bukovsky stepped out of the taxi opposite the non-descript building and entered the common lobby. He brushed past an elderly couple, almost knocking down the old woman. The old man accompanying her said sharply, 'Look where you're going'. Bukovsky turned and scowled so fiercely that the old man recoiled from the gaze, muttered something to himself and helped the old woman through the door.

Bukovsky reached a landing where a board read 'Office of Statistics'. He pushed through the heavy door, through a small reception with chairs, magazines and a small rack full of statistical publications and then through yet another heavy door into a small office. Here a woman looked up enquiringly. He did not bother to stop and went through to an inner office.

A pretty young woman in her late twenties looked up from her console. The console had displayed his photograph from hidden cameras at the entrance to the building. She had already compared his photograph and his physical characteristics with those held on file and cleared him, or he would have found himself locked in, in the front office.

She pressed the intercom and announced, 'Sir, Major Bukovsky is here'.

'Send him in', came the reply.

Bukovsky took off his overcoat, knocked on the door and walked into Mogrovsky's office.

'Good Morning Sir', he said, standing to attention after entering the room.

'Good Morning Bukovsky', said Mogrovsky, returning the greeting.

'At ease, you look well. Take a seat', said Mogrovsky.

Bukovsky walked to the settee. 'What will you drink?' Mogrovsky added.

'Vodka Sir, thank you', Bukovsky replied and continued standing.

Mogrovsky went to his cabinet, he reached in, took out two fine cut glasses and a bottle of Genghis Khan, which was his favourite. He poured out two stiff drinks. He handed one to Bukovsky. Mogrovsky walked around to the sofa and sat down. He beckoned to Bukovsky who walked across the room and settled himself into one of the single seaters facing Mogrovsky.

'We have a problem at Cerkessk, similar to the one at Riga', Mogrovsky took out his tobacco pouch to fill his pipe. 'Yes, I've heard of the problem', Bukovsky replied and moved his bulk to sit upright. He hated settees, which were soft.

Mogrovsky lit his pipe and blew a cloud of smoke towards the ceiling. 'The Interior Minister has asked me to deal with it', he paused to tamp his pipe.

'He wants this to be an example. He suspects we were not firm enough at Riga. There were too many survivors'.

Bukovsky listened intently.

'Cerkessk is a small secluded village with a small population' he remarked, 'it will not be a problem'.

'There will be an investigation. There can be no trace.' he paused. He looked at Bukovsky, holding his gaze, to say he meant business. 'If it leads back to you, you will be on your own'.

'I understand' said Bukovsky, returning the stare with his cold eyes. 'There will be no trace'.

Mogrovsky raised his glass, Bukovsky raised his. They downed the Vodka in a gulp. Mogrovsly put his glass down and stood up, signalling an end to the discussion. Bukovsky sprang to his feet.

'Good luck Bukovsky', Mogrovsky said holding out his hand. Bukovsky took the outstretched hand in a firm handshake. 'Thank you Sir, it will be done'.

Chapter 3

Date: 14th September 1999 Place: Moscow,
Time: 2.00 pm

Bukovsky knew he had to select his men from the OMON's
Special Purpose Unit.

Bukovsky made a list of twelve OMON 'Black Berets'.
These were the OMON's with whom he had worked in the
past, at Riga.

He had hand-picked them after going through their
backgrounds. He made sure, each was a loner, without
family, friends or girlfriends. Nor did they have any political
affiliations. The only quality that defined them was their
expertise in all forms of combat. They were currently with the
GRU Spetsnaz, an equivalent of the British SAS. After the
Riga operation, he had seen to it that they were dispersed with
changed identities in the many units operating in the western
part of Russia.

Bukovsky went into the records office in Moscow.
Mogrovsky had already arranged with the head of the records
for Bukovsky to go through the files, without the search
being logged. The records were in files, they hadn't been
computerised. He took a pen, writing pad, a bottle of vodka
and a glass along with him. It was going to be a long night, he
had to locate each of them, starting from the unit they were
posted to, and then work through to their current stations.

Mogrovsky chose a table at the corner, where he would be
able to observe the entire room. He went to the shelves and

picked out twelve files, carried them back to the table. He settled down, poured himself a generous shot from the bottle and picked up the first file.

The bottle of vodka was half-finished when Bukovsky looked at the clock on the wall. It was two-thirty in the morning. He rubbed his eyes, they felt like they had been glued together. He had managed to locate eleven of them, one had been killed in a covert operation in Afghanistan.

In the morning, back in his office, Bukovsky worked out a posting order for each of the eleven. They were to be assigned on special duties to his unit known as 'Special Operations' within the OMON. He made sure the move looked routine and made up a separate requisition to each unit with requirements that fitted each of the men. To avoid any comebacks to Mogrovsky, and Boris Grachev he arranged to have the requisition sent out by a Deputy Interior Minister handling personnel.

Within a week, the eleven had reported to Bukovsky. Each man was fighting fit. There was an air of excitement, they knew Bukovsky, knew what turned the man on. The one thing they all had in common was that they were killers, and enjoyed it.

He talked to them briefly on the current situation in Russia, the problems being faced by it, and the need to take action to set an example. There were no specifics, it was strictly on a need to know basis.

Chapter 4

Date: 30th October 1999, Place: Cerkessk,
Time: 9:45 a.m.

Starky, his real name Yushenko Garin, was a drunk. He was in a constant liquor induced stupor, which made him unsteady. Closer inspection would have shown a broad muscular frame. His unkempt hair and frayed clothes gave him the appearance of a tramp. He was from Riga. The people of Cerkessk tolerated him, since he was brought to Cerkessk after the massacre by Nina Andreyava and her husband, where they had found him wandering around in daze.

It was well known that he had been a member of an elite corps which had fought in Afghanistan and Chechnya, he had been decorated for his bravery, having saved many of his comrades during a firefight.

His family, a wife and a child had been killed during a massacre at Riga. The event had received wide publicity in the world and it was suspected to be the handiwork of the government. The government had put it down to a drug related war, and the case was closed. Starky had since turned to liquor for solace. His daily needs were taken care of by the state through a meager allowance, his residence was a room in the bell tower of the local church overlooking the village courtyard.

The village was built in the style of the early nineteenth century. The houses were typically made of wood. The church and the courtyard formed the main square in the village.

Unlike the Russian churches, this church stood out as one of the rare Gothic structures. Even though it had hints of Baroque detailing, it was essentially similar to the churches found in the southern parts of Germany, along the Rhine in the Black Forest region. The church had both Baroque and Gothic influences in its design, the exterior boasted of great pointed arches, inside, the walls and pillars showed off the wood work. The roof was made of stone and the sunlight filtered through beautiful stained glass windows. The church and the courtyard formed the main venue for any activity of significance in the village.

It was late morning, Starky was awakened by a cacophony of sound. He was glad he was awake. His dreams had not been pleasant. He tumbled out of his make-shift bed and stumbled as he tried to stand up, the effects of the vodka still very much in evidence. He peered through the small window. The courtyard was already full. The village folk were engaged in setting up tables and chairs.

A small stage was being erected. The village was getting ready for a celebration.

Starky grinned. Celebrations always meant plenty of food and drink. Starky pushed himself away from the window. Pulled on his shoes and half stumbled half slid down the stairs. It was mid-day and the sun was bright. Starky blinked momentarily blinded by the sun, stumbled through the doorway and into the path of a couple.

"Sorry", he mumbled, his liquor-laden breath, making the nearest man turns his face away in disgust.

'He's such a disgrace, needs to be disciplined!" said the disgusted villager,

"He's mentally unsound, and should be sent to a home", said his wife.

"It's been tried, he was sent to Krasnodar but slipped out one morning and stowed away on a freight train".

'Don't be too harsh on him' said Nina Andreyava, who was walking close by,' he's been through hell.'

Starky steadied himself, and nodded his thanks to Andreyava.

"Yuri, Irina and Dmitri should be here soon", said Nina Andreyeva, Irina's mother, trying to change the subject. "I hope they make it before four, it's usually dark by four-thirty".

They made their way to the office. The communist party office was located at the far end of the courtyard. It was the 30th of October. The anniversary of the revolution, when the workers led by Lenin had overthrown the provisional government. It was a day of celebration in the Soviet Union, the day that marked the end of the Romanov dynasty.

Starky watched for a while as the preparations were made and decided to go back for a nap till it was time.

Chapter 5

Date: 30th October 1999,
Place: Krasnodar Airport, Time: 11.00 am

The Krasnodar airport was small with parking off to one side. The main road ran along the front of the airport.

Dmitri and Yuri arrived by plane at 11 am from Volgograd. They went straight to the information desk.

Dmitri asked the girl behind the counter, 'When is the flight from Moscow due?'

'There has been a lot of fog in Moscow and the flight had to be delayed. It is expected to arrive around 1230 hours', she replied.

'Oh damn', Yuri swore under his breath, 'I hope it isn't delayed further'.

'No sir, the flight has taken off and the weather here is fine, so it should be here by 12:30'.

Dmitri and Yuri had finished their stint in the army and planned to take a break before deciding on their future plans. Irina had resigned her job as a junior political editor in Tass, the official Soviet news agency. She had decided to move into politics and was planning to spend some time with her parents at Cerkessk. They had by previous arrangement agreed to meet at the airport at Krasnodar for the three hundred-kilometre journey by road to Cerkessk.

Dmitri was tall, blond, broad shouldered and heavily built. He sported a crew cut. He was also known for his quick temper. Yuri was the opposite of Dmitri, slim, medium height, fairly long hair with finely cut features – an aquiline nose and a high forehead. He looked the classic scholar. He loved debate and had a sharp wit. Irina was tall and very attractive, with auburn hair, blue grey eyes, a firm mouth and elegant legs.

'Let's go down to the Vostok and have a couple of vodkas while we wait', Dmitri said, picking up his bag.

The Vostok was close to the airport and was one of the best eating places in Krasnodar, it boasted a large bar and a jukebox.

'Let's pick up our transport first', Yuri said pushing Dmitri towards the depot at the far end of the airport.

'We can put away our bags and won't have to spend time after Irina arrives. As it stands we will only have time for a quick lunch, we have to leave here by 2:00pm'.

Dmitri nodded, 'You're right, let's get the transport settled'.

'Which route are you planning to take?', Yuri asked.

'The Majkop-Labinsk route. The heavy rains in the Adygeja Mountains have weakened the smaller roads, so we'll have to try and make it before it gets too dark'.

They walked to the army depot, showed their ID at the gate and were shown inside the major's office. The major was a surly, middle aged man with a bloated face, from too much of vodka and too little exercise. They saluted. He sloppily returned the salute sitting at his desk.

'Good morning Comrades, what can I do for you?'

'We've come to pick up a transport Sir', Yuri said, reaching into his pocket for the warrant authorising the release.

The major read the warrant, 'Ah, so you are the sons of Ustinov and Pavlov', he said half to himself. He rang a bell and an orderly appeared. 'Release the half tonner', he instructed.

'The truck must be returned on the third day by 5 pm', he muttered towards Dmitri and Yuri.

They nodded their understanding. Yuri signed the slip the major pushed towards him.

The major reached into his desk drawer and dumped the keys on the table.

Dmitri picked up the keys, 'Thank You Sir'.

Yuri reached their half tonner and loaded his bags at the rear. The two got in, with Dmitri behind the wheel. They drove towards the Vostok.

The Vostok had not changed, they ordered vodka and toasted each other before downing them and then ordered a second round. Yuri checked his watch impatiently.

'We've got plenty of time', Dmitri said nodding at Yuri's watch, 'time for a few rounds'.

At 12:15 Yuri rose, put some cash on the table and said 'let's go'. Dmitri nodded, tossed back his drink and the two made their way to the truck.

Dmitri and Yuri entered the airport to hear the announcement that the flight from Moscow had arrived. They eagerly made their way to the arrival hall, in time to see Irina in light blue slacks looking around for them. They shouted out to her. She turned around saw them and ran towards them. She reached Yuri first, they hugged and kissed. Then she turned to Dmitri who picked her up in a bear hug and then set her down.

'Yuri, Dmitri', she laughed, her eyes sparkling with delight. 'It's so marvellous to see you'. She linked her arms through theirs while they carried her bags and made their way to the exit.

'Let's have a quick lunch at the Vostok, then we'll head for home', Yuri proposed.

'I'm starved, I could eat a horse', Irina added.

They made their way to the Vostok, and picked a table at the corner with a good view. Dmitri helped Irina with her jacket and held the chair for her. When they had settled down he caught the waiter's eye. The waiter came around with the wine list and the food menu.

'I'll have some red wine' Irina said looking at the waiter.

'Some vodka for me', Dmitri said.

'Some beer for me' Yuri replied and added, 'we'll order the food now', he looked at Irina.

She glance at the menu and ordered, 'Krasnodar roast beef and potatoes'. That was the speciality of the Vostok.

'That sounds good to me, I'll have the same', Dmitri butted in.

'Make it three', said Yuri to the waiter.

The waiter left and returned a few minutes later with their drinks.

'To the future', proposed Irina.

'The future', Dmitri and Yuri joined in.

Irina looked at them. She had grown up with them, they were more than friends. Theirs was a deep bond, they had known each other from childhood. Their parents were also friends, being prominent political figures in the region.

'A penny for your thoughts', Yuri said, looking at her face.

She smiled, 'it's so good to be back, so good to see you both', she paused. 'How long will you be here?'

'We plan to spend four whole weeks', Yuri smiled back, 'and you?' he asked.

'I'm on a three month break, decided to spend time at home. I need to decide on what I want to do'.

'So you're not planning on going back to Tass', Yuri asked.

Irina shook her head. 'No, I would like to get into politics'.

Yuri looked at her, she would make a good politician.

'How's Moscow?' queried Dmitri. 'I hear there is a lot of uncertainty in the Kremlin?'

'Yes, it's true, with the Warsaw Pact dissolved, NATO is flexing its muscles. Corruption is rampant in the government, with no solutions in sight'.

The waiter brought them their meal, served them and left.

Yuri looked at his watch, it was 2pm. 'I think we should eat and try to move on by 3pm, we only have an hour or so of sunlight, and the roads are not very good. We need to reach by eight if we are to take part in the celebrations.'

Both Dmitri and Irina nodded. They ate quickly, enjoying the food and each other's company. They finished their meal, ordered an apple pie for desert and strong black coffee, the special Krasnodar brew. Yuri called for the bill and left a hefty tip for the waiter.

Dmitri helped Irina into her jacket and the three got in the front. Dmitri took the wheel, for the ride home, through the Adygeja Mountains.

As Dmitri swung the jeep around he glanced up at the airport clock, it read twenty past three.

Chapter 6

Date: 30th October 1999, Place: Cerkessk,
Time: 5.55 pm

The two-truck convoy set out from Tbilisi on the A301 towards Kazbegi. The moon was bright and reflected off the plain canopy. The trucks had no number plates and were unmarked. To an observer they were army trucks, possibly out on an exercise.

Before they reached Kazbegi they turned off the main road taking the Ingusheta route through the mountains. The route was seldom used since it was hilly, and the roads were poorly maintained. This and the heavy rains made driving difficult and dangerous. The only advantage was that it afforded some secrecy. The route took them across the river Sanza and towards Gudermes.

The entire area was covered with pine, which provided excellent cover. During the two days they drove across the Adyejas, they did not come across a person or vehicle. They reached the outskirts of Novi Atagi in the early evening of the second day and set up camp. They came off the road onto an unpaved track suitable only for four wheel drives. The track led to a small clearing in the pine forest. They were now in a valley, separated from Cerkessk by a hill.

At 6 p.m. Bukovsky called his men around him. He pinned a map of the area and a plan of the village of Cerkessk to the canopy of a truck. The village was quite compact, with all the houses around the main courtyard. There were only three entrances to the courtyard, each of them about twenty feet wide. The church made up the fourth side of the courtyard.

All the residents of the village would be at the celebrations at the courtyard. It would be a simple operation, no resistance was expected as they would all be unprepared. It would be necessary for the group to split up and take position at the three entrances to prevent anyone getting away. The church would have to be secured which meant locking the doors into the church from the courtyard.

Bukovsky assigned two of his men who doubled as drivers the task of securing the church. The two would return to the trucks to prepare for their getaway.

The other nine men were split into three groups, each group responsible for one of the entrances to the courtyard. Bukovsky would position himself at the main entrance, from where he would give the signal to begin.

Each man had been issued with a Uzi machine pistol, twenty clips of ammunition, six hand grenades, a Walther PPK automatic with two clips, and a 'Rambo' type hunting knife. The weapons, ammunition and the grenades had no markings. The men carried no identification and wore non-descript black uniforms and balaclavas.

They got into their trucks and set out for the half-hour journey to Cerkessk. Bukovsky checked his watch, it was 7:00 p.m., the festivities would be in full swing by the time they reached the village.

Bukovsky and his men reached the outskirts of Cerkessk at 7:35 p.m., it was dark. As they crested the hill with their lights switched off they could hear music. The courtyard was lit up and decorated with streamers and balloons, the entire village population was at the courtyard.

Bukovsky instructed the drivers to park the trucks behind a clump of trees just off the main road, about a kilometre from the village. There were only two routes into the village, one through the hills that Bukovsky had taken and the other through the valley. The valley road was the main thoroughfare into and out of the Cerkessk.

The drivers parked the trucks after turning them around in the direction they had come. The others got out and checked their loaded weapons.

The two drivers, on a signal from Bukovsky, started off towards the village church making sure they stayed low. Bukovsky and the rest moved off towards the left and took position near a clum of bushes waiting for the signal from the drivers.

The two drivers reached the church by the rear. There was no one around and no lights in any of the rooms above the church. The only lights which were lit were in the church. They tried the doors at the rear of the church, which led to the living quarters and found them locked. They decided to try one of the side doors, this meant moving out in the open.

The celebrations were on full swing, the music was loud and a large group was dancing. Most of the younger folk were on the floor dancing while a group of older men and women were clapping to the rhythm.

The two moved along the wall of the church around the corner and were startled by the bark of a dog. The creature took off with a yelp frightened by their appearance. The dog ran into the courtyard, stopped and turned back to look at them. The two froze as a young boy approached the dog and started petting it. The dog started wagging its tail looking back now and then. The boy kept stroking its head and neck and after awhile, the boy and the dog walked away.

The two crept along the wall and reached a side door leading into the church. They tried the door and found it unlocked. They stepped in, closed the door behind them and quickly crossed over to the main door, locked and secured it. They went around the church locking all the doors from the inside. No one would be able to enter the church unless the doors were broken down. Each door was ten foot in height and made of solid oak. Explosives or cutting tools would be required to break down a door.

The two then made their way to the rear of the church through the living quarters of the priest. They found the exit to the rear of the church and stepped out. One of them took out an explosive device and set it up against the door. He pulled out the trip wire and hooked it across the door such that any attempt to open the door would set off the explosive. His task finished, he pointed a small pencil like object towards at the clump of the trees and pressed a button. Bukovsky, watching through his infrared binoculars picked up the signal. It signalled that the church had been secured, it was time to put the rest of the plan into action.

The rest split up into three groups with Bukovsky leading one. They synchronised their watches, the time was exactly 7:48 pm.

Bukovsky looked at his men.

'This operation should take at most half an hour, we must regroup at the trucks at 8.30 p.m. If there is any resistance, and causalities on our side, which is unlikely, I want the man or men brought in. We are not to leave any trace,' he looked around at the men, who nodded in agreement.

'Let's go', with that he led off down the hill in a crouch.

As they neared the village - the group split into three. As prearranged, Bukovsky with his team reached the dwellings at the edge of the village. They did a quick check, there was no one around, and then moved from doorway to doorway, keeping to the shadows as much as possible. As they moved closer, the music and singing became louder, they could hear clapping and shouting. It was obvious that the whole village was at the square and having a good time.

Bukovsky and his team reached the entrance to the square and moved into the shadows. He looked at his watch it was 7.59

p.m. He looked across to the left and the right, they would have reached before him. His position being the main entrance to the square was located farthest from where they parked the trucks.

Date: 30ᵗʰ October 1999, Place: Argun, Time 5.55 pm

Dimitri set off towards the Adyejas. The weather was changing, the light wind was becoming stronger. He looked up at the sky, clouds were gathering, and it started raining. It was a light drizzle, a heavy rain would slow them down substantially. He drove at a good pace, and when the drizzle stopped he was able to drive faster. The terrain and the road restricted any real speed.

They reached Argun at six. Argun was about one hundred and ten kilometres from Krasnodar. They had been on the road for more than two hours.

Irina wanted a drink so they pulled into a small eating-place 'The Yanni' at the end of the village. As was common in those parts the restaurant was a home with the front room converted into a large dining area. It was run by a middle-aged couple. The couple looked forward to visitors, it gave them a chance to get up to date with the news of the region. They ordered coffee and stretched. The man hovered around asking questions about who they were, where they came from and where they were headed. They finished their coffee and set out. The clock read twenty minutes past six.

They reached the main road, leading into Cerkessk from Armavir at seven. Though they had only thirty kilometres to go, the road crossed small hillocks and wound around larger hills so they expected to make it to Cerkessk in about an hour. A little later than expected, but in time, nonetheless to take part in the celebrations.

They reached the top of a small hillock from where they could look down into the valley and Cerkessk. As the crow flies the distance was only five kilometres, though the road took them through a full twelve kilometres, the time was seven fifty nine. Dimtri drove off the road onto the shoulder and turned off the motor. They got down from the truck and could see the flickering of the bright lights in the courtyard and the faint sounds of music.

Date: 30th October 1999, Place: Cerkessk, Time 7.58 pm

Bukovsky slid the safety off his Uzi and paused. The band had just finished a tune; the people were milling around. The girls and boys together, the men were standing around the beer kegs while others were helping themselves to vodka. The band began to play another tune.

Bukovsky pointed the Uzi towards the group of men and pressed the trigger. One man was hit as he raised his glass to his mouth, his friend turned, bewildered, the next moment his face was a mass of blood. He dropped where he stood.

As if on cue, eight other Uzis opened up, each gun targeted a group. There were shrieks and wails. The crowd did not know what was happening. People ran trying to get out of the volley of bullets. Men ran around blindly looking for their families, only to be cut down. Women ran to their children. A mother picked up her small son and turned to run, a burst caught her in the back. She was lifted from the ground, almost cut in two. The child's body riddled by armour piercing bullet fell from her hands. At the far end, a group of men shielded their women, trying to use their bodies to protect them, two Uzis cut them down where they stood.

A few of the men and women, ran to the church door, led by the priest. They reached the door only to find it locked. Bukovksy, expecting this, swung the Uzi around, catching the group in the crossfire. They stood no chance. They were dead before they hit the ground, the door of the church crimson with the blood of the victims.

It was all over in a few minutes, not a single person was standing. The whole courtyard was a mass of bodies. There were men, women and children, the whole scene looked unreal. The band and its players were cut to bits by the heavy calibre bullets, the make shift stage smashed.

Bukovsky took a quick look around, he gave a command. His men lowered their guns and reached for the grenades in their belts. They retreated back towards the direction of their trucks. When they had gone back from the edge of the courtyard, they lobbed the grenades into the courtyard in every direction, and fell flat to the ground. The grenades went off with a flash in quick succession, a string of explosions. This was to ensure that there were no survivors, if any had lived through the hail of bullets.

Bukovsky took a final look around and beckoned to his men. They regrouped and set off for their trucks. The drivers had the motors turning, and they were on their way. Bukovsky checked his watch, it read twenty five past eight.

The men would report back to their units a week later, their bank accounts considerably enhanced. There would be no group to trace.

Chapter 7

Date: 30th October 1999, Place Adyejas,
Time: 8.05 pm

Dmitri, Irina and Yuri looked bewildered. Irina turned to Dmitri and Yuri, wide eyed. She grabbed Yuri's arm, 'Wh.. What is that?', she stammered.

'It sounds like guns, its coming from the village', said Yuri, completing her sentence.

Yuri looked at Dmitri, half shocked, half in disbelief. Dmitri was staring in the direction of the village intently.

'Something's happening, let's go'. With that, Dimtri jumped into the truck. Yuri helped Irina in, and jumped in himself. Dmitri sped down the hill careening around the curves. Yuri held on to the handgrip and Irina held onto him. Dmitri drove like a mad man, the chatter of the machine guns growing louder. It seemed to go on for an eternity, then suddenly fell silent. After about a minute, or half a minute, they heard the dull thump of a series of explosions.

They tore down the hill onto the flat stretch of road leading to the main street that led to the courtyard. Dmitri drove right through the village. He slammed his brakes, the tyres screeching, as the truck came to a halt slewing around.

It was eerily quiet, there were no sounds whatsoever. The bodies were strewn across the courtyard. They jumped out of the truck and looked around, wide-eyed, in disbelief. A cry escaped from Irina as she saw the carnage. She stumbled. She grabbed Dmitri's arm, as she collapsed and fainted. Yuri reached for her as she fell and gently eased her onto the cobbled stone of the courtyard. Dmitri knelt down, his mind in a whirl.

The sight was sickening, Yuri ran to a corner feeling sick in the stomach. Dmitri looked dazed. Irina recovered and managed to stand up. The three held each other, kneeling, while Irina started crying. They knew their parents were there somewhere. They got up and walked around, looking at the corpses, the mangled and dismembered bodies, they saw the bodies of their friends, relatives and loved ones, young and old.

She found the bodies of her parents at the far end, against the wall. The bodies had been blackened by the blast of the explosives. She saw Dmitri's and Yuri's parents close by. The faces of the men were without injury, but their backs were riddled with bullets.

Irina went forward, put out her hand to touch her parents, a cry escaped her lips, a cry full of grief and despair. Dmitri looked at his father, and fell on the ground next to him.

Yuri, still in a daze, went to the phone in the village office. He dialled the emergency number and blurted incoherently to the operator, 'there has been a mass...massacre at Cerkessk, send an ambulance, ambulance', he stuttered. He repeated the message twice before the operator understood him.

As they looked at the carnage, they heard a moan from among the bodies. They quickly moved the pile of charred and broken bodies and looked down at an unkempt old man who was covered in blood. He was trying to get up. Dmitri told him to keep still and wait for the ambulance. He waved his hands and slurred, 'I'm not hurt'. The man waved his arms about in an effort to hold onto something to help himself up. Dmitri helped him up, the grip of the man strong, belying his looks, the man was well built, was not hurt, but very drunk.

Starky was mumbling something, when Irina and Yuri joined Dimitri, 'you are the daughter of Andreyava,' he exclaimed, then seeing Yuri and Dimitri, 'and the sons of Ustinov and Pavlov,' he looked around, wide eyed seeing the bodies, the bloody scene and the realisation that they were all dead,' what happened, he half said to himself, this is like Riga,' he stood up straight the sight of the bodies sobering him, 'I can help.'

Dimitri helped him to a side and made him sit down.

They went around, looking for the wounded, to try and help in any way. Yuri ran to the medical centre and using a stool rammed down the door. He came back with bandages, gauze, splints, disinfectant and anything else he could lay his hands on. Together with Irina, they moved as much of the supplies as they could to the courtyard. They started to systematically check each body for signs of life. Most of them were dead, and those that were wounded urgently needed specialist attention that only a hospital could provide. Their wounds were horrific. The three of them looked at the wounded in despair. There was no way they could save these people.

They made their way to church; they could see Father Peter's body. It was surprising that the front door of the church was locked. Dmitri realised the door was locked from the inside. He went around the church, checking each door. All were locked from the inside except for the rear door, which was unlocked. He tried the handle and it turned. He was about to push the door open but a sixth sense made him pause and look around. He a saw a faint reflection. Puzzled, he put his hand out and felt the wire. He froze, realising it was a trip wire. He saw it then, the fine trip wire at knee height that led to a small box. He recognised the explosive. The insurgents in Afghanistan had used this, it was American made, they had supplied similar munitions to the insurgents through Pakistan.

Dmitri carefully reached down to the explosive and disarmed it. Then removed the trip wire and the explosive and hid it under a nearby bush. He opened the door and went through to the main door which he unlocked. The bodies stacked against the door fell in as he opened the doors. Yuri joined him to move the bodies to a side, laying them in a line.

Dimitri cautioned Yuri and Irina that the doors could be booby trapped and told them to check for trip wires when opening any door. They moved the wounded as best as they could into the church, laying them on the church benches and covering them with blankets to keep them warm. They worked tirelessly, knowing that for most of the wounded, time was running out. The ambulances had to come from Novi Atagi, a good twenty miles away.

The first of the ambulances arrived, it had taken forty-five minutes from the time Yuri had made his call. The paramedics took one look at the carnage, exchanged a few words, and one of them stepped into the rear of his van and spoke rapidly into his wireless. Within the hour, ten ambulances and three fire engines had reached the scene with the police and the army. A helicopter landed nearby with five doctors and nurses.

Dmitri, Irina and Yuri, exhausted and numb from grief, sat slumped in a corner of the church. Near them slept Starky in a drunken slumber.

The next morning saw the arrival of senior officers from the police and the interior ministry. The three were taken to the communist party office in the village and made to sit down by a senior police officer. Present were a colonel from army intelligence and a major from the interior ministry. They listened to the questions and gave their questioners a detailed sequence of their movements in the last twenty-four hours. Dmitri showed them the explosive and the trip wire he retrieved.

In the meanwhile the police scoured the surrounding area and found hundreds of empty shells. Fragments of grenades showed no markings but were of American origin based on the design. Whoever had committed the crime had disappeared into thin air. The colonel from army intelligence and the police conferred and called in an aide to send a message to the authorities in all surrounding villages, to all airports, airfields and ports to look for anything out of the ordinary. They were specifically asked to look out for strangers moving in a group.

Chapter 8

Date: 31st October 1999, Place: Moscow, Time: 9.15 am

General Pushkin an influential member of the Russian politburo from Krasnodar was waiting impatiently for Pavlovsky, the Deputy Chief of Ukraine Security who was on a visit to Moscow.

Pavlovsky was a Russian who had been moved prior to glasnost to Ukraine. He was a staunch communist and one of the reasons for his ouster was to get him out of the way to weaken the pro-communists in Russia. Pavlovsky had his own connections, foremost was General Pushkin.

On the day after Cerkessk, Pushkin met the Intrasyn Council. Pushkin briefed them about the events at Cerkessk, and his suspicions that the hawks in the government and politburo were behind the killing.

Pushkin also listed the broad strategies for their mission. Once agreed, he would assign teams for their specific tasks. He had shortlisted the areas that would need to focus on, to bring about the collapse of the American Democratic System.

'The American people believe in success and money. These attributes are the key drivers of their economy. We need to break the confidence of the American people in their financial system. We know it is riddled with corruption, lax controls and a politician business nexus which can be manipulated to undermine federal controls', he announced.

He explained that one of the ways to do this would be to manipulate prominent corporations with a wide stakeholder base, within the American economy. The first step would be to achieve staggering growth in stakeholder value, then destabilize the corporation through market forces leading to decline and bankruptcy. Leveraging the very federal controls, which allowed them to grow in the first place. Sorovsky had identified an energy company Evron, and a communication company Wordcom among the corporations, and a bank through which the mortgage market could be manipulated. With Sorovsky, Pushkin would put together an action plan which would be discussed at the next meeting, which would specify the responsibility of each of the council members.

Pushkin heard the outer doors bang, and the gruff tone of Pavlovsky, as he talked to his secretary. He pushed open the door forcefully and stepped into the office. He took of his overcoat and scarf, slung them onto the rack and turned to Pushkin.

'Good morning sir.'

Pushkin nodded in return, then asked, 'What is the situation?'

'We don't know who was responsible, but it is the work of professionals with connections. They seemed to have vanished into thin air. They must have connections at a very high level. You can't just go around and pick up Uzi machine pistols and American grenades'.

'Exactly', exclaimed Pushkin.

'Who do you think is behind it?' Pavlovsky said, looking worried.

'It definitely has the support of the government, this is a repetition of Vilnius and Riga' replied Pushkin.

'The three who survived, or was it four?', Pushkin asked, running his fingers through his thinning hair.

'The daughter of Andreyeva, and the sons of Ustinov and Pavlov, and an old drunk, Starky who miraculously survived the shooting and the grenades', replied Pavlovkys.

'Incidentally Starky, his real name is Yushenko Garin, is a highly decorated member of the Ural Corps. He was a captain under the command of Colonel Rushenko. He has seen action in Afghanistan and Chechnya. He turned to liquor after his family was killed in the Riga massacre, a very similar incident to that at Cerkessk.'

'Their parents were good friends of mine and supporters of our movement', Pushkin said sadly.

He went to his desk and picked up the phone of his direct line. The line was sterile and was checked every day. He spoke for a few minutes, and turned to Pavlovsky. 'See that the three are brought to me, at the airbase. I'll make arrangements. I don't want anyone to know about it. We'll use Omega, see that all personnel on duty are ours'.

Pavlovsky nodded, 'It will be done'.

With that Pavlovsky took leave of Pushkin and left.

Chapter 9

Date: 31st October 1999, Place: Cerkessk,
Time: 10.00 am

Officials from various government agencies arrived during the morning. The 10 a.m. news on the radio was interrupted with a report on the massacre. The government spokesman stated that a senior delegation was being despatched to Cerkessk to study the situation. The official line was that early reports suggested the killings were related to a regional feud related to drug trafficking.

Dmitri, Irina and Yuri were shocked at the blatant falsehood being propagated. This was a ploy to divert attention from the real reasons. They sat huddled together in a corner in the communist party office. They had just gone through the horrifying task of identifying their parents and some of their friends. The bodies had been laid out in the church. The day had seen the arrival of a number of senior government officials, army generals and important politicians.

Mogrovsky too showed up, to show his concern, his real reason was to check if there were any witnesses.

There were too many bodies for an individual inquest; a mass inquest was held by the coroner from Novo Atagi. The cause of death was recorded as due to 'Fatal gunshot wounds inflicted by unknown persons'. Later that afternoon, they attended a quiet funeral for their parents.

Mogrovsky spent a few minutes with Irina, Dimitri and Yuri, conveying his condolences.

He saw Starky and went to him, he noticed that Starky was very agitated, and was in a corner by himself, the people and officials around had no time for a drunk, though it was evident that Starky was fully alert. Mogrovsky was intrigued, and needed to find out if Starky had noticed anyone or anything that night that might lead back to him or Bukovsky.

'What is your name and how long have you lived here?' he asked

'Yushenko, Yushenko Garin, I've lived here for many years after the Riga incident,' he added as an afterthought, 'I didn't have anywhere to go, Nina Andryeva brought me here and looked after me.'

Mogrovsky nodded, he needed to find out more, 'what do you know about Riga?' he asked.

'My family was killed in the massacre, I'm sure it was the same bastards behind the Riga killing and this.'

Mogrovsky nodded, 'yes we will need to find out,' saying that he left.

In Moscow, Mogrovsky buzzed his secretary, who walked in with a pencil and pad.

'I want to see Mikoslav, tomorrow,' he said.

'Mikoslav, the head of the South OMON prefecture?' she asked, since there were two Mikoslavs.

'Yes' he answered, his head was tilted back and he was staring at the ceiling. Mikoslav was one of his protégés, who could be trusted. Mikoslav walked in at 10 the next morning, and was shown in immediately to Mogrovsky's office.

'You have heard of the happenings at Cerkessk?' Mogrovsky asked him. 'Yes sir, it's in the news.'

'Do you know who is involved?", he paused, 'is there any talk of who might be involved?'

'No Sir, no one is talking about it.'

'OK, but I want to know if there are any theories floating around, on who is responsible.'

'Yes sir,' with that Mikoslav let himself out of the office.

A wailing siren heralded the arrival of another important visitor. The car came to a screeching halt, the driver jumped out to open the rear passenger door. A uniformed figure strode out. He looked around as some of the other officers walked briskly to greet their visitor, they saluted him. Pavlovsky saluted in return and asked, 'Where are the survivors?'

He was quickly led to the communist party office, to Dmitri, Yuri and Irina. 'My deepest sympathies', Pavlovsky offered his hand, the three in turn shook hands. He took them aside and lowered his voice so that others would not hear. 'Is there anything that you would like to do here, I would like you to come with me. General Pushkin would like to see you', he said.

Dmitri, Yuri and Irina looked at him. They knew that General Pushkin had been a friend of their parents and was a powerful member of the Politburo. They shook their heads, there was nothing left for them here.

Pavlovsky spoke to the officer conducting the investigation.

'I would like to see the notes made of the investigation'. The officer quickly produced a bound book and handed it to Pavlovsky. Pavlovsky went through it quickly and stopped when he came to the notes made based on the answers from Dmitri, Yuri and Irina. He tore out all the pages, took the officer aside and told him, 'this investigation is being conducted with immediate effect by my office directly. I'm taking your notes but must warn you not to discuss this matter with anyone'.

The officer nodded, 'Yes Sir, it will be treated in the strictest confidence'.

'Good, that taken care of, let's go', he beckoned to Dmitri, Yuri and Irina and towards the limousine. The three settled in the seat facing Pavlovsky. The car sped up the hill that they had only come down a day ago. They reached Novo Atagi in forty-five minutes and were in the General's plane within the hour heading towards Moscow.

They arrived at a military base in the southern outskirts of Moscow, near Podolsk. The airfield was situated in a natural valley. Irina stared out of the window blankly, still numb from the pain. They saw the runway lights lit up as the plane turned for its final descent. The plane landed and taxied to the end of the runway. It seemed to be heading directly for the hill. As it neared the hill, a huge door slid upwards. Lights inside illuminated a hangar the size of four football grounds carved into the hill. The plane came to a halt, they could hear the shrill whine as the aircraft's turbines were shut down. They had arrived at Omega.

A car pulled up alongside the plane. A soldier opened the door from the outside, which also formed a stairway for leaving the plane. The four of them were driven out to what seemed a large administration block.

They were led into the building and into an office. Standing by the chair was General Pushkin. He saw them and came forward, stretched out his arms and took Irina in a bear hug. Irina broke down. He gently stroked her hair and let her cry for some time. When she composed herself, he went to Yuri and Dmitri, hugged each of them, 'my deepest sympathies, my dear friends'.

He made them sit down in the settee at the end of the room and asked Irina, 'what will you have my dear?'

Irina answered, 'Coffee please'. He looked at Dmitri and Yuri, both nodded.

'Whoever it was, the Government is covering it up', shouted Dmitri, agitated by now. The others looked at him.

'Why else would the news suggest that it was a drug related killing. Cerkessk has never been involved in drugs. If the Government so readily jumps to such a conclusion, they have to have a reason'. He looked directly at Pushkin. 'Cerkessk has always criticised the Government and their pro-West stance. Perhaps this is to teach villages such as Cerkessk a lesson, as they did in Vilnius and Riga'.

'It was the Government', Pushkin said, softly, 'or was sanctioned by members in the Politburo, who are pro-West and anti-nationalist'.

'But surely, if we know who perpetrated this crime we can expose them?' Dmitri cried out, his voice full of anger, his face flushed, his knuckles white from gripping the chair tightly as he half rose in his chair.

Pushkin looked at them. 'There are those of us who know the happenings in Russia in the name of democracy, but we cannot do anything just now. We have to wait for our chance; we must be strong and patient.'

"You speak as though, you know what's happening and you have a plan', Yuri butted in.

'We do', Pushkin nodded. 'Our organisation grows every day; members are prepared to die for our cause'. 'We need people, young people like you who believe in our way of life, and in a strong Russia', he said, watching them closely. 'It is up to you to make the decision.'

Yuri and Irina, both nodded and went across to Dmitri. They just looked at each other, no one said anything, and they didn't need to. They each knew what the other was thinking. They had to get back at the killers. They knew that Pushkin was offering them a chance to be part of the movement. Their parents were friends of Pushkin and trusted him.

They spoke amongst themselves briefly, then turned around and looked at Pushkin, holding each other's hands. 'We are with you,' they said in unison.

Pushkin looked at them and said, 'You will run a great risk, if it is found that you are part of this organisation, it could mean your lives. Are you prepared to give up everything?' They nodded.

'Even your identities?'

They looked at each other and slowly nodded. 'We have always believed in the same things, and if this gives us a chance to work for the glory of Russia, and get at those murderers, we will do what we must', Dmitri spoke for them.

'Very well then', Pushkin nodded satisfied. He turned to Pavlovsky.

'You will see that they are taken to Kuressaare, for initial training and then to Kujvastu for advanced training and briefing'.

He then turned to the three, 'We are part of an organisation, the company goes by the name of International Trading Syndicate, also known as "Intrasyn". The headquarters is on an island in Estonia, known after the mountain, "Muhu". Kuressaare and Kujvastu are ports, both a part of Estonia', he added. 'The organisation runs a number of businesses around the world, and is very successful at it. You three however, will be part of covert operations. The covert part of the organisation is aimed at liberating Russia from its shackles and bringing back its glory'. He smiled at them and said, 'you will be told more when you are trained and ready'.

'How long will the training take?' asked Dmitri.

'About two years', Pushkin answered, 'it will be hard, but by the time you have finished you will be experts in martial arts, explosives, weapons and intelligence operations', he nodded to Pavlovsky, signalling an end to the meeting.

He shook hands with them as they left, 'the next time I see you, you will no longer be known by the names you are now', he smiled.

Chapter 10

Date: 31st November 2001,
Place: Cerkessk, Time: 5.30 am

Starky got up with a start, he was trembling and sweating, his mattress damp with his sweat. He had had a nightmare, he had dreamt of machine gun fire, and the screams of people falling over him, and the smell of death around him. The effect of the massacre and his near escape had sobered him, he had quit drinking and had taken to doing odd jobs in the local government office. He was hoping that he would receive some information about the young woman and the two men, but months passed and there was no news of them.

His mind went back to the morning after. He had seen Yuri, Irina and Dmitri talking to Pavlovsky, they had left with him in a car.

He couldn't think of anyone to turn to. With the passing of time he realised that they were unlikely to return to Cerkessk.

He thought about it, the one ton transport which had been requisitioned by Yuri and Dmitri had been driven back to the depot at Krasnodar. He decided to go to the army depot in Krasnodar, and find out what he could.

He rummaged in his old beat up trunk which held his clothes and other meagre belongings, and took out a worn leather pouch. He unzipped it and pulled out papers. He found what he was looking for, a folded booklet, the edges were tattered from constant use. He opened the booklet, the face that stared back at him was that of a smart man with an army cap, the shoulders bore the insignia of the Urals Infantry and the rank of a Captain. He tucked the booklet in his shirt pocket, and from the bottom of the trunk took the small bundle of notes that he had saved, it was not much, but enough for his trip.

The trip to Krasnodar was uneventful, he hopped off the coach and made his way to the army depot. The sentry at the gate asked for his id and the purpose of his visit. He showed him his id, and asked to see the Major. The sentry snapped to attention on seeing his rank and the insignia in the id, he opened the gate and pointed the way to the Major's office.

He walked into the office, 'Good morning Sir,' and saluted smartly.

The burly major still behind his desk, nodded, too fat to get up off his butt. 'Yes', he looked up frowning.

'Sir, I'm Capt Yushenko Garin of the 14th Urals Infantry, now retired. I am looking for information on two men who requisitioned an army transport a few months ago.'

The major leant forward in his seat, now what is this about he thought. The incident was many months ago and he had had to send a driver to pick up the transport. The curt order had come from headquarters.

'So, why do you need to know, and of what interest is it to you?' he asked.

"Sir, after the tragedy at Cerkessk, the two men with a lady were the only ones alive, and they helped me. I saw them leaving with a senior officer, and was hoping for their return."

The major nodded, he thought for a moment studying the man. This man was an ex captain of the Urals. He knew too that the 14th Urals was a distinguished battalion and had won many honours, and decided to give him some information, "They were taken to Moscow to meet someone very senior, I do not know who, but information is that they have been sent away on some assignment and are not likely to return."

'Is there any way I can obtain information on their whereabouts?" Starky asked.

The major shrugged,' Go to Moscow, and ask around, your earlier boss Colonel Rushenkov is now the Director at the Directorate of War Veterans, he will be able to help you.'

Starky broke into a broad smile, 'Colonel Rushenkov in Moscow,' he exclaimed, I'll make my way, thank you Major, I'm much obliged.'

He left after throwing a smart salute.

Starky thought about his decision to move to Moscow, six months ago, he was a changed man, after he had given up drinking, he looked fit, and there was more flesh on his frame.

He reached Moscow, his old boss colonel Rushenkov in the Infantry battalion of the Ural Corps was the man in charge of the Directorate of War Veterans. The office was housed in a small independent house, in a by lane off Gagarin Road, it was more of a mews, which had an iron gate at the entrance, manned by an old war veteran.

The events flashed across his mind.

Starky, or rather Yushenko Garin had gone up to the gate, the old war veteran asked, 'what do you want?'

'I'm here to see Colonel Rushenkov' he said.

'Where do you come from?' asked the old veteran.

The 14th Ural Infantry, which was commanded by Colonel Rushenkov,' Starky replied.

The demeanour of the veteran at the gate changed, he straightened up, looked closely at Starky. It was well known among the war veterans, that the 14th Infantry under colonel Rushenkov had been decorated and was known to have been a formidable fighting machine.

'What's your name?' the veteran asked.

'Captain_Yushenko Garin' Starky replied.

The veteran opened the gate, and ushered Starky into a small hall with chairs, he asked him to sit down, while he went into the office at the far end through two doors. Starky could see that the office inside had a receptionist who was busy typing. Starky saw her talking to the veteran, then get up and go through a door. The veteran came back. He nodded to Starky and asked him to wait, and made his way back to the gate.

Starky saw the doors of the office open and the burly figure of Rushenkov coming through.

'My God, Yushenko, where have you been all these years,' he said, pumping Starky's hand, and embracing him.

'I tried to get in touch with you after Riga, but was late. I just could not find you, you sort of disappeared. I am sorry to hear that your family was killed.'

They, Rushenkov and Starky had fought as a team, each looking out for the other, they were more like family.

Starky was overwhelmed by the affection shown by Rushenkov.

'Come on in,' Rushenkov led the way into his office.

Rushenkov buzzed his secretary, who came in with a pad and pen.

'Bring us a bottle of vodka and a couple of glasses,' he told her. She nodded and left.

They settled down, Rushenkov raised his glass, 'to the 14th, and all our comrades' he said downing the vodka in a single gulp.

Starky, took a sip, and saw the question in Rushenkov's eyes.

Starky then explained his whole story from the time the 14th, returned from Chechnya, and the rumours that Mogrovsky knew something about Yuri, Irina and Dmitri.

Rushenkov was silent for a while, 'you say that this Mogrovsky, knows something about the massacre at Cerkessk, and the disappearance of the three.'

'I'm not sure but I'll try and find out, the only way I'll be able to find out is to be assigned to his office.' Starky replied.

Rushenkov was silent for a while, 'OK, give me a couple of days, and let me see what I can do.'

Within the week, Rushenkov had seen to it that Starky had been posted to Mogrovsky's office as the clerk responsible for handling inward and outward mail.

Chapter 11

Date: 17th February 2002, Place: Moscow, Time: 12.30 pm

It was one of those quiet days, Mogrovsky left for lunch, it was 12.45 pm. Starky heard the doors close with Mogrovsky telling his aide that he would be attending a meeting called for by the commandant of Moscow's internal security, and that he would be sometime before he returned.

This was the opportunity that Starky was waiting for, a period when there would be no one in Mogrovsky's or his secretary's office. Svetlana would go for her short lunch break at 1 pm, usually half an hour.

Starky was a past master at picking locks, one of the trades he had learnt while training in covert operations, prior to his posting to the 14th Urals.

The clock read 1 pm, most of the office members had gone for lunch, Starky saw Mogrovsky's secretary reach for her overcoat, she waved to him, 'aren't you going to lunch?' she asked.

'I've had a bite already' Starky answered, 'will grab a coffee at the park, and take a walk'

She nodded and left.

The entrance to Mogrovsky's office from the outside and for visitors was through a foyer and two heavy doors before they reached the secretary, this was for screening visitors for security purposes. There was another entrance to Mogrovsky's office from his secretary's office for the office staff.

Starky went to the secretary's office and tried the door leading to Mogrovsky's office, it was locked with a simple self locking mechanism, he picked it within a minute and was inside. He had to be quick, he opened each drawer of his desk. The top drawer contained bills, the middle drawer contained files, the files contained papers of minor offenses. He put them back and looked into the third drawer. The third drawer contained more files of pending local cases. He looked all over the room, disappointed not finding anything. Across the room was a tall narrow cupboard on the right hand wall. He tried the door, it was locked.

He checked the lock, it was a good one with seven levers, and not the simple locks usually put on cupboards. It took him a couple of minutes to open the cupboard with the bent wire he had tucked behind his ear. The second and third shelves were stocked with liquor bottles.

The top shelf seemed empty, he could not look in since it was at a height, he ran his palm across the top of the shelf, along its width and felt his palm touch a thick bundle. He felt around the bundle and realised it was a file. He grasped the file firmly and brought it down. He quickly leafed through the file, pausing now and then for anything that seemed relevant. He stopped, in one page there were names of men listed along with their details, it was the names of five men all members of the politburo who were vehement in their criticism of communism. He wondered why they were listed here. 'Cerkessk' the word caught his attention, he froze, why on earth was Cerkessk listed here. It was about fifteen minutes since he had broken into the office, and the secretary would be returning soon. He decided to take the file with him.

He shut the door of the cupboard, and was in the process of trying to lock it with the wire, when he heard voices in the corridor, the secretary was returning, he left the cupboard unlocked, eased himself out of Mogrovsky's office, pulling the door shut hearing the click as it locked. He made for the door of the secretary's office and, heard her coming in. He quickly tucked the file into his shirt and pulled his coat around him. He picked up a couple of blank A4 papers from her desk and reached the door as she was opening it, 'Oh', she was startled, almost bumping into him.

'I'm sorry,' Starky said apologising profusely, 'I wanted a few blank papers, to write a letter, and went into your office.'

Svetlana, the secretary, was annoyed and frightened, 'you should have waited and asked me for the paper, you should not have gone into my office,' she rebuked him, looking around at her desk to see if any of the papers were disturbed. The desk was as she had left it, he saw that she was visibly relieved.

'I'm sorry,' mumbled Starky.

Her countenance softened,' Ok, please don't do it again'

Starky nodded his thanks and made his way out.

Starky left the office almost immediately, the security man at the gate noticed Starky with his arms around his heavy over jacket, and a balaclava covering his head.

'Hi Yushenko,' the guard greeted him, 'you look unwell.'

'I've got this bad headache, and think I'm running a fever, so I decided to leave early,' he replied.

'OK, see you tomorrow if you're feeling better, 'the guard waved him through the gate.

Starky went on his way, his arms wrapped around his body, holding the file in place.

It was 2.30 pm when he reached his flat, Starky sat down, he quickly jotted down anything that he felt was important… the names of the politburo members which was mentioned, there was a reference to clearance for action against Cerkessk, the date a month before the massacre, a few pages later there were a list of other names of politburo members, Pushkin, Albakin, Petrovsky and two others, with a question mark against them and the word 'Intrasyn' and 'Muhu' written boldly across. He was startled to see his real name Yushenko Garin, and the names of Yuri, Dmitri and Irina, Mogrovsky had scribbled…'met them in Cerkessk the morning after the massacre, and an old drunk Yushenko…who was a decorated officer from the 14th Urals….no evidence of the perpetrators of the crime'..

It was evident from the file that Mogrovsky was a part of the covert ops. Or the black ops of the government in power, the so called democrats who while mouthing pro democratic speeches and privatisation in the name of development, were in reality systematically undermining the communists by carrying out various dastardly acts and laying the responsibility at their door. The agenda orchestrated by a handful of politburo members.

The file also had details of other members of the politburo, especially prominent were the names of Yorbachev, Pushkin, Albakin, Zhirinovsky, and Pavlovsky. These were the pro-communist hardliners, a line caught his eye,……'are they connected to a company, Intrasyn, with headquarters at Muhu?' the last entry was,' need to check on Intrasyn and Muhu?'

Starky, had checked on the identity of the person with whom the three had gone that afternoon from Cerkessk, it was Pavlovsky. Pavlovsky was part of the pro communist group.

It had taken him two hours to go through the file and make his notes, the clock read 4.30 pm. The two A4 sheets of paper on which he had written were full of jottings, a lot of them did not mean anything to him, nevertheless he knew that there was something going on which he could not immediately fathom.

He did not know whom to trust with the contents of the file. He was sure that the Government or those in important positions in the politburo were involved, but did not know how deep the rot had set in. He had no idea of the events that were to occur on the 30th of October and could do nothing about it.

He knew too that the file in his hands was important and it was a matter of time before it was found missing. He had to get rid of the file and his notes.

He put the file in the drawer of the rickety table, folded the papers and put them in an envelope. He thought for a while, and then on impulse put down the address of Nina Andreyava at Cerkessk, and put his name as the sender, without an address. Nina Andreyava was dead, but the letter would be delivered to her cousin. He would be able to retrieve it when he went to Cerkessk. He stepped out and made his way to the post office, checked with the teller and put the stamps required, and dropped it in the post box. He was relieved, he now needed to put the file back in Mogrovsky's cupboard before its loss was noticed.

He made his way back to the flat, the clock read 4.50 pm.

Mogrovsky returned from the meeting on internal security, it was 5 pm. The discussions had centered around drug busts; Cerkessk was mentioned, with some members of the committee not convinced that the Cerkessk massacre was the result of a drug war. There had been murmurs that powerful people in the politburo were involved. Mogrovsky was agitated, he had jotted down events in the red file, which if found would put him in the firing line, he had been warned that there could be no comebacks from the minister. He had destroyed the letter which authorised the killings at Cerkessk. He was on his own now.

The driver got down and held the door open for Mogrovsky. As he walked into the office, he called out to Svetlana, 'Bring me the file with the red border.'

Svetlana walked across to the cupboard and took out her key, she tried the door, and was startled, the door was not locked.

Mogrovsky saw her fumbling and asked, 'Whats the matter.'

'Sir, the cupboard is not locked, I'm sure I locked it after I put in the bottles in last week, did you open it after that?'

Only Mogrovsky and Svetlana had the keys to the cupboard.

Mogrovsky sprang out of his chair, 'Damn,' he shouted, taking two strides to the cupboard, he yanked open the door, and reached for the top shelf. His palm swept the top repeatedly, exasperated, he pulled a chair and climbed on it to look in. The file was missing!

Mogrovsky face turned purple with anger, 'has anyone come into my office?' he shouted at Svetlana.

Svetlana was petrified, 'no sir, no one has gone into your office.' Then she remembered, 'I saw Yushenko coming out of my office earlier this afternoon, when I had gone for lunch, but I always lock the door between your office and mine, and it was locked. He was not carrying anything with him.' She said faltering, knowing that the matter was serious and she could be sent away at the least, or worse if he felt she had anything to do with the missing file.

Mogrovsky froze, at the name Yushenko. 'Yushenko?' he bawled, 'he was the old drunk at Cerkessk, who escaped with the three, how did he get into this office?'

'Sir, he was posted in the mail department, by the department of war veterans, more than six months ago' Svetlana explained.

'How come I didn't know about it' Mogrovsky asked.

'Sir it was a routine posting in a clerical position, which was circulated as an internal memo, it was passed by your desk as well.'

'Ok, where is he now?' Mogrovsky growled, he wasn't convinced, but that could wait for another day, 'I want him to be brought to me immediately'

'Have Marenko come in with two of his guards.'

Svetlana, immediately put through a call to security. In ten minutes, a car screeched to a halt outside Mogrovsky's office. Marenko got out as the car came to a halt.

He made his way into Mogrovsky's office.

Mogrovsky explained the situation and the missing document, 'I want that file, put it in a large envelope and delivered to me personally, no one is to browse through it, the information in it is highly confidential.'

Marenko nodded, and went out of the office.

Marenko, put a few calls to Rushenkov's office, and was informed that Rushenkov was out and would be back much later, but could be reached on his phone. Marenko did not want to wait, he made his way to Rushenkov's office, and walked into the personnel department. In a few minutes he had all the information on Starky and was on his way to the apartment.

After dropping off the letter, Starky made his way to his room and immediately started packing his meagre belongings. He knew that staying on in Moscow was dangerous, he needed to disappear.

He called Rushenkov, and told him that he needed to get back to Cerkessk, and would call him when able.

Rushenkov asked,' is everything OK, and do you need any money?'

'Thank you Sir, I have saved most of my salary these past few months, and have enough.'

'OK, take care of yourself and be careful,' he knew that Starky was onto something, Rushenkov put down the phone.

Starky had the file in his hand, and was unzipping the pouch on his back pack, when he heard the screech of car tyres, as a car braked hard in front of his apartment, he heard the car doors slam shut the door of the foyer being opened, and a gruff voice asking the porter, and then the thud of boots as men made their way up the stairs. He knew that they were coming for him, he went to the window, and looked out, there was a government car with a man standing close by, he was looking up at his window. Starky knew that he had to get out. He raised the window sill as the door to his apartment was slammed open by a heavy body. He had half stepped out of the window when one of the men was on him, he swung his fist which caught the man full on the face and sent him sprawling, the man was strong, he got up and came after him, Starky was almost out of the window, and was still unbalanced for the long drop to the ground, he had the file in one hand, and the other was holding the edge of the window. The man behind, swung his heavy rubberised baton, the force caught him full on the shoulder, he lost his grip, and his feet slipped off the edge of the sill, he felt himself falling, plummeting to the ground, head first. He tried to twist his body to land on his shoulder, there was no time, the last thing he saw was the earth rushing at him, he crashed head first to the ground, his head taking the full force of the fall, he was dead on the spot, the file still clutched tightly in his hand.

Marenko bounded down the stairs, and reached his body. He pried open his fingers and took the file. He called Mogrovsky, 'It's done, I've got the file'

'Good work, bring Yushenko in, I want to talk to him"

'I'm sorry he's dead,' Marenko explained the circumstances.

'OK, have his body taken to the morgue, and arrange for it to be cremated, do it quietly, do not make any entries in the registers, if there are questions, call me, I'll talk to them, I don't want any information leaking out.'

'It will be done.' Marenko signed off.

Chapter 12

February 2002 Time: Place: Muhu

The training in Kujvastu and Kuressaare had been hard and so were the lessons. The camp was run military style, training handled by ex-KGB field officers, each an expert in his field. The camp was under the control of a commandment with the rank of a Colonel.

They came back to Kujvastu for final training in soft skills for their chosen areas, at the end of two years. Dmitri trained as a bodyguard, he was well suited for the job. Yuri, turned to his first love, photography. He studied books on photography and worked hard. His expertise reached the level of a professional. Irina who had studied to be a journalist, turned her attention to psychology, studying important Government personalities and office bearers. Her list consisted of Generals, the heads of security and the Presidents of the previous Soviet republics. All those who were pro-west and anti-communist, she focussed on their weaknesses.

It was a bright sunny morning, it was early spring, when the three were called to the camp commandant's office at Kujvastu. They stepped into the office and were surprised to see General Pushkin; he greeted them warmly and shook hands.

'I have been informed that you have finished your training, and are ready to go into the field'.

The three smiled. 'Yes Sir', they had waited long enough, they were itching for some real action.

'Before you set out on your assignments, you have a week off to enjoy yourselves. Arrangements have been made at the Hotel Volga in St. Petersburg, with all expenses paid. You are not to talk of what you've been through to anyone.'

He looked at them. 'Any questions?', he asked. The three shook their heads, smiling.

They found themselves in St. Petersburg the following day. The Volga was a well known five star hotel, the bars and restaurants were elegant and the nightclub had a terrific Deejay. It brought back nostalgic memories of their student days. St. Petersburg was like a second home, they knew the city like the back of their hands, they knew the back streets, and the small eating joints which served delicious goulash.

They each had a room to themselves. It had been hard after Cerkessk, the two years at Kuraasaare and Kujvatsu had blunted their grief. It would be a week with gay abandon. Irina loved both men, and they both loved her. She had decided not to choose, she wanted both men, time was too short and the future too uncertain.

It was the end of the week. Three vehicles were ready for them that morning as they left the hotel, their destinations different and unknown. They knew that they might not see each other again. With their changed identities they were not expected to recognise each other if they happened to meet.

Irina hugged and kissed both men passionately, 'I love you', she said, 'take care', tears in her eyes. Yuri and Dimitri nodded, turned to each other hugged and shook hands.

Chapter 13

Date: 1st March 2002, Place: Minsk,
Time: 9.00 am

The Forgery and Record section of the KGB, was moved from the basement in Dzerzhinsky square to a modern building in the same area. The new building was equipped with the latest electronic gadgets.

Most of the personnel were old and their methods outdated. The Minister for Internal Security decided to modernise the department by inducting young graduates and training them. A Russian Recruitment Agency, Moscowa Handlowych, was retained to handle recruitment and training. Since this was a sensitive department the agency received clearance from the highest levels. The President of the agency, Valentin Ligachev, was a Director of Intrasyn.

Ligachev had received a call from Pushkin, during the week the three were spending their vacation in St. Petersburg. Ligachev had instructed his protégés in the Forgery and Record section of what they needed to do.

Records of those killed in action were painstakingly studied, to find those that fitted the description of Dmitri and Yuri.

Dmitri's new identity was that of Anatoly Chernov, a Belarusian lieutenant who had been killed in action in the war in Afghanistan. The records were altered to show that though initially thought to have been killed in action, he had survived.

His records showed that he had been a paratrooper in a commando squad of the GRU Spetnaz and the KGB Special Forces, code-named 'Zenit'. These commandos had seized Kabul and killed Amin, the Prime Minister of Afghanistan in December 1979. Four mechanised Russian divisions had rolled into Afghanistan and seized key centres while Soviet advisors had immobilised Afghan units. The Soviets had seized Afghanistan with a mere seventy casualties.

He had been promoted to captain in special operations and then to a senior operative in the third Chief Directorate handling Military Counter Intelligence. Anatoly had been the bodyguard of the Chief of Counter Espionage.

Date: April 2002 Time: Place: Moscow

Boris Pugo had been a war correspondent and photographer, reportedly killed while filming action in the Kandahar region of Afghanistan. Boris was the only son of a miner, who had died when Pugo was in his early teens. Of his mother, there was very little information. A search had shown that she too had died a few years later. Boris Pugo had no other known family connections. He had grown up in the ghettos of St. Petersburg, with little formal education. He had been an avid reader, spending as much time as he could in libraries. He had started photography as a hobby when he was fifteen, had later enrolled as a student in the Russian Academy of Arts. After college he had been offered a job in a local newspaper in Tbilisi in Georgia and volunteered for photographic assignments in Chechnya and Serbia. After a few years in Chechnya and Serbia he wanted to see real action and volunteered as a war correspondent in Afghanistan.

He was fearless and was a fixed appendage to the Russian Infantry. He was where the action was, his photographs were of real action taken close up in the midst of the heat of battle. He seemed to lead a charmed life, escaping almost certain death many times. Nemesis did catch up when he was filming an attack by the Russians in Kandahar on a Taliban stronghold. The attack had gone wrong, the Russian patrol was ambushed and had retreated as best they could, but a number of the members went missing.

It was alleged that he was seized by the Taliban and later killed, though his body was never found. His camera was found by a ground patrol, in one of the Taliban's hideouts captured by the Russians. He was listed as missing in action. The film when developed provided the world some of the best photographs of the Russians in action.

Records were reconstructed to show that Boris Pugo had been later found badly injured, and suffering from amnesia. Boris had been a long-term patient in the military hospital in Kiev. He had recovered physically and mentally, working his way as a free lance photographer. Yuri was now Boris Pugo.

Yuri or Boris Pugo as he was now known had been put through a course on practical and theoretical photography. His appearance had changed, his hair was slicked back and he wore a pair of horn-rimmed glasses.

He had sent photographs taken during the Afghan war to western magazines and set about visiting various western cities. He was provided money and contacts that brought him into high society in places like London, New York, Paris and Frankfurt. He held exhibitions, where a number of his photographs as a war correspondent were displayed. His social circle grew, his manners and knowledge found him many admirers.

Chapter 14

Date: September 2002,
Place: New York, Time: 9.30 am

It was a foggy morning in New York, Boris had mixed himself a coffee from the tray, room service had brought in. He was glancing through the Herald Tribune, when the phone rang.

'Mr Pugo?' the caller enquired over the phone.

'Yes, it is he' answered Boris.

'I'm Dick Verglas from the News de Internacionale, if you recollect we met briefly at the Governor's media dinner last Saturday.'

'Oh yes, I remember,' Boris answered.

'I would like to discuss a business proposal and was wondering if we can meet over lunch on Wednesday,'

Pugo knew the News de Internacionale, a magazine rated to have the highest readership in the western world. Its photographers were rated to be the best in their field.

'Wednesday the third?' asked Boris.

'Yes, if it is possible,' answered Verglas.

'Can you please hold a minute, while I check my diary?'

'Certainly' answered Verglas.

'Yes, I'm free and would be pleased to meet you.' Boris replied.

'Very good, I'll book a table at the Hilton Intercontinental, at the La Casa restaurant for noon,' Verglas answered.

'See you on Wednesday,' Boris put the phone down.

Chapter 15

Date: 5th August 2002,
Place: Kaliningrad, Time: 4.00 pm

It was a bright sunny morning, the shimmering Baltic Sea made it difficult to see the boats which set out with their water skiers behind them. A couple of boats with couples in them were languidly tossing around in the slight swell.

Nikolai Molotov stretched out on his deck chair with Vodka in his hand at his dacha at Kaliningrad.

He leaned forward, pointed the remote to his Hi Fi set and turned down the volume. He wanted to think, and liked soft music in the background.

Nikolai Molotov was a career KGB officer, he believed in the old system. He had been thoroughly disillusioned with 'Perestroika'. He had followed the course that had taken the Union of the Soviet Socialist Republic from being a world power to a Russia that had to barter its honour for its existence.

The words of an Army officer in an election meeting in 1995 still rang in his ears.

'For what did we make these sacrifices? So that European politicians can tell their people they have won, so that our enemies can hail our own leaders as saints; So that the achievements of the Soviet people and soldiers can be thrown away in months?'

It was all an empty dream; the west was getting away with everything giving nothing in return. It was evident from the

57

last G-7 meeting. The west had succeeded in making Russia destroy all its tactical nuclear missiles.

Molotov thought about his meeting in early 1997 with a distinguished looking gentleman at the Maximillian Platz in Munich. They had both chosen a spot next to the fountain, waiting for the grand clock in the square to strike at noon. A simple exchange of greetings had led to polite conversation. When they realised that they were from St Petersburg, it had led to a serious discussion on Russia. They had ended up at the Hofbrauhaus for a beer and a light meal. He shared the gentleman's dreams of Russia. By the end of the evening, he had joined the movement. That had been a long time ago. Much had taken place since then. With time a firm conviction had grown, that for Russia to get off its knees and to hold up its head it would have to break off the shackles of the west. It would then and only then regain its original status and glory.

In the months and years he had been prepared and knew what was expected of him. The last meeting at the chateau was still fresh in his mind.

Belarus with Estonia, Latvia and Lithuania with ports in the Baltic Sea were strategically important to Russia. The three had very close ethnic ties and had formed a Federation in December 1991.

Belarus was responsible for the security of this Federation. This Federation was part of the Commonwealth of Independent States known as the SNG or the Sodruzhestvo Nezavisimyhk Gesudarstr. Subsequently in May 1992 at Tashkent the Commonwealth was declared dead and Belarus with its three neighbours declared themselves independent, and announced their intention to establish their own national armies.

The three Baltic States re-organised their internal security arrangements. The erstwhile KGB's facilities and personnel were transferred under the supervision and control of the central government, with the service being split into three separate services.

The government at Belarus formed its own Federal Security Agency and the VIP Protection Squad. These organisations were under the direct control of the Interior Minister Mr. Chebikov, a very pro-west supporter of democracy.

The structure was simple, the Chairman of the Security Committee was the Interior Minister, under who were the Chiefs of the three services.

It was a well-known fact that the Interior Minister was in fact the power behind the Belarus government, with the President a mere figure head. It was also acknowledged that the Soviet President conferred with Chebikov on all matters of state.

In the build up to the G7 summit in 1991 in London; one of the requirements was that the Soviets destroy their entire arsenal of tactical nuclear missiles in line with the INF Treaty, to enable the Soviet President to be invited to the G7 summit. The summit was important, the Soviets were to make a pitch for a one and a half billion-dollar grain credit. Chebikov was widely credited with having taken the initiative in the Belarus and the other Baltic States in meeting the deadline for the destruction of the missiles.

It is now history that all the President of Russia came back with was a piece of paper conferring a Most Favoured Nation status with the USA and nothing else. The G7 had once again shown its weak leadership. There was no leader within the G7 who had either the vision or the leadership required to push decisions to support the democratic movement in Russia. The Europeans were in any case puppets in the hands of the Americans, with the British qualifying for first place. The only country among the G7 to voice its concerns were the French, they were a minority.

Chebikov was a tough ex-KGB officer from the Belarus. The President of Russia had seen to it that he was appointed as the Interior Minister. His deputy was Molotov, whom

Chebikov brought in when the KGB was modernised and reorganised from being an instrument of terror to a protector of the Soviet system. The KGB was now a watchdog of the armed forces, especially in dealing with dissidents and nationalists; however it continued to maintain its primary role of espionage and counter espionage. It was the KGB that often fought corruption in the Soviet Government and economy.

Kaliningrad was a part of Russia though it had Lithuania as its neighbour to its north and east and Poland to its south. The Black Sea was its western border. Molotov had arrived late on Friday night from the Belarus capital of Minsk after a meeting with the President of Belarus, Vladimir Dukovsky and the Interior Minister Chebikov. The meeting was concerning the Arms Treaty between Russia, Ukraine and Belarus. Chebikov had, as expected, dominated the proceedings. Belarus was crucial to the reduction that was required of the SS-20 Intercontinental Ballistic Missile deployment. This was one of the conditions for the upcoming Treaty. The treaty once signed would give Russia leverage when dealing with Europe and the United States of America.

Belarus had large radar installations at Hrodna and Vicebsk built to detect incoming US missiles. The array had been specifically built to counter the Strategic Defence Initiative or the SDI of the United States of America.

The Russian President was depending on Chebikov to have the Belarus government hand over control of their nuclear arsenal, their Black Sea Fleet and ports, and control of the radar installations to Russia.

Nikolai Molotov had been briefed by Pushkin on Dimitri's assignment. He assigned Dimitri or Anatoly as he was now known, to the Fourth Chief Directorate, which was responsible for VIP protection.

As was the custom Nikolai Molotov, introduced Anatoly to Chebikov. Chebikov as Interior Minister was the boss of the Fourth Chief Directorate of Belarus.

'Anatoly has been assigned to your detail from the third Chief Directorate,' Molotov announced to Chebikov, as they entered his office.

Viktor Chebikov was a big burly man with bushy eyebrows, built like a bear, he had a broad fleshy face. There was very little fat on him, he was strong and as broad as a door.

He turned to Anatoly, 'So why do they send you to us?' he asked in a gruff voice.

Anatoly replied, 'The third Chief Directorate, directed me to report to you, Sir'.

Chebikov studied Anatoly for a while, and picked up the file, handed to him by Molotov. He went through the file, 'I was in Afghanistan', he said, 'where did you see action?'

'At Kabul and Kandahar, Sir', Anatoly replied.

Chebikov nodded, he glanced through the file in his hand and spoke to Molotov, 'I guess he will do'.

He turned to Anatoly, 'Go down to the office and meet Brakov, he will assign you to your detail'.

Anatoly threw a smart salute. 'Thank you, Sir', turned and left.

Brakov, the chief of the Security Detail for VIP movement was an Intrasyn man and had been briefed by Molotov. He assigned Anatoly now a bodyguard as one of the chauffeurs to Chebikov.

Chapter 16

Date:2nd October 2002 Time: 11:30 a.m.
Place: New York

It was 11.30 am on Wednesday, Boris went down to the foyer, nodded to the concierge who waved and called out, 'Good Morning Mr Pugo, How are you sir?'

Boris smiled, 'Good Morning, Harry, I'm well thank you, and you?'

'Very well, thank you Mr Pugo,' he sang out.

As Boris stepped out Fred the doorman asked, 'Can I get a cab for you sir?'

Boris nodded. Fred spoke into his mike. A minute later a cab pulled up in front of Boris. The doorman smartly opened the door for Boris and closed it behind him.

'Thank you, Fred,' Boris nodded.

Fred was the smart old doorman, though he was seventy, he didn't look a wink past sixty. A cheerful chap, dressed in his smart hotel livery. He had a brilliant memory and didn't miss a thing.

The cab drove Boris to the Hilton Intercontinental, pulled into the hotel porch. Boris paid the cabby and included a generous tip. The cabby, obviously very pleased, turned back at him and smiled, 'Thank you, Sir, have a good day.'

Boris nodded to him, 'You too' and stepped out.

He checked his watch as he made his way into the hotel, it was five to twelve. He had been to the hotel before so he knew the layout and made his way to the La Casa.

The restaurant had a warm décor. It was tastefully furnished, the woodwork, mahogany, with deep red upholstery. The restaurant had a bar to one side, with the other facing a garden with a fountain. There were many guests standing at the bar. Most of the tables were occupied.

He approached the door and a steward came to him smiling, 'Mr Boris Pugo?'

'Yes' answered Pugo.

'Good afternoon sir, will you follow me please.' With that he led the way to a table which had a splendid view of the garden, fountain and the bar.

As they approached the table, a figure stood up. Boris recognised him, as the person he had been introduced to at the Governor's dinner.

'Mr Pugo' Verglas, he held out his hand.

The steward waited till both men had settled down in their seats, then asked,' Can I get you gentlemen something to drink?' and handed them each the wine list.

Verglas turned to Pugo, 'What will you drink?'

'A Gimlet, but with Vodka 'Pugo said,

'Make it a Dry Manhattan for me 'Verglas said, 'with plenty of Ice.'

When the steward had left, Verglas turned to Pugo, 'It was good of you to accept.'

'It is my pleasure,' Pugo said. 'Besides, I know of your magazine and am a great admirer of it. I think your magazine is different.'

'In what way do you think we are different? 'enquired Verglas.

The waiter arrived with the drinks, after he had served them, he asked.

'Would you like to order sir?' he asked Boris.

'I'll have the Tempura Trio for starters, followed by a Cesario Steak, the steak to be very rare', the waiter nodded and made his notes.

'I'll have a Funghi al Forno with tempura butter for a starter and a Hoi Sin Duck, with black olives.' Verglas, peered up at the waiter, looking over his half moons.

'May I suggest a good wine to go with the meal sir,' the waiter asked.

'Yes sure,' Verglas answered.

'I would suggest the Combelle Chardonnay 1962 with the starter and the Carinena 1966 with your meal sir,' the waiter said.

Verglas nodded, 'Excellent choice.'

As the waiter left Verglas, removed his half moons and put them back in its case, which he put into his jacket. 'We were discussing, why you find News de Internacionale different.'

'I find that your magazine has captured every major and minor happening, as it has unfolded. It means you are a magazine prepared to give your readers the best story and the best pictures.

This is close to my heart.' Boris explained, taking a sip from his Gimlet. He nodded in appreciation, it was the way he liked it, with Vodka.

Verglas nodded, he understood that Boris being a professional appreciated good work.

'I have seen your photographs as a correspondent. The events that you have covered, from the time you started in Estonia.' Verglas said.

'It is one of the reasons why I requested this meeting,' he paused. 'Our magazine has an excellent set of correspondents in the west; we cover the world from the Americas to Asia and Australia. The one area where we are not adequately staffed is the Baltics, from the Balkans, and the area stretching as far as the Hindu Kush Mountains. You know the area well and have worked as a correspondent in many of those parts, you know the language and the people.'

The waiter had come with the starters and the wine, pushing a small trolley. He put down a plate in front of each and removed the cocktail glasses. He showed the label to Verglas and proceeded to open the Chardonnay. He sniffed the cork and poured a little into Verglas's wine goblet. Verglas sipped the wine, paused and nodded. The waiter moved around to fill Boris's glass before filling Verglas's. He wished them a 'Bon appetite' before putting the bottle into the bucket of ice.

'I understand the freedom you have as a freelance journalist and photographer, however I believe there are advantages in working in an organisation which can give you the same level of freedom in your work and movement, and provide you more time by organising the routine.'

They finished their starters. The waiter watching from a discrete distance, cleared the plates and shortly thereafter came with the trolley with the main course. He uncorked the Carinena, and served them both.

After the waiter had left, Boris looked at Verglas and smiled, 'Are you making me an offer' he asked.

Verglas smiled, 'Yes, I would like to make you an offer to run the network covering the area from Estonia in the west to Afghanistan, Tajikistan and Kyrgyzstan in the east.'

He thought he saw Boris hesitate and added.

'You will have all the freedom you want, and there will be staff and managers to take care of the administration.' Verglas continued as he started on his Hoi Sin Duck.

'How is the Cesario Steak?' he asked of Boris.

'Excellent, it is one of the best I've had,' Boris replied.

'The chef here is Italian, and he is one of the best.'

The restaurant had filled up, the bar was full, it was 1 p.m. The restaurant was a favoured place for important business luncheons.

Boris put down his knife and fork, wiped his mouth with the napkin, took a sip of wine turned to Verglas, smiled and said, 'I would be very happy to work for the News de Internacionale.'

'Welcome to the family' Verglas beamed he said raising his glass.

Boris raised his glass, 'To News Internacionale' and downed a good portion of the contents with the first sip.

They spent the next hour savouring the main course and the excellent Carinena. They finished off with a cappuccino. Verglas called for the check and left a big tip as was evident from the face of the waiter. They decided to sort out the details in the next few days.

From his hotel, Boris put a call to the office of the Chairman of Carg Agra, the commodity giant. Carg Agra was a subsidiary of Intrasyn, its business was world trade in grains and edible oils.

'The Chairman's office, may I help you?'

Boris thought that the woman would be about thirty-five, she sounded efficient.

'I'm Boris Pugo, the photographer, may I speak to the Chairman.'

'I'm afraid he is rather busy, can I help at all,' she asked.

'I need to speak to him, it's important. Can you tell him it's Pugo?' Boris' voice sounded impatient.

It could have been the tone of his voice, or something else which she could not place, she reluctantly agreed. 'I'll see if it is possible.'

A few moments later, she was back on the line. 'I'm sorry to have kept you waiting, I'll put you through to him right away.'

'Hello Boris,' the voice of Vicktor Trubin boomed. 'You are a long way from home, how are things with you, anything I can do?'

Boris grinned. 'Hello Vicktor, no just thought I'd let you know that I've signed up with News de Internacionale to handle the Baltic end.'

Vicktor, knew what it meant. 'Oh good,' then added,' Boris if are you free one of these days, we can meet and catch up on the news.' The invitation was not meant to be taken seriously.

'Thanks, I'm tied up at the moment,' with that Boris disconnected.

Another cog in the wheel was in place. Pushkin and the council would know before the day was through.

Chapter 17

Date: 9th May 2002 Time: 10:30 a.m.
Place: St Petersburg

The car with Irina headed towards the main railway station of St Petersburg. As they left the driver handed her an envelope, she tore it open. It contained a letter and an identity card. The face that stared out at her from the identity card was hers, but the name was Nina Zaslavskaya.

She opened the letter and read," Reservations have been made for you. You will proceed to Moscow by the Transalpine 748 leaving from Gleis 3 at 11:15. At Moscow change to the Transalpine 632 leaving from Gleis 5 at 14:05 to Kiev. Tatyana Ratushinskaya will receive you at Kiev. She is your friend and you will live with her. Tatyana will tell you what is to be done."

There were instructions to destroy the letter after she read and understood it.

Irina now under the name of Nina, was dropped off at the main station, it was 1045 in the morning leaving her half an hour to find her train and carriage.

She walked down the main entrance, with a brisk springy step drawing appreciative glances from the men who turned around to look at her as she walked by. She took out her ticket, the carriage number and her seat number were clearly written.

She walked to the large station monitor situated at the entrance to the platforms, and found her train. It was expected at the platform in ten minutes. She walked to the newsstand and bought a copy of Pravda. She glanced at her watch it was

11:00, almost immediately the station public address system announced the arrival of her train. She walked briskly with her suitcase, to her coach and settled down in her seat. The coach was quite empty so she took off her sable and spread it on the seat next to hers. She placed the suitcase over her seat on the rack. Sitting down she crossed her legs and checked her watch. The time was 11:14, the express was due to depart in a minute. She was tense so she opened the newspaper and pretended to start reading.

She forced herself to relax and glanced through the paper. She was a different person now, and would know very soon what was expected of her.

The train started and a short while later the conductor came through. Irina picked up her bag to get her ticket, the conductor in the meanwhile looked on appreciatively at her shapely legs. As he punched the ticket, Irina said,' I have a connection at Kiev,'

The conductor nodded,' The Transalpine to Kiev leaves from Gleis 6 at 14:05, this train arrives at Gleis 5,' he smiled noticing her frown, 'There is a dining car on the train towards the locomotive, and the food is good.'

Irina, or rather Nina thanked him as he left.

The journey to Moscow passed swiftly. Nina was not hungry, she had a coffee and a sandwich from the refreshment trolley and read the Pravda.

The change at Moscow was uneventful. Two young men, businessmen, evident from their pinstriped suits joined the train at Tula and decided to sit in her coach. They looked at her smiled, and asked 'May we sit here?'

'Sure thing,' Nina moved her bag off the seat next to her.

The men decided to sit opposite her, it was easier to talk, and certainly a better place to look at her.

'We are going to Kiev' the taller one said, 'where are you headed?'

'To Kiev' Nina replied.

'This is our first visit to Kiev' the shorter one volunteered, 'Are you from Kiev?'

'No I'm visiting a friend' Nina replied, and picked up the paper to end the conversation.

'Do you plan to stay long' the shorter one persisted.

'I'm not sure 'Nina replied, without looking up from her paper.

The shorter one gave up trying to draw her into a conversation.

The train went through some breathtaking scenery. On its stretch from Nizhyn, as it passed Brovary the tracks wound along the lake formed by the river Dnieper, the lake stretching for about five hundred kilometres from Chernobyl in the north to Nova Kakhovka in the south. The river emptied itself into the Black Sea near Kherson, about a hundred kilometres along the coast east of the port Odessa. There were a number of dachas along the lake, with motor boats moored at the marinas. This was the inland playground of the rich and famous in the Ukraine, the other being along the Black Sea.

The Transalpine pulled into Kiev at 17:03, two minutes ahead of schedule. The two men got up and brought her suitcase down from the rack. She smiled a thank you. They both grinned, 'have a good time in Kiev.'

'Thank you, you have a good time too,' Nina smiled back.

She saw them shrugging as they left, to them it was a missed opportunity.

Nina, stepped down from the carriage and looked around. She saw a figure wave at her. Tatyana Ratushinskaya came at a brisk walk and held out her hands and hugged her. To an onlooker it was two good friends or sisters greeting each other.

'Did you have a comfortable journey?' Tatyana asked.

'Very comfortable' replied Nina.

Tatyana led the way with Nina following. This was the final stop for the train, all the passengers were getting off. The platform soon filled and they had to walk slowly.

Tatyana led the way to the car park, and opened the boot of her Lada. Once the suitcase was stowed away, Tatyana opened the passenger door and let Nina in. They drove towards the south west of Kiev taking the road along the lake.

'Have they explained what you will be doing?' Tatyana asked.

'No, only that you will brief me 'replied Nina.

'You are to be my cousin, the daughter of my mother's sister. You will live with us, at the house where I live with my parents. You will tell my parents that you have a job at the Institute of languages, which is at Kiev. Diplomats and senior members in the Ukraine and Russian government often use this institute. Your real assignment is to be with 'The Rose' she paused.

'The Rose?' Nina asked with some surprise, it seemed an odd name.

'It is run by a Madame, and caters to the senior politicians and bureaucrats in the Government.' Tatyana replied slowly.

Nina looked shocked, 'What, do you mean......a brothel?'

'Yes, a very exclusive one,' replied Tatyana.'

Nina's head was in a whirl, she had never thought that the assignment would be anything like this.

'Are you alright,' Tatyana asked noticing that Nina had turned ashen and suddenly fallen very silent.

'Yes...yes' Nina mumbled, 'I didn't expect this.'

Tatyana nodded, 'I know its hard, but it's the only way. I tried, but I'm not attractive like you, and Gorky, likes young beautiful women.'

They reached Tatyana's parents home, it was a modest house. They made her welcome. Tatyana made the introductions. Nina was shown to her room where she washed and came down for supper.

After supper Tatyana and Nina took a walk, along the narrow country road opposite the house. The street was unlit but the moonlight provided sufficient light.

'We will go to the Rose tomorrow to meet, Laila,' Tatyana said.

'Do I have to start so soon? 'Nina seemed disappointed.

The next morning, Tatyana and Nina left for the Rose. The Rose was a large Dacha, situated on the side of the lake on small hillock at Irpin. Irpin was some twenty-five kilometres from Kiev. The dacha was set back from the road, by about a hundred yards. The pine trees along the wall that surrounded the dacha kept it out of view of passersby. The road leading to the dacha opened out into a large courtyard. There were rest rooms and a self-service coffee bar at one end of the courtyard, the other end had open space that served as a car park.

The dacha itself consisted of a large lobby, with alcoves. Each alcove with a large comfortable settee, while providing privacy afforded the occupants a view of the bar and the piano. A large bar was situated on the far side, in an extension to the lobby, there were no barstools, it was not meant for single men. Tables were provided in the bar area for guests. One side of the lobby had a row of French windows, through which the lake and the surrounding hills were visible.

The dacha had suites on the first floor, ten in all, furnished opulently. The beds were king-size four poster types, the walls fitted with mirrors. The mirrors where provided with blinds, which could be drawn over the mirrors when required. The mirrors could be moved to any angle that the occupant might prefer.

The dacha boasted a kitchen run by Franco a well-known chef from France. The cellar contained some of the finest wines from France and Italy, with membership to the Rose strictly by invitation.

Tatyana and Nina, had lunch and left for the dacha. Laila the Madame who ran the Dacha woke only after 11 am. She would be ready to meet them after lunch.

It was a weekday and the dacha was not busy. Weekends were very busy, guests were required to make advance reservations. Tatyana drove through the open gates, to the parking lot. They stepped out, Nina self-consciously tugging her dress. Tatyana had made her wear a dress that accentuated her figure. The dress was an excellent fit, though a little too short for Nina's liking, Tatyana didn't seem to think so. In any case Nina carried it off superbly.

Tatyana led her in. A steward, who recognised Tatyana, looked approvingly at Nina and led them to a table. Tatyana was obviously expected.

The steward offered them a drink, Nina ordered lemonade with soda, and Tatyana an iced tea.

Laila came down the curving staircase, smiling and held her arms out for Tatyana. They kissed and then Laila turned to Nina.

'So this is your lovely cousin, I'm so happy that she has come. I'm sure you are going to be very happy here,' she said reaching for Nina's arm.

'We will talk about everything, but first let us relax and get to know each other a little more.'

Chapter 18

The two mechanics, chosen were from the KGB, started with the undercarriage. They finished within the hour.

'It's clean' they spoke to no one in particular, though Anatoly and Valentin were close by.

They then proceeded to fill in the paper work.

Chebikov was a careful man, he had survived two assassination attempts and no detail was too small for him. He always chose the route, one of three just before he got into his car. No one, not even Nikolai Molotov knew the route.

The only common areas of the three routes were at the start for about a mile, and the final two miles that took them into the city leading to the government offices.

That morning's briefings saw Anatoly as the bodyguard and driver, with the other bodyguard, Valentin Solovyov, riding as a passenger in the front seat.

Both were standing outside the gleaming Zil limousine. The Zil, specially built, had armour plating that could stop a high velocity rifle bullet at 30 yards. The car had a five-litre turbo charged engine and churned out a whopping three hundred and fifty-horse power. It had a top speed of a hundred and thirty miles per hour.

Chebikov stepped out from his official residence and looked around. He pulled on his gloves and walked to the limousine. Anatoly held the door open for him.

'Take the Mausoleum route' instructed Chebikov as he got into the limousine.

'Yes Sir' Anatoly replied, closing the door. He dropped the keys, they clanged on the concrete pavement.

Chebikov, looked out of his window as Anatoly bent to pick up the keys. The other bodyguard got into the passenger seat in the front.

Chebikov did not see the small red disc that Anatoly dropped with the keys, but did not retrieve.

A man in balaclavas and hood in a bedroom on the 12th floor in a tower block three streets away focussed through a pair of powerful binoculars. He spoke into a microphone, 'It's red.....the mausoleum route.'

'Acknowledged'.

The man put his binoculars away, and took the express elevator to the underground parking lot. A few minutes later he was tearing away at high speed on a high powered motorcycle through by lanes.

The mausoleum route would bring the limousine through the park. The motorcade for Chebikov consisted of two motorcycle outriders in front of the limousine and an identical limousine with security personnel bringing up the rear. The bodyguard next to Anatoly had his handgun on his lap.

A man with a hooded jacket at the junction spoke briefly into his hand held phone.' It's at the Park entrance.'

About a mile later, Chebikov ordered the motorcade to stop. He asked the accompanying limousine to go ahead with the outriders. The darkened glass of the limousines made it impossible to make out who was in the limousines.

Further along the road inside the park a innocuous van had pulled up its hazard lights flashing, apparently broken down on the side of the road. The driver had driven the van over the kerb onto the grass to allow room for traffic. The road inside the park curved right, making it difficult for vehicles coming into the park to see the van till they were almost on the van. The van had put out a red triangle. The triangle was only some 30 yards behind the van, but being on a curve was out of sight of oncoming motorists. Motorists had to brake hard to avoid hitting the triangle. Some of them lowered their windows and shouted at the driver who was apparently trying to fix the van, he was stretched out under the chassis they could only see his legs.

Across the road from the van, was a large clump of bushes. A keen eye would have seen two men with what seemed to be a short wide pipe, nestled in the bushes, they wore dark green hooded jackets which merged with the vegetation.

The wail of the sirens grew closer as the motorcade approached. The outriders came around the bend, the closest braked hard seeing the triangle in front of him, the bike skidded, the motorbike slipping away from under him, the momentum taking it across the tarmac where it bumped the kerb and stopped, its engine spluttered and died. The rider rolled and came to his knees.

'Bloody hell' he shouted looking wildly around him.

The second outrider also braked hard but was able to control his skid. He managed to pull the bike across as it skidded. The bike came to a halt facing the kerb away from the van. The limousine came up behind, but as if sensing something the driver stopped a good ten yards from the outrider who was in his path.

At that instance the van doors were flung open, revealing two men in balaclavas and hoods each manning a heavy machine gun. One of the machine guns blasted away at the outriders, the outrider on his bike caught by the heavy calibre bullets was lifted like a rag doll before crashing back on the tarmac, mangled beyond recognition. The machine guns in the van then swung around pumping an endless stream of bullets into the limousines. The front tyres of both were shot to bits as the high velocity bullets from the machine guns tore into them.

The second outrider still on the ground, pulled out what seemed to be a flare, and pointed it at the van, at almost the same instance one of the machine guns turned on him. The burst from the machine gun tore into the outrider's head, the helmet and his head disappeared. A flash was seen from the outrider's hand, as he squeezed off a shot from his pistol grenade. The grenade went right into the van. A flash accompanied the explosion inside the van, blowing out the top, the machine guns and the two gunmen.

A blue-white flame spurted from the bushes across the road. The shoulder fired antitank missile tore through the windshield of the first limousine. The explosion that followed lifted the car in a massive ball of flame. It crashed back to the tarmac a twisted heap of metal, mangled and black with flames licking out on all sides. There were no signs of the four men in the car, or what was once a car!

Anatoly braked hard, seemingly to make a 180 degree turn; the limousine skidded and started swinging, as the rear wheels slid across the road.

The rear of the limousine crashed into the mangled heap that was once a security car, its rear wheels spinning.

Chebikov had dropped to the floor of the car, the armour plating protecting him from the machine gun fire.

Valentin the bodyguard opened the front passenger door and dived out rolling as he hit the tarmac. He shot at the men in the bushes. His bullet caught the man with the anti-tank gun in the chest. The man pulled the trigger as he staggered back. The front of his chest turning crimson, the gun slipped from his lifeless hands. The missile shot out, hit the tarmac in front of him and exploded, blowing him, and his partner to bits. Valentin felt the heat and blast of the explosion as it lifted him up, he came crashing back to the tarmac, his left arm limp and bleeding, and his shirt shredded with thin strips clinging to his body.

Anatoly reached for his handgun, and turned off the engine.

'Why did you turn the engine off?' Chebikov barked, fear making his usually gruff voice shrill.

Anatoly calmly replied, 'All the assassins are dead,'

Chebikov grunted and heaved his frame off the floor and sat back in his seat.

Anatoly turned around and shot him thrice in the head. The back of Chebikov's head exploded from the soft nosed bullets, spraying his brain on the rear windshield. Chebikov slumped forward, dead.

Anatoly saw a movement through the corner of his eye, he turned, his gun still pointed at Chebikov. Valentin, was at the open door, blood dripping from his left hand and glassy eyed, his clothes, face and arms blackened from the missile blast, his gun lined up on Anatoly. Anatoly swung his arm around, they fired simultaneously. Anatoly saw Valentin's head rear up as he slid to the ground on his knees, swaying and toppled face first. Anatoly felt something slam into his chest, he felt a tearing sensation then a numbness, he tried to swallow but couldn't, his shirt was drenched, it was red and felt sticky, the gun suddenly felt too heavy, slipping from his hand, he could hear the wailing of the sirens. He died as his face fell forward on the steering wheel.

The fire brigade, the police and the ambulance arrived in rapid succession.

That night it was reported that the Interior Minister of Belarus, Vicktor Chebikov had been assassinated and Nikolai Molotov had been appointed the new Interior Minister.

Strangely no mention was made of the assassins, or the group to which they belonged.

Chapter 19

Date: 30th May 2003 Time: Place: Kiev

It was the summer of 2004, the sun was bright the temperature in the mid sixties. The sky was cloudless, the light breeze whisked away the few leaves dotting the pavement.

Gorky looked out of his window and whistled a tune, while dabbing on some cologne. He looked at the bottle, it was 'Polo' by Ralph Lauren and smiled. Nina had given this as a present for his birthday a couple of weeks ago.

He stepped out of the door, he was a handsome figure, tall well built, with greying hair. He was dressed in a smart pin striped Seville row suit, a silk designer tie and shoes by Bally, a sign of the change since the days of Soviet Russia.

The driver of the gleaming Zil limousine snapped to attention and opened the passenger door. Once his passenger was seated he went around to the front.

'The Dacha, Gavril', ordered Gorky.

'Yes Sir,' Gavril started the motor. The Zil glided out and sped towards the outskirts of the town.

Gorky was the Head of Security in the Ukraine. He had risen swiftly and was reportedly close to a senior member of the Russian Politburo. Gorky was an outstanding student at university and had been selected by the then head of security Vladimir Rosky. Gorky had risen through his brilliance and helped by the fact that he had married Rosky's daughter. His position afforded him the means to indulge himself with regular visits to the 'Dacha', as it was popularly known in the corridors of power. The Dacha provided a variety of experiences, predominantly sexual. It was an expensive whorehouse.

There was no routine, however Gorky indulged himself at least once or twice a month. The visits were made under the ruse of official business. It was usual for him to spend the night at the dacha when he visited Kiev.

The Zil pulled up at the Dacha. The Madame, Laila who ran the place was from Turkey, she was very discreet, it was only high-ranking officials who visited the place. It was a private club. Those without proper connections were appropriately discouraged. Gorky had had the Rose investigated as part of his first job. Laila was an attractive woman and used the opportunity to show Gorky the substantial benefits available. Gorky had been a staunch supporter since then.

As the Zil pulled up Laila opened the door. As Gorky stepped out, she went forward arms outstretched. 'My dear Gorky, how good to see you' embraced him and led him inside. At the door she beckoned to Irina 'Here is your man'.

Irina smiled at Gorky who put his arm around her waist and led her towards the stairs.

Gavril Popov, Gorky's driver and bodyguard moved the Zil to the car park away and to the left of the Dacha. He lit up a cigarette. It would be a long wait before he could turn in himself. The Madame had made arrangements for the drivers, to get something to eat from the kitchen and some bunk beds to spend the night.

Irina led Gorky up the steps to her suite. The suite was tastefully decorated, in blue. Blue reminded Irina of the clear blue skies of Cerkessk in summer. The suite consisted of a lounge with a bar at one end, leading to the bedroom, the bedroom had a dressing room and an on suite bath.

She took his jacket and made him sit in his favourite sofa.

'Will you have a drink' she asked.

'The usual', Gorky replied, stretching himself, he felt relaxed, he planned to spend the night here. He thought back, it was almost a year and six months since, Laila had introduced her to him, he had not been with any of the other women at the dacha since. Irina was educated, very attractive and surprisingly shy, very unlike the other women at the dacha. He had asked Laila where she had come from, all he had gathered was that she had come with a suitable recommendation.

Irina came to Gorky with his drink. She fixed a fruit punch for herself, and settled down in the sofa next to him. He reached out to hold her hand, squeezed it, 'Will you play for me?'

Irina smiled 'Of course' what would you like me to play?'

'Anything', Gorky said with a smile.

Irina stood up placed her glass on the mantelpiece, smoothing her full length dress as she walked to the piano. She selected the piece and began to play. Gorky loved music and the theatre, he leaned back and closed his eyes as Irina played. When she finished Gorky clapped 'Bravo that was beautiful' Irina rose, smiled at Gorky and made a small curtsey.

She looked at the clock above the mantelpiece turned to Gorky 'It's past eight, will you have something to eat?'

He nodded 'something light please'.

They sat together for a meal consisting of a salad, a small portion of roast beef, mashed potatoes and boiled vegetables. Irina chose an excellent Bordeaux for the meal. The meal ended with a chocolate soufflé, Gorky's favourite. After the meal Gorky helped himself to one of the Havana cigars, and settled himself in the sofa while Irina brought in the coffee.

It was 10 p.m., Irina rose picked up the cups which she deposited on the table and made for the bedroom to shower and change. Gorky slipped off his shoes and socks, went to the cupboard for his dressing gown and pyjamas.

Irina walked out of the bath. She had changed into a sheer silk nightdress the light behind her accentuating her figure. Gorky smiled at her, she was stunning. Irina gave him a coy

81

smile and went to her dressing table and sat down to do her face and hair.

Gorky walked up behind her, slipped his arms under hers, bending down as he always did, kissing her ear and neck, his hands gently squeezing and caressing her breasts. She felt him lean against her as he cupped his hands over her breasts.

'You are tense today,' he playfully nipped her ear.

'It's, just that my back hurts a bit,' she said, 'I'll be fine.'

Gorky tightened his arms around her and lifted her up.

As she rose, Irina leaned forward and picked up a folded handkerchief with her left hand and held it over her nose, with her right she picked up a lipstick and pointing it towards Gorky's face pressed the top. A small puff of vapour shot out into Gorky's face and nose. Gorky gasped, straightening up, his hand clutching his throat, his eyes bulging, he was choking. He staggered back and crashed to the floor. The cyanide vapour had caused a heart seizure and resulted in almost instantaneous death.

Irina screamed as she jumped up, knocking down the stool and most of the contents on the table, she dropped the lipstick on the floor among the other cosmetics, and rushed to the door shouting hysterically, 'Help, help get a doctor...doctor'. She rushed to the door.

Laila heard Irina's scream, the crash of the stool and the sound of something heavy falling to the floor. She ran up the stairs taking two steps at a time, reaching the door as Irina opened it. She saw the distraught Irina and rushed past her into the bedroom. She saw Gorky's crumpled form on the floor, his eyes bulging out of their sockets his tongue sticking out as though he had been choked. The only clothes on his body were his dressing gown. She felt for a pulse and found none. Laila rushed to the phone and dialled a number that put her directly through to the head quarters of Internal Security. She informed them that Gorky was having a heart seizure and needed an ambulance immediately.

The number was the Special Branch of the Ukraine Security Service. They handled all matters concerning high-ranking officials. In minutes two unmarked cars one with Pavlovsky the Deputy Head of Ukraine security the other with security personnel headed out to the dacha. On the way an ambulance joined the two cars with the personal physician of Gorky. The motorcade made its way to the dacha their klaxons wailing.

Laila heard the wail of the sirens drawing closer, even as she looked out through the window she saw two Zil limousines turn into the driveway with an ambulance. They screeched to a halt. Even before the Zils had stopped the doors were flung open and four men in plain clothes jumped out and made for the front door.

The ambulance came to a halt behind the Zils. The doctor stepped out and made his way to the front door while the two paramedics came out of the rear of the ambulance with a stretcher and equipment.

Pavlovsky turned to the doctor, 'Lets go' and led the way in. Laila opened the door and they gave her a questioning glance. She pointed up the stairs. They ran up the stairs and into the room. They saw the body of Gorky lying face down next to the overturned stool.

Gorky had not been moved. Laila knew that he was dead from the moment she had felt for a pulse. Irina was sitting in a corner sobbing, her hair in total disarray, and her mascara running.

The doctor knelt and felt Gorky's neck for a pulse, there was none. He gently turned the body over and with his pen torch checked the pupils, there was no movement. He turned to Pavlovsky, shook his head, then beckoned to the paramedics. They brought in a stretcher and moved the body to the ambulance.

Pavlovsky's men had taken control and were noting down the identities of all occupants. Irina and Laila were instructed to wait for him in Laila's office. Noticing the glances that Irina's flimsy nightie attracted, Laila brought her a wrap and led her into her office.

Pavlovsky took the doctor aside.' How did he die?'

'Can't say, seems to have been a severe heart seizure. I'm surprised; he had his last check up only a month ago and was fine. I·checked the body, there are no signs of any injuries. I'm puzzled, the girl said that he was gasping for air and then collapsed. I'll see what the post mortem brings up.'

The doctor had thirty years of practice to his credit. He had been chosen as the personal physician of a number of the top brass and had in his long career investigated some very sensitive cases involving violent and accidental death. To him Gorky's death was puzzling. As the medical orderlies lifted the body onto the stretcher he turned to Pavlovsky, 'We will have to notify his family.'

'Yes, as soon as I have had a word with the Minister, I'll let you know.'

The doctor nodded, he would be the one who would have to do it. He would have to think of something appropriate. The family could not be told of Gorky's extra-curricular activities.

After the doctor left in the ambulance Pavlovsky went to Laila's office where Irina and Laila waited. He settled himself in the chair behind her desk and looked at them, 'Alright, let's have it, what happened tonight?' Laila explained the events from the time Gorky arrived with Irina filling in.

'You mean to say that he suddenly collapsed and died?' he asked.

'We've told you everything that happened and everything that we know' Laila said indignantly, Irina nodded in agreement.

'Let's go to your bedroom' Pavlovsky stood up, Irina led the way.

Pavlovsky looked around at the place where Gorky had fallen. The cigar in the ashtray still smouldering caught his attention. The ash of the cigar was half an inch long, he picked it up and smelt it, it was an excellent Havana. He went past the upturned stool and stood at the dresser, the area near the upturned stool was strewn with bottles of lotions, perfumes and lipsticks, which had been knocked over.

He turned to Laila. 'I'll need to close and seal this area, I will decide if we need to investigate further'. He spoke to his aide who promptly went out and returned with a companion. They left the room. The men closed and sealed all doors.

Pavlovsky took the men aside and spoke to them. He turned to Laila, 'these men will remain here, no attempt is to be made to enter this area.'

Laila nodded, 'Please do what is necessary, I'd like this cleared up as soon as possible.'

Pavlovsky turned to Irina, 'We may want you for further questioning', Pavlovsky left in a Zil with one of the security men.

Pavlovsky reached his office, dismissed his aide, walked to the communication console and put a call through to the Interior Minister.

'Are you sure it was a heart attack?' the minister asked disbelief in his voice.

'That's the opinion of the doctor Sir, there was no signs of violence. It seems to have been a massive attack, he must have died immediately'.

'I'll wait to hear what the doctor finds. Keep me informed of further developments'.

'Yes sir', Pavlovsky was about to put down the phone, when he heard the minister say, 'Pavlovsky, I am appointing you as Head of Security, the official notification will follow, after I have appraised the President'.

Chapter 20

NATBAL

Date: 1st July 2003, 9:00 a.m.
Place: Washington D.C.

The end of the USSR as it existed before Glasnost and the birth of the CIS, led to the subsequent changes or rather phasing out of key agencies associated with the cold war. The proposal made by the heads of NATO security, had led to the formation of an autonomous agency named the "North Atlantic Baltic Watch," formed with members drawn from NATO countries. The Heads of Security of the NATO members were apprehensive of the state of affairs in the CIS. The agency nicknamed NATBAL had its headquarters in an office run by an electronics company known as "Q Systems". Q Systems was a Government Organisation and was known to be closely connected with the Central Intelligence Agency of the United States and had as its legitimate business the development of advanced electronic gadgetry for missiles and defence related space programmes.

The hawks in the American establishment had their suspicions about Soviet Russia and wanted to continue clandestine surveillance and intelligence gathering. The Aldrich Ames affair was seen as especially damaging to the US intelligence community.

The current chief of NATBAL, Brian Turner was an ex-chief of the branch of the CIA specialising in disinformation.

The security chiefs of NATO knew that in spite of the changes in the KGB and despite 'Glasnost' the KGB continued the use of disinformation. Disinformation was a process by which a Government spread damaging information resulting in the diversion of resources and energies of Opposition Governments or Agencies leading to the destabilisation of governments.

The chief of NATBAL was an expert in intelligence gathering and was widely credited with having passed on information to Yorbachev about the October plot by pro Communists. However as matters turned out, Yorbachev and his Politburo members disregarded the information which led to the events which has since created history.

Brian Turner was a shrewd man and worked like the chairman of a large Corporation. Reports needed to be precise and typed on one side of an A4 sheet of paper with each finding and conclusion clearly put down. Nothing of importance that went on in the erstwhile USSR escaped him. He liked men who could think and arrive at conclusions based on logic and 'gut feel'. He would often explain that 'gut feel' was really a result of knowledge and experience of the territory. If he needed explanations or if information of a substantial nature was to be disseminated, he called for a meeting.

He walked into his office, in Washington DC, on the Monday morning. The weather was cold and damp, he glanced out of the window and he could see the trees stripped of their leaves, dripping as the drizzle intensified. His secretary walked in with his morning coffee. He liked it dark and strong.

'Good morning Sir, awful day isn't it?'

'Morning Mary, terrible weather', he busily tamped the tobacco in his pipe, and picked up the report that Mary had put on the table.

'Came in this morning', she said and left.

Brian glanced at the report and frowning spoke into the phone, 'Mary, can you please bring in the Red folder'.

Mary knew exactly which red folder he was referring to. It was Brian Turner's habit of putting papers which his 'gut feel' said were important and connected, but which on the face of it seemed totally disconnected in a Red, signature type folder.

Mary walked in with the folder, left it on the table and left. Brian was deeply engrossed in the first report, puffing vigorously on his pipe.

The intelligence report on his table was about a wagonload of roubles that had passed through Poland in transit to Greece. The roubles were transferred to a truck at the Polish border and moved across the Balkans to Greece. In Greece the truck had turned up in a scrap yard with the interior stripped. German intelligence had reported that the truck was escorted by two men who were later recognised as KGB officers attached to the interior ministry from files held by them. A trace put out found that they were no longer with the KGB with current whereabouts unknown.

Brian frowned, and called out, 'Mary can you get me a fresh cup of coffee, the darn coffee has gone cold.'

He then reached out to one of the reports in the red folder and started reading. Colossal sums were being laundered. These were the profits of crime mainly narco-dollars. The Mafia was funnelling resources into legitimate business by buying them out and setting up trading companies. One of them was listed as Intrasyn which traded in commodities and crude oil. Shell companies were set up in tax havens and the profits, which were in some cases phenomenal, channelled to them from various transcontinental deals. All transactions were on a high seas basis, with documents being switched. A product sold in Frankfurt was delivered in Thailand, and being a high seas transaction, were not subject to local taxes or the need to file returns - a most effective cover for the narco -dollars and profits that were being realised.

Mary walked in with a fresh coffee, 'you're not drinking your coffee, no wonder its cold'. She left a steaming cup on the table and picked up the cold one.

'Thanks, Mary, hand me that report will you.' He stretched for the third report from the red folder and continued reading. With the Russian economy staggering from hyperinflation, roubles were highly devalued and the Russians were looking for dollars. An offer made by a Russian high ranking officer of rockets, anti-tank missiles and 'enriched uranium' to Iraq for a sum of five million dollars had been intercepted. The merchandise would be delivered at Bandar Abbas, where Mafia connections across borders ensured speedy and uninterrupted movement of goods. This trade was so efficiently managed that legitimate trading organisations would have been proud of the system. Delivery was guaranteed and money was always collected, there were simply no defaults. Defaults meant a very sudden death.

Brian Turner froze when he saw the photograph and the note at the bottom. It read. "Photograph taken at 19:30 hours at Geneva by Interior Furnishers," an undercover surveillance company set up by NATBAL. The photograph had been taken from a high rise building facing the chateau. The chateau was listed as the Austrian residence of a director of Intrasyn. The photograph was not clear, it was only of half the face, but Brian Turner knew that it was of Alexander Zhirinovsky.

'What the devil is this fellow doing here', Brian spoke out aloud. Was this the first time that Zhirinovsky had come to the west incognito or was this the first time intelligence had been able to obtain a photograph? He wondered. This meant that Intrasyn had connections with the old Russian Communist machine.

Brian Turner, put the three reports together, there was something going on out there, he could feel it in his gut... something big. He decided to call a meeting of the NATO Heads of Security.

'Mary', he called out. Mary came in with her pen and pad ready to jot down notes.

'Call a meeting for Monday next week', he said, and returned to puffing his pipe, the pipe had gone out, 'Damn' he mumbled, rummaging in his desk for a box of matches. Mary came around picked up a box of matches from behind the tray and handed it to him.

Mary put the envelopes marked 'Most important' and sent it out by the diplomatic bag. Each NATO head of security received the message the next morning, read it and destroyed it.

Chapter 21

Date: 8th December 2003 Time:10:00 a.m.
Place: Washington D.C.

The NATO security chiefs of the member nations arrived one by one. They had each come in a military aircraft. The pilots having been briefed an hour before takeoff on the destination and the flight plan, and indeed the identity of their passenger. The chiefs from Europe had taken off shortly after dark in the wintry evening, while their American counterpart had taken off some 5 hours earlier. They landed at the military airfield. They were met on the tarmac by an unmarked limousine driven by a sergeant and accompanied by a senior NATO officer.

The first to arrive was the American chief, followed by the German and then the others. The last to arrive was the Turkish chief.

The limousines swept out towards the south of the city. They entered the city outskirts, and swept into a wide driveway through a set of open gates. The road led into an estate. A hundred yards from the first set of gates they came to a halt at a set of high wrought iron gates. The driver put his palm on to the sensor that was on a pedestal erected ten yards from the gates on the driver's side. He removed his palm at a prompt that appeared on the screen. The gates swung open and the limousine passed through the gates. A careful observer would have noticed the small camera that recorded and transmitted the images back to a security block inside the building.

The sensor itself had been calibrated to check the palm and compare the signature of the print with those stored in the system. If the print did not match, the first set of gates would have closed behind the vehicle, trapping the vehicle between the two gates, while setting off an alarm at the guardhouse. These were simple precautions but very effective.

The chiefs were ushered in by a member of the security detail and led to a large room with a round table. The room was equipped with all manner of gadgetry and a sophisticated video projection and presentation system. At one end there was a large map of the world with the borders of NATO highlighted.

There was a simple writing pad, a pen and a carafe of water and a glass at each seat. Each member was escorted to his seat.

Once all the chiefs were seated, Brian Turner turned to them.

'Gentlemen thank you for coming' he put down the three reports. 'Over the past ten years or so there have been a number of incidents. They involve the movement and laundering of large sums of money from Russia. Traces have shown that these sums are being transferred to an account in Switzerland. The account is in the name of an organisation, "Intrasyn", a major trading conglomerate.' He paused, and took a sip from his glass. He would have dearly loved to light up, but all meetings were strictly non-smoking.

'We have had a routine surveillance report filed from a watchdog agency of a meeting at a chateau in Geneva. The chateau has been under surveillance for the last three months. This was after a small time narcotics dealer was picked up for questioning and had a piece of paper in his wallet which had the address of the chateau. A photograph taken has captured a partial photograph of what we believe is a Russian politician Alexander Zhirinovsky, a hard-liner. What was he doing in Geneva? A quick check on all airports and marinas was done of the days immediately before and after the date of the photograph. There is no record anywhere of entry or exit under his natural name. When we requested the logs the following day, they were reported erased. The person responsible didn't have a clue how the logs were erased'.

'The photograph was studied by an agent of NATBAL and he immediately recognised Zhirinovsky. Headquarters then ran a check on the chateau, the occupant and his organisation. The chateau belongs to "Intrasyn", the same organisation to which funds are being channelled. The occupant is the local representative'.

Brian Turner looked around him at his guests. Some were making notes, the others waiting for him to continue.

'Intrasyn,' he explained is short for 'International Trading Syndicate'. Its activities cover international trading in commodities. Storage and movement of Industrial raw material, including radio-active raw material such a uranium and thorium, grain, oils, and currency'.

'Intrasyn, is a major conglomerate and has a turnover in excess of 60 billion dollars, with a major share of the world grain and oilseeds trade. Its other activities include shipping. It owns and operates container vessels, tankers and break bulk carriers.'

He picked up a piece of paper, 'Gentlemen I have here a report which was part of an investigation by an undercover investigator which reads as follows, "A trader could if he had the connections obtain Roubles through the black market or through normal market channels. Buy a ton of crude petroleum in Russia for the rouble equivalent of seven dollars and sell it for one hundred and forty dollars in Western Europe. The foreign crook would need to have connections with a Russian Politician. With the help of the politician the foreigner could open a Russian bank account and a licence to buy roubles at huge discounts." He put the paper down and continued.

'The company is quoted on all major stock exchanges and enjoys a very good reputation. It is staffed by some of the brightest students from Ivy League colleges and has contributed substantial sums for good causes and charities.'

He paused. Some of his colleagues were leaning forward in their seats. 'The headquarters is in Muhu an island off Estonia in the Baltic Sea. The island incidentally is part of Estonia', he paused, took a sip of water and looked around at the faces at the table. There were frowns around the table. Those around the table were used knowing, and found it uncomfortable to be learning of an organisation and its activities at this stage.

'Muhu, gentlemen' he continued, 'Is well placed for travel, by sea, air and has the advantage of being rather out of mainline traffic', he paused, 'If you see what I mean. The island has excellent communications systems, and is linked with all major trade centres.' We have monitored their activities, such of those that we are aware of for some time now. Intrasyn has branches in all European capitals, in the United States, in Iran and Iraq, all in the guise of subsidiaries'. He held up his palm, when some of the members annoyed asked.

'Why haven't you told us about it?'

'It would have been premature, and I assure you that every single activity of theirs is legal', he paused.' The activities and the movement of currency and goods have quadrupled during the last twelve months, and particularly after the collapse of the Russian economy. We have run a check on the directors of Intrasyn and its subsidiaries and have found that the key directors are of Russian origin and are or have been members of the Communist Party.'

He shuffled his papers, picked out a single typed note and began. 'I have learnt last week that the administration of the storage and movement of all fissile material in Russia has been entrusted to Intrasyn. And that there is no clear record of the quantities held. He heard the deep intake of breath around the table.

'Gentlemen, the reason why I called for this meeting was to brief you on Intrasyn and its activities. The photograph that we received last week, I believe, is of Alexander Zhirinovsky. What was he doing in Geneva? There is something out there Gentlemen, and we need to find out what.'

Brian Turner looked around, 'That's all gentlemen, any questions?'

The NATO Security Chiefs left one by one. Escorted to their cars by their bodyguards and driven away to the airport; all following separate routes. They were driven directly to the tarmac to their planes. Each plane taxied to take its place among the queue for takeoff.

Chapter 22

INTERNATIONAL TRADING SYNDICATE- INTRASYN

Date: 18th December 2003, Place: Muhu,
Time: 5.45 pm

It was twilight when the first of a series of limousines swept through the bright glare of floodlights to a barrier that was manned by a guard inside a glass fronted cubicle. The guard was armed with an Uzi machine pistol. There were high wrought iron gates beyond the barrier, the entrance to a winding road up a hillside into a wooded area. The limousines had dark tinted windows. It was impossible to see the inside even when the reading light was turned on. The limousines stopped before the barrier and the driver, who inserted the palm of his left hand into a slot, lowered the window. In a few seconds a green light flashed in the cubicle and the guard operated a switch which lifted the barrier. Careful observation would have shown that the glass of the cubicle was bullet proof and that there were two heavy machine guns mounted on either side of the wrought iron gates. The guns were pointed at the driver of the car and the front tyres. These could be operated remotely by the guard from inside the cubicle.

The limousines went through the gates and continued up a steep winding road. The road ended where it opened out to a large courtyard. The limousines stopped at the entrance to a large mansion. The mansion was built in the fashion of the palaces in Great Britain, similar to the Blenheim Palace in Woodstock.

A guard escorted the lone passenger in each limousine into the palace. The driver parked the limousine at a designated parking slot. After parking the vehicle the driver stepped out and stood by his vehicle. The drivers did not nod or acknowledge the presence of the other drivers. There was a marked similarity in their builds and manner. Each was at least six-foot plus, well built, and dressed in black, with close-cropped hair. They were handpicked bodyguards, and owed total allegiance to their masters.

Each member was taken through to a large room panelled in oak, on the walls hung a number of rare paintings of the masters. As members entered, Zhirinovsky greeted them with a warm handshake. Drinks were being served from a sumptuous bar at the end of the room. The table was set for dinner, there was light talk among the members who arrived. They had come from various parts of the Western Hemisphere and included, drug barons, arms merchants, Russian Generals, and principal shareholders of some arms producers. They had all travelled under false passports. Their official itinerary would have placed them in another part of the globe. If investigations were made, records would show that a person of the name and description had in fact travelled to the specified destination.

They took their seats after all of them had arrived and proceeded to enjoy a delicious meal starting with a sea food cocktail, followed by a first course of Pollo Picante and a main course of a rare Chateaubriand made from Scottish Angus. The meal was complimented with a selection of the finest wines. Dessert, consisted of a choice of some delicious soufflés and chocolate pastries. As soon as the tables were cleared and the brandy and Havanas taken around, at a signal from Zhirinovsky, the waiting staff left closing the doors behind them.

Vladimir Sokolov, the chief of Intrasyn, rose and addressed the guests.

'Comrades, you have met comrade Zhirinovsky as you came in, I am pleased that he has taken time off from his busy schedule to join us. There are a number of things to be done to achieve the goals that we have set for ourselves. I am happy to inform you that our plans are progressing as scheduled'.

He turned to Zhirinovsky, and said 'I request Comrade Zhirinovsky to address the gathering'.

The members applauded as Zhirinovsky rose. He looked around at those at the table.

'Dear comrades, I will come straight to the point. You are aware there has been a lot happening from the time we last met. The whole state of the Russian nation is in shambles, we find ruin and decadence in every aspect of our society and life.'

The 2002-2004 financial crisis affected us badly. We have been able to withstand the downturn through the leadership of Vladimir Pushkin.

He was breathing heavily, his face puffed. 'We have been exploited by the West, the so called Democratic Governments. They promised Yorbachev money and aid for reforms, but let us down. They have seen to it that the men elected to government are mere puppets who toe the line of the Americans and the Europeans. As a result Russian manufacturing is being broken up, and being sold off. The retired Russian farmer, soldier or factory worker finds that he has no savings and no welfare.' He paused and took a sip of water.

'Russian farms are being broken up as part of the "New Order". This is an idea of Western Capitalist land reform experiments. This move suggests a determination to uproot a system of collectivised agriculture implemented by Stalin in the 1920's. Young people are leaving the countryside. The equipment is broken down and sold by corrupt officials, with the proceeds going into their pockets.'

His audience some sipping their brandies and puffing their cigars were listening with rapt attention, they knew that Zhirinovsky was an ardent Russian and those who had arrived from the West knew that what he said was true. The west was frightened of the Russia after the breakup of the CIS. The only Russia that they could deal with was a Russia that was bankrupt and corrupted. This short-sighted thinking was behind the dirty deal they dealt Yorbachev promising him money when the reforms were in place but in the end they sent him back empty handed, leaving him no room to manoeuvre politically in his country.

'Gentlemen', Zhirinovsky continued. 'Look at what we have become, a third rate country, where is our pride. The cities are filthy, there is no security, and even crime is less organised in the hands of petty criminals and bosses.' There was a chuckle around the table with the drug barons exchanging glances and smiling.

'We are not the power we once were, the western alliance is breaking us up, worried about Russian nationalism. They are taking steps to see that we do not reclaim our sphere of influence in the Baltics and Eastern Europe.'

Zhirinovsky, leant on the table, picked up his brandy and had a short sip, choked on it and spluttered, 'Excuse me', wiped his face with a tissue and continued.

'If we don't fight the danger now, we are lost and comrades, your businesses are lost too'.

He looked around at the arms dealers and the arms producers all of whom had a major interest in promoting conflict, and the cold war.

Zhirinovsky continued. 'Without the cold war our economies will go down in ruins.' He gestured to the American arms producer. 'Your Government has already cut back on defence programmes, has cut back on research, the space programme. I can go on gentlemen'.

He paused. 'You need conflict like the gulf war, to test your arms and to sell your arms. You need a Vietnam. You need Communism to make your Government put funds into NATO and maintain a nuclear deterrent. How is the world to progress?'

He looked around the table. 'Comrades, politics is all about lies and terror, my country cannot afford a democracy. We have to protect the world from the spread of those extremists from the Middle East and Pakistan. We are beginning to see the effects in Serbia and in Chechnya.'

There were nods around the table, extremists were creating problems in the west as well.

Zhirinovsky paused, the air around the table was still with expectancy, he had a way with his audience, and was known for making shocking statements.

'Comrades, the time has come to act. The people are ready and we must set the stage to take over and bring back the glory of Communism and re-establish a Greater Russia.'

There were cheers and thumping of tables, the Russian General stood up. 'Comrade, I pledge myself to the cause. Our people are being put into place. Our comrades who believe in our cause, are everywhere and will give their lives for the struggle.'

Zhirinovsky went around the table and handed them each an envelope.

'Comrades this is the plan, read it, commit it to memory, especially the dates and destroy the note.'

Each of them read and re-read the note, there were sharp intakes of breath, one by one they burnt the envelope and the single sheet of paper.

Zhirinovsky stood up. 'Gentlemen I wish you all a safe journey back, we will be in touch as usual through the channels we have set up. There are specific tasks that have to be done.

Comrade Sokolov has briefed you on the actions that need to be taken, and even as we speak the stage is being set in motion.'

Zhirinovsky and Sokolov stood at the door as each of the members filed out. They shook hands, and were escorted to the front door to their waiting limousines. They left without a further word to each other, aware that in the days ahead there would be demands made which would have to be met.

Chapter 23

Date: 14th January 2004,
Place: Washington D.C, Time: 4.45 pm

It was five in the evening. Brian Turner was getting ready to leave when Desmond Bain, NATBAL'S Chief of Information for the Baltics, walked in. He handed Brian two typed sheets. Brian puffed on his pipe, reading the papers.

'I've been looking for a pattern, the sightings of Zhirinovsky, and the reports. I think that there is trouble brewing in the Baltics.' Desmond ventured, 'I'll see you in the morning'.

Brian respected Desmond's judgement, he nodded, 'I'll read them and give you a call.'

With that Desmond left.

Mary walked in with Brian's coffee and placed it on the table. 'I'm planning to leave is there anything else?'

'No thanks Mary, I'll see you in the morning', he settled down with the papers Brian had given him.

The pages contained a series of news items reported in leading international newspapers.

A report from the Ukraine where the President had decided not to seek a second term had cast a shadow over the deal to rid the Ukraine of nuclear weapons.

The President of Russia when he addressed the Duma after his election in 1993 had stated. 'We do not consider a single country or a coalition in the West or East to be our enemy. Our Foreign Policy is to create a belt of good neighbourly friendly states. The new military doctrine and new military ideology of Russia should proceed from these premises'.

'It is necessary that in the post Soviet world, Russia control as great a share as possible of the old Soviet Russia's strategic assets'.

Brian read the notes made by Desmond.

The most important of these strategic assets were the 25000 nuclear warheads. A mix of intercontinental ballistic missiles, intermediate range ballistic missiles, land and submarine based missiles, tactical and battlefield weapons. Battlefield weapons were those which were fired as artillery shells. The majority was based in Russia, a little over one thousand six hundred in the Ukraine, a thousand five hundred in Belarus and one hundred in Kazakhstan. Among the nine main air bases, three were in the Ukraine, one in Kazakhstan and five in Russia. All the nuclear submarine based missiles were based in Russia, in ports in the East and the West.

Russia had signed the START-II, the Strategic Arms Limitation Treaty with the United States in June 1992 and had committed to reducing its intercontinental ballistic missiles from 21000 to 3500 by the year 2009. START-II had envisaged that Russia, the Ukraine, Belarus, and Kazakhstan would reduce their arsenals as agreed. Russia as the major partner of the CIS states had agreed to enter into treaties with the three Balkan states to effect the reduction. With Kazakhstan having transferred its arsenal to Russia it was now between Russia, the Ukraine and Belarus.

The Presidents of Russia, the Ukraine, and Belarus had agreed to work out the details of the treaty to be signed at a summit meeting to be held in Kiev. The summit was to be attended by the Presidents of Russia, Ukraine and Belarus. A special invitation had been extended to the President of the United States of America. The date was fixed for the 30th of October 2011.

Brian turned to the other notes.

The cover story on Pravda read 'As per the terms of the Treaty, Ukraine would relinquish its arsenal of more than 1600 nuclear warheads would hand over control control of over 350 ships of the Black Sea Fleet to Russia; and Belarus would merge with Russia to form a two-state community, a European Union style body.' The article continued, 'however there was wide spread disagreement from the Ukraine public who saw this as a move by Russia to control them.'

The Treaty would pave the way for the formal signing of SALT-IV, which envisaged the destruction of all missiles with a range of more than 3000 miles whether land or submarine based.

The treaty would also remove any ban on the development of the ABM, the Anti Ballistic Missile or Star Wars type of testing, development and deployment.

Brian sucked on his pipe, it had gone out, he frowned, there was a lot happening and decided another meeting of the Security Chiefs was necessary. The information he had received and the reports from the Central Intelligence Agency of the United States of America made it imperative for NATBAL to take immediate action.

Chapter 24

Date: 18th January 2004,
Place: Washington D.C., Time: 9.15 am

Brian had seated himself at the table awaiting the arrival of the Security Chiefs. They entered one by one and took their seats around the table. Brian nodded to each of them as they came in. When all had been seated he rose.

'Good afternoon Gentlemen, I have here your reports after the last meeting. I have discussed the reports with my colleagues here and the time has come for us to look at the series of events, which on the face of it seem disjointed.'

'We have studied the reports received from you and have found a pattern.'

'The reports have originated from Thailand, Laos, Burma, China, Afghanistan, Columbia, Jamaica and Nigeria.'

"A series of drug busts, there was a distinct pattern. Heroin from the Far East via Afghanistan, the modes of transport by truck in areas where border controls were lax and where officials could be easily bribed. Then via the Baltics into Europe"

He cleared his throat, took a sip of water, he touched the pipe in his pocket, and continued.

"Cocaine and Cannabis came in from Nigeria through couriers. Colombian cocaine cartels were shipping drugs into the Baltic States. Who route them into Europe. Consignments were hidden in fruit, and grain sacks. When they arrived at a port they were transported under bond to Baltic destinations without inspection, to addresses which did not exist. On arrival at the destination the shipping company would put up the merchandise for auction to realise payment, minus of course a few sacks or crates which held the contraband. The shipping company was legally safe since it carried goods based on a declaration. A random inspection would confirm the goods to be as per the manifest. Once at the destination the transfer was simple, especially if the officials concerned looked the other way."

'NATBAL's investigations had shown that all customs officers at the Baltic ports used by Intrasyn were on Intrasyn's payroll and all shipping companies which had auctioned merchandise were owned and operated by Intrasyn.'

Brian paused looked around at the intent faces. They were waiting for him to continue.

'Further investigations have shown that Intrasyn conducts all transactions through banks in Switzerland, Luxembourg, and the Channel Islands. Documents were always forwarded to offshore accounts. More details were not available in spite of legislation enacted to curb laundering of drug money. Moreover since Intrasyn carried on a huge volume of transactions which were perfectly legal it was impossible to track such transactions. The subsequent transfer of funds to other numbered accounts was legal and handled by reputed firms with impeccable credentials. A check on the personnel in these firms had come up with a blank. All executives were clean and came highly recommended. Intrasyn had set up a foolproof system to launder its drug money.'

Brian went on. 'Intrasyn is a professionally run company where policies are set and monitored by a corporation that is privately held. Intrasyn provides Estonia a country with a population of 1.6 million and a GDP of 2.1 billion dollars, more than half its GDP and provides employment for a quarter of its eight hundred thousand workforce. Intrasyn in short controls Estonia, its government and its policy.'

Brian Turner picked up a report surveillance had filed, he continued,

'When we last met we discussed the meeting at the chateau, and the presence of Zhirinovsky in Geneva.'

He paused,' and the sudden death of the Head of Security of the Ukraine from a heart attack, a few years ago, and the assassination of the Interior Minister of Belarus.'

'There was a encrypted transmission right after the Ukrainian Head of Security was assassinated, which we are trying to decipher.' He went on, 'Reports suggest that the Cerkessk incident in 1999, might be connected.

He looked around him, 'Gentleman I don't think that the death of the Ukrainian Head of Security and the transmission was a co-incidence.'

'He was a reformer, unlike his former compatriots who were from the KGB. I for one will personally miss him and the influence he wielded in the Kremlin.'

Brian moved to a large map of the Baltic region, which had coloured flag-pins stuck in them; he picked up a pointer.

'These red flags mark the route of the drugs and contraband, and the green the flow of money. We know where the drugs are going. Our traces have shown that money is moving into the very areas where we have noticed a marked increase in the activities of the Russian Mafia and where the Russian Nationalist movement is strongest.'

He paused, 'the origin of the money gentlemen we know is from Intrasyn. They buy commodities at exorbitant prices, from corporations controlled by nationalists when they can obtain it for a fraction of the cost elsewhere; one way of transferring money across borders legitimately.'

There was pin drop silence when Brian Turner finished.

Brian turned to the American head of Security.

'Donald, will take us through some of the CIA findings.'

Donald nodded to Brian, stood up, cleared his throat and began.

'Some time ago, shortly before the Soviet Union broke up, a Russian Military intelligence officer Oleg Penkovsky with the rank of a colonel defected to us. This was around the same time as the arrest of Aldrich Ames, the CIA man accused of spying for Moscow. I have gone through the transcripts of the de-briefing, where Oleg mentions that contracts for the storage and accounting of fissile material were entrusted to Intrasyn, even though this was against the recommendations of the Defence Ministry. The politburo member who swung the decision in favour of Intrasyn was General Pushkin.'

The Security chiefs of NATBAL knew of Pushkin as a vehement hard-liner, they nodded to themselves, this was as expected.

Donald went across to the map and looked at it, finding the place he wanted, went on.

'There is however an interesting connection. This Pushkin is from Cerkessk. The same Cerkessk where there was a massacre, similar to the killings of Riga and Vilnius. In both cases the murderers disappeared without a trace. It is widely believed that the pro-democrats were involved, and that it had sanction at the highest level.'

'There are other reports of the increasing polarisation within Russia, with the nationalists increasing in strength. Our analysis points to a movement that is gaining strength, a pro-communist movement.'

'Can we infiltrate Intrasyn?' Farhan of Turkey asked.

'I'm afraid that is impossible', replied Brian. 'The operative will get as far as a legitimate manager in a corporation, the controls are outside. We infiltrated an operative as a manager into the organisation sometime ago.'

'Where is he now?' Farhan asked.

'Dead', replied Brian. 'He had a nasty accident during a water skiing vacation in the Black Sea. The facts were not available, his wife and family were taken care of financially by Intrasyn and the matter closed.'

One of the members wanted to be excused, so Brian decided to stop, it was time for dinner and the group moved to the dining room which had been laid out.

The staff came around serving drinks from the bar. Brian was served his favourite gin and tonic. The chiefs had all been served their drinks and were talking to each other, exchanging notes. The meal was excellent, served with a French Chardonnay and an Italian Chianti. After dinner they moved back to the main room where they were served Remy Martin and Havana cigars.

Brian looked around to see if all had been served and then preceded.

'Let us now take a look at the happenings in Russia, especially of the hawks in the cabinet. We see Russia's intent to reabsorb what it calls "near abroad", all the component parts of the old Soviet Empire from the Baltics to Central Asia. An important factor is that twenty five million Russians live outside Russia's borders, spread in the Baltic States. We have received reports of plans to merge Russia with its western neighbour the former Soviet republic of Belarus.'

He reached down for another sheaf of papers.

'Let's take a look at the political arena. We have the expansion of NATO, and the American stance that adding former Warsaw Pact allies into the ranks of the NATO alliance is a good idea. Many in Russia, especially the hard-liners see this move as a step to undermine Russia's influence and authority. The Russian's have clearly stated that they are not prepared to live with any of the former Soviet republics inside NATO. Russia's Parliament sees any move by the Government to toe the western line as anti-Nationalist.'

'The split within Russian politics has resulted in two groups, those that are pro-west and pro-reform and those that are pro-Nationalist and pro-Communist. The pro-West, democrats have failed the people, and are being propped up by the west.

He picked up a remote control and pressed a switch, the lights went dim and a picture was projected onto a screen that had slid down automatically at the far side of the room. Some of the members closest to the screen moved their chairs around to get a better view.

'This is the photograph of the person who was seen at the chateau. As you can see it is not a full frontal picture. Have a look at this.'

He pressed the remote and another photograph was projected, this was a full frontal view of a man, the person bore a good resemblance to the man in the first picture.

'This man,' Brian continued, 'Is Alexander Zhirinovsky, the rising Czar of Russia, and these are some excerpts from his speeches:'

"American Zionists offered me one hundred million dollars if I left politics"

"All we want is three countries, Afghanistan, Iran and Turkey. Russia can save the world from the spread of Islam"

"I may have to shoot one hundred thousand people, but the other three hundred million will live peacefully."

"We must deal with ethnic minorities as America did with the Red Indians and Germany did with the Jews"

"I will immediately declare a dictatorship. The country cannot afford democracy for now."

'That's the information gentlemen. We have to decide on our course of action.' Brian sat down and picked up his pipe, stuck it in his mouth unlit.

There was a murmur from around the table, the information put together sounded ominous.

'We have a situation where, there is a definite connection between Intrasyn and the Communists and Nationalists in Russia. And possibly a connection between Intrasyn and the attempted assassination of Shevardnadze.'

'Is there any connection with the death of the Chief of Security of Ukraine?' The US chief asked.

'Can we investigate the death of the security chief' asked the British chief, 'Perhaps it can throw some light on the circumstances at his death. Do we know where it happened?'

Brian chuckled, 'He was visiting an exclusive brothel maintained for high-ranking officers, politicians and politburo members. Membership was by invitation only.'

'How do we investigate a situation inside Russia?' the German chief asked. 'Besides, NATBAL does not exist, at least for the real purpose, as far as the Russians are concerned.'

Brian sucked on his pipe.

'Perhaps the time has come to use the services of Markes.' There were questioning looks around the table.

'Markes Trubin, Gentlemen is one of our operatives in Russia. He has been inactive for some time now.

'We need an operative who Ames did not know about. As it stands most of our operatives in Russia have been compromised.'

There was some more discussion, future action and plans were discussed and finalised.

Brian rose. It was almost 11.30 p.m.

'Thank you for coming gentlemen, no doubt we will see each other again.'

They left as they had arrived, with their bodyguards and in the same cars, to the air force base, for their journeys back to their stations.

Chapter 25

Date: 2nd January 2005, Place: Amsterdam, Time: 9.15 am

Boris Pugo walked into the office of "News de Internacionale", at its Atlantic headquarters in Amsterdam. It was a cool sunny day in spring, he had just completed an assignment in Turkey. His travels had taken him into the Kurd held areas. His report and the photographs of atrocities meted out to the Kurds had made the western world sit up and take notice. Turkey being a front line NATO State had enjoyed US support for many years, but with the information and photographs that News de Internacionale had published, Amnesty International had made a damning report in its annual findings. The US administration had immediately sent The Secretary of State to Turkey to try and help it resolve its differences with the Kurds.

Dick Verglas was in Amsterdam, his move to Amsterdam had been made shortly after Boris had joined the magazine and was in recognition of his contribution.

A meeting had been called by the Chairman, to kick-start the opening of the East European headquarters at Warsaw.

Boris walked into Dick's office, it was not the normal sort of furnishing one would expect in an office. A solid rose wood desk stood in one corner, facing the window, the door on the left led to his secretary's office. The carpet was deep, and there was a single chair, straight backed in front of his desk. It was clear that he didn't enjoy people sitting around if there was no work to be discussed. At the end of the room near the entrance stood a peculiar coat hanger, made from the trunk of a small tree, it had been painted or coated with some sort of resin, its branches serving as coat hangers. Dick's hat, scarf and woollen overcoat was slung across it. The window overlooked a canal, and a small park across it.

Dick frowned and looked up at the sound of the door being opened.

Boris and he had become good friends, and respected each other's ability. There was no formality between them. Boris had not knocked and neither had his secretary buzzed him.

'Ah, the master in his den.' Boris strode across to Dick. Dick smiled and got up out of his chair, his right arm stretching to shake Boris's hand.

'Hi Boris, good to see you' Dick said, as they pumped each other's hand vigorously.

The side door opened and a flustered secretary walked in. 'I'm sorry Mr Verglas, I didn't send him in,' she stopped realising that Dick wasn't unhappy with the situation.

'This is Mr. Boris Pugo, I'm sure you've heard of him', he turned to Boris, 'This is Lana my secretary'.

'Pleased to meet you', Boris shook hands with Lana. Lana was pretty, perhaps in her mid thirties, with dark hair and a swinging walk, which accentuated her well, shaped hips.

'Can I get you something to drink, 'she asked looking from Boris to Dick.

'Some coffee will be great', Boris answered. Then added,' black please, and one sugar.'

'I'll have some coffee too', Dick told her. She knew he liked it with a lot of milk and one sugar.

Lana left, swinging her hips, Boris looking appreciatively after her. 'Nice girl,' he commented.

'Don't know what I'd do without her', Dick said.

Boris settled down in front of Dick.

'You might have guessed why we called you down here', Dick asked.

'Is it to do with Warsaw,' Boris asked.

Dick nodded, 'The Chairman is keen that we establish the Warsaw office as the headquarters covering Eastern Europe and Russia, the erstwhile Union of the Soviet Socialist Republic'.

'He wants you to head the office. You will run it independently, on the same lines that I run this office,'

Dick smiled. 'It's a promotion, I hope you like it.'

Boris's face broke into a broad smile. 'I didn't expect to head the office.' Boris replied, 'It's an honour.'

'The Chairman will make the announcement shortly,' Dick replied.

'You will need to make arrangements, my office here will help you in sorting out details, bank accounts, accommodation and the rest of the necessities. You will need to look for staff and others who are going to help you run the place.' He paused, 'I know it's not what you expected in a manner of speaking, you will have some administrative responsibilities, but look at it this way, all the real plum coverage will be yours for the taking.'

Boris's face relaxed, he smiled, he hadn't thought of it quite like that, what Dick said was true. It would make matters easier to handle.

'It sounds fine now', he replied, 'For a moment I thought I'd be tied to a desk.'

A month from the day Boris met Dick, the Warsaw office was up and running. Boris had chosen his staff carefully, his second in command was a woman, Andrea, who had a stint with Tass in Moscow. She had been recommended by Sokolov of Intrasyn.

Chapter 26

MARK RICARDI

Date: 29th January 2005, Place: Odessa,
Time: 5.50 am

Mark Ricardi now known as Markes Trubin, was a western mole. He was secreted into the Soviet Union, many years ago by MI 6, the Secret Intelligence Service of the United Kingdom responsible for international clandestine activities and national security. Markes's files had been transferred to Brian when NATBAL was formed.

Mark had been recruited by MI6, as a fresh graduate. He had a diploma in computer engineering. Was a keen sportsman, and made his mark in the university rugby team. He was of medium height, loose limbed and blond, with sharp features. He walked with a swinging gait.

He had been put through the SAS course and trained in unarmed combat, explosives and in all types of arms. He was a natural with a handgun and qualified as a Markesman. His natural aptitude with computers had helped MI6 in hacking certain sensitive sites in the course of its activities in Saudi Arabia.

Unknown to the royal Saudi family, every activity of each member was catalogued and secreted away. MI6 would use the information in the event the Saudi's refused to co-operate.

During his service in the Middle East, Markes had learnt Russian. It was a necessity to assess the Afghanistan situation and Russian involvement. He had been infiltrated as a computer technician employed by the United Nations.

After the Russians left Afghanistan, MI6 felt that with the upheavals predicted in the Soviet Union it would be prudent to have an agent secreted away as a mole, to be activated if and when necessary.

He was sent to Samsun a port and a fishing village in Turkey on the Black Sea coast directly across Odessa. He had spent six months as a fisherman running a trawler and in the process making friends with the Russian fishing trawlers operating in the Black Sea. The truth was the trawlers did a very profitable side business in the transport of drugs and contraband. Markes with his fluent Russian soon made friends with the group which operated their trawlers out of Skadovsk a village on the Black Sea about fifty kilometres to the east of Odessa, on the eastern bank of the mouth of the Dnipro.

Markes had on occasion joined his new found friends on trips to Odessa where they whiled away the night at the 'Petrovsky' a seafront bar frequented by hard drinking sailors, fisherman and the whores, waiting to be picked up. There were border checks at Odessa, though no one ever stopped the fishermen. Packages would frequently change hands at the seafront with the police standing by. They were well looked after and even joined the fishermen at the Petrovsky for a drink on the weekend.

Markes was woken by the shrill call, from a loudspeaker to the Morning Prayer from the nearby mosque. It was a dull grey morning and surprisingly warm for the part of the year. Markes had told his landlord at Samsun the night before that he was moving out. He had settled his account the night before. He got up, packed his meagre belongings in his travelling case. It had all his worldly possessions, two sets of underwear, a pair of black jeans, a clean shirt, a thick fleece jacket and his laptop. The laptop was his most prized possession. It was custom built and had been loaded with customised software, software which had been developed by Markes himself. Software that could be used to hack into systems, search for passwords, and download masses of data.

He had walked down the quay to the fishing boats, waved to a bunch that were standing around a mast that they were fixing. He walked on till he came to the boat that he worked on, 'The Yasmin.'

'Haallooo', shouted the familiar voice of Cavit. Cavit was busy checking the engine of the trawler with Yusuf his assistant.

'Hi', said Markes returned the greeting.

They had agreed to meet for the crossing to Odessa. Cavit had another reason for going to Odessa. He had to deliver a package that night for one of the Mafia bosses in Istanbul. Markes had accompanied him on many trips earlier. Cavit was always happy when he volunteered to join him. The trip would take twelve to fifteen hours depending on the weather. He would need to put into port and deliver the package at an address near the port.

'Are we ready to leave?' Markes asked.

'In some short time, we be ready,' Cavit replied, and resumed whistling a tune which Markes had never been able to follow.

Markes went to the stern to check the nets. They would troll a little just so that they had some fish to take ashore at Odessa. A few good-sized fish with a couple of bottles of vodka was always met with approval from the guards at the port.

They set off, it was six in the morning, Cavit at the helm. He set course for Sevastopol. From Sevastopol they would sail along in sight of the coast to Odessa.

As they moved out into open waters, they could see the sun peeking through the clouds. The clouds were breaking up with the light breeze that blew in from the south. Markes rigged the main sail, it would help them along. They picked up some speed, a steady eighteen knots.

Cavit was looking around. He had checked the readings on his radar and sonar and signalled to Markes to lower the trolling gear and nets. Markes went around to the back with Yusuf, as Cavit reduced speed. They trolled for the next two hours, the catch was good, especially the twelve large lobsters! The guards would be delighted with such a gift. They decided to stow away the trolling gear and nets. Markes and Yusuf set about packing the fish and lobsters in the icebox. They brought up the nets, stowed them away and hosed down the deck.

The trawler picked up speed as Cavit raised the revs, they were doing good time. At the rate they were going they would make Odessa by nine that evening. It would be easier to get ashore and go about their business, especially since it was a Friday.

They saw the coast and Sevastopol in the distant. Markes waved to the fishing boat making its way back to one of the many fishing villages along the coast, stretching from Alupka to Jevpatorija. It was getting close to twilight and would be dark soon. Cavit raised the revs a couple of notches, he did not like to travel these waters after dark.

It was a quarter past nine when they saw the lights of Skadovsky and Odessa. They still had a good hour to go.

Cavit cut down the rev as he approached Odessa. The fishing harbour was to the right. He had to take adequate care to see that he wasn't in the way of bigger boats. The marina was almost full, most if not all the boats had returned. Cavit chose a space at the far right end of the quay. He aligned the boat as he approached the quay, put the propeller into reverse to check his speed. He raised the revs as the boat slowed down quickly. It bumped lightly into the tyres slung on the side of a moored boat and moved into the slot. Yusuf jumped out on the quay with the rope in one hand. He deftly slipped a knot around the mooring peg while Cavit, turned off the engine.

Markes, Yusuf and Cavit joined the group at the Petrovsky. It was midnight, they had had many rounds of Vodka. Yusuf had found himself company for the night in the form of a busty red haired woman. Cavit had settled down with the group around a table at the far end of the room, intent on their card game. Markes left unobtrusively, not that anyone cared. Most of the customers were three deep at the centre of the room around a table on which a girl was dancing accompanied by a man on a banjo singing a folk song. She was young, her skirts whirled up and around her legs, showing a good pair of legs, and lace knickers. The men roared at every glimpse of her knickers clapping and singing with the banjo.

Markes left the bar, walked to the end of the corridor and retrieved his travelling case. He looked around while lighting up a cigarette and then stepped out into the street. He turned left and walked a hundred yards and then stepped into the shadow of a doorway and waited. He waited for a full five minutes, cupping his hand around the cigarette so that the lighted end did not show. No one followed. He stepped out of the shadows and walked at a brisk pace to the train station. The train station was in a plaza about a mile from the port. He walked on the road that ran along the tracks from the port to the main station. The track was owned and operated by the port. The large cranes in the port cast their shadows across the deserted road. The sky was clear, he could see the Great Bear clearly.

It was a weekend, and after midnight. The train station had a sizeable number of people around. Markes had dressed casually, in blue jeans and a navy blue fleece, a denim jacket and a cap. He looked like any young man making his way home after a night in the city, the only difference was his travelling case.

Markes bought a single ticket for Mykolajiv from the counter. The bored assistant at the counter barely looked up when he handed him his ticket. The train, a shuttle service between Odessa and Mykolajiv was already on the platform. He got into a non-smoking car and looked for an empty compartment. He swung his case up onto the carrier and sat in the seat across the aisle next to the door of the compartment. Non smoking cars had fewer passengers than smoking cars. He had pulled his cap down in front so that it hid most of his face, stuck his legs out to discourage anyone from entering the compartment and pretended to be asleep. A few passengers boarded the car, glanced at his compartment, and moved on, seeing him stretched out.

The train started on schedule and soon they were trundling out of Odessa, along the coast. Markes glanced out of the window and could see the reflection of the moon on the Black Sea. He would soon reach what would now be his home, for as long as was necessary.

Chapter 27

Markes's identity had been painstakingly built up from records that had been taken from the county office in Odessa months earlier.

It appeared to be a robbery that had gone wrong, the thief had dumped all the records near the window through which he had entered. No one realised that Markes Trubin's records were missing. Officially he was not dead anymore.

Markes's bank account was activated and transferred to Mykolajiv, which was a hundred kilometres from Odessa. During the following months, there were transactions into and out of the account. Records would show that an apartment had been rented by him, the rent for which had been paid for out of his account, as were bills for all utilities.

Markes arrived at Mykolajiv early in the morning. He had memorised the layout of the town from photographs and a map that he had been sent with the keys of the apartment. The apartment overlooked the mouth of the river Novyj on the banks of which Mykolajiv stood.

He stepped out of the train station, and recognised the hotels and bars across the station. He turned left and then crossing the street turned right. The sights were familiar, his attempts at memorising the photographs and maps were paying off.

He entered the plaza next to the shopping mall just off the high street. The plaza opened out into a small courtyard, where a number of cars were parked. Presumably they belonged to those who lived in the apartment block. He walked up to the third floor, and went down the corridor on the right. The apartment number three was to his left. He entered and turned on the lights.

The apartment was well appointed, it had a fireplace at one end. The side of the room next to the fireplace had a large window that overlooked the river. The floor was carpeted. A three-piece suite with side tables was spread out in the room. Table lamps and a few photographs of friends were on the mantle piece. The apartment had a large single bedroom with a bath next to it. The kitchen was fully fitted.

Markes enrolled in the University of Kiev, travelling back to Mykolajiv over weekends. He spent two years, receiving a Masters in Politics and Sociology. He had signed on as a free lance journalist for the Demokratichna Ukraine. His specialisation was the Baltics. His work had been brilliant. He was well liked and was soon a regular at social gatherings in Odessa. His work took him across the whole of Russia and the erstwhile Union of the Soviet Socialist Republic.

Rosinsky had been a fisherman in the past. He was a shrewd man. He walked with a limp, a result of one foot being shorter than the other. He had broken his leg when he fell off a mast during a gale. This had all but ended his career as a fisherman. He did odd jobs for a living. Markes had befriended him and found he had a sharp mind, didn't talk much and had a family to look after. Markes had recruited him through a lengthy process that had started by buying him a drink at the Petrovsky on one of his early forays into Odessa. The casual acquaintance, soon turned into a solid friendship. Markes learnt of Rosinsky's problems and gave him money at regular intervals for information initially on the movements of drugs and contraband out of Odessa. In a short while thereafter Rosinsky was reporting on the movements of the Black Sea fleet. Rosinsky was a faithful fellow and did as he was told.

Markes had also loaned him money to buy a house. There was little chance he would pay it back, it just ensured Markes his loyalty and that was all Markes needed.

Markes had one hobby, computers, he loved designing and building them. His current lap top model had a processor with a high speed chip capable of running at 20 giga hertz, a hard disc with a capacity of 1000 GB, and a random access memory of 250 GB, a very potent piece of equipment that he had built from parts smuggled into Odessa through a variety of means.

The focus of MI6's activities had been the Russian threat, but with the end of the cold war the operational efforts in the Commonwealth of Independent States was reduced by more than two thirds.

MI6 was relocating staff to intelligence activities against Britain's European partners under operation 'Jet Stream'. This had had a set back with the discovery by France of the theft of a submarine tracking device from the French Navy. MI6 had used a front company at the naval base at Brest to obtain information from an engineer.

There were other gaffs by MI6 when Norman McSwain the 50 year old chief of MI6's Moscow station was exposed on Russian television when he attempted to make contact with one of his moles in Russia, Platon Obukhov.

MacSwain's career ended and Platon ended up with a hole in his head in a cold grave somewhere in the Urals.

Markes's communication was organised through the radio. He had linked his computer to tune into a predetermined frequency on one of the satellite channels. The computer downloaded messages, which could only be accessed through a password. The software was programmed in a manner that the downloaded files were hidden, coming up only when the programme was accessed with the password. The downloaded messages were encrypted. Markes would use a further programme that had to be loaded in a special sequence to enable it to decipher the message.

Markes was careful to avoid any serious relationships, they were too risky. Zoya was the daughter of a local politician Ivan Usov, and was in love with Markes. Markes and Zoya had known each other for some time now. Zoya had invited Markes to a dinner an occasion to felicitate her father Ivan Usov. The host Yevgany Grishin was the owner of the refinery that had been privatised. Ivan had seen to it that Yevgany was offered controlling interests by leaning on a bank to lend Ivan the necessary finance and guarantees. Grishin a shrewd manager had turned the company around, helped by contracts to supply the Black Sea Fleet, with gasoline and diesel. Ivan had seen to it that contracts for Crude oil supplies from Russia over five years at a discounted price, were offered to Yevgany in exchange for providing employment to ten thousand workers. The arrangement worked well consolidating both Ivan's and Yevgany's future in the region.

Zoya was a very attractive woman, she was tall and well built, her auburn hair cut close. She wore a black evening dress cut low in front, it showed off her lovely rounded shoulders and her full bosom. As the evening wore on, Markes found himself out on the patio with Zoya. Before they knew it they were in each other's arms, kissing passionately. Zoya slipped off her shoes, picked them up in one hand, took Markes's right hand in the other and led him through the side doors to the staircase away from the party. They went up the staircase, the sounds of the music fading as they made their way up into her bedroom. They entered the bedroom, Markes closing the door behind him. Zoya turned to him, their lips met, their tongues probing. Markes picked her up and placed her on the bed, kicking away his shoes, while she tugged his jacket, tie and shirt off him. She turned on the bed to let him unzip her dress. He felt her warmth as she slipped out of her dress, the sight of her naked body and her hands as they roamed over his, exciting him. She undid his belt and he let her pull his trousers off him. He pressed her back onto the bed his hands running over her breasts, his mouth on hers. His palms stroking her thighs and hips. He went down on her, his tongue probing, feeling the moistness. She moaned and arched her back. She pulled him up onto her, her hands stroking him as he entered her.

It was late morning when Markes woke with a start. He tried to orient himself, looked to his left and found Zoya curled up still asleep. He gently pulled back the covers and slipped out, looked for his boxer among his clothes strewn on the floor, and pulled them on. He went into the bathroom and steadied himself as he stood over the john. He stepped into the shower, braced himself as the cold water hit him. The water soon turned warm and then hot. He turned off the shower, wrapped a bath towel around him. He heard the door open, looked up and found Zoya with nothing on. He felt a stirring as she walked to him. He kissed her, shaking his head. He was on dangerous ground, he was attracted to her as she was to him. He reminded himself, no emotional relationships.

By the time Zoya was out of the bath, he was dressed and ready. Zoya, walked over, pulled at his tie. 'Stay', she said.

Markes shook his head, 'No, I'd better go, I've got an appointment'.

'When will I see you again?' she asked, looking serious.

'Soon, perhaps,' Markes replied, 'depends on my work.'

There was a knock on the door. 'Enter', Zoya called out.

The door opened and a maid walked in with a tray, of coffee and croissants, 'Good morning Zoya,' she turned and nodded to Markes.

'Good morning, Naina,' Zoya wished her.

Markes nodded, 'Good Morning'.

Naina left the tray on a table near the two-seater settee, and left.

Zoya poured out the coffee, added a dash of milk.

Markes liked his coffee strong, without sugar.

Zoya handed him the cup.

She picked up her cup and cradled it in both hands. 'Will you call me when you're back?' she asked.

Markes nodded, 'I will'.

The coffee was good. Markes finished and put his cup down.

Zoya went to him, they held each other and kissed.

Chapter 28

Date: 9th April 2007, Place: Odessa,
Time: 4.30 p.m

Markes entered his apartment. As was the usual routine on weekends he switched on his computer, to access the update from NATBAL.

The computer whirred into action, the screen changing images as the computer went through the process of booting up.

He clicked on the programmes and went through the process of loading the de-cryption programme in reverse. Once the programme was loaded, he entered his password and logged onto the web. On the web he accessed a special site, where he had to enter a further password to gain access. Finally he had to place the little finger of his right hand, in a specially adapted sensor. The screen remained idle for a full minute and then flashed into life.

Markes looked at the screen, and realised with a start that there was a message for him.

It read, 'Nostradamus'.

Markes knew that 'Nostradamus' meant. He was being activated. As was pre-arranged he would have to wait at the Petrovsky on the first Friday night after the activation at 8 p m. He would be approached by his contact who would brief him. The contact would say the words, "This senile lady has lost her position". This was a reference to Nostradamus and his prediction of the blitz of 1940, with St Paul's Cathedral being the senile lady.

He felt elated at the thought of being activated. Information on the movements of the Black Sea Fleet was no longer important enough to have an agent on standby. It was Brian who had convinced him that he would be needed.

He had heard of the Aldrich Ames episode, the cover of many agents in Eastern Europe had been compromised, especially those that were active under MI6 control. Markes was off record, and therefore safe.

Markes made his way to the Petrovsky at 7 p.m. Zoya had called during the week and left many messages. He did not call back.

The Petrovsky was busy, the fishermen and the sailors had converged. He stepped into the smoke filled bar, the music was blaring loudly. The girl was twisting and jerking to the music. A sailor who was already drunk was trying to get himself up on the table helped by equally drunken friends. He didn't succeed. The song ended, the girl bowed and waved to the crowd. She stepped off the table, swinging a cape over her shoulders and pushed through the crowd who cheered and clapped. The music started again. A fresh-faced young girl emerged from the door next to the bar, walked through the crowd which parted to let her through. She swung up effortlessly on the table and started swaying to the music. The cheering and clapping began.

At the far end of the room were the hard-core gamblers, with drinks by their sides, cigars clenched between their teeth, oblivious of the music and the commotion.

Markes looked around, walked to the bar and waited till he caught a waiter's eye.

'Vodka', he said.

The waiter poured out his drink and placed it on the bar. Markes paid him, pocketed the change and took a sip.

Markes peered around the dim smoke filled room, it was slowly filling up. He didn't have the faintest idea who his contact would be.

It was 5 p.m. and still cold and damp and very still. The fog that had formed in the late afternoon lay thick, with visibility down to 30 metres. The old man cleaning his small fishing boat heard the powerful growl of a boat approaching the fishing pier of the marina at Odessa. It was a Friday, soon the marina would be full. The fishermen would be returning before it was fully dark.

The boat eased itself into a slot, near another large boat. The old man heard the slosh as the anchor hit the water and the clanging of the chain as it fed out. The old man saw a lone figure step out, he couldn't quite make out the face, the man sported a beard. The figure shuffled along the pier and disappeared around the corner. A figure came out on deck, he was probably one of the fishermen. Lit a cigarette, blew out the flame then flicked the match into the water. The old man sloshed the water in his pail along the deck, the water washing over the side. He hung the pail to a hook, on the railing that ran around the rear of the boat. Stamped his feet then stepped from the boat to the pier. He walked past the boat that had just moored, peered at the side to read the name 'Siren' which was written in Italics, he waved to the man on the deck who waved back.

'Where have you come from?' he asked in Russian.

'Turkey, Samsun,' the man replied.

The old man looked at the boat, it looked like an ordinary fishing boat. The clean lines of the Siren, and the shape of its hull pointed to a boat designed for speed. He noticed the bulge of the auxiliary diesel tanks along the deck, as was customary for boats built to stay out.

It was a few minutes past eight. Markes felt a nudge on his left, and moved a bit to allow a rough looking bearded man to take up space next to the bar. He had large bushy eyebrows joined in the middle, this gave his face a sinister appearance. Markes moved aside to let him move up to the bar. The stranger asked for some vodka and was served. Took a sip, then wiped his face and beard with the back of his sleeve. No one took any notice, the bar was full of bearded rough looking fellows, it was a port and known for its traffic in contraband and drugs. Those who plied their trade came from various parts of the erstwhile USSR and from Turkey, especially Kurds, who needed money for their fight against the Turks.

He turned and put his back to the bar, looking at the girl on the table. As the music stopped, the girl pulled a shawl over her. She stepped off the table. One of the young sailors, put his arms around her, as she lost balance, and fell, pulling the young man with her.

The bearded man next to Markes grinned.

'The senile lady has lost her position', the man pointed to the two on the floor as he spoke to him amidst the din, the words barely audible, then laughed aloud waving at the two on the floor, the young man trying to stand up while helping the girl. The young man had had a few drinks too many under his belt, which didn't help. The man downed his drink, turned to the bar, waved to the barman and asked for a refill.

Markes looked closely at him, he was dirty and looked a tramp. His eyes though were bright and intelligent.

'I'll meet you outside in ten minutes', Markes said and moved away from the bar.

He moved towards the gambling tables, brushed past a girl who grabbed his arm.

'Want some company handsome?'

Markes made his way to the toilet that was at the end of a corridor which led to the back door. He stepped inside the toilet, looked around, there were two men sharing a joint, the smoke had an acrid sweet smell, he recognised it as marijuana. He walked into one of the cubicles, waited for a few minutes and then pulled the handle. Then walked out and turned right, glancing over his shoulder to see if anyone seemed interested in his movements. There was no interest at all. He stepped out into the cool night air. He walked across the street and stood in the shadows. In a short while the bearded man pushed through the front door, slouching, looked around, caught sight of Markes, and shuffled across the street.

'Let's find a quiet place', he said, his accent clearly English.

Markes led the way towards the rail station, along the open road running along the pier. The road was deserted.

They walked for a mile, then turned off the road to the sandy strip that led to the water. When they were clear of the road, the bearded man, straightened up, gone was the shuffling and the slouch, he reached up and pulled off his beard and what seemed his eyebrows. His appearance had changed completely.

They found a spot close to the water, and sat down.

'I'm Daniel Mason,' he stated briefly, 'but here I'm Andreas Amalrik. We will see each other only when absolutely necessary'.

Markes nodded. Mason would be his control.

He then proceeded to brief Markes on the situation.

'NATBAL and the security chiefs are convinced that there is a larger plot, with support from within the Politburo'. He paused when he heard the motor of a van along the road behind them. The revs increased as the driver changed to a lower gear as he approached the bend. They saw the headlights sweep around the corner and heard the tyres screeching. They heard the revs changing as the driver moved up again around the bend and sped away.

'There is a lot at stake, especially the treaty between the Ukraine, Belarus and Russia, which takes place next year'. He looked at Markes.

'NATBAL has evidence that a large international company Intrasyn, is involved in major illegal activities, with its headquarters in Estonia. We have evidence to show that key

Politburo members are behind the company, not officially, but are the authority behind it.'

He took out a tissue and wiped his nose.' It's a form of state sponsored criminal activity.'

'The Chief of Security of the Ukraine was replaced by a hard-liner, sometime ago'.

'How did that happen?' Markes asked.

'He died of a heart seizure,' Daniel paused,' He was in good health, but died suddenly. You will need to investigate, we will make our evaluation after we receive your findings. Our information shows that there has been steady infiltration of hard-liners in key positions in the states having access to the USSR's nuclear arsenal.

It was well past two in the morning when they finished.

Amalrik and Markes exchanged addresses on the net; they were web sites. They agreed that they would access the web sites once a week. Messages requesting a meeting would be simply listed as "Call us at this number for further information", they would ignore, the first and last two numbers. The third and fourth numbers would indicate the date and the fifth and sixth numbers the time on a twenty four-hour clock. There would be a reference to the location in the bottom three lines of the web page. They had agreed on the venue at each location. If they failed to make it on the date specified, the next date would be three days hence, until they met, unless there was a message on the web.

They walked back to the road and towards the Petrovsky. They came to a crossing, and went in opposite directions.

Chapter 29

Date:11th April 2007, Place: Odessa,
Time: 6.30 am

Markes decided to move out of Odessa. His cover as a
freelance journalist was well suited for his new role. He knew
that he would be alone, and if he were caught, there would be
no one to turn to. He thought of Zoya, she was his only regret
in leaving. He would drop her a note. She would forget in time.

Markes made his way back to his apartment. Markes lay
for a long time on his bed, he couldn't get to sleep. He was
excited as well, the time had come to put his training to use.
He went into the kitchen and made himself a strong black cup
of coffee, then settled himself on the settee, going through the
details of the briefing. Markes decided that he would check out
the death of the Ukraine Chief of Security, his cover would
hold and from what he had heard it was good tabloid material.

He finished his coffee, then decided to take a short nap.

He must have drifted away. When he woke he felt the glare
of the sunlight through his window. He checked the time, it
was 7.00a.m. He called Rosinsky and asked him to keep the
apartment cleaned. He explained to Rosinsky that this would
be a lengthy assignment. His neighbours were aware of his long
absences from time to time.

Markes had a quick shower. He cooked himself a large
breakfast of eggs, bacon and toast. He didn't want to stop
to eat, at least till dinner. He packed his laptop and a few
clothes into a bag that he slung over his shoulder. Pulled the

door behind him and stepped out into the corridor. It was a Saturday and no one was around, it was too early.

He walked to the train station and bought himself a ticket to Kiev. The train journey was uneventful, the whole compartment had a dozen people, some of them dozing and others reading the papers.

Markes looked back at the meeting he had had with Daniel. He would check out the story on Gorky and then take it from there. There were too many loose ends, Intrasyn, the presence of Vladimir at the chateau, the death of Gorky and the Central Intelligence Agencies findings on Intrasyn. It was true that Russia was polarised between the pro Communists and the Democrats or reformers. It seemed that matters in Russia were progressing as would a country as big and as powerful as Russia transiting from communism to democracy. The date for the treaty between Russia, Ukraine and Belarus had been fixed. The treaty would go a long way in allaying fears of control over Soviet Russia's nuclear arsenal.

It was mid-day when the train reached Kiev. He picked up his bag and stepped off the train. He heard the public address system announce the arrival of the train from Odessa. He went to a corner and took out his camera from his bag, then made his way to the coach terminus, a short walk from the train station.

On the way a taxi driver hailed him, taking him to be a tourist 'Can I give you a ride, sir, I'll show you the sights.'

'Thank you,' Markes shook his head, replying in Russian, 'I'll take the coach.'

The taxi driver, smiled, 'Have a good day.'

Markes waved to him, and made his way to the coach station.

Markes reached the coach station and checked the display. Irpin was on the route for all coaches to Korosten and Cherniv. The coach to Korosten was in ten minutes. He went down to the kiosk where he ordered a coffee and a smoked salmon sandwich. He munched slowly looking around the coach station. There were a number of cheap lodgings that he could rent with no questions asked.

The coach arrived soon afterwards. He helped an old lady onto the coach, she thanked him and went up front. Markes settled himself in the rear, where he proceeded to remove the cover of the camera.

The coach wound its way out of Kiev. Soon they were on the road skirting the lake to Irpin. The town soon gave way to rolling hills, thickly covered with pine and other evergreens. As the coach wound its way through the hills the lake came into view, stretching as far as the eye could see. Markes took a few photographs. They arrived at Irpin twenty five minutes later.

The coach dropped him at the only stop in Irpin, opposite the square. The town's café, a small place was directly opposite the coach stop. The square was in front of the church, with a few shops built around it, and as in all small towns in Russia served as meeting place with the district records office, the revenue office and the post office situated around the square.

Markes walked to the café, knowing that he would be able to pick up the local gossip. He walked in, saw there was no one at the café, except the owner.

'Good afternoon,' He wished him.

'Good afternoon, Sir', The café owner returned his greeting.

Markes sat down at one of the tables and put his bag on the chair next to him, and his camera on the table.

The café owner came to him, wiping his hands on his apron.

'Tourist?' he asked, his gaze taking in the camera and bag.

'No, I'm a journalist,' Markes answered. 'My paper asked me to check out a story'.

'Ah,' the owner said, 'but why here, this is a small town?'

'Is there a dacha where an important man died some time ago?' Markes asked.

The man nodded, 'Yes the Rose, a man died here a few years ago, and for many days the police and politicians from Moscow and Kiev, were here.'

'Here?' Markes asked.

'No, I meant they were going to the dacha.'

'How did he die?' Markes asked.

The man laughed, 'the girl was too young for him, must have died of exhaustion.' He stopped laughing and becoming serious explained, 'the dacha is for important men from the government, so we don't ask many questions.'

'Can I go there?' Markes asked, 'I can pay'.

The man's eyes brightened, 'I will ask my nephew to take you, and he knows a girl there, who is the Madame's sister, I will see what he can do.'

The man disappeared and returned with a young man, 'This is Vitali, he will help you. I have told him that you will pay him some money.'

Markes nodded to Vitali, 'Can we go now?'

'Give me a few minutes, I will fetch the meat'.

'Vitali supplies the meat to the dacha,' the owner explained, seeing Markes's questioning look.

Markes heard the sound of a motor, turned to look out of the window and saw Vitali in a beat up Lada pick up. The rear was loaded with a large basket covered with a white cloth. Vitali waved to him. Markes left, nodding to the owner, opened the passenger door and sat in the make shift seat. It was actually a long stool, serving as a seat for the driver and passenger.

Vitali grinned at his discomfort, 'You will get used to it.'

'Who runs the dacha,' Markes ventured,

'She lives in the dacha, her name is Laila,' Vitali answered.

'How do I get to see her?' Markes asked.

'Very difficult,' Vitali said.

Markes opened the flap of his shirt and took out a wad of notes, he handed a few to Vitali, whose eyes popped out.

'Do you think this will help?'

Vitali nodded, 'I'll see what I can do. My girlfriend works there, perhaps she can help.'

Markes nodded, 'OK, we'll meet your girlfriend.'

It took them ten minutes to reach the dacha. Vitali drove in and parked near a service entrance.

Vitali switched off the motor, got out and picked up the basket in the rear. He told Markes to stay in the car till he returned.

A few minutes alter he heard a giggle, and saw, Vitali with a plainly dressed young woman, coming towards the Lada.

The young woman got in first and slid along the seat and Vitali got in behind her.

Vitali set off, turning right at the gate instead of left, the road taking them away from Irpin. After a couple of miles, Vitali turned off on a dirt track, which led to an orchard at the edge of the lake.

Vitali stopped and they all got out.

Vitali turned to Markes, 'She is Natalia, works at the dacha. I have spoken to her, she will talk to you, but you cannot say who gave you the information.'

'Agreed,' Markes looked at Natalia.

'It was reported that a senior man from the government died here suddenly', Markes asked her.

Natalia, looked for a while at Markes, then turned to Vitali, 'but that was a long time ago. Besides, we were told that we should not talk about it,' she said.

'These government people are all the same,' Vitali said.

'They are worried that his wife will find out', he grinned.

Natalia smiled, 'What do you want to know?'

'Who was he, and how did he die?'

'His name was Gorky, he was the chief of security in the Ukraine,' Natalia said. 'He was with one of the young girls and he died of a heart seizure.'

Markes, said, 'you said young girl, do you know who she was. And how are you sure that he died of a heart seizure?'

'The new girl Nina, was introduced by Tatyana. Laila was told to take this girl by someone from Moscow.'

'Who is Tatyana?' Markes interjected.

'Tatyana is a girl who lives in Kiev, she has been with us for nearly seven years.'

'Do you know who recommended Nina from Moscow?'

'Madame said it was someone very important, a Politburo member, General Pushkin.'

'Is Tatyana still in Kiev?' Markes asked.

'Yes, Tatyana still works here, she is here usually only on the weekends.

'I'd like to meet Tatyana,' Markes told Natalia.

'I'll ask her and let you know. Where will you be staying?'

'I'll take a room at a lodging house in Kiev.' Markes told her. He took out a large wad of notes and handed them to Natalia.

'I'll come back tomorrow at the same time, is that alright?'

'No', Natalia said. 'This is the weekend, and we are very busy. It will be best if you come on Monday afternoon, the day we are closed.'

Markes nodded, 'Fine, I'll see you on Monday afternoon'.

They drove Markes back to the coach stop at Irpin.

Markes arrived at the coach stop at Irpin at 7, on the Monday morning. The sky was cloudy, the air felt dry. A light breeze stirred the leaves on the ground. Markes stepped out onto the dusty pavement, waved to the driver and made his way to the café.

'Good morning' bellowed the owner with a bright smile, he recognised Markes.

'Morning' Markes returned the greeting.

'Coffee?' enquired the owner.

'Yes please' Markes replied, making his way to a table near a window.

The owner brought a carafe of coffee with a cup and saucer to the table and set it down.

'How was your visit to the dacha?' he asked.

'Good,' replied Markes, I'm meeting your nephew today'.

'Ah, but be careful, there are many important men who come to the dacha, and it is not wise to find out too much.'

Markes nodded, 'Thank you for telling me, I'll be careful'.

The owner went to the bar and returned with a plate of biscuits, which he placed on the table. It was customary to serve coffee with biscuits, in those parts.

Markes poured a cup of coffee and sipped it. It was strong and black, the aroma was different, but good.

He heard the clanging of Vitali's car as it came down the narrow road leading to Irpin from the hills.

Vitali pulled up, across the street. Vitali and Natalie made their way to the Café. They opened the door saw Markes, waved to the owner and made their way to his table.

'Good morning', Markes greeted Vitali and Natalie.

They greeted him in return.

'Coffee?' Markes asked.

Vitali nodded and beckoned to the owner for two more cups.

The owner brought the cups, there was plenty of coffee in the carafe!

Vitali helped himself to a biscuit as Natalie poured out two cups. He turned to Markes, 'We will go to the farm, Tatyana will meet us there.'

Markes nodded.

They finished the coffee, Markes, paid the owner and left.

The road wound around the hills, there was a steep section which soon gave way to a flat valley, they could see the farm in the distance. A stream running through the valley provided the farms fresh water for the livestock.

They soon reached a farm building, made of stone with a sloping roof and tiles of slate. Slate was in abundance, as was evident from the outcrops of layers of rock with a dark bluish hue.

A small car was parked next to the house.

'Tatyana, is waiting for us.' Natalie observed, 'That's her car'

Vitali pulled up alongside the car.

They went into the house, which had a fireplace at one end of the room. The fire had a pot hanging over the centre of the fireplace. The room was large and L-shaped. The fireplace was at centre of the larger section of the L, with the dining table near the door in the smaller section that led to the kitchen. There were two settees around the fireplace. Tatyana rose from one of the settees. She was tall and had an oval face. She was dressed in a long skirt with a printed top. The dress accentuated her figure, her hips and long legs. She looked a little tired. Sunday was normally a very busy day at the dacha.

She looked at Markes, noticed his gaze and smiled. She was used to men looking at her.

'This is Tatyana', Vitali introduced Tatyana to Markes.

Markes went forward and shook hands. Her palms were warm, her smile open and welcoming.

They spoke generally about Markes and his work.

'Vitali has told you about my interest in Gorky's death.' Markes ventured.

'Yes..yes, he has,' Tatyana replied, she moved in her seat, obviously a little uncomfortable.

'I understand he died of heart seizure,' Markes volunteered.

'Who is Nina?' Markes asked abruptly.

'She was a friend. We both came to the dacha together.' She replied.

'Where is she now' Markes asked.

'She left after this happened, haven't seen her since,' Laila the Madame didn't want her to work here anymore. Gorky was a very important person, and when he died, it created a lot of problems, with all the government people and others coming here.'

Markes nodded, 'I understand'.

'Do you know who the doctor is, and can I meet him?'

Tatyana looked surprised, 'But the doctor is dead, he died about a month after Gorky died, it was an accident, he was killed when his Jet Ski overturned.'

Markes was startled, but he didn't show it. 'Has the doctor any relatives?'

'He has a sister who lives about two hours from here.'

'Where was the inquest for Gorky held?' Markes asked.

'The records are at the local district office', Vitali replied.

'Do you think I can see them?'

'It can be arranged for a fee', Vitali replied.

'Where is Nina now?' asked Markes.

'I don't know', Tatyana replied, her expression changing, 'I have to go now.'

'Don't be alarmed,' Markes replied. The question on Nina had obviously disturbed Tatyana.

'I just wanted to know, since she is the person who saw him die.'

'She left, and went away, I don't know where.'

'You said that you started work at the dacha with her, when was that?'

'Some years ago.' Tatyana replied. 'I've got to go now she said,' getting up.

Markes knew he wouldn't get anything more out of her, and that she wasn't telling them all she knew.

Vitali looked at Markes and shrugged his shoulders, 'She has a mind of her own, and besides she doesn't want to talk about it'.

Markes, was looking into his cup, frowning. He was aware of Tatyana leaving the room, Natalie followed her out of the door and saw her to her car. They heard the car start up and leave.

Natalie walked back into the room, 'I'm sorry, but talking about the incident disturbs her, she agreed to come because of me and Vitali.'

'Thank you, I understand,' Markes replied.

'Do you think, I can see the record of the inquest. I can really make it worth your while?'

Vitali looked at Natalie, she shrugged and nodded.

'I will obtain a copy from the office, I know a person, but it will cost you. Of course I too need some money, it is dangerous to look at such records of a senior government official.' Vitali explained, spreading out his arms, his palms turned upwards.

'When will I have the copy,' asked Markes, pulling out a sheaf of notes from the inside pocket of his jacket. He split the package into four, handing a quarter to Vitali. Vitali's eyes popped, he hadn't expected anything like this.

'You will have it in two days,' he said, grabbing the wad of notes and shoving it into his jacket.

Markes held up a sheaf of notes,' I'll give you this if you take me to the doctor's sister.'

Vitali's eyes gleamed. 'I'll find out where she is, and arrange for her to meet you. I'll let you know when I have the copies ready.'

Markes stood up, 'If you take me to the coach stop at Irpin, I'll be on my way.

Chapter 30

Tatyana, thought about her meeting with Markes. One of the reasons she had agreed to meet him was to find out what he wanted to know. There had been a number of journalists, who had come through with questions, but Markes's questioning was deeper, there was more to Markes than journalism. It was necessary to get word to General Pushkin.

Tatyana put a call through to the number that she was instructed to call if there was a problem.

'Hello, Dr Rushkov's surgery', bellowed a voice at the other end.

'This is Tatyana, from The Rose, I need to fix an appointment', she said.

There was a pause at the other end, Dr Rushkov understood. 'Can we make it on Thursday next week?

'No, doctor, I need to see you earlier,' Tatyana replied.

'OK, come in tomorrow in the morning,' Dr Rushkov replied, realising that the matter was urgent.

Vitali was grinning when he met Markes at the coach stop two days later.

He shook hands with Markes and they both went into the café for a coffee.

'I have the papers, they are transcripts of the records. I had to pay a lot of money to the clerk in the office, so that there is no record that he has given me a copy.'

Markes nodded, quickly scanning the two sheets, 'Good work Vitali'.

'There is the other matter', Vitali butted in, 'The sister of the doctor'.

'Yes', Markes looked up from the papers.

'She will see you, we will go there tomorrow. I have told her that you are not from the government. She hates government people, they treated her very badly after the doctor died.'

Markes smiled, 'That's good work Vitali, you're earning your money.'

'Yes, I need the money. I want to buy a new car and marry Natalie, so she can stop working in the dacha.'

Markes read the report before him, it had various medical jargon. The inquest had found that Gorky had died of a massive heart seizure. There were no internal injuries, the only external injury was a bruise on the face to the upper lip and nose, consistent with injuries a person would have suffered when falling on his face. The report stated that Gorky had died of natural causes.

Markes was picked up the next morning by Vitali at Irpin. They made their way through the hills to Bojarka. The route through the hills reduced the distance by almost half. They could have taken the highway that would have meant going back to Kiev and then taking Highway 131 to Zitomir. Vitali knew the roads well. The scenery was breathtaking, the road wound around hills, crossing many mountain streams, with small wooden bridges built across them. The road was for the most part wide enough for one vehicle. There was little or no traffic in the hills. The occasional tractor pulled over to make space to let them pass.

They reached Bojarka by noon. Vitali drove through the town and pulled up near a boarding house, or so it said on a board. Vitali beckoned to Markes to get out, and led the way in. A large woman an apron tied around her waist greeted Vitali and led them to a table near the fireplace.

The woman seated them then left and returned with a bottle of vodka and two glasses. Vitali spoke to her briefly in a dialect which Markes had difficulty following. He gathered that Vitali was ordering a meal for them.

The meal consisting of a large steak and potatoes arrived with a bowl of boiled vegetables. The food looked good and smelt even better. They were both hungry after the drive, and tucked in, washing the food down with the vodka.

The woman brought a carafe of coffee and two cups, clearing the plates as she left.

'When do we meet the doctor's sister?' asked Markes.

'I've told her to expect us sometime early afternoon. We will go to her place from here, she should be at home.'

Vitali paid and thanked the woman. Markes waved his thanks as they left.

It was a short drive to the doctor's sister's house. It was situated on the first street leading off to the left from the high street, at the northern end, after the community centre.

They parked the car opposite her house. There were no parking restrictions. There weren't many cars around in any case. Vitali led the way to an independent house with a low hedge at the front. The entrance was through a wrought iron gate. The gate squeaked as he opened it. A curtain was pushed aside inside the house. Markes could see a face looking out of the large front window. The door opened as they approached. Markes could see the figure of a middle-aged woman of medium height, with a shawl wrapped around her. She looked tired and anxious. She opened the door and looked up and down the street, as if to see if there was anyone taking any interest in her or her visitors.

She beckoned them to enter. Vitali went in and Markes followed. She turned requesting Markes to close the door behind him, then led the way into a large sitting room.

Vitali turned to her and introduced Markes, 'This is Markes he is a reporter'. He turned to Markes'. This is Mrs. Andreyeva, the sister of Dr. Shekov'.

Markes nodded in her direction.

'Markes is doing some research into Gorky's death and is planning to write an article. He wishes to ask you some questions.'

Mrs Andreyeva nodded in his direction, 'I will tell you all I know, she dabbed her eyes. They killed him', she blurted.

Markes was astonished at her statement. He looked questioningly at Vitali, then asked Mrs Andreyeva,' Why do you say he was killed?'

'He was so afraid,' she blurted. 'It started after he had done the report on Gorky's death'.

'You mean the coroner's report?' Markes asked.

'Yes'.

'Why do you say that the doctor was killed?' Markes asked her in a softer tone.

'In what way, did he tell you anything?'

'No, but in one of his letters to me he wrote that he feared for his life.'

'Did you ask him about it, and why he feared for his life?'

'He said that he was told not to talk to anyone about his report', she sniffed, Markes offered her his handkerchief. She blew loudly into it.

'After the report he was always looking over his shoulder when he went out. He was sure he was being followed.'

'Did he go to the police?' asked Markes.

Mrs. Andreyeva looked at Markes and then at Vitali, exasperation on her face.

'It was the authorities that were following him.' she said sharply.

'I'm sorry for asking but I needed to know. Did he ever talk to you about Gorky's death?' Markes asked gently.

'No', she dabbed her eyes with the edge of her apron.

'Is there any information that you think would help,' Markes asked her.

She thought for a moment then said hesitantly.

'I have some of his papers that I have not looked at, would you like to look at them?' she asked.

'That's very kind of you, 'Markes replied, 'It could help.'

Mrs Andreyeva, went in, they heard a desk being opened and sounds of papers as she rummaged around. She returned with a bundle that she put down on the coffee table in front of them.

'These are some papers of his. I found these papers hidden in his clothes. His clothes were the only personal belongings of his that were not taken by the authorities. He used to read a lot, but none of his books were returned.'

Markes picked up the bundle.

'May I look at the papers?' he asked.

She nodded.

Markes opened the bundle there were some old letters, the postmark was many years ago. Markes handed them to Mrs Andreyeva. She looked at the address on the back and said. 'These letters are from his wife who died many years ago.'

Markes, looked at a black leather bound book. When he opened it he realised it was a diary, he flicked through it, stopped at the dates when Gorky had died.

He saw the entries, they merely described Gorky's state at the dacha, an entry," Died of natural causes…heart seizure..?' caught his eye…why had the doctor put a question mark.

Markes, flipped through the pages to the date when the autopsy had been done, an entry which had been underlined caught his eye. "Though, the symptoms were of heart seizure, some blood vessels inside the nasal orifice were ruptured, and traces of a cyanide compound were evident….." The doctor had made a footnote "autopsy report". Markes knew that this piece of information was not in the copy of the coroner's report that he had received.

Vitali and Mrs Andreyeva had noticed the change in Markes. 'Did you find something?' Mrs Andreyeva asked.

Markes pretended that there was nothing of interest, not wanting to upset them, he brushed it aside by saying.

'No, only some routine information, but nothing that makes any difference to the situation', Markes put the diary down. He did not want to arouse her curiosity.

'Will you have some coffee,' Mrs Andreyeva asked.

'Yes please,' Markes replied.

When she left to make the coffee, Vitali asked.

'Do you want to keep the book?'

Markes nodded.

'I will return it, but I would like to go through it.'

Mrs. Andreyeva returned with a tray containing a pot of coffee, cups, milk, sugar and biscuits, which she placed on the coffee table.

'Markes would like to take the book to study it further; he will return it later', Vitali paused, looking at Mrs Andreyeva's reaction.

'He is willing to pay for its loan. He pays very well too'.

Mrs. Andreyeva nodded her acceptance.

'I do not want to go through any of his papers, Vladimir, changed so much after the death of Gorky, and I think that the reason Vladimir hid these papers was because he had written something in it.'

They had the coffee and the biscuits. Markes pulled out a sheaf of notes and handed them to Mrs. Andreyeva. She looked at the bundle.

'That's too much,' she said.

'Please keep it,' Markes said, 'It will come in useful'.

Markes and Vitali left, it was late afternoon.

Chapter 31

Date: 15th May 2007, Place: Kiev,
Time: 9.30 am

Markes went through the diary. It was clear that the doctor had found traces of cyanide in Gorky's nasal passage and hair, especially in the follicles, though surprisingly there were no traces in the blood stream or the lungs.

Markes made his way to the local library. He went in to the medical section and was soon engrossed in toxicology. It was mid-day before he found what he was looking for. It was studies done on victims of gassing. The studies inferred that a small amount of cyanide gas would kill if directly inhaled. The victim would die as a result of a collapse of the nervous system leading to heart seizure. If the amount of cyanide was small, there would be no traces in the body or the blood stream.

The doctor had checked on the cyanide because he had noticed a discoloration in Gorky's inner nose. His colleague, the local doctor had put the discoloration to the injury Gorky has sustained as a result of falling and striking his nose and upper lip on a hard surface.

Dr. Shekov had been correct, Gorky had indeed been murdered, that finding had cost him his life, of that Markes was sure.

Markes knew that he had to speak to Nina, the girl who was with Gorky when he died.

It was late evening when Tatyana left the dacha. She decided that the General had to be informed.

Tatyana drove her car to the coach stop at Irpin. She parked her car behind the café, and went in to keep out of the cold.

The café owner greeted her, 'Good evening, coffee?'

'Yes please,' she seated herself near the window. She would be able to see the coach as it came up the hill towards Irpin.

She was served her coffee, it was black and hot, and she sipped it gratefully. She had had very little sleep the previous night.

She thought about the events in the past year and more, the killing of the doctor, the investigation by the authorities and the publicity that the dacha had received. It had nearly resulted in the closure of the dacha. Now when they thought that everything was under control, here was this prying reporter.

She thought of Nina. Nina would be in Muhu, preparing for the final operation.

Her thoughts were interrupted by the sound of the coach's engine as it changed into a lower gear to climb the slope.

She quickly drained the cup and put the money on the table, waved goodbye to the innkeeper and stepped out just as the coach came to a halt, throwing up a cloud of dust.

A couple stepped out of the coach, nodded to Tatyana as she climbed in.

'Good afternoon,' the coach driver wished her.

She smiled at him, 'Kiev return please' and handed him the money.

She walked to the rear of the coach, and picked a window seat. She wanted to be by herself.

She must have dozed off during the trip, and was awakened by the driver's gentle nudge. 'We have arrived at Kiev.'

She woke up groggy, shook her head to clear it. Quickly brushed her hair, looked at herself in the mirror she carried in her handbag, then touched up her lips with a bright red lipstick, picked up her overnight bag and was the last to leave the coach.

She walked to the Sashlik Hotel. Business travellers to Kiev frequented this hotel. The hotel was clean, had a decent bar and restaurant, and was modestly priced.

She went up to the desk, stated her name and was given a registration card that she filled up. She picked up her key and made her way to the elevator.

She had a quick shower and changed into a plain evening dress, so that she wouldn't draw too much attention, checked her watch, and went down at 7.30 p.m. to the bar.

Dr. Rushkov was a big man, with a gruff voice. He was leaning against the bar having downed his first vodka of the evening. He had ordered another when he spotted Tatyana. He waved to her and beckoned her to join him.

'Fancy seeing you here', he said in mock surprise. 'You look great.'

'Thank you, it is a pleasant surprise doctor.' Tatyana replied as he kissed her on the cheek.

'What will you drink?' he asked her.

'Some wine, red please,' Tatyana answered.

'Why don't we sit at a table,' he signalled to the bar tender to have the drinks sent over.

They spent some time over a couple of drinks, after which they made their way to the restaurant for dinner. After dinner he suggested that they take a stroll along the canal.

Tatyana explained to Dr. Rushkov, the events of the last few days and the activities of Markes. She explained his obtaining the transcript of the coroner's report and his visit to the doctor's sister.

Dr. Rushkov frowned, 'A diary he said half to himself, Our men should have gone through all of his papers, I am surprised they didn't find anything. Do you know what was in it?'

'Vitali and Mrs. Andreyeva don't know. Markes took it with him, said he would return it later.'

'What about Markes, where is he from? Do you know who he represents?'

'All that he has told us is that he is from Kiev, though I think he has come from further south. His accent is different.' Tatyana explained.

'The General and the council will have to be informed', Dr. Rushkov muttered half to himself.

'Keep a watch on Markes and let me know if anything else develops, you can call me at the surgery. If the nurse answers, just say that you are Mrs. Zaslavskaya from Kiev.'

Dr. Rushkov and Tatyana walked back to the Sashlik.

Chapter 32

Date: 14th May 2007, Place: Kiev,
Time: 3.30 p.m

Markes, called the innkeeper and informed him that he would like to meet Vitali at Irpin the following day.

The innkeeper called back and left a message at the hotel, that Vitali would be able to see him the next day.

Markes arrived as usual on the coach, the battered Lada of Vitali was parked near the inn. Vitali grinning came around to the door of the coach as the coach came to a stop.

'Good morning, how was the ride?'

'No different from the earlier rides,' Markes answered.

'So what do you want to do today,' Vitali asked.

'I would like to see Nina, the girl who was with Gorky when he died,' Markes answered.

Vitali's expression froze.

'But that is impossible,' he said.' She left a week after Gorky's death, no one knows where. Laila the Madame was very upset, with all the publicity that she decided to send Nina away.'

'Would Tatyana know where she went?' Markes asked.

'I don't know, we can ask her.'

'What about Laila the Madame,' suggested Markes. 'She might be able to help.'

'I'll see what I can do 'Vitali shrugged.' You should wait at the café, I'll have to go to the dacha and see whether we can meet Tatyana and Laila.'

153

Markes, nodded.

Vitali returned a half-hour later.

'We are in luck, we can meet Tatyana and Laila, this afternoon.'

'Great job, Vitali', Markes slapped him on the back. 'Let's have a bite to eat, we have plenty of time.'

Vitali and Markes pulled up at the yard at the Rose. It was early in the afternoon, too early for any activity.

A girl met them as they entered, smiled at Vitali and nodded to Markes. She beckoned them to follow her and led the way up the stairs into a large study. The room was tastefully decorated, with paintings on the walls. There was a large shelf containing books, and a small bar at one end of the bookshelf.

They made themselves comfortable. The girl offered them a drink which they politely declined.

Tatyana and Laila entered shortly thereafter. Tatyana smiled and shook hands with Markes, and Vitali. She turned to Laila and introduced her to Markes.

'This is Laila, she is the owner of the Rose,' then turning to Laila she introduced Markes.

'This is Markes Trubin he is from Kiev and is a journalist', she paused, 'from which newspaper?' she looked questioningly at Markes.

'I'm a free lance journalist,' Markes answered, taking a couple of steps to Laila to shake her hand.

Laila was a tall woman, she was well built and good looking. She wore a loose fitting printed dress. She would stand out in a crowd, it was more her bearing. She was an intelligent woman, one could tell from her eyes. They didn't miss a thing.

'I have heard that you are here to discuss the events around Gorky's death,' she came straight to the point.

She pointed to the settee, 'Why don't we make ourselves comfortable.' She settled down with Tatyana on a settee.

When they had seated themselves, a girl appeared as if on cue.

'What will you drink,' she asked.

'Some coffee please,' Markes answered.

She looked at Vitali.' The same for me please.'

'Make it four,' she looked at the girl, who smiled in acknowledgement and left.

'What do you wish to know,' she looked to Markes.

'I would like to meet the girl who was with him at the time of his death,' Markes answered.

'You mean Nina,' Laila asked.

'Yes, that's what I understand.' Markes replied.

'I don't know where she is, besides I don't want to know. We had so much of publicity after Gorky's death that our important clients almost stopped coming.' she replied,

'How did you come across her in the first place? You must have some system before taking her in. You have very important people coming here.'

'Yes, we take girls only if they are recommended by someone we know very well.' Laila replied.

'Can you tell me who recommended her?' Markes asked.

'Tatyana, knew her for many years, and when she came to her in Kiev, Tatyana brought her to me.'

'I heard that she was recommended by someone from Moscow?' Markes prodded.

Tatyana's expression changed, clearly agitated.

'Who told you that?'

Markes shrugged, feigning disinterest, 'I just asked, it doesn't matter.' He changed the subject.

'Can I see the room where Gorky died?' Markes asked.

The girl brought in a tray with coffee and biscuits. She poured out the coffee, placed the milk, sugar and biscuits on the table and left.

They helped themselves to the biscuits and the coffee.

'I'll show you the room,' Laila rose.

Markes followed with Vitali and Tatyana.

They entered a large suite that consisted of a large bedroom, leading to a dressing room and a bathroom. It was beautifully furnished.

Markes walked to the mantelpiece over the fireplace, and looked at a framed photograph of a young woman, with blond hair. She had fine features and intelligent eyes. She was very attractive.

'I didn't even know where to send her things,' Laila continued. 'She left in a hurry and didn't even tell us where she was going.

Markes looked at Tatyana,' Would you have any idea where she might be?

Tatyana shook her head, 'She just wanted to get out, I have no idea where she is or what she's doing.'

Markes picked up the photograph and looked at it. He would remember her face if he came across it again.

Tatyana and Laila made some small talk. Markes realised that he wouldn't get much further.

'Thank you very much,' he said, turning and smiling at Laila, 'I think I have learned enough.'

Vitali dropped him off at the coach stop.

They heard the coach as it came up the hill.

'Good luck to you and Natalie', Markes said as he shook hands with Vitali. Vitali nodded smiling.

Chapter 33

Date: 14th May 2007, Place: Kiev,
Time: 7.30 p.m

Markes was back in his lodging house that evening, from where he sent a message to his control. He needed to know the status of the leads that NATBAL was working on.

Less than a week later Markes was meeting with Amalrik. It was a Sunday, they had chosen a park in Kiev. It would be quite full on a Sunday evening, and they would be less noticeable. They had travelled to Kiev, arrived there in the morning and had made eye contact at a pre-designated place. After the initial contact they had moved off in separate directions. As prearranged they had each taken turns to check if the other was being followed. One of them would go into a restaurant for a coffee. On his exit, the other would observe the area to see if there was a tail. If there were any interest, the rendezvous would be called off.

Markes shared his findings with Amalrik.

'What do you know of General Pushkin?'

'NATBAL's information is that he is the one behind Intrasyn, in fact he is the head honcho.'

'Where is he from,' asked Markes.

'He's from Cerkessk,' Amalrik stated, he was frowning, and said half to himself, 'It's the place where there was a Riga style massacre a long time ago.'

'I've been thinking about that,' Markes said.

'There were rumours that it was state sponsored, by the pro-democrats. The population in Cerkessk were pro-Communist.' Amalrik explained.

Markes nodded. "Yes that was true, it was organised by someone in the government, but the whole thing was hushed up. The Politburo is made up of two factions, each as powerful as the other, with its own supporters in the rank and file.'

'This Nina, was she from Cerkessk?' Amalrik asked.

'Yes, that's what I understood.' Markes replied.

'Perhaps, Cerkessk will have some answers'.

'I was thinking of that', Markes replied, 'I will sort out a few things here. We will stay in contact the usual way.'

They parted company, without shaking hands. Amalrik left first, Markes waited, for a full half an hour, and went in the opposite direction.

Chapter 34

Date:27th May 2007, Place: Kiev, Time: 3.30 p.m

The old man in the corner in a torn raincoat straightened up as the radio in his ear crackled.

'Status?', he heard the gruff voice through the receiver.

'One of them, the bearded man left about half an hour ago, and now the reporter has left too. We have Andreas and Krushenko with their teams tailing them'.

'OK, but just observe them, find out whom they meet and where they go. I want to know everything about them.'

'OK, understood.' The old man, took off the raincoat and straightened up. He was a young man in his early thirties.

Markes, walked around the corner, and entered the shop. He was taking no chances. Though Amalrik and he had checked to see if they were being followed before they met, he checked constantly. The corner being at right angles did not give the tail much of a chance to observe where Markes had gone. The young man turned the corner and looked down the street, which was empty. He turned back and ran around the corner. Markes observing the street through the store window that offered an excellent view saw the young man. He could see the exasperation on the face of the man, and his frantic look. Markes realised that the man was following him, which meant that someone was onto him and Amalrik as well. His mind raced, what could have set this off. He knew that his forays into Irpin, and his inquiries would have given room for suspicion. He could not go to his room now, till he was certain that he had lost his tail. He could see the young man looking around at the parade of shops and speaking into a microphone, attached to his collar. He was obviously looking for back up. Markes moved to the rear of the store. Found a toilet and went in, he pulled out a grey wig, removed his jacket and turned it inside out. He pulled out a pebble from his pocket and a wad of chewing gum from his jacket. He put the pebble in his shoe, the pressure would make him limp as he walked. The limp was real, the pressure of the pebble in his shoe made him wince when he stepped too hard. He stuffed the wad of gum into his mouth, and worked it to either side. His cheeks bulged but not unnaturally, changing his appearance. He put on a pair of round glasses that he carried with him. His transformation was complete. He limped out of the toilet, stooping a little. He heard shouts and the young man who was tailing him came barging through the store, and ran to the rear. He scarcely gave Markes a glance. Markes picked up a book and went to the counter to pay.

The owner a middle aged man cursed at the young man under his breath.

Markes paid for the book, stepped out and made his way to a coffee stall across the street. The street was buzzing with activity, a car drew up along the kerb and spilt out three men who went down the street that Markes had come up half an hour earlier checking the shops. Markes finished his coffee and left, limping along the street with the book clasped under his armpit.

Once out of sight, Markes pulled off his shoe and threw the pebble away. He walked briskly towards the town centre. He pulled out his mobile phone and called Amalrik. Though they had decided not to use mobile phones for communication this was an emergency.

Amalrik had taken the usual precautions, to check for a tail. He had failed to spot the man who was dressed simply in the outfit worn by the men in those parts. He approached his apartment block, turned to take a quick look around, and then opened the door. As he was entering, a young man came running up, and ran through the door before it closed. He nodded to Amalrik, who nodded back in return. They both took the lift. Amalrik looked at the man, he was dressed in a plain shirt, tucked into a pair of designer jeans. He wore a thick navy blue woollen jacket. He was of medium height and had broad heavy shoulders. Amalrik pressed the button for the 4th floor, though his apartment was on the 5th, the man pressed the button for the 3rd floor. The lift stopped at the 3rd floor, the man went through the door fishing in his pocket, for his keys. Once the lift doors had closed, he turned quickly and bound up the stairs to the 4th floor, he heard the lift stopping at the 4th, he pressed himself against the wall to keep out of sight of anyone peering down the well of the staircase. He heard the lift doors close, then heard the fire doors of the staircase next to the lift open, and the heavy tread of a person climbing up the stairs. He waited, then made his way up behind Amalrik. Amalrik went through the fire doors at the next floor into the corridor. He went to his apartment, looked briefly around as he bent to insert the key into the lock. As he turned the key he felt the change in the pressure of the air around his ear. He turned and took the full force of the blow on his temple. He crumpled in a heap, the young man held his body before it hit the floor. The young man pushed open the door and hauled Amalrik's body into the apartment. He let the body slide to the floor and felt for a pulse, there was none. He cursed under his breath, he had bungled. He had meant to knock him out.

He heard the mobile phone in Amalrik's pocket ring. He rummaged in Amalrik's pockets for the phone, looked at the display to see if the callers id was displayed, it wasn't, so he let it ring.

Markes heard Amalrik's phone ring, there was no answer. After the usual rings the phone's voice mail was activated. Markes heard the message and shut down his phone. He knew that something had happened to Amalrik.

He made his way to his apartment. Checked to see if he was being followed, he wasn't. He quickly put his things together, he would have to move out, whoever they were, they were professionals, and he was a target. He slung his bag with the laptop strapped to the bag over his shoulder. He had paid for the week, he looked around the apartment, there was nothing of his there. He pulled the door shut, and was out of the lodging house in five minutes. He dropped the key into the clerk's mailbox and left.

He crossed the busy street, making his way to the far corner. The corner was adjoining the entrance to the subway. He went into the self-service café, and went to up to the first floor. There were a number of tourists around with bags similar to his. He blended well with the crowd. He picked a spot near the window and watched the street below. He had a clear view of the lodging house from where he sat. He waited, twenty minutes passed when he saw the same black car draw up alongside the lodging house. Three men stepped out. They stood outside the lodging house as one of them used a key to gain entry. They disappeared into the building. The door opened again after fifteen minutes, and one of the men got into the car and sped off.

Markes's thoughts went back to his first briefing. NATBAL were not sure if there was something brewing in the Baltics, any doubts he had were dispelled. He thought of Amalrik and wondered whether he was alive. There was no time to find out. He had to get on with his investigations. He had to visit Cerkessk.

Chapter 35

Date: 19th May 2007, Place: Tallinn,
Time: 9.30 am

Boris, had shifted his headquarters to Tallinn. It was conveniently placed from Muhu. The connections were good and allowed him easy access to Russia and Europe. His connections with Intrasyn ensured that he was given access to photographs and stories that were instant front pagers. He quickly became the blue eyed boy of News de Internacionale.

Boris received a call from Pushkin.

'The council is meeting at Muhu, I think it's time you met them and we briefed you on the mission.'

Boris was thrilled, he had waited long enough, he had heard that Irina was at Muhu, now co-ordinating Baltic activities. He had heard of the death of Dimitri. Irina would have been devastated. The thought of seeing Irina again made his heart pound. He buzzed for his secretary.

'I need to travel to Haapsaalu, please make the arrangements.'

'How long will you be gone', she asked.

'I should be away for about a week or two at most, post any message for me on my site.'

She nodded, she knew the drill. Boris did not like to be contacted on the phone. He had one of those satellite trans-receivers, a sophisticated piece of communication equipment which did not need any phone lines. Boris could set up his system in a desert and communicate via satellite. In the same way he could access his mail from his website, and send replies. This gave him the freedom he wanted without compromising his location.

He would fly to Haapsaalu, from there he would be taken by boat to Muhu.

Boris looked out of the window as the plane took off over the Gulf of Finland, then made a turn south, making a full circle setting course for Haapsaalu. He marvelled at the beauty of the Gulf of Finland. It was a clear day, he could see the yachts, and the other boats leaving their wake in the deep blue water. The plane climbed, and soon there was nothing below except clouds. The pilot's voice came over the intercom, welcoming them. He gave them some information on the height and the weather en route, and the weather at Haapsaalu. It was a short flight. He asked for a coffee, refusing the breakfast tray the flight stewardess brought. He looked through the News de Internacionale, there was nothing of significance.

The intercom came to life as the pilot asked the crew to take up landing stations. The plane banked to the left. Boris could see the Island of Muhu as the pilot made his turn in preparation for his final approach. Boris felt the small jolt as the wheels touched. The engines revved up again as the pilot put the thrust in reverse.

The airport at Haapsaalu though small was capable of handling large transcontinental aircraft. It had a long runway and had adequate hanger and fuelling facilities. This was partially due to the presence of the Estonian air force. Prior to the break up of the Soviet Union, Haapsaalu was a base for the Russian 'Bear' squadrons, a crack strategic bombing command, with nuclear capability. It was also home to the 'Genghis' fighter squadron, which had the latest Soviet MIG 32 fighters, capable of speeds of Mach 2.5 at sea level, with over wing missile platforms, and the latest avionics. This base was linked to the Soviet High Command, and was connected to the Soviet and Warsaw Pact Early Warning Systems. The base and its capability was one which had every NATO commander worried when there was any confrontation.

Boris stepped out of the plane, walked down the stepladder that had been rolled up to the plane. The airport did not have any aerobridges. He boarded the coach to the terminal. The formalities were perfunctory, he was expected and the two men at immigration waved him through. Every person who entered the terminal was photographed, and the digital image transmitted to a mainframe computer that matched the photograph with known and suspected western intelligence agents. A match would in the least result in a twenty-four hour tail and a thorough search of the person and his belongings.

A man in a plain grey suit met him at the exit. The man wore sunglasses and a hat angled to cover his face. Boris had been briefed, the description given was accurate. The man moved towards the exit, and as instructed Boris, followed him. The man led him to a Zil limousine, which had the motor running. They got in and he was driven to the quay. The ferry between Haapsaalu and Muhu was getting ready to leave. They boarded the ferry. The crossing took twenty-five minutes. He heard the engines revving as the screws were put into reverse and almost immediately felt the boat slow down as the pilot eased the ferry into its slot.

His companion saw him to the exit and then abruptly left him. Boris was taken aback, and looked around for him, wondering what this was all about.

It was then he saw her, looking radiant and beautiful. He remembered the way she looked when he had last seen her at St Petersburg, when the three of them had parted. He saw her wave, he dropped his bags and ran towards her. She was coming towards him, she ran into his arms, he lifted her up, put her down, his lips on hers. They kissed long and hard, hungry for each other. He felt her body against his, he ran his fingers through her hair, and felt her nails digging into his back. Time stood still, and so did a few bystanders, smiling as the lovers kissed and kissed again.

Boris, held her from him. Irina was crying, 'I thought I'd never see you again.'

'Shh,' Boris calmed her down, stroking her hair, and kissing her face. 'I'm here now.'

'We'll never see Dimitri again', she broke down sobbing.

Boris felt a lump in his throat, they would never see Dimitri again.' Yes, we'll never see him again, but he will always be with us in spirit.'

Irina composed herself, Boris dried her tears, and gave her his handkerchief to blow her nose.

'I've been assigned to take care of you', she said proudly.

Boris looked at her lovingly, 'That's the best thing that's happened to me in a long time.'

'I've got a car, I'm to take you to the dacha and we spend the rest of the day together. Your briefing starts tomorrow. The council meets two days from now, when you will be briefed about the assignment.'

Boris grinned, put his arms around her, and together they made for the car.

Irina drove him to the dacha, it was on the coast, on a hillock, overlooking the sea.

Intrasyn owned the island, and ran the place. The rules were laid and enforced by Intrasyn. No one entered or left the island without clearance from Intrasyn security.

She parked the car on the driveway. They got out, they didn't see anything around them, all they saw was each other. Boris came around to her and took her in his arms and kissed her. He lifted her up and pushed through the doors of the dacha. He took her into the bedroom, closing the door with his foot and put her down gently on the bed. She pulled him on top of her, holding him tight in her arms. He kissed her lips, her face and stroked her hair. She tugged at his jacket and shirt. They moved apart, taking off their clothes and throwing them across the room. He saw her body, her long shapely legs, her breasts round and firm. Her hair was spread out on the pillow, her eyes bright and shiny, she was beautiful. He lay down beside her and held her, his palm over her breast feeling their firmness. He stroked her thighs, they kissed, their tongues probing. He kissed her all over, running his lips and tongue over her nipples, her navel and between her thighs. He felt her touching him, stroking him and feeling him grow as his desire mounted. She felt him in her. He heard her moan with pleasure. They were oblivious of anything but each other. They enjoyed each other till they were exhausted, and fell into a deep sleep in each other's arms.

Chapter 36

Date: 27th May 2007, Place: Kiev,
Time: 7.30 p.m

Markes knew that the airports, the coach stations and the rail stations would be watched. He needed a change in identity, both physical as well as in the papers he carried. For the time being Markes had to disappear. In the months that he was being prepared he had developed many identities. Each one had an appearance, bank accounts, bills with his name and address, all dating back at least six months. These identities were painstakingly built with locations in different regions of Russia. He had to find a place, but lodging houses would be watched too. With his backpack he could pass off for a hitchhiker. He made his way to the downtown area of Kiev, the high street was closed to traffic. The sides of the cobbled street were lined with shops and cafes. This was where the tourists came in the evenings, and where the prostitutes openly solicited business. Markes needed a place to stay the night, to change his appearance and to make contact with Amalrik if he was still alive, and with NATBAL.

As he walked past the brightly-lit shop windows a young blond came up to him, she smiled.

'Would you like to have some fun?' she asked. She obviously thought she saw some interest and said,' I can do anything you want,' she looked down at his crotch, licking her lips.

Markes smiled.' How much will it cost me?'

'Fifty dollars, for an hour, plus the room charges,' she said.

'How much for the whole night, at your place,' he asked.

She brightened up, the guy would probably spend two hours with her and then fall asleep. It would give her a chance to rest too.

'Make it three hundred dollars and I'll take you to my place' she said.

'Done, lead the way,' he replied, taking her arm.

A couple sitting at one of the cafes, tourists by the look of things, were observing them. Markes turned to them and smiled. The woman turned away, the man smiled back.

'Let's buy some whisky.' Markes led the way to a wine store, where he picked up a bottle of Ardbeg. She led the way through narrow streets to a door which she opened and led the way into a small hall, from where stairs led to the apartments. A lift provided an easier way of climbing up. They entered the lift and went up to the fifth floor. She opened the door to her flat which was the first flat on the left and turned on the lights. It was a modest apartment, tastefully but sparsely furnished. It was self contained and had a small sitting area adjoining the kitchenette, which had a breakfast table. The apartment had a bathroom, and a decent sized bedroom with a king sized double bed. A door led to a small balcony overlooking the entrance to the apartments.

She kicked off her shoes, and went into the kitchenette to get a couple of glasses and an ice bucket that she filled with ice cubes. Markes had settled himself on the settee. She came in and stood around waiting. He asked her to join him.

'I must have the money first,' she said apologetically.

'Oh, I'm sorry, I didn't realise.' Markes said, pulling out a wad of notes from his jacket. He counted out three hundred dollars which he handed to her.

She walked across the room to her dresser where she put the money.

She looked at him,' Ice?'

'Yes please,' he answered.

She half filled the glasses with ice and poured two generous shots of whisky. She handed him a glass, then sat down next to him.

'To a good time,' and took a good swallow.

Markes took a sip, letting the whisky flow over his tongue, savouring the smoky flavour.

She snuggled closer to him, her glass was half-empty. She drew her legs up on the settee, hitching her skirt up, showing a lot of leg and some.

'Why don't you change into something more comfortable,' Markes suggested.

She looked at him, and broke into a wide smile.

'Sure thing baby', she winked at him and stood up, turned and asked him to unzip her. She made her way to the bedroom.

Markes, pulled out a flat container from the inside pocket of his jacket and took out a small pill which he dropped into her glass.

She returned a few minutes later, in a very short pink nightie, minus the pyjamas. She stood in front of him with her legs spread apart, hands on her hips and a 'come hither' smile.

'You look terrific' he said.

"Thank you,' she smiled, 'why don't I make you comfortable.'

'Sure thing, come on here', he patted the cushion on the settee next to him. 'Have another drink'.

She sat close to him, her legs and thighs rubbing his. Markes felt a stirring. He composed himself, this was no time to get romantic, and he had work to do.

He kissed her, she kissed him back letting her tongue wander in his mouth, probing. She took his hand and put it on her thighs. Markes let his hand rest on her thighs for a while, then reached for the bottle, and topped up her glass. She felt for his belt buckle with her left hand and undid his belt. Markes reached across the settee for her glass and handed it to her. She took a large gulp, some of the whisky trickling down her cheeks.

Markes picked up his glass, which was still quite full, and took a sip.

'I need to go to the bathroom.'

She smiled at him, 'Come back quick, I like you.'

'Sure thing,' Markes replied. He could she was slurring her words, the drug was taking effect. She would be fast asleep in a few minutes and wake up after about 12 hours with nothing more than a mild hangover.

He came back from the bathroom, and found her on the settee, her nightie riding high on her hips. She was lying face down, fast asleep.

Markes carried her into the bedroom and laid her on the bed, pulling the covers over her.

He put his bag on the settee and set up his laptop, using her telephone to log onto the Internet and his website. He checked to see if Amalrik had replied, he hadn't, which meant that he was in trouble or worse. He had to contact NATBAL. He was to access a site only in an emergency and when there was no other alternative available. He logged on to NATO, the website welcomed the viewer and presented the viewer with a number of options. He carefully used the options that he had memorised. He had to use a password at each stage. At the final stage, he had to scan the palm of his left hand with the scanner and transmit the scanned image. There was no prompting for the last part. It was a means to safeguard the site from unauthorised access. The image was checked and verified after which he was given access to his site at NATBAL. The connection enabled him to contact NATBAL and Brian if need be directly.

He quickly sent out his findings and conclusions after the last meeting with Amalrik. He advised them that Amalrik was compromised, and that his cover was blown. He was now under identity three, a Russian clergyman.

He was planning to visit Cerkessk, on the anniversary of the massacre. As a clergyman he would be able to talk about the incident without raising any suspicion.

Brian was in the office when the transmission came through from Markes. His chief of communications came into his room.

'We have Markes,' he announced and made his way back to the communications room.

Markes's message came through clearly.

Brian dictated the reply, which was typed in by the communications officer.

The message was simple.

'Noted, developments, acknowledge, Tristar,' the Tri meant identity number three, and star stood for clergyman. The 'Star' was the idea of Edwin Noble, the chief of NATBAL operations, who was a Russian Jew by origin. He wanted the Star of David to be incorporated in some way.

It went onto read, 'three, four, two zero' it simply meant, check your website, three weeks from now, on the fourth day at the end of three weeks, at two in the morning. The zero was there just to confuse a hacker, or the opposition.

Markes opened his bag and took out a clergyman's smock, and collar, and a box. He needed to change his appearance. The box contained all the ingredients for a makeover. It had false beards, mustaches, stage glue and a special type of chewing gum, which could be stuck to the gums, changing the shape of the cheeks. He went to the bathroom and proceeded to dye his hair black, he stuck on a mustache and a beard. When he had finished his makeup he dressed, putting on the collar and the smock. He looked at himself in the mirror; he did not recognize the person who peered at him from the mirror.

Markes quickly cleaned up, it was late, he decided that he would take a short nap. He stretched out on the settee and set his alarm for five in the morning. The alarm woke him up, he glanced at the blond, she was still asleep. He used the bathroom, splashed some water on his face to freshen up, and left closing the door behind him.

He walked down the stairway; the lift made too much noise. He made his way to the underground train station, it was still dark. The station was almost empty; there were a few commuters. He put some coins in the self-service ticket machine and punched a few buttons and picked up his ticket. The coach was empty except for two elderly ladies, who greeted him. He returned the greeting and made his way to a seat at the end of the coach away from the ladies. He pulled out a worn leather bound Bible from his bag and started to read.

As the train moved away he saw the man dressed in black. He was sure he was part of the group who had tailed him and Amalrik. The man was checking each coach. Markes saw him enter the coach and make his way through the coach towards the ladies, after which he made his way through the coach towards him. He came up,' Good morning Father.'

'Good morning son.'

The man nodded and went on his way. The man had not been suspicious. Markes was pleased, the masquerade was working.

At Kiev, Markes made his way to the mainline station and bought himself a ticket to Charkiv. He was certain that they would check with the ticket counter for tickets to Krasnodar, Armavir or Cerkessk.

The train conductor announced that the train would be arriving at Charkiv, Markes walked to the toilet and quickly removed his collar and smok and stuffed them into his shoulder bag. It was dusk and the city centre which was close to the rail station was crowded. Markes made his way to a public toilet and stripped away his mustache and beard, which he stuffed into a garbage can.

Markes's uncle had been a clergyman he had been very close to his uncle. His uncle would take him into the church whenever possible and and show him the rountine of priests, and explain to him the responsibilities they had.

Markes decided that he would have to move close to Armavir if he were to obtain information without drawing attention to himself. He checked at the coach station and found a service which left in half an hour for Armavir. He made his way to a sandwich bar, ordered a roast beef sandwich and coffee which he ate slowly taking in his surroundings. The coach arrived which he boarded for the short drive to Armavir.

At Armavir he made his way to a cheap lodge paid the clerk and made his way up to the bed room. The following evening he made his way to the church. He knelt praying for all intents, much after the congregation had left. The priest noticed that Markes who was new to the church visited the church every evening and spent a great deal of time in prayer. On the third day he approached Markes,' Son you are new here, where do you live and what do you do?'

Markes explained that he had been away from the area for the past twenty years and had returned to spend the rest of his time in and around Krasnodar with the village folk, and that he wanted to serve the church. The priest, father Joseph was overjoyed with Markes's interest in the affairs of the church and his knowledge. It was difficult these days for the church to find young men to join the cloth. The world outside offered the young so many opportunities and distractions. He was pleased that a man so young had decided to come back to the village from the city. He welcomed him into his home, and insisted that Markes move into a room above the priest's quarters in the churchyard.

'From henceforth you will be known as Father Markes.' Father Joseph blessed Markes and handed him a priests' smock.

Markes felt ashamed for cheating the priest. The priest trusted him and had accepted him. He had a job to do and the room offered to him in the church offered the perfect place to set up his satellite communication apparatus, it was on the first floor and had a separate entrance. Being a priest's room the possibility of anyone entering his room was remote. Further, as a priest he would be able to move around the area freely.

Chapter 37

Date: 3rd June 2007, Place: Washington D.C., Time: 1.30 pm

Brian immediately put a call to the chief of the Central Intelligence Agency.

'Tom, there have been a few developments in Russia concerning Intrasyn, would it be possible for you to have your Sigma II satellite take some photographs of Muhu, especially the entrances to the harbour and around the old submarine base?'

Tom's voice boomed down the sterile line.

'Sure thing Brian, the satellite is due to make a pass over the area in 12 hours, we'll work the orbit so that we have at least 5 passes to cover the whole sector. I'll see that the photographs are sent to you in the bag.' He paused and as an afterthought asked,' I read the report, which was sent to the President. Intrasyn has stepped up its activity; it would seem that they are planning something big.'

'The only big thing coming up is the signing of the treaty between Russia, Belarus and the Ukraine, which is later this year.'

Brian knew that Markes would be on his own, he would have to move in another 'Sleeper' into the system, as a backup since Intrasyn were onto him.

Brian walked to his desk, and picked up the report that he had received on the assassination of the Interior Minister of Belarus. It had been put down as an assassination by a rival political group; those who had been ousted in a failed coup attempt a year ago. After the coup attempt, every coup leader had been hunted down and executed by the Interior Minister's squad. There was no trial, it was reported that they had been shot down in cold blood, some in front of their wives and children.

There were many questions that came up with the report. No one had claimed responsibility for the assassination. The person who had benefited was Molotov, who was pro-Communist and a good friend of Pushkin. He was a known hard-liner. The President of Belarus was a weak man, controlled by the Minister of the Interior. There were conflicting reports from the investigation; it was believed that a rifle shot had killed the minister. Further probing through informers, was that the fragment of the bullet recovered from the ministers body was believed to be from a handgun. Ballistic reports leaked out placed the bullet from a handgun issued to one of the bodyguards. This led to the theory that his own bodyguard had killed the minister.

Antony, the second secretary for Trade and Industry of the British High Commission at Belarus, had developed a relationship with a girl working in the trade and Industries department at Belarus. The girl's brother was a driver in the Federal Security Agency. He had told his sister and Antony that the minister had in fact been killed by one of the bodyguards. An investigation had been launched, but had never been completed. When Molotov had taken over, the investigation was abruptly dropped. However, it had been established that the bodyguard who was thought to have been the assassin was Anatoly, who had joined the VIP Protection Squad a year before the assassination. It was reported that Molotov had had a hand in recommending Anatoly. The investigation had shown that Anatoly was an impostor. The real Anatoly had been killed in action in Afghanistan, sometime in 1985. Another piece of evidence was that a chain recovered from the impostor, was a rare piece. Such chains had only been made in the Krasnodar region.

The Second Secretary had dutifully reported the conversation to the First Secretary who in turn had passed it on to London. The paper found its way to MI6. The chief of MI6 decided to inform Brian.

The moment Brian heard of Krasnodar, he knew that it concerned Cerkessk. He did a little investigation of his own. He had instituted a department to keep track of hard-liners within Russia that were part of the erstwhile Soviet System. Molotov owed his rise in part to Pushkin. Brian had his department check the agencies that recruited graduates as bodyguards and the VIP Security Squad. The company was Moscowa Handlowych, the Director Valentin Ligachev. Further checks showed that Valentin Ligachev was a Director of Intrasyn.

Brian had the origins of the particular type of chain checked through the Cultural Affairs Secretary of the United Kingdom Embassy in Moscow. The whole exercise had been conducted under the auspices of collecting information for an exhibition of local art and craft. The chain in particular was listed as having been made for a certain Ustinov family in the early thirties.

Brian had established the connection between Anatoly and Cerkessk as well as between Anatoly and Pushkin.

It was imperative that Markes investigate Cerkessk. Cerkessk could provide vital clues to Intrasyn's plans. There was something being planned.

Molotov had made many changes after he had taken over, all personnel in key positions were handpicked by him, and all were pro-Communist and anti-reform.

After the death or rather the assassination of Gorky, Pavlovsky had been appointed the Head of Security for the Ukraine. All matters concerning security, including that of the President and other VIPs was now the responsibility of Pavlovsky.

Brian had received detailed reconnaissance photographs from Tom. The resolution was very high and it was possible to pick out people. The photograph showed the island, which was approximately 60 kilometres in length and 40 kilometres in width in great detail. The island was a natural fortress, there was no beach. The land rose perpendicularly out of the sea to a height of approximately one hundred feet, except at one point, where for a distance of about a kilometre, the land sloped gently into the sea. This was the port and the terminal for the ferry between Haapsaalu and Muhu. Entry to the island was via the ferry, or by air. The island had a landing strip, capable of handling medium sized jets.

High walls, which served as breakwaters ran back from the sea to the island. The reinforced concrete walls were a good thirty feet high and twenty feet thick. The island was perfect for the purpose it was acquired. The port area was a natural harbour with a deep draught, which enabled ocean-going vessels to berth. The area around the port had huge warehouses, storage tanks for oil and silos for grain. The port was laid out to cater to various type of cargo. One side had piers with piping and pumps, for unloading oil tankers, the second for handling grain. All loading and unloading was mechanised. To load a vessel with grain, a compressor would transfer the grain from the silos to the vessel's hold at a rate of twenty thousand kilograms per hour, or could suck grain up into the silo at the same rate. There were specialist cargo areas, which handled sensitive and hazardous material. The storage areas were guarded, by machine gun toting guards. The whole area was under electronic surveillance as well, the satellite pictures showed the CCTV cameras and towers.

Brian turned his attention to the Southwest side of the island. This was the disused submarine base. The whole area was unstable. From earlier intelligence reports he knew the Russians had carved out huge caverns in the rock face, capable of housing three submarines per bay. There were six such bays, the seventh bay was very large which had cranes and other engineering equipment fitted along the pier. This bay was used to repair and refit submarines. The sea around the area was rough and choppy. Access to the base on the landside was through a tunnel cut through rock. On the landside, the tunnel led to a large concrete bunker located in a compound surrounded by buildings which housed armament stores, living quarters for naval personnel and a large engineering workshop. The Russians had abandoned the base after an earthquake had brought down the roof of many of the underwater bays, and some of the bunkers. Casualties if any, were not reported, it was rumoured that the Russians had lost two submarines, the reactors of which had been subsequently taken out, but the hulls had been left behind. Access to the island via the disused base was not an option.

Brian's department that kept track of hard-liners had been working on the assassination of the Interior Minister of Belarus. Through an informant they had been able to obtain a scanned photograph of Anatoly the bodyguard who had been assigned to protect the minister. The scan had reached them via Turkey. A considerable amount of money had exchanged hands, with a clerk in the record office of the Second Chief Directorate in Minsk where Anatoly had been first appointed.

Markes moved into the room in the church above Father Joseph's room. This would be his home for the time being. Markes set up his equipment, he turned on the equipment and followed the protocol to log in, the screen flashed to life giving him access to NATBAL.

Brian's communication officer transmitted the information on Muhu, and Anatoly's photograph with an instruction that the data would self erase in 120 seconds. Markes memorised the photograph and the information on the island.

NATBAL had provided him with as much information as it had, it was up to him now to find out more and report back. Markes was aware of Brian's growing frustration at guessing Intrasyn's plans. He did not for a minute doubt that there was a greater plan.

Chapter 38

Date: 20th May 2007, Place: Muhu,
Time: 8.15 am

Boris or rather Yuri, woke up, he blinked, the sun was bright. He looked at his watch on the bedside table; it was past eight in the morning. He felt a movement next to him, turned and saw that Irina was awake too. She smiled at him and came into his arms. They kissed, just touching lips at first, and then more passionately. They reached for each other, aroused. He reached for her she came into his arms their naked bodies merging as they made love hungrily.

Irina moved back from him and looked at him as they lay spent. She smiled and ran her finger along his lips. He smiled back. They didn't have to say anything, they understood how they felt.

'I'll shower and change,' Irina said, sliding across the bed taking the sheet with her.

Boris felt the sheet move away, made a grab for it, but it was too late, Irina had slipped out of bed taking the sheet with her. She looked back at him, smiling at his nakedness. She mouthed him a kiss and went into the bathroom.

She came out fresh looking terrific.

'Will you shower and change, I'll fix breakfast.' She said.

Boris looked at her, and nodded. He was enjoying her company. She was all he wanted.

Boris, came out of the shower, picked a clean pressed shirt from the dresser. The dresser had been filled with clothes of his size and taste. He had an idea that it was Irina's work.

'Breakfasts ready,' Irina called out from the kitchen.

Boris could smell the coffee, the bacon and eggs. He felt ravenous.

They ate together, and talked. When he asked her where she had been and what she had done, she turned very silent, and he could see her eyes turn watery with tears. He touched her hair, stroked her face and changed the topic. It was obvious that she was troubled with what she had done. He would raise it, but not now. There would be a time and a place for it.

Irina drove him to the main office which was only a couple of kilometres away.

They went through a gate manned by men in security uniforms. The security personnel knew Irina by sight, but stopped them nevertheless and checked Boris's papers. They were waved through to the main office block. Irina took him into the complex, punching codes at every door to gain access. The office was like any other corporate office, managers and staff going about the legitimate business of Intrasyn. All personnel were of course screened prior to being taken in, and unknown to them kept under surveillance for a period ranging from a couple of months to a year depending on the information they had access to. The real business of Intrasyn, the trade and transport of fissile material the laundering of money, and the drug related transfers of money was controlled by a small core group who were housed in another office. Their support systems, the computers and their network was separate from the general office. No one had access to the other building except the personnel working there. The one exception was cleaning and maintenance staff.

Irina took him to through to the office of the Administrator. The Administrator had overall responsibility and had been picked by Pushkin. In all matters concerning Muhu, his word was final.

Irina stopped at the desk of the Administrator's secretary. She was a stern looking woman, who did not approve of pretty young women doing men's jobs. She looked at Irina and Boris, 'he's expecting you', she said.

'Thank you', Irina said politely and smiled.

The demeanour of the secretary changed just a little. Perhaps these young women were not so bad after all.

They walked into the office.

Gregory Gromanov rose from his desk as the two walked in. He walked around his desk, and stretched his hand in welcome to Boris.

'Welcome to Muhu,' he said grabbing Boris's hand, enveloping it in his. He was a big man with large hands.

'My pleasure meeting you, Sir,' Boris replied. He knew that Gromanov was one of the members of the Intrasyn Council.

'Was your trip comfortable, this young lady has been impatient for your arrival,' he turned and grinned at Irina. Irina was blushing. Boris felt a warm glow looking at her blush. She looked so young and vulnerable.

'Please sit down,' Gromanov sat down himself.

'Irina has been assigned to take you through the office; you will in particular meet with the Advanced Prototype Team. The team is highly competent, and has experts from areas such as electronics, explosives, engineering, materials and the lot. During the following week they will show you some special photographic equipment which will play a crucial part in your assignment. You will meet the council after you finish.'

He rose signalling that the meeting was over.

They rose, shook hands and left, Irina leading him to the Advanced Prototype section.

He was introduced to the whole team. There were some thirty of them, all experts in their own fields. Intrasyn was credited with the procurement of the drawings of the Anglo-French Concorde, which led to the building of the Russian Tupulov 144, the Russian equivalent. The Russians were able to test fly the Tu 144 ahead of the Concorde. The Exocet Missile system was another feather in the cap of Intrasyn. The scientists at Intrasyn had designed the Russian version of the Exocet with designs obtained from French technicians for a sizeable consideration. This led to the development of the Russian ANZ 33 anti ship missile system well before the French had launched their own.

The scientists were grouped under a lead chief, depending on the work at hand and the requirement of the project. Boris and Irina were assigned to the group dealing with Imagery Analysis Protocol. They were taken to a room that had a huge array of sophisticated measuring devices. There were many cameras from all over the world. Boris was dumbfounded, he loved cameras, and here was the largest and the best collection he had ever seen. He was like a boy, asking questions. After the tour, they were taken to a briefing room. Boris and Irina were shown various types of cameras used by reporters, especially the ones with long range telescopic lenses and the other wide-angle lenses. They had modified the bodies of each. The experts showed Boris what seemed to be a normal camera, he was asked to handle it, and take photographs. The camera was no different from what he had used, with the exception that it was much heavier.

The expert took the camera from Boris, turned the lens anti clock wise, and an inner ring clockwise till both clicked into position. The camera with its lens looked no different. The expert mounted the camera on a stand and then focussed it at a potted plant placed about twenty feet away at the end of the corridor. He pressed the shutter, the pot exploded. The bulletproof plate glass that separated them from the pot, protecting them from the sound, and force of the explosion. Boris and Irina were surprised, how did the pot explode, and what did the camera do?

The experts explained that the camera when set to the 'L', L standing for Laser, position as they called it emitted an invisible high energy laser beam which transferred a burst of energy to the object. The energy transfer was in done in nanoseconds, the high amount of energy transferred in a short space of time worked like a detonator. If the object was made of material that had a sufficiently high-energy bank, such as research development explosive commonly known as RDX, or even high concentrations of urea, the sudden release of energy or detonation would cause an explosion.

The camera needed a high-energy battery source, which was provided from a battery pack; similar to the pack carried by photographers. The additional electrical circuits and coils, and capacitor for the laser were the reason for its higher weight. The camera when checked was no different from a normal camera and would pass inspection under airport security systems. The components in it were the same, except that it had two sets of circuits, one for normal operation and one for covert operations. Since the transfer of energy through the beam was affected by distance, it was necessary for the person using it to be relatively close. This meant that the person risked being blown up with the object.

Boris was taken to the design and engineering section. The camera was ready, the scientists wanted to raise the energy transmission rate. It was expected to be fully operational within the next fortnight, well ahead of schedule. Boris spent the rest of the day with the engineers and scientists studying the design and the functioning of the camera. The camera had been designed using material that was easily available in a camera or an electric store. He could now fix it himself if necessary. He was shown how to take it apart and reassemble it. To pass the test he had to be able to take it apart and put it together in the dark.

The electrical circuits were more complicated. For ease of maintenance, the engineers had made it in the form of sub-assemblies for the more intricate and computerised parts, the chips used were readily available in most computer stores or from mail order catalogues.

At the end of the week Boris was ready, he could strip and re-assemble the camera in fifteen minutes. He was given a miniature multi-meter with which he could check component parts and when necessary change them.

For Boris and Irina, the days together was pure bliss. That evening as they were driving back, 'You're quiet,' Boris remarked, looking at Irina's profile as she drove.

She turned, glanced at him, trying to muster up a smile. He saw a faint glisten in the corner of her eye, and knew that she was close to tears.

Boris ran his fingers along her cheek, and brushed a strand of hair. 'Let's go down to a quiet place away from the dacha,' Boris suggested.

Irina drove to the foot of the hillock and instead of turning to the dacha drove on ahead. They soon reached a clump of trees, she drove off the road and behind the clump of trees. The trees were shaped in the form of a semicircle, and once inside the semicircle the car was not visible from the road or the approaches.

She turned the motor off and sat still, Boris put his arm around her, 'What's troubling you?' he asked, kissing her on the cheek.

She turned in her seat, holding him tight, burying her face in his chest. He gently stroked her hair.

She drew back, 'Tomorrow you meet the council, and then you will be leaving,' she stopped, close to tears.

'I'll be back as soon as I finish the assignment. I want to spend the rest of my life with you,' Boris cupped her face in his palms.

'Do you know what you have to do?' Irina asked.

'No, do you?' Boris asked her.

She shook her head.

'What did you have to do,' Boris asked her gently. The occasions he had brought this up earlier had made her very unhappy.

She looked at him, looked down at her hands, she seemed to withdraw into herself. Boris reached out, held her close, she let him.

She took a deep breath, 'I had to work as a prostitute in a dacha, for almost a year and a half, and then I killed the Security Chief of the Ukraine.' She sobbed, holding him tight, 'I felt so dirty, being used by strange men.'

Boris felt a lump in his throat, all he could do was hold her tight, stroking her hair. He let her cry, she needed to get it out of her system. The sobs racked her body.

'I love you, Irina,' Boris stroked her cheeks, kissing her eyes and face.

She stopped after a while, composing herself,' I have thought about it for days and nights, it's been haunting me, till you came here.'

Boris looked at her, 'That's behind you, no one is going to keep us apart now.'

She nodded, 'But you still have the assignment, and I'm frightened.'

They were both quiet for some time. Boris had a faraway look in his eyes and had fallen silent. 'Anything the matter', asked Irina. 'Nothing', he said, 'nothing, I just remembered something'. He paused, then said, 'Dmitri and I would always argue over who you would choose.'

Irina put her arms around him, and hugged him tight.

They hugged each other and cried.

That night, they went back to the dacha for a light meal. Irina was impatient. She felt liberated after she had told Boris about her role in the dacha, as Nina. She wanted Boris, wanted to have him close to her, feeling him, his closeness. They went to bed early, and made love into the early hours.

'You better get some sleep,' Irina told him smiling and looking at the clock on the mantelpiece, it was quarter past two in the morning.

After breakfast Irina drove him to the Administrator's office. They had been security cleared and the guards showed them through. Gregory's secretary seemed to have thawed somewhat and even managed a smile.

'Good morning,' they heard Gregory from behind them. He had walked out of the conference room.

'How did you find the last week, I understand that you have become quite the expert with the camera?' Gregory thumped Boris on the back.

'I had some excellent teachers, Sir,' Boris replied.

Gregory looked from Boris to Irina, smiling,' I hope you've taken good care of him,' Gregory knew how Irina felt about Boris.

'The Council will arrive shortly, we have a preliminary discussion, and after that you will be called in for a briefing.' Gregory explained. 'Make yourselves comfortable, Raisa will organise what you need'.

Gregory disappeared into his office.

Boris and Irina, moved into an adjoining office after requesting Raisa for some coffee.

The council consisted of Pushkin, Zhirinovsky, Gregory, Sokolov, Sorovsky, the chiefs of two prominent Swiss banks, a well known arms dealer, the Chief Financial Officer of one of the world's leading producers of military aircraft, three well known Mafia chiefs with operations in the United States of America and Sicily, and an international shipping magnate from Greece. They arrived separately and were shown into the Administrator's conference room.

The meeting started immediately, Raisa served members with coffee and refreshments.

Gregory welcomed them and handed over the proceedings to Zhirinovsky. Each of the council members briefed the gathering on the status of the various activities, ranging from the movement of drugs, the status of money laundering to the sale and transport of nuclear fissile material to rouge states. Each area was discussed and the next stage of action agreed between the members. It was a business meeting with the policy makers reviewing the status and agreeing on the next course of action.

Pushkin rose, 'Gentlemen, we have progressed, we have our people in place in the Ukraine and the Belarus, we have finalised our plan of action on the day of the signing, we have to agree our actions after the treaty, or rather the day of the treaty.'

'I have with me the young man, whom I would like you to meet who is key to the success of our plan.'

Pushkin sent for Boris.

Boris was ushered in to meet the Council, he came in, looked around the table nodding. Each of those present nodded, raised his hand in acknowledgement, or returned his greeting.

Pushkin explained to them the background and training that he had been through, and his current assignment with the News de Internationale. The council was impressed.

Zhirinovsky, looked at Boris,' Do you know what you are expected to do?'

'No Sir'.

Zhirinovsky nodded, 'The assignment has to be accomplished, irrespective of the cost, the future of Russia depends on it, do you understand the significance?', he was waving his hands as he spoke, his face turning red with the excitement.

Zhirinovsky continued, explaining the task that Boris would have to carry out. Boris was prepared for the worst, Irina, Dimitri and he had sworn to each other to avenge the death of their parents. He knew too the dangers of the task he had on hand. He knew he would be lucky to get out alive.

Boris was shown out of the room. He made his way to Irina, thinking of the future.

Irina jumped up when he walked in. He seemed tense. She held his arm, 'Are you okay? Did they tell you? She asked out of concern.

Boris nodded, and explained.

'But, you will never be able to get out', she cried,' You will be killed.'

'That's a chance I'll have to take,' he said,' Don't worry, I don't want to be a martyr, I'll make it back to you somehow.' He said, seeing the concern and fear on Irina's face.

Boris left for Muhu early the next day. Irina dropped him off at the ferry. They had lain in each other's arms the whole night barely sleeping. Irina was frightened. He calmed her as best he could. He had been offered Irina as a backup, he had refused. Irina did not know of his refusal.

He was tempted to tell her, she would have jumped at the opportunity, it would mean they could be together, but that would expose her to unnecessary risks.

He would catch the afternoon flight into Haapsaalu. He knew what he had to do, it was now left to him to execute the plan.

After Boris had left, the council sat down to discuss the plan for the day after the treaty.

Pushkin, rose, he buzzed and Raisa walked in. She sat down plugged in her lap top, and turning it on punched a few buttons. The screen behind Pushkin lit up. It was a large map, a Warsaw Pact map, showing the order of battle for a 1983 military exercise. It depicted, areas of Northern Europe from Poland on the right to the United Kingdom on the left. There were red and black arrows depicting movement of troops, the red for the Russian forces and the black for NATO forces. Various types of armaments and ground support systems were depicted with signs. Pushkin referring to the map explained the time based action plan. They spent the rest of the afternoon, discussing and finalising details. The whole plan was stored in the system in the Administrator's office. The system was a standalone Local Area Network, with no connection to the Internet. This protected it from hackers working through the Internet. Access to the LAN system was by means of a series of passwords, entered consecutively. The system was in a secure building on the island. Pushkin and the council had every reason to feel comfortable.

Chapter 39

Date: 29th September 2007,
Place: Armavir, Time: 7.00 am

It was a Sunday, Markes had attended the church with father Joseph, who introduced him to the congregation and asked for volunteers to show Markes around the area. Many volunteered. Father Joseph organised for one of them who had a jeep to take Markes to Cerkessk on the 30th of October, the anniversary of the massacre.

Vaino Valjas was a farmer who owned a few acres at Armavir. Father Joseph and Markes had decided that it would be best to leave a day earlier; Markes was keen to reach Cerkessk the previous night, it would give him a chance to get a feel of the place. He knew that he had only the day to complete everything he had to do.

Father Joseph decided that he would join Markes and Vaino to Cerkessk for the journey on the 29th. Vaino's jeep, was of Second World War vintage, the engine was in good condition, Vaino took pride in his mechanical abilities, the body however was well past its prime. The narrow mountain roads, though reasonably well paved, had been damaged by the rains. Though the suspension was passable they had to hang on tight, as Vaino tried to avoid the potholes and dips. The lights of Vaino's jeep were not in the best shape either and it took all of Vaino's concentration to keep them moving at a reasonable pace.

They arrived in Cerkessk at eight that evening. Though it was late being a full moon night there was sufficient light to see the arrangements that had been made for the meeting in the morning.

Father Joseph was met at the village church by the local priest and the local party leader. The truth was that most of the inhabitants of Cerkessk were new. The party had invited people from the nearby villages after the massacre to make Cerkessk their home. Father Joseph introduced Markes to the priest, Father Benjamin who had been at Cerkessk for about a year. Father Benjamin showed them to their quarters, which was a row of buildings on the far side from the church.

'We have a meal ready, and would be very happy if you will join us,' Father Benjamin said.

'Viktor will come for you, in about fifteen minutes to show you to the dining room.' He excused himself, 'I will see to the arrangements, while you freshen up.'

Father Joseph nodded, 'Thank you, we will be very happy to join you.'

The meal was simple, consisting of bread, and a meat stew. There was plenty of meat, potatoes and cabbage.

They ate well, quite famished from the ride.

After they had finished, Father Joseph asked, 'Are you planning to hold a service tomorrow?'

'Yes, I spoke to some of the relatives of those who had died, they wanted a service.'

Father Joseph nodded in agreement.

Father Joseph checked his watch, it was 9.30 pm and decided to turn in. Markes, left them, 'I'd like to take a walk around the village, it's too early for me.'

Father Joseph, turned to Father Benjamin, 'I'm ready to hit the sack.'

Father Benjamin nodded, and led the way.

The village was quiet, the walls of the church and the party office had been scrubbed and whitewashed, but the pock marks made by the bullets were still visible, all one had to do was take a close look.

Markes walked around to the party office, he saw the lit window, and he made his way towards it.

The office door was shut from the inside, but he could hear music. He tapped on the door,' Hello, anyone there?'

The radio was turned down, he heard the grating of a chair being moved. The door opened and a figure, looked towards him.

'Who is there?'

'I'm Markes, I've come with Father Joseph from Armavir for the anniversary service.'

'Oh' the man grunted, 'Do you want to come in?'

'Yes, if it's no problem,' Markes replied, moving towards the door.

The man held the door open for Markes to enter.

Markes went in, turned to the man, putting out his hand. The man took it, 'I'm Leonid.'

'Have you lived here long, I mean in Cerkessk,' Markes asked.

'No, my uncle died in the shooting, and there was no one else in the family. The government asked me to come here and take over my uncle's land and property. I didn't have a job so I came here.'

Markes looked around at the office, it had the photographs of party officials on the walls. The office itself was neat and tidy.

'I heard that there were some who survived the shooting,' Markes asked casually while looking at the photographs on the wall.

'I heard there was only one, an old man named Starky.'

'I heard that four survived,' Markes said.

'No, I heard that the three were the first to arrive after the shooting. It was two men and a girl, their parents were also killed in the shooting.'

'Are they here, I would like to meet them.'

'No father, they have left, the old man also left, I heard he went looking for them sometime back, but has not returned. We have not had any news of the three or the old man.'

'Are there any relatives of the them here,' Markes asked conversationally. He did not want Leonid to think he was looking for information.

'It would be good if there are relatives at the service.'

Leonid nodded, 'Yes it would be good,' he went on, 'I'll check tomorrow morning to see if any of their relatives are around.'

Markes, shook hands with Leonid,' Thanks Leonid, we will meet tomorrow.'

'Good night father,' Leonid closed the door. Markes heard the music as the radio was turned up.

The morning saw the entire courtyard in front of the church fill up. A small stage had been erected with a pulpit to one side.

Father Benjamin started the service with a prayer. His sermon was touching. The village had organised a light meal for all those who attended. Many of those who had lost loved ones wanted to meet with Father Joseph, Father Benjamin or Markes. They wanted to be able to talk about their loved ones and their loss.

Markes found himself counselling young and old that had been affected. They could not comprehend the reason for such an atrocity. No one had taken responsibility and neither had the government done anything about the killings. It had been conveniently forgotten.

'Father Markes,' he heard someone calling.

Markes turned to see Leonid with three women, 'Hello Leonid'.

'Father, you wanted to know if there were relatives of those who had survived, this is Valeri Ustinov, Sophia Andreyava and Raisa Pavlov, they are the cousins of Sergei Pavlov, Irina Andreyava and Dmitri Ustinov."

Markes's felt his heart thumping in excitement.

He put out his hand, 'May the Lord grant you peace', he said. They took his hand in turn kissing it.

'We arrived here last week, and are staying at the house of Sergie Pavlov', Valeri said, 'We have not decided what to do with the house.'

'Don't they have any children?' Markes asked.

'Yes, each of them have a child, but no one knows where they are now. They were here just after the shooting. It must have been horrible for them, seeing their parents dead like that.' Raisa dabbed her eyes as she spoke.

'Have you tried talking to the authorities, they should be able to find them for you.' Markes suggested.

'We have tried everything, it's almost if they have disappeared', Valeri said. 'I have a photograph of Dmitri in the house, which I showed the police who came to investigate, they didn't even look at it.'

As an afterthought she suggested, 'Why don't you come to the house father, I'll make you some tea.'

'Sounds like a good idea,' Markes smiled.

They arrived at the Ustinov residence, which was at the edge of the village. The house was built on a large plot of land, the gardens were well tended, with flowerbeds along the walkway to the house. The rear of the house had a high stone wall and backed onto farmland. The house was solidly built. Markes entered the house, the door was short so he had to stoop to enter.

'It was made low to keep out the cold,' Valeri volunteered. It made sense, since the door faced the direction in which the wind was blowing. Having the entrance in any other direction would have spoilt the plan.

Valeri made them sit in front of the fireplace. The settee was large and very comfortable

Valeri excused herself to make the tea, and Sophia went with her, they came back almost immediately each clutching an envelope.

'These are photographs of Dmitri, you can have a look at them while I make the tea,' Valeri said, she then added, 'an envelope was surprisingly addressed to Nina Andreyava, by Yushenko, who we know as Starky, a long time ago, and this was after the incident at Cerkessk, so Starky knew that it could not be delivered to Nina Andreyava, perhaps he had a reason for addressing it to her. I have been holding on to it, in the hope that when Starky came back I'd give it to him,' Sophia held out the envelope, 'perhaps this will help'.

Valeri went back inside to make the tea.

Markes's heart was pounding, he was about to receive information, all of it by chance. He took both the envelopes. The one addressed to Nina Andreyava was brown and discoloured, the post mark showing the date as 17th of February 2002.

Markes, opened the envelope with the photographs first, he looked at the photograph, and took a quick deep breadth. The man in the photograph was identical to the person in the photograph sent to him by NATBAL via the Internet. The man in the photograph was the bodyguard who was thought to have been responsible for the killing of the Interior Minister of Belarus.

Valerie walked in with tea and biscuits.

'I heard that there were three who came here after the shooting,' Markes asked.

'Yes, but we don't have photographs of Yuri and Irina' Sergei said, 'We can perhaps go to their homes, and see if we can find some old photographs to show you.'

Markes opened the second envelope, and found two folded A4 sheets, the sheets were filled with notes, almost at random. He quickly scanned through the sheets, the words 'Cerkessk' caught his attention, there was a lot more information on the two sheets, but that would require careful reading.

'Can I keep these papers, there is some information which might lead me to Starky?' he asked of Sophia.

'You can keep the papers father,' she said. 'I really have no use for it.

The biscuits were passed around, they were homemade and Markes found himself helping himself a second time. They finished their tea.

Valerie waited till Markes had put his cup down.

'Would you like to go to Sergei's house father?' she asked.

'Yes I'd like that', Markes replied.

They made their way to Sergei Pavlov's house.

Once inside, Raisa Pavlov, went through a chest with glass shutters. She checked the inside and the drawers, 'There are no photographs, here,' she said disappointed.

'That's fine, it was only out of curiosity,' Markes replied.

They heard loud tapping on the door. 'I wonder who that is.' Raisa exclaimed,' he seems to be in a great hurry.' She made her way to the front door.

'Oh, hello, why don't you come on in, we have Father Markes with us, and we are showing him a photograph of Dmitri.'

'No, I can't come in just now, I've to see to some work, I just came to give you this,' he held out a photograph of Irina and Yuri.

Raisa came in with a great big smile, 'Look what we have found, a photograph of Irina and Yuri.'

She handed the photograph to Markes.

Raisa saw the startled expression on Markes's face when he saw the photograph.

'Have you seen them before father?' she asked', you seemed startled when you saw the photograph.'

'It's just that she resembles someone I knew a long time ago,' Markes pointed to Irina.

'She's a very attractive woman,' he said.

Raisa smiled,' Yes father, if you had seen her before you took your vows, you might have changed your mind.'

Markes grinned, 'Yes, I know what you mean.'

They spent an hour together, with Valeri, Sophia and Raisa talking about Irina, Dmitri and Yuri. The three were well known and the village was proud of them and their achievements.

Markes, took leave and went back to father Joseph.

Father Joseph was busy and talking to Father Benjamin, so Markes took out the papers he had been given by Valerie, which were written by Starky. He quickly went through them, from the notings this was the first solid evidence, or rather confirmation that the Cerkessk incident was sanctioned by members of the politburo, and carried out by an insider, someone the politburo used for black operations. There were oblique references to certain members in the politburo, all supposedly staunch democrats. What surprised Markes even more was the revelation that Intrasyn was not behind these incidents. The common denominator was that the members of the politburo who had sanctioned the killings, had interests in companies where the Russian state was divesting its holdings for a mere pittance. The beneficiaries were these very same politburo members.

He had the information he wanted, Anatoly was actually Dimitri, and the girl Irina was none other than Nina, or rather Nina was actually Irina. That left only Yuri. More importantly he had information on the people behind the Cerkessk massacre.

It was also clear that Intrasyn had used these three as a means to their own end. The fact that they were infiltrated into sensitive positions that needed a high level of clearance pointed to the involvement, of people such as Zhirinovsky and Pushkin.

It was also clear that the Cerkessk massacre were sanctioned by members in the highest levels of government.

Father Joseph had finished his talk with father Benjamin. 'Shall we leave?' father Joseph asked Markes.

'I'm ready,' father.

They got into the Vaino's jeep for the bumpy ride back to Armavir.

That night Markes logged onto the website, to transmit his findings to NATBAL.

The message was received by Brian's communications officer and was on Brian's desk immediately.

'The first part of the puzzle, has fallen into place, what is Yuri up to, I wonder?' Brian thought aloud.

Markes's transmission had come through clearly. The three, two men and a woman were from Cerkessk, and had been recruited by Intrasyn.

The pattern of developments, the assassinations, the re-positioning of key security personnel in the Belarus and the Ukraine, seen in the context of the Treaty was disturbing. NATBAL needed more information. There was only one place, where the answers lay, in Muhu the headquarters of Intrasyn.

Mary came in, 'this has just arrived,' she handed Brian a large envelope. It was from Interpol.

Brian opened the report, and pulled out a sheaf of papers and some photographs. He picked up the photographs, going through them, rapidly. He looked around and picked up the Interpol report. Surveillance at the ferry terminal at Haapsaalu had shown that there was a change in the schedules on a particular day. The terminal had been shut down for the general public. The only craft going in and out were Intrasyn yachts. The report talked of a number of limousines that had taken passengers from the Airfield to the ferry terminal.

The photographs were of Zhirinovsky and Pushkin, and a few others who could not be identified though the photographs had been enlarged.

This was the second time that Zhirinovsky had come out to a meeting, and with Pushkin. The answers lay in Muhu. Brian decided that he would have to risk sending Markes to Muhu, there was no other alternative.

Brian sent a message back to Markes, 'Visit to Muhu imperative. Need information on recent meeting of 'Brotherhood'. The code Brotherhood was taken from the 1980 exercise code-named Waffenbruderschaft or Armed Brotherhood, which combined the East German National People's Army and the Polish and Soviet forces. The Brotherhood now referred to the Russian Political-Intrasyn combine.

Markes, read and re-read the message from NATBAL. The instructions were clear, he had to visit Muhu, that's where the answers were. Markes knew the odds were stacked against him, if he succeeded in getting in, the chances of getting out were even lower.

The message from Brian ended with the details of a back up, another mole of NATBAL in Viljandi.

Markes knew he had to find a good excuse to move away from Armavir. Father Joseph was depending on him to carry on his work. Markes spent a further two weeks with him before he found the right moment to discuss with Father Joseph his desire to study Theology at one of the Russian Universities. Father Joseph was very pleased and suggested that he study at the University of St Petersburg, Markes gently told him that he would like to spend some time at a few of the universities before deciding where to study. Father Joseph immediately wrote half a dozen letters to various friends and accquaintances introducing Markes and requesting them to assist Markes in selecting a University.

Markes decided to take leave of Father Joseph after the Sunday service.

Markes, woke early, Father Joseph was up as usual. 'Good morning father,' Markes went to Father Joseph and kissed his hand.

'May the peace of the Lord be with you,' Father Joseph murmured.

They made their way to the dining area and partook of a simple meal of bread, cheese and coffee.

Father Joseph handed Markes a bag. 'Some food for your journey,'

'Thank you Father.'

Father Joseph handed him a small envelope. Markes opened it and found money in it.

'Father, I don't need any money,' Markes protested.

Father Joseph smiled, 'Money has its uses, son and you will need it.'

They heard Vaino's jeep as it turned into the church courtyard. Vaino had volunteered to drive Markes to the Armavir railway station.

Markes bought himself a ticket for Riga; after some discussion the railway clerk issued him the ticket via Moscow.

The train to Moscow arrived at 7.10 am. Markes entered the compartment, it was quite full, no one took particular notice of him, most were dozing. The train was carrying commuters to offices and factories in Kropotkin, Tihoreck and Pavlovskaja. The train would be quite empty after Pavlovskaja.

Markes found himself a seat made himself comfortable and promptly fell asleep. He felt a gentle tapping on his shoulder and awoke to find that the train had stopped at a station.

The conductor apologised, 'Sorry Father, just checking to see whether you want to get off at Pavlovskaja?'

Markes smiled back,' I'm on my way to Moscow,' he reached into his tunic for his ticket, the conductor, waved at him and went on his way.

Chapter 40

Date: 2nd October 2007, Place: Muhu, Time: 1.30 p.m

Pushkin had received information on Markes and Amalrik, he knew that Amalrik was dead, 'The blundering idiots', he rasped.

His aide standing by kept silent, he knew that Pushkin was in a foul mood.

'I want to see Dudayev', he growled at his aide.

'Yes Sir, when should I call him'.

'The day after tomorrow, here in the office,' Pushkin replied, waving his hand dismissing the aide.

Dudayev was a KGB officer assigned as the head of the Kremlin Guard force. The Kremlin Guard force protected important government centres, and also controlled the Government Communication Troops, which provided the states secure communication lines.

Dudayev arrived at 10 a.m. and was driven directly to Pushkin's office.

He entered Pushkin's office, 'Good morning Sir'.

'Good morning Dudayev,' Pushkin replied.' We have a problem. We have information that there has been substantial interest by outside parties in Intrasyn and Cerkessk.' He paused, 'We think that he is a western agent, no one on our files, so he must be off record. He was last seen at Kiev, one of his accomplices was in our hands but was unfortunately killed while being apprehended. I haven't got time for amateurs. I want you to take over the investigation. The agent is to be apprehended and if that is not possible neutralised, and any accomplices with him.'

He pressed a button, his aide walked in. 'See that everyone is suitably briefed. Dudayev is working under my direct authority, he is to be given whatever he needs.'

Dudayev knew that the meeting was over, he had been given wide powers but had to deliver.

Dudayev proceeded to set up a team for the task, he requisitioned, ex KGB agents who had worked in the field. He set up headquarters at Moscow with special branches at Kiev, Haapsaalu and Odessa. He had access to any information that he required, if clearance was required all he had to do was inform the aide who ensured that it was done. The entire organisation was ready in a week's time, he chose Yevgany as his second in command.

Dudayev met with his team and went through the movements of Markes, his meeting with Amalrik in Kiev and his subsequent disappearance. They had access to information passed to Pushkin on Markes's visit to the Rose, his meetings with Laila and Tatyana, as well as his visit to the doctor's wife. The file ended with Amalrik's death and the disappearance of Markes.

Dudayev addressed his team, 'We need to find out where he is, he seems to have disappeared into thin air.'

He spoke slowly,' we have a description and a photograph, let's start by checking all airports, rail stations and coach stations in Kiev, someone could have seen him.'

Dudayev turned to Yevgany a seasoned KGB field agent, 'What do you think, Yevgany?'

'If you look at what he is trying to do, he is gathering information, which centres on the death of the head of security of the Ukraine. He has visited associated places. He has also shown interest in Nina. Where did Nina come from?'

'She was from Cerkessk,' Dudayev replied.

'We should check to see if he has shown any interest in Cerkessk.'

Dudayev nodded, 'Ok, we'll meet early tomorrow'.

They met at Dudayev's office early the next morning, the field agents were good, the team working on Cerkessk had come up with the arrival of a young priest Father Markes, his stay at Father Joseph's church and the visit to Cerkessk on the anniversary of the massacre. They knew that Father Markes had met with Dimitri's and Irina's relatives, and had visited Yuri's home as well. They had checked the story that Markes had told Father Joseph. Nothing checked out. The description given by Father Joseph was close to the man in height and size they had tailed and lost at Kiev.

'He's definitely our man', said Dudayev.

Yevgany nodded. 'He's good at changing his appearance. We will have to look for characteristics which he cannot disguise.'

He turned to one of the men. 'See that the surveillance photographs at Kiev are studied by the bureau, I want to know anything in his appearance, his walk or movement of his head or hands which can be used as a means of identification.'

'He has been on the trail of Irina and Dimitri and Yuri.' He said half aloud, almost as if to himself. 'Yet there is no sign of him checking Dimitri's whereabouts.'

'I want to know where he went after he left Cerkessk.' Dudayev turned to Yevgany. Yevgany nodded, 'We are checking on that at this moment, the operatives are at railway stations, ports, coach stations and with taxis.'

'Let me know as soon as you receive any information.'

Chapter 41

Date: 2nd October 2007, Place: Moscow,
Time: 1.30 p.m

The train reached Moscow, the halt would be for half an hour. Markes got off the train and made his way to the front to the sandwich kiosk.

'Good afternoon Father,' the kiosk owner greeted him.

'May the blessings of the Virgin Mary be with you,' Markes blessed him.

'What can I do for you?' the stall owner smiled.

'May I have a corned beef sandwich and a beer', he handed the money to the owner, picked up the sandwich and the beer and made his way back to his train. He realised he was quite hungry and ate quickly. He washed down the last mouthful with the beer, deposited the bag and the bottle in the garbage can and checked the station watch. He still had a few minutes; he walked across to the newsstand and bought himself a copy of the News de Internacionale.

He settled himself in the train and started reading the paper. The News de Internacionale was a recent magazine in these parts, he couldn't quite remember when it had started circulation. It made interesting reading.

He must have dozed off. He awoke with a start, in time to hear the train conductor announce that the train had arrived at Riga Central. He looked around, there was a lot of commotion. He peered through the window, the train was emptying.

Markes picked up his bag, stepped out of the train and made his way to the monitor on the platform. He checked the connection to Viljandi and found it was on the suburban service route. Trains were frequent, every fifteen minutes at peak times. He made his way to the suburban section of the station. A train was ready to leave, the guard standing by to wave it on its way. He checked the monitor, and made his way into the crowded compartment. The run was short, it had taken thirty minutes, he checked the station clock, it read 6.30 p.m.

Zonta, was another of Brian's moles, he had been an agent of the Estonian Secret Service, trained by the Russians in clandestine activities, explosives and counter espionage. At one time during his career, Zonta had served in the Third Chief Directorate of Estonia, which in Estonia had responsibility for Military Counter Intelligence and VIP Security. Brian had recruited him, after the fall of the Berlin wall.

Markes did not know of him till he received Brian's message, this would have been the same with Zonta. Zonta had co-ordinated the information gathering activities of NATBAL around the three Baltic States. Brian was risking blowing Zonta's cover, since Markes's cover had been blown the remotest contact with Markes would immediately bring Zonta under investigation.

Markes, stepped off the train at Viljandi and made his way to the coach station. He could have walked, but wanted to give the impression that he had some distance to travel. The coach was a service to Parnu. He got off the coach about two miles from the station and made his way to the northern sector of the town.

He knocked on a door that had no name board but carried the number 302. He heard a shuffle, and waited, it seemed a full minute before the door opened. There was no one in sight. Markes stepped into the house, and looked around. He felt a presence and turned to find Zonta moving out of the shadows. Zonta was a careful man, he did not utter a word, but motioned to Markes to take a seat. After a few minutes he stepped out of the door and took a quick look around. Satisfied that Markes had not been followed he stepped back in quickly and shut the door.

Markes looked around at the room. It was sparsely furnished, the main room had a three piece settee, a couch, a couple of chairs, a writing table, a bed in an adjoining room, which had an attached bath and toilet. The kitchen was at one end of the main room, adjoining it was a small dining area with a table and four chairs.

'You had better get rid of that smock, it stands out like a sore thumb' Zonta said bluntly. His irritation showing.

Markes nodded, looking at Zonta who was about the same height and build as himself.

Zonta understood, 'I'll get you some of my clothes, they should fit.' He disappeared into the adjoining room and came back, beckoned to Markes. 'I've laid out the clothes on the bed, you can shower and change.'

Markes peeled off the false beard and moustache, shaved, showered and changed. He felt refreshed, looked into the mirror feeling reassured in finding a familiar face.

Zonta had cooked some pasta and mince. He had set the table for two and had put out two glasses and a bottle of vodka on the dining table in the kitchen. Zonta poured two generous shots. They downed the first drink and poured themselves a second round. They helped themselves to the food, and vodka, there was no talk till they had finished the meal.

Zonta lit a cigarette, offered one to Markes who shook his head. 'Brian told me that I was to give you whatever assistance you required.'

'Tell me all that you know of Muhu,' Markes asked.

Zonta, stood up and walked back into his bedroom without saying a word. He returned with a large rolled map that he spread on the table. It was a reconnaissance map of high resolution covering the ferry terminal at Haapsaalu, and the whole of Muhu. Markes saw the writing along the margins; Zonta explained were the schedules of the ferry service from Haapsaalu. The checkpoints, the security cameras, the layout of the island and its entrance, the administration buildings were all very clear.

'I have to visit Muhu,' he said, and saw the surprise on Zonta's face.

'That's suicide,' Zonta exclaimed, 'it's a fortress, and there's only one way in, which is constantly monitored. There's no way you can get in without being noticed.'

'What about the south side, the Old Russian Naval base?' Markes asked.

'It's disused now, and there's no way in, besides the sea is very rough and the rocks very dangerous. The currents are very strong. The only way in is on the ferry or by helicopter.'

'I'll have to find a way.' Markes said.

Zonta fell silent thinking, 'There is a slim chance,' he said almost to himself, 'You might be able to get away with it. The only problem is how you will get out.'

Zonta looked at the map, studied it for a moment and explained to Markes.

Chapter 42

Date: 2nd October 2007, Place: Muhu, Time: 2.00 p.m

Dudayev had sent a team to requisition all that had been taken from Amalrik's place in Kiev. The team returned with the items taken and the report filed by the local investigating officer. There were details of bank accounts, and signatures, all of which checked out as Amalrik's, one of the numbers did not. A check showed that it was of a different bank. Further checks showed it was in the name of Markes Trubin. A team was sent to investigate, the bank officer was only too willing to help, having been persuaded by a call from the Interior Ministry. The personal details of Markes Trubin were passed to Dudayev, including a photograph. The photograph was similar to the one that the surveillance agents had taken of Markes.

A further check at the record office showed that Markes Trubin had died many years ago. His records had mysteriously disappeared during a robbery that had taken place about a year after the fall of the Berlin wall. The current Markes Trubin was an impostor.

Yevgany put a team to check on Markes Trubin's life. Every aspect of his life from his early days at Mykolajiv, his stint at the University of Kiev, his affair with Zoya, his love of computers and his flair for disguise was recorded.

Dudayev and Yevgany concluded that Markes had to be a western mole. Pushkin would need to be told immediately and Markes neutralised.

Yevgany looked at the photograph of Markes for a while, he picked up a pen and inked in a beard, moustache and a pair of horn-rimmed glasses. The face that they saw was very similar to that of a priest. Show this photograph to Father Joseph and ask him if this was Markes.

The team returned in an hour, they had scanned the photograph and sent it by email to their contact in Armavir who had shown it to Father Joseph. They had received the confirmation that it was indeed Markes.

Dudayev turned to the men in the room.' See that every one of our operatives has a copy, I want all airports, stations, and every public place, under surveillance. I want to know where he is in the next twenty-four hours.'

He paused, then turned to Yevgany. 'Have we received the surveillance tapes from Kiev?'

Yevgany nodded, 'They are ready to be screened.'

Yevgany and Dudayev made their way to the screening room.

Dudayev and Yevgany settled down in the projection room. The lights were turned off and the projector started with a signal from Yevgany.

The tapes showed Markes, alone and then his meeting Amalrik. The video had been taken with a long-range camera, the images were sharp and they could clearly make out his face.

Yevgany signalled for them to stop and asked the operator to project the photograph of Markes Trubin from the bank. The person in both photographs was identical.

'Continue,' Yevgany said lighting up a cigarette.

The projection showed Markes walking towards Amalrik. He walked with long strides, his hands swinging backwards in an arc.

Yevgany asked for the film to be run and rerun, he could not find anything special. He asked for close ups of the face, of the forehead, of the chin, nose and lips. He was looking for any distinguishing characteristics that would stand out under a disguise. He could not find anything. He asked for a close up of his arms and hands.

Yevgany sat upright, he asked for the close up of the right hand to be frozen, there was a characteristic that seemed different, Markes' right thumb was large, quite large. On close examination it showed that he had two thumbs which were conjoined.

Chapter 43

Date: 2 nd October 2007, Place: Viljandi,
Time: 8.30 p.m

Zonta and Markes, decided that they would turn in early and start work early next morning. Markes stretched out on the couch, it was long enough for him to stretch.

They woke early, had a heavy breakfast, it would have to see them through the better part of the day. Markes had changed his appearance. He used a wig to change his appearance to a grey-haired, middle aged man with a slight paunch. He dressed in overalls, following Zonta's instructions as someone looking for casual work. His shoes were heavy and worn.

They took the coach from Viljandi to Haapsaalu. The ride took them an hour and a half. They got off at the square near the terminal that had all the warehouses.

Zonta made his way to one of the tall buildings near the church. As they made their way up the stairs Zonta said.' We will be meeting the contractor who supplies loaders and cleaners to the warehouses, the port and the local offices.'

They stopped on the fifth floor, pushed through the doors and found themselves in a foyer, which was crowded. Zonta pushed his way through and catching the eye of one of the men in the cubicles waved at him. The man waved back, obviously he knew Zonta.

Zonta looked back, 'Follow me and don't say anything. I'll do the talking, if he asks you your name tell him its Sergi. He'll then ask you for your papers, say that you lost them.

The place is full of men who are looking for work with no questions asked. They are paid very low wages, but no one complains.'

Zonta pushed the door of the cubicle open.' Hi, Kozyrev, how's it going?'

'Not too bad, have you got anything for me,' Kozyrev looked meaningfully at Zonta.

Zonta nodded, 'but first I want you to meet a friend, 'he needs a job, a cleaning job.' He reached into his jacket and pulled out a plastic bag, it was about two inches square, flat and packed tightly. It contained a white powder. Markes guessed it was Heroin. He saw the wide smile on Kozyrev's face as he reached for it. Zonta drew his arm away. Kozyrev face fell.' What do you want?'

'I'll give you another packet as well, if you can send my friend to the island.'

Kozyrev shook his head. 'Its too much of a risk.'

'You just have to put him on the detail on Friday, just like you do every week.'

Kozyrev thought for a moment, looked at Markes. 'Hey you, are you good at cleaning?' he asked.

Markes nodded,' I'll clean your office for you this evening, and you can see for yourself in the morning.'

Kozyrev reached for the packet, 'You will have to return with the detail in the evening, I want no tricks, or we'll both end up very dead.'

It was Wednesday and they had two days for preparations. Markes followed Zonta as he made his way to various warehouses, talking in whispers with the men he met. Money and packets exchanged hands. Zonta had by the end filled a sizeable bag with the items he had collected.

'Lets get back, I've got all the stuff I need,' he said as they made their way back to the coach stop.

They reached Zonta's place and settled down for a final once over. Zonta reached up over his cupboard and took out the large rolled map which he had shown Markes the previous day and spread it on the table. It was the reconnaissance map covering the ferry terminal at Haapsaalu, and the whole of Muhu.

Chapter 44

Date: 2 nd October 2007, Place: Cerkessk, Time: 9.45 am

Andropov headed the team sent to Cerkessk. He went to the church, and knocked on Father Joseph's quarters. The door was answered by Father Joseph who smiled and held the door wide open.

'Come in son,' and seeing his companions said, 'bring your friends with you'.

They followed him into Father Joseph's room. It was very sparsely furnished and had only two chairs.

'You are not from these parts, can I get you some water to drink?'

'No thank you father, we are here for some information.'

Father Joseph looked questioningly at Andropov.

'What is it that you wish to know?'

'Father, there was a priest, Father Markes who was here with you for some time, do you know where he went?'

Father Joseph looked surprised, it was the second time in two days that someone had questioned him about Father Markes.

'Father Markes decided that he needed to study Theology, I have given him letters of reference to present to various people that I know. He said he was planning to visit various universities before deciding where to study. He is a fine young man and we are fortunate that he has chosen to serve the Lord.'

Andropov nodded. 'Do you know how he travelled?'

'Vaino dropped him off at the Armavir railway station,' Father Joseph replied.

Andropov thanked him and made his way to the railway station.

Andropov didn't waste any time. He showed the railway clerk his identity. The clerk was suitably impressed and blurted. 'I can check my records, this is not a very busy station, most of the tickets were to Vilnius or Moscow,' the clerk was checking his records when he stopped, 'yes, I do remember this one, he bought a ticket for Riga via Moscow, which was not usual.'

Andropov went to the nearest phone booth and spoke to the operator. Within a minute he was talking to Dudayev.

'We should have our operatives in Moscow and Riga check to see where he is headed.'

Dudayev was silent for a while. He wondered whether Markes's destination was Muhu and Intrasyn's headquarters.

'Yes, go ahead and keep me informed.' He instructed Andropov.

Chapter 45

Date: 18th October 2007, Place: Muhu,
Time: 10.30 am

Pushkin called Boris on his direct line.

'Hello Sir, it's a pleasure to hear from you.' Boris answered.

'We are having a meeting of the group, I want you join to us, the members will be briefed on the status and you will have a chance to meet them.'

'Yes Sir, certainly,' Boris replied.

'I'll see you,' Pushkin hung up.

Boris pressed the intercom button.' Carla, can you please come in.'

He heard the side door of his office open as his secretary walked in. 'Yes Mr Pugo.'

'I will need to be out of the office for the next week or so.'

'Yes Sir, for the Treaty?'

'No, I'm leaving tomorrow, to Haapsaalu. I'll leave from Haapsaalu for Kiev.'

'Do you want me to make any reservations for you.'

'Yes just the ticket to Haapsaalu. I'll make arrangements after that.'

'Is there anything else?' she asked.

'If there are any calls for me, inform them that I'm not available till after the Treaty.'

She nodded, Boris was used to doing things on his own and his office let him.

The next day saw a lot of activity at Muhu. A steady stream of business jets landed early in the morning. Their flight plans having been cleared from Haapsaalu the previous evening. No details of the passengers were given and none were asked. The planes were on charter to Intrasyn, and had originated from various points in Europe.

The lone passenger and his bodyguards were met on the apron by a limousine, and taken to the building adjoining the administration building. Vladimir Sokolov the chief of Intrasyn met them.

Sokolov addressed the gathering.' Comrades we are at the beginning of the most important phase of our plan. Everything is in place for the day of the treaty. Once accomplished we will have our people in place for the next phase of achieving our Legacy, The Bolshevik Legacy comrades.'

He nodded to Zhirinovsky, who rose to a round of applause.

'Comrades, our men are in key positions at this very moment. The Chief of Security of the Ukraine, the Interior Minister of Belarus and the Chief of Army staff in Russia.' He nodded to Pushkin who nodded in acknowledgement.

'In a short while you will see our men in the top slot in the three republics, paving the way for our taking back what is rightfully ours. And you gentlemen,' he waved to the arms dealers and the drug barons will be back in business. I will let comrade Pushkin take you through the details.' He sat down to a round of applause.

Pushkin stood up and moved to the far end of the table. He signalled to an aide at the end of the room. A switch was thrown which was followed by a hum as a screen descended from the ceiling. A projector lowered itself from the ceiling simultaneously.

'The next phase of the plan gentlemen as explained is to replace the heads of government of Russia, Ukraine and Belarus. This will be done on the day of the Treaty.'

He waved to Boris to join him.

'This young man, who you have known as the correspondent for the News de Internacionale will see to it.'

Pushkin proceeded to explain the plan. There were smiles and nods in Boris's direction. All of them approved.

'I have brought him here today so that you know him. I expect all of you to give him any assistance that he might require.'

He nodded to Boris, who made his way back to his seat.

Pushkin continued.' The plan you are about to see will take place a month after the Treaty, I will personally notify you. However, after the day of the Treaty you will all be on a four hour standby.'

He raised his arm. The aide dimmed the lights and the screen lit up.

'What you are about to see is the starting point for us to claim our legitimate Legacy.'

The projection started, the heading read, 'The Order of Battle'. Computer generated graphics showed the launch of nuclear attacks with the names of cities targeted. Figures on the screen illustrated the damage to NATO troops and cities. This was followed by invasion forces illustrating heavy armour and armoured personnel carriers. The projection continued. Pushkin sat down, there was no need to explain. The projection ended and the lights came on. Boris looked around, there were many around the table that had their mouths open, their jaws slack, surprised and unbelieving. Some were shuffling in their seats. One fact was clear, none of them had expected anything like this.

Pushkin stood up, 'Gentlemen, are you awed by what you just saw. This is for real. Are there any questions?'

There were murmurs around the table, and smiles as the plan dawned on them. One of them started clapping, which was joined by the others, till the room resounded with cheers and the thumping of the table.

They went back to their limousines for the ride back to the airfield, and to their private jets.

What they had seen would change the destiny of the world.

Chapter 46

Date: 20th October 2007,
Place: Haapsaalu, Time: 5.00 pm

It was early evening on Thursday when Markes and Zonta made their way to Haapsaalu, on the coach. Zonta had spent the day assembling various types of miniature explosives that Markes would need. They reached Haapsaalu around six in the evening and made their way to Kozyrev's office. The office was a part of the apartment where Kozyrev lived. Kozyrev had closed for the day. They knocked, heard a gruff voice asking who it was. The door opened, Kozyrev was in his vest and pyjamas holding a bottle of Vodka.

'Come in,' he waved to them, they were expected. He pointed to the settee. 'Make yourselves comfortable, Vodka?' He asked.

They nodded. He went to a liquor cabinet and took out two glasses. He handed one to each of them and filled it half full with vodka.

He raised his glass.' The stuff you gave me was good, very good,' he said and took a large sip.

They finished with Kozyrev and returned to Zonta's apartment, It was close to midnight when they turned in, after a light meal.

Date: 21ˢᵗ October 2007,
Place: Haapsaalu, Time: 5.00 am

They awoke at four, washed changed and checked that their disguise was intact. They made themselves some sandwiches, washing it down with strong hot black coffee. Their belongings were packed into briefcases. Zonta made sure that he packed two sets of his old uniforms. They looked like early morning commuters making their way to the train station.

Zonta took a length of trip wire and strung it at three different places. He saw the questioning look on Markes's face.

'They will think the place is booby-trapped. They will spend time looking for the explosive. Just buying time,' he grinned.

They made their way to the street taking separate routes and arranged to meet at the rail station. They would buy return tickets, Markes for Novgorod and Zonta for Saint Petersburg. They would get off at Pskov and buy return tickets to Smolensk. From Smolensk they would make their way to Kiev.

'Hold it,' Zonta turned to Markes.

'We need cash to buy tickets, we'll take it from one of the cash machines.'

'ATM transactions are recorded, they will know we were here' Markes said.

"I know, but do we have a choice?'

Zonta withdrew a sizeable sum, which he split in two, handing one half to Markes.

Zonta looked at Markes. 'I'll see you on Sunday night,' he said, shook hands and walked away towards the coach stop.

Markes reached Kozyrev's office, and was given a pair of overalls. 'This is standard, no one in the cleaning gang is allowed to enter wearing anything other than in this uniform.

The colour of the uniform identifies the contractor supplying the labour.'

'What about cleaning material?' Markes asked.

Kozyrev nodded. 'That's standard as well.'

Markes, took his laptop out of its case, and put it into a special black plastic bag that he zipped up.

Kozyrev showed Markes the cleaning trolley. Markes rolled the trolley to the end of the room to get it ready. The room downstairs was filling up with the rest of the cleaning detail. He filled the tank with water, looked around, saw that no one was looking his way, and slid the laptop and a small carry bag into the water tank. He looked down into the water and could not see the bag or the laptop..

Kozyrev was busy filling the forms that would have to be presented at the terminal at Haapsaalu and again at Muhu. He handed each of the detail a badge with a number on it.

Chapter 47

Date: 21st October 2007,
Place: Haapsaalu, Time: 5.30 am

It was a quarter to six as they made their way to the terminal for the six o'clock ferry to Muhu. The ferry would take an hour to cross. Their work would start at 7a.m. and end at 7p.m, during which time they would have had to clean all the administration buildings.

The trip into the ferry terminal, the crossing and the entry into Muhu were smooth. The guards were obviously bored. They saw the uniforms and the badges and waved them through. One of them came around and looked at the trolleys, none of them were frisked. Markes was not sure whether they did a head count at all.

Their tasks had already been assigned. Markes had the responsibility for cleaning the administration building adjoining the main building, this was more by design than by chance. They split up as soon as they entered the main campus. Markes looked around, Zonta's map had been very accurate, the security cameras and the lights were exactly in the locations as in Zonta's map.

Kozyrev had organised that Markes was assigned one of the regulars as his team-mate. His teammate was the head of the group, the others listened to him without any questions. The men were paired and the cleaning schedule was laid out.

They made their way into the complex. Markes was surprised that there were no coded locks on doors between departments. Perhaps it was the knowledge that they had complete control of the island that made Intrasyn decide against such precautions.

They decided to start with the rest rooms, and move across the outer corridors working their way into the building by evening. The schedule was such that, they would have access to the office at five when the office closed. They then had two hours to clean up and leave. The last ferry to Haapsaalu was at 7.15 p.m.

Markes and his companion decided to work around the block in opposite directions, meeting at the middle at the rear.

Markes went into the rest rooms that were situated near the reception area and away from the main office. He had a quick look around, there was no one around. He checked for hidden security cameras, found none and went into one of the cubicles. He removed his right boot and twisted the heel till it came off. He removed what seemed a flat disc that seemed to be some sort of wax. There was a strip of very thin shiny metal wound around the disc. He unscrewed one of the bulbs in the cubicle, inserted the disc and screwed the bulb back on, it lit up.

He quickly cleaned the bowls and the washbasins. A few men dressed in suits walked in, had a smoke, washed and left. He worked steadily till lunchtime. The group gathered at the rear of the building to eat their packed lunch. They set to work immediately afterwards.

At four the office started emptying, it was a Friday evening and most of the men and women were hurrying to get back. By five the office was entirely empty. Markes and his companion had decided that, they would take opposite ends of the building and as soon as they finished they would make their way back to the ferry independently.

Unseen by his companion, Markes removed the laptop, placed it under a desk and pushed the trolley towards his companion.

'I don't need the trolley, anymore', he said.

His companion had been instructed not to interfere with anything that Markes did. He quietly took the trolley and moved away.

The office was exactly like any other office he had been to. There were workstations and computers. At one end of the office there was a row of glass fronted cabins. The workstations had phones, one at each station. He lifted the receiver, and was immediately answered by a voice, he replied that he was part of the cleaning gang and had accidentally lifted the receiver. He was curtly asked to put down the receiver.

The work station terminals had been switched off. Markes started cleaning the office. It was close to seven, he looked towards the reception area when a bright flash lit up the area in front of the administration building, and all the lights went out. The emergency lights came on. Smoke was billowing out of the front. He heard a babble of voices as the cleaning detail came running out of the building and gathered around the front. The circuit had been shorted, resulting in an electric fire. It was a small one and would soon be put out, but afforded a diversion. A car screeched to halt near the reception area and a voice over a loudhailer instructed the workmen to leave the area immediately. He looked out and saw the men of the cleaning detail running to the ferry terminal. There would be no head count with this commotion.

He pressed himself against the wall in the shadows inside the office as a guard came around the outside locking doors. The security guards were trained in fire fighting and had brought up special fire extinguishers to put out the fire.

He heard the hoot of the ferry's horn as it left Muhu. Markes looked at the clock in the office, it was 7.15 p.m.

The commotion lasted for an hour, then all turned quiet as the guards and the car left. Markes picked up his laptop and made his way into the computer room. He carefully checked to see if there were any cameras, or infrared sensors fitted in the room, there were none. This was the heart of the Intrasyn operations, at least the legal part. The adjoining administration block was isolated from the block he was in. The buildings and the walls reminded him of a security enclosure. He guessed that it was out of bounds for most personnel in the main administration block. Markes walked around the office. From what he could make out, the computer system was very advanced and linked both sections. It would be possible to access the files used by the clandestine section of Intrasyn if the codes or passwords could be cracked. Intrasyn had not linked their system to the Internet. All external lines went through operators.

Markes crouched low and made his way into the computer room. It was cool, the temperature was controlled. He removed his overalls and dumped them in a corner, decided that he would eat and then start. He picked a spot and opened the packet, his dinner consisted of corned beef sandwiches and cheese. He saved most of the cheese for the next day, he knew he would have to last for two days on what he had. He heard a boot kick a stone and froze. He waited, the guard was on his rounds. Markes saw him as he came around the corner. The guard had a large powerful flashlight that he shone at random into the office. Markes slid to the floor near the corner out of view from the guard. He saw the beam light up the corner near the area where he was crouched. The guard passed.

Markes drank some water from the office water dispenser, wiped his face and hands and took the laptop out of its case. He found the power lead and plugged it in. He walked around to the rear of the computer to look for the parallel ports to plug in.

He found the parallel port that he was looking for and plugged in. He turned on his laptop, the screen flashed into life. He quickly changed the protocol, entered the password as the program was loaded onto the hard disc. Markes set about loading the macro that he had written. The programme was designed to work on combinations under the password protocol, by retrieving and storing all names, then combinations of words and numbers, in the hard disk. The programme then applied each name, or set of characters so retrieved as the password. Markes had tried this and it had worked very well, the only issue was the time it took. Though the computer worked at a very high speed, the vast number of such names and combinations in a system meant it took time, in some cases, days. Markes knew he had till 8 p.m. on Sunday before he would have to leave for his rendezvous with Zonta.

Markes checked his watch, it was just after 8.30 pm. He had a little more than forty-eight hours to crack the system.

He knew that organisations such as these with large in-house systems had a series of checks and passwords for access depending on the level of the operator. It would mean that his decoding programme would need to be run at every level, if it worked. He also knew that the computer's internal log would record the programs that he accessed with the date and time. He wasn't sure whether the system was monitored from any other point in the building or block.

He had to enter a password to enter the user protocol.

He clicked 'enter' and the screen filled with a list of names; after a moment, a new set of names replaced the old set. Markes pulled up a chair and sat down looking at the screen, as it kept flashing with sets of names.

He must have dozed off and woke with a start. He had dozed off for an hour or so. "Incorrect Password" stared at him from the screen.

Markes was at a loss, his programme had worked on many occasions. He checked the mouse of the computer, and found a sensor with a built in fingerprint scanner. He examined the system minutely and found that there was no way in which to break in from a terminal. The server was wired such that if he tried to enter the system physically, it would cut off access to the mainframe.

Markes knew he had to find a solution and fast. He knew that a system is only as secure as its weakest link. The system was secure from a software point of view, but what about physically. Markes traced the wires from the terminal around to the junctions. He traced the cable carriers under the floorboards. They led to a large heavy looking door with a large single handle and a digital read out. He realised that it was a walk in vault. He checked the sides of the digital dial. It had the ports he was looking for. The vault itself, was not very sophisticated, and had a combination dial. He studied it carefully, it would take time but he could crack it.

He walked back to his laptop unplugged it from the terminal, and took out a set of wires. He plugged the wires into a port in the digital dial, punched at the keyboard for a few minutes. Then reached across and pulled a chair close to the door on which he placed the lap top. The numbers on the digital read out flashed as the computer ran various combinations.

In the first half-hour the first digit had been fixed on the digital readout. It was two hours later that all the eight numbers on the read out were fixed. Markes heard the click as the last digit stopped flashing. The vault had been cracked. He turned the handle and pushed very lightly. The door was well balanced and required very little force. He stepped into the vault, it was cooler than the room outside, the temperature control here better. Though it was dark inside, he could see the lights of the mainframe flashing.

Markes made for the data banks of the mainframe. He checked to see if they were wired to an alarm. They were not. He checked the adapters required to plug them into his laptop. Then unzipped a side pouch on the carrier bag and took out the adapters that he needed. The mainframe was an IBM. He plugged into the hard drives and set to work on the keyboard. He had to find the passwords which would allow him access to the hard drive, and using the operating systems he had loaded on his lap top he would be able to download the data.

The main frame was huge and its capacity was humungous, he had to check the data stored, decide what he needed and copy it. He had made a calculated guess and had grouped the data under various topics such as "Foreign Transactions, Plan, Nuclear Fissile Material, Treaty and so on." The program he had written scanned each hard drive for a pattern matching the database he was looking for. The programme was arranged under various headings. When he entered a word under topic, the programme would select the database that it would use to scan the disks for a pattern.

He opened the front panel of the computer, there in front of him were the hard drives of the mainframe. They were arranged in series. He had seen many large mainframes in his career, but this mainframe was huge there were twenty-seven hard drives. He realised at once that it would be a mammoth task to first scan the drives for the topics and then copy the data he wanted.

He checked the drives and the mainframe to see if they were wired to alarms. He found none. He selected the first drive from the right hand side, he had to start somewhere. He plugged in the adapter. The hard drive was now connected to his laptop.

He worked on his laptop, and after a few attempts, found the operating system that the main frame was using, it was Linux. The screen went blank for a few seconds and then came to life. A prompt appeared which read 'Select Topic,' he entered "Assassination". Then clicked on 'GO'. He was relieved when he saw 'Scanning Files'. He knew it would take some time. He pulled up another chair and sat down.

The programme ran for some time, after about twenty minutes, the words, 'No Match Found' came up. Markes swore, he went back to 'Topic' selected 'and punched in "Nuclear". The programme ran for around ten minutes, and came up with a blank.

Markes was getting impatient, he was not getting anywhere. He entered "Location" then sat back.

The programme started its scan, it must have been a good ten minutes or so, he was tired and must have dozed off. He heard a distant pinging, he awoke with a start, as the screen came alive with 'View Data, the options were Yes and Exit' He clicked on the 'Yes'

The screen filled with a series of names, some with a radioactive symbol next to them, clearly denoting storage of Plutonium- Fuel and Plutonium-Weapons Grade, Markes was shocked, he was fully awake now. He double clicked on the Weapons Grade icon, a table appeared on the screen, giving locations, quantities stored, quantities shipped, and the recipients. He saw Iraq, with Bill Broadham next to it. Bill Broadham was the designer of the Super Gun for Iraq, it was reported that the Agency had assassinated him about three months ago.

Markes quickly entered the protocol for downloading the files to his laptop. The process took half an hour though his laptop ran at an amazing five thousand giga hertz per second.

After a further two attempts with the second hard drive, he entered 'Transactions'. The file listed trades in all types of material. Markes was stunned, listed were 'Commodities', under which were listed 'Fuels', 'Oils' and others. Markes knew that there was a whole lot of information, involving transcontinental transactions in Nuclear Fuels, Banned Substances, Grain, Sugar, Edible Oils and other commodities. There was enough evidence to destroy Intrasyn, if he could expose it. However his primary task was to uncover the plan behind the trail of death that he had been sent to investigate.

He had finished with the third hard drive, and started on the fourth, his third attempt was successful when he punched in 'Plan', under topic.

Date: 23rd October 2007, Place: Muhu,
Time; 10.00 pm

Markes double clicked on 'Plan' and watched the screen came to life with the words Phase I, Phase II and Phase III. He held his breath and clicked on Phase I.

A series of dates appeared on the screen, there were some words next to each date, but this made no sense to Markes. They were codes. He stared at the dates, trying to make sense. Then it struck him, one of the dates was the date when the Head of Security of the Ukraine, was assassinated at the Rose.

The other date tied in with the date when the Interior Minister of Belarus was killed.

He checked the other dates, they didn't strike a bell. He looked again, they were in chronological order.

There was an entry against the 30th October, it was the day the Treaty on Nuclear Arms between Russia, the Ukraine and Belarus was to be signed, the President of the United States of America was an invitee to the occasion. He sat there dazed for a few minutes. He moved the cursor to one of the dates and double clicked, a short paragraph appeared.

'Phase I, Belarus assignment, Mission accomplished, Interior Minister in position'.

He clicked on another date, a paragraph appeared. 'Meeting confirmed, and Head of Security in place, Phase I, Ukraine assignment complete.'

He clicked on a third date, it read,' Operative in position for Phase I, conclusion.

He clicked on the 30th October, it read,' Phase I, on schedule, will be 'Framed in Eternity.'

He realised that Intrasyn or whoever was controlling it had a larger plan, the Interior Minister of Belarus had been killed and replaced, as was the head of Ukraine security. The assassinations had been meticulously planned, and Intrasyn's personnel had been infiltrated systematically. He wondered how deep the rot had set.

The 30th of October, was only three weeks away, he had to get out and get the information to NATBAL, or to the local authorities.

He went back to the initial prompt which had given him the options of Phases I, II and III.

He double clicked on Phase II, the title read, 'WWW'. He was shocked, WWW was an acronym for World War III. The start date was listed exactly 4 weeks after the 30th of October.

The words that stared back at him from the screen was an instruction, which stated that the attached document headed 'Information' was to be circulated to the Russian, Ukraine and Belarusian people before 'The action under WWW' in the second attachment was implemented.

Markes double clicked on the second attachment, he froze at the picture on the screen and felt the hair on his neck stand up. The title read 'The Battle Plan'.

The Battle Plan showed a Map similar to the Warsaw Pact map. It showed the order of battle. It depicted northern Europe from the Ukraine on the right to France on the left. Pictures of tanks, showed the movement of the invasion forces, small missiles with an 'N' mark indicated the launching of tactical battlefield nuclear weapons.

The Plan was listed day wise.

Day one was to be a surprise tactical nuclear missile attack on major NATO bases, in West Germany, and Turkey.

The attack was to be followed up by a million troops from Russia, Ukraine, Belarus and the East European countries, supported by armoured personnel carriers, and heavy tanks. Air cover would be provided by MIG fighter bombers and helicopter gunships.

A warning was to be sent concurrently to the United States of America that if they intervened, Intercontinental Ballistic

Missiles that were targeted at fifteen major cities in the USA would be launched immediately.

Day two, West Germany is occupied and is taken over by the Russian and the Warsaw Pact alliance.

On the same day, tactical nuclear missiles are fired at major ports in Holland, Belgium, Luxembourg and Denmark.

Among the documents were many Russian military exercise maps classified as 'Sekretno' or secret, showing the Limit of Strategic and Operational Tactical Nuclear Strikes. There were other maps that showed key NATO installations marked with Red Bomb and Rocket symbols, all targeted for destruction, and in all cases by tactical nuclear weapons.

All armed forces, the army, navy and the air force were to be combat ready effective the 30th of October, on a two-hour stand by.

Markes's hands were shaking as he worked his laptop. Before him was the master plan for World War III and the destruction of a large part of Europe.

There were lists of senior army, air force and navy personnel with their positions listed. In each case there was a notation listing the person who had been replaced. A date, which presumably signified the day they took over, was listed. In each case the takeover had been pre-planned.

The battle plan covered a period of 30 days at the end of which Russia and the Warsaw Pact Alliance reached the Atlantic coast.

The plan listed a great amount of detail, listing those who would handle the administration with names, rank and responsibility. Markes realised that the current administration in Russia, Ukraine, Belarus and possibly most of the East European countries had been compromised. There was a parallel administration, really in control.

Markes checked his watch, it was 9.30 p.m. He had a couple of hours before his departure. He knew he had to have some evidence to show the world what was being planned.

He set his laptop to download the Plan document.

He worked back to the initial prompt which had given him the options of Phases I, II and III.

He double clicked on Phase III.

The screen flashed to life with 'The Bolshevik Legacy'

There were a series of dates and activities; he could not connect them with any happenings. He recognised the names, Yorbachev, Pushkin, Petrovsky, Albakin, Shakalov, Zhirinovsky, Sorovsky, the names of a few prominent Swiss bankers, international arms dealers, the president and council members of the DSA in America and the PES in Europe, he recognised the names, and knew that all had communist leanings.

Markes's mind was in a whirl; he had stumbled onto something which was much bigger than his original assignment. He had to take some evidence back; evidence to convince the United Nations Security Council to start an investigation, the world's security and freedom was at stake.

He worked his laptop to download Phase I, The files were huge. The downloading took an hour for the laptop. The planning, the organisation and the attention to detail staggered him. It was a meticulously planned exercise. The immediate task was to get out and get word to NATBAL, he had to stop them from carrying out the October 30th task. He knew now that it was the assassination of the presidents attending the signing of the Treaty at Kiev.

He was still in the dark on the identity of the assassin or the actual plan for the assassination. The computer log would have recorded the downloads. Markes set about to erase the log of the downloads of the Legacy and the Plan document.

He heard the commotion outside, and dogs barking, he slid across to the window and lying down, looked out. The courtyard had been lit up. The security guards were leading leashed and muzzled guard dogs, they were Dobermans. The dogs were being led to the guardroom across from the entry to the ferry terminal.

Markes's mind raced, there could be only one reason to have guard dogs taken out on a Saturday night. The floodlights too had been put on. He looked around and beyond the courtyard. The areas leading to the cliff edge were sparsely lit. The area for fifty yards from the administration buildings was cleared, but beyond the clearing there were trees and undergrowth. He decided to leave immediately. He had not erased the logs, he had to let it be, there was no time to lose. He quickly unplugged the laptop, slipped the adapters and the laptop into the pouch and then slung the bag around his shoulders so that it lay across his back. He picked up the rope and the small carry bag. He crept to the door away from the lights, and eased open a door. He heard the chopper and looked up to see its lights as it hovered and made its descent to the landing pad.

He was about to open the door and move out when he heard voices coming towards him, he froze. There was no way of getting past them before they spotted him. The helicopter had landed and he could hear shouts. The guards passed the door, voices raised, and broke into a run. They didn't give the building a glance, they were on their way to the landing pad.

Markes eased open the door and crouching low, ran towards the trees and the undergrowth. He had barely reached the trees when he saw the group with the guard dogs led by two men in civilian clothes go towards the administration building that he had just left. Markes opened the pouch and took out a coiled length of nylon with a tube attached at one end, and a pair of gloves. He unscrewed the bottom of the tube and pressed a button, three prongs sprang out of the body. He screwed the base back on. He now had a three-pronged climbing hook with a line. He took out two long objects that Zonta had fabricated. He ripped open the tape on the side of the tube and flipped open a lid. He flicked the switch and lobbed the object away from him into the clump of trees. He did the same with the second object, but lobbed it further away than the first.

He was watching the group, the two men who had gone in from the group came barging through the doors, waving some clothes. Markes realised that they were his overalls. One of the men shouted to the dog handlers. The guards removed the muzzles and let the dogs sniff the overalls. Markes knew that the dogs would be after him. There was no way he could outrun the dogs, nor could he kill all three Dobermans. He put on the gloves, unzipped the pouch, and covered his nose, bent low and sprinkled the contents on the grass, in front of him and around where he stood. He stepped back from the patch where he had sprinkled the powder and broke into a run, towards the trees and the cliff edge.

Just as he took off, the first object he had lobbed exploded, he heard a shout, the group headed towards the explosion. Thirty seconds later the second device exploded

The group started towards the explosions, except two of the group who stayed put waiting for the dogs to pick up the scent. He could hear the dogs barking, excited by the explosions. They circled around the front of the building trying to pick up his scent. Markes was running towards the edge of the cliff and the line of trees. He saw the dogs pick up the scent and break into a run across the clearing towards the trees. He heard a shout from the two men who had not followed the group, they had spotted him, the dogs were running towards him. He heard a shot ring out and heard the whine of the bullet as it missed him by a good two feet. The saving grace was that the shooters were no marksmen. He reached the edge of the cliff, there were trees along the edge. He chose a tree leaning out over the edge and swung the nylon rope with the hook around the base and fastened the rope. It was dark at the edge of the cliff, the closest perimeter light was a good thirty yards away.

The dogs barking loudly came at a run to the clump of trees, where he had stood a couple of minutes ago. The three dogs, sniffed the ground where he had sprinkled the contents of the pouch, the next instance the dogs were whimpering and rolling on the ground, convulsing and frothing at the mouth, they were dead inside of a minute. The powder he had sprinkled was dried blood mixed with sodium cyanide powder.

Dudayev, Yevgany and the men arrived a few minutes later. Dudayev was fuming, he saw the dogs, and stopped.

Some of the men bent down with their flashlights inspecting the ground.

'There is some red powder, looks like blood,' one of them said.

Two of the security guards bent down to feel the powder.

'Fools, you will kill yourselves, can't you see that the dogs are dead, he has used some sort of poison.' Dudayev shouted at the men.

The men stepped back quickly looking sheepish.

'Look for him you idiots,' Dudayev shouted,' split up and check around the trees and along the edge of the cliff in both directions.'

The men broke into a run, fanning out along the cliff, a group was running towards him, he heard one of them shout and knew he had been spotted. There were no spotlights along the edge of the cliff, only sodium vapour lamps at thirty-yard intervals.

The light though dispersed, was sufficient for the men to make out the figure at the cliff edge.

The men opened fire at him, he heard the staccato of several machine carbines. Heard the bullets as they thudded into the trunks of trees close to him.

He gripped the rope and swung out, something slammed into his back, the force knocking him off balance. He regained his balance, felt no pain or discomfort and realised that he was unhurt, the bullet had hit the computer pouch which he had slung across his back. He gripped the rope hard as he felt his body swinging out over the edge of the cliff face with the force of the blow and his own momentum. He loosened his grip and rappelled down the rope. He used his feet to check his descent, and to keep his body away from the sides of the cliff. His descent was too fast, he could feel the heat of the rope burning through the leather of his gloves. He heard the roar of the waves below him as they crashed against the cliff face; the sounds increasing in crescendo as he descended. He looked down, he could see the white froth of the breakers as they pounded the cliff. He knew from his study of Muhu and the bathymetric charts that the cliff rose straight out of the water, there were no rocks below, the ocean floor was flat except for minor undulations. The water here was deep going down to over a hundred feet.

He was fifty feet above the water when he heard voices of men shouting above him, his pursuers had reached the top of the cliff. He let go of the rope and fell the remaining fifty feet. He hit the water, just as the men above loosed off a volley, the bullets spraying the rope where he had been a moment ago.

He went feet first into the water, hastily taking a deep breath. He was in the water and still in one piece, he kicked his legs and moved his arms, the bag slung across his back and the pouch helped slow his descent. He swam away from the cliff for as long as he could hold his breath, and cautiously rose to the surface, he surfaced, gasping for breath. He heard the staccato of machine gun fire, and looked back at the cliff. He was more than a hundred yards away, his swimming and the current had moved him away from the cliff. He could make out the silhouettes of his pursuers. Some were using flashlights to look into the water, while others were spraying the water randomly with bullets.

The sea was calm which helped as he swam towards the lights of Haapsaalu. He checked his watch the luminous dial read 10.15 p.m., he was on schedule. He stopped, tread water and looked around every few minutes, then he saw it, the small flashing light. He gave a shout and made his way towards the light.

Zonta had noticed the commotion on the cliff and the firing. He opened throttle and the rubber dinghy surged through the water towards the cliff. Zonta had heard the shout from the water and pointed the light in the direction of the shout. He saw Markes swimming towards him. The dinghy pulled up alongside Markes, Zonta reached down and helped him up.

'Are you OK?' he asked.

Markes nodded, 'Yeah, yeah, I'm fine.'

Markes swung the laptop from his shoulder, felt a jagged edge, alarmed he swung the pouch around. A jagged hole, about eight inches in length and four inches in width had been punched out in the centre of the pouch, he felt along the jagged edge with his fingers, he could feel the mangled mass of wires and metal.

'Damn' he swore, he grabbed the torch from Zonta and examined the laptop. The back had been gouged out, he could see portions of the hard disc and the motherboard, a twisted heap of metal. The heavy calibre bullets had ripped through the laptop. The computer had saved his life, but was a total write off. It was a piece of junk.

'What's the matter,' Zonta asked.

Markes held the laptop to him, Zonta could barely make out in the dark. 'The laptop took a couple of bullets meant for me' he said.

He looked at it ruefully and chucked it overboard. All he had to go by now was in his head.

Zonta handed him a packet that contained a waterproof jacket and trousers. Markes stripped and changed quickly, throwing the wet clothes over the side.

'We must move fast,' Zonta said opening the throttle. The dinghy front rose in the water as it surged forward, the twin outboards each churning out a whopping three hundred and fifty-horse power.

'They will be after us. They would have alerted their patrol boats, actually gun boats, which are capable of speeds of up to forty knots and are equipped with the latest electronic gadgets. My reckoning is that they will have a helicopter up in the air soon.'

Zonta handed Markes a packet, and a flask. 'There's some roast beef sandwiches and coffee, you might as well eat when you can.'

Markes was ravenous, he settled down at the back of the dinghy across from Zonta, and proceeded to eat, washing down the bread with gulps of coffee. Zonta changed course and made his way south.

'Where are we headed?' Markes asked, noticing that Zonta was moving out to sea.

'They will be waiting for us at ports, and landing stations, along the coast.' Zonta replied.

Markes saw a long arc of light swinging over Muhu, making its way towards the sea. 'They've got a chopper with a spot light.'

'They will have a patrol boat out as well, which will work in tandem with the chopper, the speed boat giving readings from its radar to the helicopter, enabling the helicopter keep track of its target.'

Markes nodded, noticing a fast boat its searchlights skimming the area ahead of it making its way towards their general direction.

'Can't this go any faster?' Markes asked.

Zonta grinned. 'Watch this,' and he opened the throttle. Markes was knocked back as the dinghy surged ahead, skipping across the waves.

'What's it doing? He shouted above the roar.

'About fifty knots, there is very little drag on these boats. They are especially good when the sea is calm.

They could see that they were distancing themselves from their pursuers. The helicopter was doing a zigzag across the water.

'I thought that they had electronic devices such as radar and sonar which could pick us up?' Markes asked.

'They can't pick up this contraption. The body is rubber, the engines have been covered by a special rubberised compound that gives it stealth characteristics. We can't be picked up by thermal imaging devices since the exhausts have deflectors which act as heat sinks.

'So does that mean they cannot spot us?' Markes asked

They heard the chopper moving closer to them, the calm sea had the advantage that their wake was visible from the sky! They heard the rattle of what sounded like a 30-mm gun, and heard the whine of the shells as they overshot the dinghy.

Zonta took evasive action, he started weaving the dinghy in a zigzag fashion, and he turned the boat heading north. The patrol boat was straining to keep up as Zonta opened the throttle fully. The dinghy reared up, only the tail end and the screws in the water. The boat was unstable and the slightest imbalance could cause it to overturn. They were literally skipping over the water, leaving little or no wake. The patrol boat continued south. The patrol boat had lost them at least for the time being. Zonta kept course for the next fifteen minutes after which he turned the boat back to the original course. The helicopter had lost them too, judging from the direction it was going. Zonta's ruse had worked.

'We will make our way south around Saaremaa and then head towards Parnu, through Irbenskij Proliv and through the Gulf of Riga.'

'I need to get in touch with NATBAL,' Markes explained his findings to Zonta.

'No location is safe; every place will be under surveillance and all calls monitored. There is no direct dialling facilities in the whole of the region, all calls are through switchboards.'

Zonta thought for a moment then said. 'From Parnu, we'll make it to Viljandi. We might be able to make a call from my place.'

Zonta and Markes looked back, the patrol boat was nowhere in sight, and the helicopter's searchlights were far behind. They had lost their pursuers.

Chapter 48

Date: 24th October 2007, Place: Muhu,
Time: 1.00 am

Dudayev was losing patience. The temperature had dropped and a haze was forming over the water with visibility down to five hundred feet. He had seen the wake through his night glasses, the wake had been barely visible, but suddenly it had disappeared, 'Where is that damned boat,' he shouted at the pilot. 'I thought you said that you could pick them up with the electronics that you had'.

'I'm sorry Sir, I've checked with the patrol boat, we can't pick them on radar or sonar.'

'Have you asked them to check with their infra red imaging devices, they are in a speed boat which should give off some heat.'

'No sir, they can't seem to pick them up on the infra red cameras either, and with the fog building up, its going to make it near impossible.'

Dudayev cursed loudly at everyone in general.

'They are in a small speedboat, possibly a rubber dinghy of some sort. This also means that they can't go far. They must be planning to get ashore soon.'

'Let's head back for Muhu,' Dudayev instructed the pilot.

There was pandemonium in Muhu, Sakarov had been informed, who in turn had called Pushkin and Zhirinovsky. Pushkin and Zhirinovsky made their way immediately to Muhu.

They landed at Muhu at 1.30 am.

'Take us to the administration building,' Pushkin instructed the driver.

He turned to Sakarov,' I want the systems man there as well.'

'He's there already checking to see which files were accessed' Sakarov replied.

Pushkin turned to him in alarm. 'What do you mean accessed. I thought that the system was protected by all sorts of passwords.'

'Yes, but, the man who broke in has been able to hack into the system,' Sakarov replied apologetically.

The cars brought them to the administration building.

Pushkin, Zhirinovsky and the others made their way into the computer section. They saw the open vault and the opened panels of the main frame which housed the hard drives, and a cable which was left on the chair.

'Can you tell me what he has accessed and if he has made copies of any of the documents?' Pushkin gasped. His face contorted and puffed.

'This is a cord to connect a computer, I'd say a lap top to the hard drive.'

'So what are you telling me?' Pushkin asked, exasperated by the technical jargon.

'I've checked the logs sir, he has copied the Legacy Document and The Battle Plan. The logs do not show that any of the other data were copied.'

'Are you absolutely sure?'

The systems man looked down at his feet and shuffled around. 'Sir it is possible for him to overwrite the log.'

'Do I take it that I have to assume that he copied all the files?'

'No Sir that is impossible, since he would not have had the space in his portable computer.'

They heard the helicopter landing, and before long a car pulled up. In walked Dudayev and Yevgany.

They saw Pushkin and Zhirinovsky and stopped short.

'Come in Dudayev,' Pushkin called out.

'The bastard has come all the way from god knows where. Gives our agents the slip. Gathers information from the Ukraine to Cerkessk and finally makes it inside Muhu. All this under the noses of our security, and escapes after spending a day or two inside the heart of our operations.'

Pushkin's face was red, his eyeballs looked as if they would fall out of his head. He controlled himself.

He turned to Dudayev, 'I want him neutralised before the 30th. Use whatever means you have to, but make sure he is dead.'

Dudayev and Yevgany made their way into an office in the administration block. They would use this office and the office at Haapsaalu.

'Send word to all operatives. Look for two men possibly more, along the coast of the Gulf of Riga, and from Haapsaalu to Riga in the south.'

'I have sent out word already, with a photograph,' Yevgany replied.

'We need to find details of his associate. I want everything on the rubber dinghy. Find out anything unusual, such as a boat leaving or arriving at an odd hour. See that our lookouts are posted at all public transport facilities and inform our operatives at the exchanges. I want to know of all international calls booked or made in the last twenty-four hours and during the next two days.'

'I want to look at the cause of the fire in the toilet,' Dudayev said.

He turned to the security chief of Muhu.' Make sure this man is brought here as soon as possible.' he handed the man a piece of paper with the name. 'Use my authority, find him, and make sure he is flown in.'

They walked into the toilet, the burnt section had been sealed off. Dudayev looked at the burnt and blackened wire, and the holder.

'How can a bulb suddenly cause a short circuit,' he wondered aloud.

'Gregory, should be able to find an answer,' Yevgany referred to the person whose name Dudayev had scribbled on the piece of paper. Gregory was an arms and explosives expert, who had worked in clandestine operations.

'I want to take closer look at site of the explosions at the cliff edge,' he walked to the door, Yevgany and the others following.

The men walked single file in a long line, each carried a powerful flashlight. It was turning light when they finished. The men had found the casings of the two devices, mangled and torn. They collected them and sealed them in a plastic bag. Yevgany checked his watch, it was five thirty in the morning.

'It's not a conventional type of explosive, it is a miniature napalm bomb. Very difficult to make, unless the person is an expert.' Yevgany said, inspecting the case and handing it to Dudayev.

Dudayev held it to his nose sniffed it and nodded, 'definitely napalm.'

There was a shout from one of the men.' I've found a piece of metal and plastic.' He said, holding up an irregular shaped object about eight Inches by four inches.

Dudayev and Yevgany studied the object.' It's a piece of metal covered on one side with plastic.' Yevgany said.

'We'll check it in the office'. Dudayev said putting the piece into a plastic bag.

They returned to the administration building for a quick wash and some coffee. They heard the noisy rotors of a helicopter as it made its descent to Muhu. Dudayev and Yevgany were in the dining hall, when Gregory walked in.

Gregory, saluted Dudayev, and then nodded to Yevgany.

'Where did they contact you?' Dudayev asked.

'I was in Moscow,' Gregory replied.' We are developing some delayed action munitions.'

'Delayed action? How will this new munitions help' Dudayev asked.

'We can trigger the munitions with high frequency electromagnetic waves. When the munitions are fired they don't explode on impact, and can be triggered using the wave.'

'We have a problem here,' Dudayev proceeded to explain the fire and the explosions at the cliff edge.

Dudayev pointed to his aide. 'He will take you to the lab, and the toilet, I want a report in an hour, is that possible?'

'Yes sir.' Gregory replied, and left.

'Before you leave have a look at this,' Dudayev pulled out the piece of plastic with the metal from the bag.

Gregory examined it. 'Its ABS plastic similar to that used in computers and electronic equipment. The metal here stuck to the plastic is really a separate part. Energy released as a result of impact has glued them together. We can examine it in the lab.'

Dudayev looked at him. 'Are you sure?'

'Absolutely,' Gregory replied.

'OK, let's check it out in the lab.' Dudayev turned making his way out of the door, the others followed.

Gregory went with the aide to check the toilet.

The lab technician took a look at the piece of plastic. 'This is from a computer, or rather a lap top', he said.

'Are you sure', Dudayev sounded excited.

The technician put the piece of plastic under a microscope.' There's no doubt, the piece of metal is from a hard disc, there are fragments of lead as well.' He pointed to the microscope.' You can see for yourself.'

Dudayev and Yevgany looked and saw for themselves.

'One of the bullets must have hit him or the laptop. If the hard disc is destroyed, the data he downloaded is safe!' Dudayev thought aloud.

Gregory returned an hour later.

Dudayev moved over to the settee in the office, sat down, 'let's have it'.

Gregory asked,' Was an investigation done earlier?'

The head of Muhu security nodded,' yes, our electrical personnel checked it, it was a short circuit.'

'It was a short circuit that caused the fire,' Gregory paused. 'But the short circuit was not accidental, it was caused.'

'How' asked Dudayev.

Gregory proceeded to explain. Then added, 'A similar type of device has been used by us in clandestine operations. I've analysed the silver foil used in the disc, it is of Russian origin.'

'What does that mean,' Dudayev asked.

'The person who made this device, was trained in Russia, and by covert operations.'

'I've checked the devices used in the explosions, at the cliff. They are specialised devices, not used commonly. There are only a few who have this knowledge.'

'How many', Dudayev spoke, clearing his throat.

'I would say, about fifteen in all. This explosive was developed during the Vietnam War. This is a high incidenary device to start fires in installations where the material is flammable but has a high flash point.'

Dudayev turned to Yevgany.' I want a list of names of personnel trained and institutions where this training was given.'

Yevgany nodded and moved towards the lab with Gregory.

Yevgany called up Colonel Druskayev of Military Counter Intelligence, Moscow. Druskayev was responsible for training and recruitment.

'Druskayev,' the voice announced, at the end of the line.

'Hi Druskayev,' Yevgany replied, 'How are you,'

'You son of a gun,' Druskayev, guffawed, 'Its been a long time.'

They exchanged pleasantries. Druskayev knew that Yevgany would not call him without a purpose.

'What can I do for you?'

'I need list of all personnel trained in 'Code Beta.''

He heard Druskayev take a sharp breath, 'Why, is there a problem?'

'Yes, there is and we need to locate one of them quickly. I need the list of all trained, with current locations. Where they live, eat, drink, their family, their girlfriends, mistresses, bank accounts, the works.'

'OK, where do I reach you?' Druskayev asked.

'I'm at Muhu,' Yevgany hung up.

Chapter 49

Zonta knew that they would have to get ashore before it was light. He checked his watch, the luminous dial showed it was four in the morning, the stars had disappeared. He had to reach shore and dump the dinghy.

Kuressaare was an old fishing port and the draught was low, so no large boats or ocean going vessels ever came to it. The ships usually anchored in the Irbenskij Proliv and barges brought cargo to the ships. Some of these barges went all the way from Kuressaare to Ventspils in Latvia.

Across the Gulf of Riga from Kuressaare was Ainazi, on the border of Latvia and Estonia. The coast here was similar with islands strung along the coast from Riga in the south to Viljandi in the north.

The coast was dotted with fishing villages. The islands allowed the fishermen a natural shelter from the open sea, and a staging ground for their clandestine activities. While fishing was their livelihood, many fishermen made a few extra bucks running contraband and drugs between the Republics, Sweden, Finland and Norway. Helsinki was only a hundred kilometres from Tallinn and the innumerable islands between Turku, Helsinki and Stockholm made surveillance quite impossible. Questions were never asked. It was just as easy to get a knife in your back if one was careless walking the streets in any one of the towns along the waterfronts.

253

Zonta, slowed down the dinghy, the powerful outboards could hardly be heard. He was approaching a cluster of islands off Ainazi. He looked around at Markes who was curled up in a corner fast asleep.

Zonta could see lights on the bigger islands and the blurred images of boats moored around the islands. He checked his watch, it was four thirty. He needed to find a place fast before the fishermen set out.

He skirted the first two islands. He was looking for a small island with vegetation, but shielded from view from Ainazi. He found the perfect spot. The island was small with sufficient vegetation to hide the dinghy, and close to a larger island that had boats moored at the roughly made quays. The larger island was close enough for them to swim across.

Zonta gently shook Markes, by the shoulder. 'Time for us to leave.'

Markes woke with a start, fully awake and trying to orient himself.' Where are we?'

'Just off Ainazi,'

'Ainazi,' Markes exclaimed. 'I must have been out like a light.'

'You were, right after we lost our friends.'

Zonta eased the dinghy into a small inlet on the island, it was a stream that emptied into the sea. He killed the engine and jumped out followed by Markes. They pushed the dinghy upstream till it was half out of the water and in the thick vegetation. Zonta stepped back and looked, the dinghy was not visible.

Zonta went back to the dinghy and unzipped a side pouch. He took out two small life jackets and three pouches. He handed one of the life jackets and a pouch to Markes.

'This will help us to swim to the next island, where we'll be able to buy passage to Ainazi.

'The pouch has a set of dry clothes.'

'How will we buy passage?' Markes asked.

Zonta showed him the third pouch.

'What's in it?'

Zonta unzipped the pouch and showed Markes the small plastic pouches containing a white powder.

'Heroin, they'll assume we are in the business, and won't raise suspicions. The only problem is we'll have to watch our backs. This lot has a street value of over fifty thousand dollars.'

Zonta and Markes slipped the life jackets over their heads and set out for the larger island. Though it seemed close it took them half an hour of steady swimming. It was getting light, Zonta checked his watch, it was ten minutes to five. They could see a lot of activity in the fishing village, so Zonta made for the port away from the fishing village. The port was small and consisted of a large wooden pier with several pontoons leading off at right angles. The boats were moored along the pontoons. The port was quiet, except for the creaking of boats at their moorings rocked by the light sea breeze. Zonta reached one of the boats and made his way along the boat to the pontoon, with Markes following. Zonta reached the pier, he grabbed the edge. He reached up to swing himself up on the pier when they heard a cough. Zonta froze and waited, half out of the water and hanging from the pier. A man came to the edge of the pier and was looking out over the water. He spat into the water. Had he looked down he would have seen them. They heard a woman calling out. The man turned and made his way back into the building at the shore side of the pier.

Zonta swung himself over and then bent down to help Markes over. They stripped off the life jackets and stuffed them into a garbage bin near the building from which the man had come out. The building was a café. They could see the dim shapes of the man and a woman through the frosted window. They made their way away from the pier towards a clump of trees, stripped and changed into dry clothes. They removed their shoes, which were light leather joggers made for running, wrung them and their socks and slipped them back on. They stepped out of the vegetation, looking unshaven, dressed in faded jeans and a coarse shirt. They looked no different from those who frequented the waterfront.

The day was breaking, as they made their way back towards the cafe. They could see the fishermen making their way to the boats. In the distance Markes could see a couple of boats heading out to the Gulf.

They pushed open the door, the room was large and warm. The place was empty. They could smell the coffee and the bacon.

Zonta walked to the bar and rang the bell, a head poked itself out of the door.

'Be with you in a moment,' she said.

A few minutes later the door opened and the woman came through, an apron tied around her waist.

She mumbled something, Markes thought it was good morning, and nodded back.

'What will you have?' she went behind the bar to fill up a jug of coffee.

'Breakfast please' Zonta replied.

'Take a seat, I'll bring it to you,' she motioned to the tables behind them.

Markes and Zonta settled themselves at a table near a window. The woman brought the coffee and two mugs.

She returned a while later with two plates heaped with potatoes, eggs and bacon.

Zonta and Markes started on the food, they were hungry and proceeded to demolish the food, washing it down with strong black coffee. The place was filling up, with the port workers and sailors, no one took any notice of them.

A man walked out of the kitchen, poured himself a mug of coffee and leant against the bar, took a sip and then lit up a cigarette. Zonta got up, walked to the wash room and a few minutes later came out and went to speak to the man.

'I need to get to Ainazi,'

The man looked at Zonta, at the scruffy shirt and trousers.' How will you pay?'

'Zonta unzipped the pouch and took out one of the small packages.

'With this,' he held out the heroin.

The man's eyes widened, he looked around to see if anyone else was listening or looking their way. No one was. He reached for the pouch, opened it and took a pinch. He rubbed it in his left palm with his thumb and then inhaled.

'Good stuff,'

'OK, there is a freighter leaving this evening, you wait here and I'll see if Ramirez is willing to take you.'

He shouted out to the woman, gulped down his coffee and left.

He returned in fifteen minutes, walked over to their table.

'Ramirez will take you,' he proceeded to explain.

Markes and Zonta left the café and made their way to the far side of the pier, where the larger vessels were moored. They looked for the 'Kolguev.' They found it. It was a fifty-foot vessel, which had seen better days, the paintwork was badly scarred, and the gear was run down. A gangway, which was just planks tied together was the entry into the vessel. They looked up at the bridge and saw a figure looking down at them. He had a cap pulled low over his face, he was chewing on a cigar.

'We are looking for Ramirez,' Zonta shouted.

The figure disappeared, a few minutes later he reappeared on the gangway, and walked down to them. A couple of rough looking guys had appeared on the deck.

'I'm Ramirez, Claudio told me you want to get to Ainazi.'

Zonta nodded,

'We leave at this evening, and payment in advance,'

Zonta nodded, handing him a small pouch.

Ramirez proceeded to check the stuff as Claudio had done, 'Good stuff,' he said half to himself.

'You can come on board now, settle yourselves in the cabin.' He led the way up the gangway.

They set out shortly after five, Ramirez piloting the vessel through a series of turns and twists, avoiding the sandbanks and shallow spots. He knew the waters like the back of his hand. Before long they were out in the open sea heading towards Ainazi. The Kolguev though old and rusty had large powerful diesels, they could feel the throbbing as Ramirez opened the throttle.

They made steady progress, the deck hands checking on the crates and ropes, tightening those that had loosened. It was turning dark as they neared Ainazi, the lights along the coast gave them some idea of their heading. They could see the trawlers returning, their lights dotting the sea around them

They reached Ainazi without any incident. Ramirez's freighter was obviously known in these waters. He waved to passing vessels, some which tooted their horns.

Ramirez eased the Kolguev into Ainazi, a small modern port. The piers had better equipment and most of the loading and unloading was mechanised. They felt the slight bump as the Kolguev lined up against the pier.

They nodded to Ramirez. 'Thanks, for the ride,'

'Anytime, 'Ramirez smiled,' If you can get this stuff on a regular basis, 'he waved the pouch,' come and see me, we can do some good business.'

Zonta nodded, making his way to the gangway.

He checked his watch, it was seven. He looked around, no one seemed to be taking any notice of their arrival.

They made their way towards the rail station, which was the quickest way to reach Viljandi. The ride would take them about four hours. They could get something to eat at the rail station and then settle down.

The streets approaching the rail station was badly lit. Zonta and Markes had walked a couple of hundred yards when they heard footsteps behind them. They turned and saw two men, with caps pulled low over their faces, each carried a knife, the light reflected off the blades. They turned to face them, then heard footsteps behind them, they looked around to find two more men, with knives.

'I'll take these two,' Zonta said, 'you take care of the other two.'

Markes nodded. Both pulled off their belts. The belts had big buckles.

Markes and Zonta split up to draw their attackers towards them.

The first one lunged at Zonta with his knife. Zonta side stepped, and hammered the man on the neck, he gave a grunt and collapsed in a heap. The other circled Zonta. Zonta wound the belt around his arm, feinted to the left and then swung the buckle as the thug moved to his right. The belt catching him full in the face. The buckle caught behind his left ear. Zonta pulled hard, the buckle tore through the ear and across the man's face, ripping through his jaw. The man screamed and dropped his knife, clutching his face.

The other two attacked Markes simultaneously, trying to cut him. He swung around right leg stretched in a karate style kick, his heel catching the jaw and neck of one of the attackers. There was a dull thud and a cracking sound as his neck broke. The man crumpled in a heap.

The other attackers suddenly realised that they were dealing with seasoned fighters, looked at each other, wide eyed, turned and ran.

Markes and Zonta looked around to see if they had attracted any attention, there was no one around. They broke into a run to get away from the scene. They slowed to a walk as they saw the lights of a larger street.

'Just thugs, we are lucky,' Markes said.

Zonta nodded. 'For a moment I thought that Intrasyn had got to us.'

'They must have got wind of the heroin.'

'One of them looked familiar, he might have been on the Kolguev,' Zonta added.

They reached the rail station, and Zonta went to the ticket counter and bought two tickets to Viljandi, then made their way to the kiosk and bought themselves some ham rolls and coffee, settled down on the bench near the departure board awaiting their train.

Chapter 50

Date: 25th October 2007,
Place: Haapsaalu, Time: 6.00 pm

Kozyrev was closing down for the day, when he heard cars pull up outside his apartment. He heard loud voices, and heard his name being called. He looked out of his window, the men were dressed in civilian clothes, but he guessed they were government agents, from the way they carried themselves. His mind raced, going over the happenings in the past few days, was there something that he could not explain.

He heard the knock on his door.' Open up.'

Kozyrev, ran to the door, opened it. 'Please come in gentlemen, what can I do for you?'

'We want some information,' Yevgany stated, walking in and looking at Kozyrev's desk, and the papers on it.

'Anything you want, 'Kozyrev replied.

'You sent out a detail on Friday to Muhu.' It was more a statement.

'Yes.'

'Do you know all the men who were on it?'

Kozyrev felt uneasy. He had not been comfortable with the man Zonta had brought with him.

'Yes I have their records,' Kozyrev opened the draw of the filing cabinet, and pulled out a file.

'I want a list of all the names and the addresses,' Yevgany signalled one of his men.

'I have the addresses of all but one,' Kozyrev replied.

261

Yevgany turned to him in surprise. 'How is that you took on a man without verifying his details?'

'He was brought to me by a man I know quite well.'

'And who is this man you know quite well?' Yevgany's voice had taken on an edge.

'Zonta, 'Kozyrev replied.

'Do you know where he lives,' Yevgany asked.

Kozyrev hesitated. 'No, I've no idea, but I've done business with him.'

'What business?'

Kozyrev's palms were sweating, his podgy face was flushed with fear, beads of sweat were running down his face and nose. He knew that there was no point in lying.

'He..he.. supplies me with heroin,' Kozyrev stammered. 'It was only very recently that I got into contact with him.'

'How long ago? Yevgany asked.

'A month ago…he made me an offer one day, it just happened. He dropped into the office after seeing the board offering cleaning services. He wanted to have his office cleaned.'

'Did you get to clean his office?

'No, we…we discussed the other business.'

'Take him, I want all the files with him moved to Muhu, 'Yevgany ordered his men.

They bundled Kozyrev into the second car. One of the men spoke into the phone. Ten minutes later a van pulled up with men carrying plastic tubs. They stacked all the files in Kozyrev's office into the tubs.

Yevgany walked into his office in Muhu. He had briefed Dudayev and assigned men for going through the records of Kozyrev's cleaning gangs. Yevgany's office had direct access to the record section in Haapsaalu. The personal details, of the men on the lists were checked starting from their earlier occupation, their bank accounts, their family, friends, and girlfriends were checked. All of them drew a blank, the men who made up the cleaning details were generally unemployed, on benefit and had no connections, direct or indirect.

'A call for you, sir,' Yevgany's aide came in.

'I'll take it here,'

The aide, went out to instruct the operator.

'Druskayev, how are you my friend, I hope you have some news for me.'

'Yes indeed, we have checked with Special Branch, and have been able to reach nine of them. They are deployed in various sectors. None have been away from their stations in the last week.'

'How many received this training?'

'Eleven, of which nine are accounted for, one was killed in action in Afghanistan.'

Yevgany held his breath, 'What about the one who has not been accounted for.?'

'He was part of the Estonian Secret Service, he saw service in the Third Chief Directorate. He left the service after his girlfriend was killed in an accident.'

'When?'

'About four years ago.'

'Who was his girlfriend, and where did she live?'

'She was a German girl, who had come to do a thesis on the social anthropology of the Estonians. She lived at the Halls, at the University of Haapsaalu.'

'What is the name of this fellow, and what was his last known address?'

'Andreas Komanovsky, he had an address at Haapsaalu. I've checked the address, the building was demolished and a shopping centre put up. The owner of the place, did not have a forwarding address.'

'What about his bank accounts and his identity card details?'

'We've drawn a blank, he closed his accounts, withdrew all the money in cash. It's as if he wanted to drop out of sight. There are no records anywhere.'

'OK, can you scan a photograph of his, and have it sent to me right away.'

Yevgany went across the room to Dudayev.' We know the identity, or are at least reasonably sure of the man behind the explosives. We should have a photograph sent to us in a couple of minutes.'

An aide walked in and handed a sheet of paper to Yevgany.

Yevgany showed it to Dudayev.

'Lets show our friend here and make sure.'

Dudayev and Yevgany went into a room. Kozyrev was tied to a chair, his hands spread out and his palms on the table, face down.

Dudayev put the paper in front of Kozyrev. 'Have you seen this man before?' 'Kozyrev, looked at it and nodded, Yes its him, he was the one who brought his friend.'

'But you don't know where he lived, or his address.

'No, I didn't ask him.'

'Did he ever mention where he was from, or when he would return, or how long it would take him to reach his place.'

Kozyrev thought for a moment, he knew he was in deep trouble, and wanted to help as much as possible.

'Once when he came to my office, he said that he needed to go back to his place but would return by the evening.'

'Do you remember the time when he visited you?'

'It was in the morning before lunch.'

'OK lock him up, we'll see if we need him anymore.'

Dudayev turned to Kozyrev. 'The only reason you're not dead is because we might need you for more information.'

Dudayev went into his office followed by Yevgany.

'If he said he would return in the evening, his base has to be close to Haapsaalu, perhaps an hour or two by coach or train.'

He took a black marker, and drew a circle.

'A hundred mile radius from Haapsaalu, covers Tallinn in the north and Ainazi in the south. The motor dinghy was making its way south. Double the surveillance at all ports, I want the smallest incident reported, and a round the clock update.'

Yevgany nodded, and made his way to the communications room.

In less than an hour, Yevgany walked into Dudayev's office,' We have information from Ainazi.'

'OK lets have the story. 'Dudayev got out of his chair, and started pacing the room.

'The police have reports of one man killed and one injured in a street brawl. Four junkies set out to mug these two guys who had just got off a freighter. The freighter incidentally is the Kolguev, registered at Parnu, run by a crook, Ramirez. Ramirez needed some persuasion, he now has a broken leg and a pair of crutches. He picked up these two guys at one of the bigger islands off Ainazi. They made payment with heroin. He recognised both Andreas Komanovsky and the other chap, the one who made it out of Muhu from the photographs we showed him.'

'When did this take place and where did that street lead to, the one where the brawl took place?

'About two hours ago, the street led to the rail station. I've put some men on the job, we should be hearing from them.'

Dudayev checked his watch.' If they are still on a train we should be able to intercept them at the destination. As soon as you hear from your Ainazi detail, have a squad at the destination. I want them captured if possible, or if there is the slightest problem, shoot to kill. I want this wound up today.

Chapter 51

Date: 26th October 2007, Place: Ainazi,
Time: 7.30 pm

Markes and Zonta finsihed their sandwich and the coffee, shortly thereafter they heard the public address system announce their train.

'The Riga Central Tallinn Port express is expected shortly on Gleis three.'

Markes looked up at the station clock, it was 7.50 p.m.

The train trundled into the station, the gleaming turbo charged diesel locomotive reflecting the light from the station overhead lights. The coaches winding back along the track. The doors opened as soon as the train came to a halt.

After the passengers exited, Markes and Zonta got into the nearest coach, found two seats across each other near a window and sat down, they would be able to keep a look out on all sides.

Five minutes later the public address system in the train crackled to life.

'Good evening ladies and gentlemen, this is your senior conductor speaking, this service is for Tallinn stopping at Voru, Parnu, Viljandi, Haapsaalu and Tallinn. We expect to arrive at Tallinn at eleven p.m. The next station stop is Voru. Refreshments are available at the front of the train between the first and standard class.'

The train trundled out of Ainazi, picking up speed.

'May I see your tickets please?' they heard the conductor.

Markes and Zonta showed him their tickets which he promptly punched.

'Can you tell us when this train will arrive at Viljandi?' Zonta asked him.

'In an hour and a half,' he replied.

'And at Parnu?' Markes asked.

'At nine fifteen, Parnu is a short distance from Viljandi.'

He nodded at their thanks and moved on.

Chapter 52

Date: 26th October 2007, Place: Ainazi,
Time: 8.50 pm

The car with Yevgany's men screeched to a halt at the train station at Ainazi. The doors were thrown open and three men jumped out and ran inside. The clock showed 8.40 p.m.

One of them went to the station superintendent.

'Have there been many trains leaving in the last hour?'

'Three trains, one at 7.30pm, the other at 8 p.m. and the one which just left at 8.30 p.m..'

'Can you tell us the destinations.' One of the men asked.

'The 7.30 p.m. train was going south, to Riga, the 8 p.m. to Tallinn and the 8.30 service to Pskov.'

The men thanked him and went to the ticket counter.

The leader of the group took out two photographs and showed it to the clerk.

'Have you seen these two?'

'The clerk shook his head looked bored and went back to the paper he was reading.

The leader reached across the counter, caught the clerk by his coat lapels and lifted him up.

'I asked you a question, you son of a bitch, if you don't answer me, I'll break your neck.'

The clerk's face turned red, he blurted. 'I just came on duty, I swear it I didn't see them'.

'Who was on duty before you?'

'He is by the kiosk, there,' he pointed to a chap who had a hat and had a scarf around his neck. The chap had just finished his coffee and was about to move on, when he heard his name called.

He turned and bumped into the leader who had come up close.

'Yes, what can I do for you?' he asked.

'Have you seen these two?' the leader of the group asked.

The man put his hand in his pocket and took out a pair of reading glasses, he put them on and squinted.

'I have seen this chap,' He pointed to Zonta, then paused, 'there was another fellow with him, I did not get a good look at him, I'm not so sure it was this chap.'

'Do you know their destination?' the leader asked.

'Yes for sure, this guy bought two tickets to Viljandi.'

The leader went to a phone, he waited for awhile, then spoke into it.

'They are on the way to Viljandi on the 8 p.m. service from Ainazi. The train should reach Viljandi by 9.30 pm.'

'We'll have a reception committee waiting' Yevgany hung up.

Dudayev reached for his jacket from the coat hanger.

'Lets get down to Haapsaalu, we'll take the chopper.'

He paused at the door. 'Call Haapsaalu and have them send Miloslevic and his men to the station, I don't want any screw ups.'

Yevgany picked up the phone.' Get me Haapsaalu.'

'Miloslevic?' he asked. 'Have you received the photographs?' he paused then added. They are on their way to Viljandi, they are on the service which arrives at 9.30. Take them alive if possible, if not kill them.' He hung up.

The chopper was ready and waiting, its rotors turning. It lifted off as soon as Dudayev and Yevgany got in, heading for Haapsaalu.

Miloslevic and his men arrived in two cars at the Viljandi rail station.

Miloslevic went to the stationmaster, showed him a card. The stationmaster rose from his desk.' What can I do for you?'

'I want two of my men at the exits checking tickets, and two on the platform at either end. Can you arrange it?'

'I'll move my men out and your men can take their place.' He said.

Miloslevic showed him the photographs.' These two are on the service that comes in at 9.30, can you find out the coach they are in?'

He checked the clock. 'The train is expected any minute now at Voru, I'll phone the station master, he'll be able to check and let us know.'

He reached for the railway telephone on his desk. The line connected him directly to the stationmaster at Voru, he spoke into it then hung up.

'The train is arriving at Voru in a few minutes, he'll call us back.'

Miloslevic pulled up a chair then lit a cigarette. 'How many exits do you have?'

'Two on this side of the platform and two on the other side across the tracks.'

'Is there any other way of entering or exiting the station?'

'Yes through the service entrance of the restaurant, and at the end of the platform leading to the siding where goods are unloaded.'

Miloslevic turned to his assistant. 'Post two men at each exit, two at each end of the platform, and two each at the service entrance to the restaurant. I want two men across the street from each exit, and two at the taxi stand.'

Miloslevic had just finished his cigarette when the phone rang.

The stationmaster picked it up. 'Hello, yes..yes OK thanks,' then hung up.

'They are in coach F, which is around the middle of the train, on the platform side. They have window seats, facing each other.'

Miloslevic reached for his machine pistol, and worked the mechanism, but kept the safety on. He was ready. He checked the clock, the train would arrive in just under twenty minutes.

Chapter 53

Date: 27ᵗʰ October 2007, Place: Voru,
Time: 8.20 pm

Markes and Zonta pretended to be asleep, they had just pulled out of Voru. A railway employee had entered their coach at Voru, he had looked at them and hastily moved away.

Markes and Zonta exchanged glances, got up and moved out of their compartment, through the sliding doors separating the seating area and the space near the exits. There was no one standing around since the area was not heated.

'I think our friends are on to us,' Zonta remarked leaning forward to Markes's ear to make himself heard above the noise.

'I'm sure they will have a reception committee waiting for us at Viljandi. They must have checked with Ainazi. What is the stop before Viljandi?'

'Parnu, the station is quite small and has a platform for each track. The entrance and exit to the station is on one side only, the other side leads to a river and a marina.'

'Just what we need. Its dark and we can work the lock on the door on the other side,' Markes added.

They looked through the sliding doors on either side to see if there was anyone taking an interest in them. By the look of it no one was.

Zonta took out a piece of wire and inserted it into the door mechanism on the right exit. The station platform would come up on the left. He worked at the mechanism for a few minutes, then nodded to himself.

'Its ready to be sprung. As soon as the train stops at Parnu, the release mechanism will be operated for the doors on the left. We can at that time spring this lock and let ourselves out on the right.'

It was 8.50 p m, and dark, they heard the senior conductor on the public address system.

'Ladies and gentlemen, we are a couple of minutes away from Parnu our next station stop.'

They heard the train starting to apply its brakes, and the subdued grinding noise as the cast iron brake blocks ground against the wheels.

Zonta stood near the door, as the train came to a stop. A few passengers came through the sliding doors from the compartment. Markes made way for them. They opened the door on the platform side and stepped out. Markes closed the door after them. Zonta worked the wire, there was a click as the locking mechanism was released. Zonta pressed the lever and the door swung open. Zonta jumped out first, using the door to propel himself forward. Markes followed, the doors swung shut as Markes released the door, he steadied himself and jumped, the drop to the ground, was a good five feet, it was dark and they had to lunge forward to be clear of the ballast. They landed and rolled, to absorb the force of the fall, got up checked with each other, dusted themselves and then moved quickly towards the adjoining tracks.

They crossed the tracks and ran towards the river and the marina picking their way carefully. The perimeter lights were few in number, and the ground uneven. They reached the edge of the marina when they heard the commotion behind them. It was a good five minutes since the train had reached Parnu. Something was holding up the train. Markes and Zonta guessed that it was their absence.

The phone rang in the stationmaster's office at Viljandi, he picked it up. 'Yes?' then stood up and placed the receiver down, he turned to Miloslevic. 'They have got off the train.'

'What?' shouted Miloslevic,' When..where?'

'The stationmaster at Parnu checked the whole train. They are not on the train. No one saw them at the station. It's a very small station and only a few people got off. The stationmaster checked the door of the compartment on the marina side and found that it had been opened. It's his guess that they got off at Parnu.'

'What's on the other side?' Miloslevic asked.

'It's a river with a marina.'

Miloslevic thought for a moment, then went to the phone and spoke for a few minutes. He came back, his face red.

He spoke into his walkie-talkie, in a few minutes the whole squad was around him.

'The bastards have given us the slip, they must have got off at Parnu. Make for the marina at Parnu, take the dogs, I want every nook and corner checked.'

Chapter 54

Date: 27th October 2007,
Place: Haapsaalu, Time: 7.15 pm

Dudayev and Yevgany arrived at Haapsaalu, they had received the message that the two had jumped off the train at Parnu.

'I want every station, coach stop, public place, and eating joint under surveillance. They had planned to make it to Viljandi, my guess is that they will.' Dudayev walked to the desk behind him, picked up the phone and spoke to Pushkin, appraising him of the position.

A military orderly came in with a message for Yevgany. He looked at the piece of paper, and took it to Dudayev.' It seems that Komanovsky is living in Viljandi. The interior ministry tracked down a friend of his German girlfriend in Haapsaalu; this girl would go with Komanovsky on weekends to Viljandi.'

Dudayev thought for a moment. 'Viljandi is a small place, have his photograph taken to all the banks in Viljandi, there can't be more than a couple of dozen. Show the photograph around, once he is recognised it will be simple to obtain his address.'

'We'll have to wait for morning, till the banks open. Miloslevic and his squad are at Parnu at the marina, with the dogs.'

Dudayev went to the map on the wall, he looked at it for a few minutes.' The chances are they will steal a boat, the marina will be deserted at this time, and there are many small boats.' He traced the river till it came to a road, he looked at Yevgany.

'What would you do if you needed to get to Viljandi, if you were in their shoes?'

Yevgany walked to the map, looked at it.' There is only one point where the river can be left easily.' He pointed to the point where it crossed under the bridge.' The banks are too steep everywhere else for fifteen miles or so, till it passes Viljandi.'

'Set up road blocks at these two points,' Dudayev pointed at the road map before and after Viljandi.

'Have the road patrolled. Tell them to stop and check everyone, all males are to be detained. I want information on an hourly basis.'

Markes and Zonta, came to the pier and decided to make their way to the far end. The pier had boats moored alongside, they could see lights in some of the cabins, and twice they saw people on the deck. It was too dark, no one paid any notice.

They were nearing the end of the marina, the boats at the end were smaller.

Zonta stepped from the pier into one of the small boats.

'They'll be after us and soon, the streets are unsafe, we'll be spotted. The boat will take us downstream towards Viljandi. We'll leave the boat on the outskirts of Viljandi and then walk to town.'

Markes nodded, the idea sounded good. He stepped into the boat.

They looked around and saw that there was no one around. They found a pair of oars at the bottom and started to row.

'We should try to change our appearance, The chap at Voru knew who he was looking for. I've got a makeup kit with which we can quickly change our appearance, we'll use it just befoe we leave the boat.'

Zonta laughed, I'll settle for a paunch, dark hair and a cigar.'

'That's sure to change you enough to avoid any casual observer from recognising you. The simplest disguises are the most effective since it doesn't make it seem that you have been done up.'

Markes quickly used a few items he carried to make small changes in their appearance.

They rowed the boat to the centre of the river, away from the bank. The night was dark so there was little chance of being seen. In any case one side was hilly with a lot of vegetation and the other had the rail tracks, on a raised bank. Both were fit, they rowed with slow deep strokes, without splashing.

Zonta and Markes were facing away from the direction they were moving, so they had to look back at intervals to correct their course. The river was almost straight, enabling them to see the lights of Parnu in the distance.

They continued rowing, Markes noticed a set of lights moving towards them from Parnu, it was a long way off.

'What's that, looks like we are being followed.'

Zonta looked at the lights, they were alternatively dim and bright.

'They are checking the banks with spotlights, the lights seem to be blinking since they are pointed downstream at intervals.'

They started pulling at the oars harder and quicker, the boat sped along.

'We've got a head start and they are moving slowly, we'll be at our spot soon.'

The river swept under a bridge over which the rail tracks and the road leading into Viljandi had been laid.

'Lets stop the boat here,' Zonta said, and stopped pulling. Instead he put his oar in and paddled in reverse. Markes followed his action.

The boat came to a stop under the bridge. Zonta nudged it towards the bank and into the tall grass.

'This is the only spot before Viljandi where we can climb out to the road. The next spot is after we pass Viljandi.'

The river bank on both sides was overgrown with tall grass, and the depth of the river near the bank shallow enough to allow them to wade in the water. They pushed the boat into the tall grass, till the boat was covered from all sides and the bridge hid it from view from above. In the dark it was impossible to see the boat, the person would have to come alongside on the river, and would need a powerful flashlight to see the boat among the tall grass.

Miloslevic and his men arrived at Parnu and made for the marina. There were many boats moored along the narrow wooden pier. The boats were of all shapes and sizes. The lighting was poor, making it difficult to find their way. The ground was soft and slushy, making progress difficult. They split up and started combing the area from the rail tracks to the river and along the river on both sides. They had powerful flashlights. The dogs whined and strained at their leashes, finding the scent. The guards had to run, tripping over stones to keep up with the dogs.

Miloslevic followed. The dogs ran up the pier and started running along it.

The commotion and the lights brought out some of the boat people on deck.

'What's the matter?' one of them asked.

'Have you seen two men in the past hour?' Miloslevic asked.

The couple who had come out shook their heads. 'No, no one has come by this way.'

Miloslevic waved and followed the dogs. The dogs had jumped into one of the boats, The handlers remained on the pier.

'Follow the dogs, lets see where the scent takes them,' Miloslevic told the handlers.

The dogs jumped from the first boat to the second then stopped and started whining.

'They must have taken a boat from here,' Miloslevic, moved back to the pier and ran along it. The marina office was closed. He spoke into his walkie-talkie to the Parnu police, then waited.

His walkie-talkie crackled. 'Yes,' he answered then swore at the man at the other end.

'Lets get back to town,' he told to his men.

They reached the Parnu police station. Miloslevic walked into the inspector's office.

The inspector had been briefed. He jumped up out of his seat as Miloslevic entered.

'The inspector at Viljandi has been informed about these men. Patrols have been deployed and road blocks have been set up.'

'Good,' Miloslevic nodded in appreciation.

'I want a motor boat, to check the river between these points.' Miloslevic pointed to the map.

'It will be arranged immediately.' The inspector said. He picked up the phone and spoke rapidly into it.

In a few minutes a policeman walked in.' The boat is ready sir.'

Miloslevic nodded his thanks to the inspector and made for the marina.

The motor boat roared into life, Miloslevic and his men grabbing the handrail as the boat surged forward.

'Move slowly, and check the banks' Miloslevic instructed his men and the crew of the boat.

'Swing the spotlights in a slow arc, along the banks.' He had posted two men on either side as lookouts.

The boat made slow progress, the river was wide, about fifty yards across. They stopped frequently. The dark night with the spotlights bouncing off the water, the rustling and movement of the grass made the lookouts imagine they saw movement.

Chapter 55

Date: 27th October 2007, Place: Parnu,
Time: 10.00 pm

With the boat hidden in the tall grass, Markes and Zonta quickly took off their shirts, and turned them inside out; the colour of the insides were different, though it was difficult to tell in the dark. Markes took out his mini make up kit, and a small torch. He applied some colour to Zonta's hair turning it from blond to black. He did the same with his hair, then added some grey by using a powder, which he smoothed in with water from the river. He took out a moustache and a pair of folding glasses. When he had put them on, Zonta could not recognise him. Markes held the long rubber balloon, which he inflated partially and wrapped it around Zonta's stomach, Zonta tucked it into the top of his trousers to hold it in place, and tucked in his shirt over the bulge. He would pass off for a paunchy middle aged man. The whole process had taken them five minutes. Both knew that they had to move fast.

They clambered up the steep embankment, at times on all fours. The embankment was overgrown, so no tracks would be visible. They reached the road, dusted their clothes for any tell tale signs, and started walking towards Viljandi at a brisk pace.

'They will soon be after us, we'll stick to the road for the time being. The trees and the shrubs on the side of the road offer cover, we'll use it when necessary.' Zonta said leading the way.

They made good time, the road was winding, through hilllocks. Zonta was in familiar surroundings.

'There are many small tracks away from the road, which we can walk along, but it will slow us.'

Miloslevic and his crew, came around the bend slowly. The bridge was ahead and the river here was narrower.

'Check the banks on both sides' Miloslevi raised his voice, impatiently, 'this is the place where the embankment is flat enough to climb out.'

The men nodded in agreement, and shone the powerful flashlights to and fro across the grass on both sides. The boat had slowed to a snail's pace.

One of the men shouted, 'There is something there, can you see that?'

'Where,' Miloslevic peered through the darkness to where the lookout was pointing.

'Keep that bloody light still' Moloslevic roared at the man handling the spotlight.

'Sorry sir, it's the boat that's rocking.'

They saw what looked like a red slash on a white background.

'Take her closer,' Miloslevic ordered.

The boat edged towards the tall grass. They were within ten feet of the grass, a small red object was visible through the gaps in the tall grass.

'Its not a boat' one of the men said.'

'Take the boat closer' ordered Miloslevic, 'lets have a closer look.'

The boat moved closer, moving into the tall grass. They were about five feet from the object when flashlights showed the white hull, with the red slash which the light had picked up earlier.

They could now make out the shape of the boat from where they stood, hidden by the grass. The red slash was the Z in 'Zhivago' the name of the boat.

Miloslevic grabbed his Walkie-Talkie and spoke quickly.

'Lets head back to Parnu, and full speed.' He instructed the boatman.

The helmsman turned the boat around and opened throttle. The boat surged through the water, making the return journey to Parnu in fifteen minutes.

Markes and Zonta saw the horizon light up in the distance. The hazy glow of a distant headlight coming up a hill towards them from Viljandi.

'I think we had best get off the road, it must be them. Our friends back there would have found the boat and radioed Viljandi.'

Zonta led the way. He left the road and moved into the vegetation, Markes following. They reached an outcrop of rocks and went behind it, pushing their way through the scrub surrounding it. They waited. The lights were from an open jeep moving slowly. The jeep had powerful headlights and a movable high powered light mounted on the roll over bar, which a man was handling. He was moving the spotlight from one side of the road to the other. The jeep passed them and continued.

Markes and Zonta knew that once the jeep reached the bridge, it would turn back. It was too dangerous to be on the road anymore.

They were looking for them. Word would've gone out. They would have to be very careful, all entry points to the city would be under surveillance. Zonta would have to use the by lanes.

They worked their way through the shrub forest reaching the edge of town. There was an old disused barn on the edge of the forest. Zonta made for it. They could make their way from the barn to adjoining buildings and then to the smaller lanes. It was mid week, the time 10.15 in the evening, a little more than an hour since they left the train. It was autumn and quite cold, there were not many people about.

'There's less chance of being noticed, if we use the small lanes.' Zonta said and led the way.

They made their way through a maze of lanes which were cycle tracks, wide enough for a small cart. The tracks wound through the town, skirting playgrounds and finally reaching the northern section of the town; at times passing quite close to the larger streets. They could see jeeps and security personnel, people were being stopped and possibly questioned. A full-scale check was in progress.

They were across the courtyard from number 302. Zonta stopped and waited, they moved into the shadows and watched for a full ten minutes. They waited and watched, observing the windows, the place around, looking for a flash of light in a window or any movement in and around the house, or for any signs which would indicate surveillance. There was none.

'OK lets go,' Zonta led the way. He reached the house and they entered. Zonta looked around the insides, checking to see if any of the contents had been moved or disturbed, or for any change, he checked to see if the hair he had stuck across the bedroom door was intact. It was.

'Lets pack what we need, we will not be able to come back here,' Zonta said,' They will find my address, its just a matter of time.

'How do we get information to NATBAL, do you have a scrambler on this phone?'

Zonta shook his head.' Intrasyn controls everything, they will be here in minutes if you ask the operator for a long distance call. We should eat, then plan our moves, and get some sleep when we can, and leave here before sunrise.'

They busied themselves fixing some food and brewed a pot of coffee, Markes filled in Zonta with his findings. They carried the food and coffee to the table and started to eat.

'I don't know yet how they plan to carry out the assassination, or by whom. My guess is that the assassin trained for this is Yuri. He explained to Zonta his reasons. 'The plot seems to revolve around the three who survived the massacre at Cerkessk.'

'I am still puzzled by the phrase, Framed in Eternity.'

'Perhaps it is something to do with a photograph,' Zonta suggested.

Markes nodded. 'Perhaps.'

'The treaty is just three days away, at Kiev. We need to get this information to NATBAL.'

'We should make our way to Kiev.' Zonta suggested.

Markes walked around the room, he picked up an ashtray, it looked very familiar. Zoya had a similar one in her bedroom.

'I can speak to a girl I know. Her father is a local politician and has contacts in the government. She'll be able to have this information sent to NATBAL.'

Zonta shook his head. 'You are signing her death warrant the moment you involve her.'

Markes nodded.'I understand the risk, but the situation is desperate and we need to take desperate measures.'

Zonta did not look convinced.

Markes decided that he had to try. He saw Zonta shake his head as he went to the phone.

He dialled Zoya's private number, only her friends had been given it.

'Hello' he recognised her voice, though it sounded distant.

'Hi Zoya, its me, Markes.'

He heard the sudden intake of breath. 'Markes, my God, where have you been, I've been so worried. Are you well, I want to see you, can you come now?' there was a torrent of words.

'Hey..hey easy, I'm fine, I'm not in Odessa?'

'Where are you?' she asked. 'I've missed you so much.'

'Listen carefully, I need you to do something for me,' Markes explained.

'Are you in trouble?'

'No..not exactly, but I need to lie low; I cannot be seen.'

'I need you to come to Kiev tomorrow, tell you father that you are meeting friends, don't mention my name. Book yourself a double room in the Spola, as Mrs Usov.'

'Are you in trouble?' she asked again.

'I'll tell you about it when we meet, I can't talk to you on the phone.'

'Will you come to the hotel?' she asked

'No, you will have to pick me up at the rail station'

'Ok,' she paused, he knew that she was thinking. 'I'll be there at the station, in a rented car. Which train will you be arriving on?'

Markes gave her the details and added. 'Zoya, remember do not tell anyone that you spoke to me.'

'OK, I'll be there, do you want me to bring anything else?'

'No,' he paused. 'Zoya, wear a blue scarf around your head and stand by your car.'

'Why?' she asked,

'I've got a friend with me. One other thing, I am in disguise,' he explained his disguise to her and that of Zonta's.

He heard her giggle. 'I'll be there.'

'Zoya,'

'Yes'

'Thanks.' He hung up.

Chapter 56

Date: 28th October 2007, Place: Viljandi, Time: 4.15 am

They awoke at four, washed changed and checked that their disguise was intact. They made themselves some sandwiches, washing it down with strong hot black coffee. Their belongings were packed into briefcases. Zonta made sure that he packed two sets of his old uniforms. They looked like early morning commuters making their way to the train station.

Zonta took a length of trip wire and strung it at three different places. 'They will think the place is booby-trapped. They will spend time looking for the explosive. Just buying time,' he grinned.

They made their way to the street separately arranging to meet at the rail station. They would buy return tickets, Markes for Novgorod and Zonta for Saint Petersburg. They would get off at Pskov and buy return tickets to Smolensk. From Smolensk they would make their way to Kiev.

'Hold it,' Zonta turned to Markes.

'We need cash to buy tickets, we'll take it from one of the cash machines.'

'ATM transactions are recorded, they will know we were here' Markes said.

"I know, but do we have a choice?'

Zonta withdrew a sizeable sum, which he split in two, handing one half to Markes.

'See you in Kiev.'

Chapter 57

Date: 28th October 2007, Place: Viljandi,
Time: 10.00 am

The car drew up outside the Bank of Estonia in Viljandi. One of Dudayev's men walked in, while the other waited in the car outside, the motor running. The man who walked in was dressed in a suit. The bulge under his arm was visible. He was armed. It was 10.00 in the morning.

At the door he was stopped by the bank's security guard. The guard had worked a shell into the chamber and had the safety off. His associate, moved to the far side of the bank, keeping the line of fire clear.

'Stay clear of the door,' he shouted at a customer making his way to the door.

The customer, turned frightened by the tone. He took one look at the man who had entered and the stance of the bank's guards and ran to a side.

Dudayev's man put his right hand up and put his left hand in his left shirt pocket. The bank's guard following every move carefully.

He pulled out a badge that he shoved at the guard.

The guard took it and looked at it. To him it made no sense.

The commotion had brought the bank's manager to the front.

'What is it?' he asked.

287

The guard gave the badge to the manager.' This man is armed and this is his identification.'

The manager looked at the badge, recognised it for what it was.' Its Ok, let him in.'

He beckoned to the man.' What do you want?'

'I'd like to talk to you in private,' the man replied.

The manager nodded. 'Follow me,' and led the way to his office.

The man following, locked the door behind him.

'Why did you lock the door?' the manager asked, his voice turning shrill with fright.

The man ignored him, and put the photograph of Andreas Komanovsky in front of him. 'Do you recognise this man?'

'Why, yes, he is the well known journalist Zonta of the Demokratichna Ukraine, and a customer of ours.'

'I need his address.'

'I'm sorry, I can't do that. It's confidential.'

The man leaned across the desk and took hold of the manager's lapels. Lifted him from his seat, and head butted him.

'Ahh,....,' the manager screamed.

The manager's nose had flattened, spewing out blood, his nose broken.

The man released the lapels of the manager and let him drop back into his chair.

There was a pounding on the door.

'Tell them its OK,' the man said, pulling out a Walther PPK.

The manager, his eyes wide with fear shouted.' Leave us alone.'

The pounding ceased.

'Now, will you give me his address?

The manager nodded, he was holding a tissue to his face. 'I'll have to ask the clerks.'

The man nodded, walked to the door and unlocked it.

The manager buzzed and his secretary walked in. She saw the manager's face and the pistol in the man's hand and screamed.

A bank guard came running his gun drawn.

'Stop,' the man pointed his gun at the guard.

The guard stopped.

'Put your gun down, and move to the corner,' the man ordered.

The guard did as he was told.

The man turned to the manager. 'Now tell your secretary what I need. Also tell her to find out the transactions during the month.'

The secretary ran out, sobbing. The man sat on the edge of the manager's table, and put away his gun.

The secretary ran back a few minutes later with the details on a sheet of paper.

She handed the paper to the man. He glanced at it.

'How far is this address?'

'About a mile from here, in the northern part of town.'

The man glanced at the transaction sheet.' What's this?' he pointed to a transaction dated that morning.

'It's a withdrawal, done today, very early in the morning.'

'Withdrawal from where?' the man rasped.

'From a cash machine, near his address.'

The man grabbed the phone on the manager's desk, and spoke quickly, giving all the details. He then hung up and left the bank, without another glance at the manager.

Dudayev and Yevgany, received the message in Haapsaalu. Their men had covered four banks, all of which had drawn a blank.

Yevgany took the call.

'We've found him.' he explained the findings to Dudayev.

They went to a map of the square around Zonta's apartment. The map of Viljandi had been set up in the room.

The map showed a number of small lanes leading to and from the square.

'Send a squad to the address. Have men posted all around the house, down the lanes. Are there any rail or coach stations within a mile of the apartment?' Dudayev asked..

'There is a rail station a mile to the south, towards the town centre. The coach station is next to the rail station.' Yevgany explained.

'Once the men are in position, I want four men to go up to the apartment, the rest are to stay.'

Dudayev, picked up the phone, and dialled.

'This is Dudayev, I want the telephone number of', he read out the name and address of Zonta..' I want a list of all telephone calls made from that number during the last six months.'

The phone rang, Yevgany picked it up,' Yes' he listened.

'Send all the records you have on Andreas to me today.' He hung up.

'We have positive identification that Andreas Komanovsky is the person known as Zonta. He withdrew a sizeable sum of money this morning, very early in the morning.'

Dudayev looked at the map of Viljandi.

'There's a railway station within a mile of the apartment. It's my guess that they are on a train.'

Yevgany picked up the phone and talked to the leader of the squad at the railway station.

'They have not been seen by any of the men.'

'They could have split up, and even changed their appearance.' Dudayev replied.

'One of them has read the plan. They know that the next phase will take place in Kiev. Its my bet that they will try to reach Kiev and pass the information to anyone in authority in the United States Embassy, or for that matter in the Russian government.'

Yevgany nodded.' I was thinking the same thing.

An aide came in.

'A despatch rider has brought some records for you, sir' he spoke to Yevgany.

'Send him in.'

Yevgany took the official looking bundle with seals on them and signed for it. He broke open the seals, unwrapped the paper and took out two thick red files. He flicked through the pages, stopping now and then to read.

'This Andreas Komanovsky was with the Estonian Secret Service, where he trained as an explosives expert. He has seen service in the Third Chief Directorate. He is quite accomplished and has been decorated.'

'Explains the explosives used at Muhu.' Dudayev said.

The phone rang, Yevgany picked it up.' Yes, who's speaking,' he listened. 'Its for you.' He handed the receiver to Dudayev.

'OK, how many calls were made from that number during the last week?'

'One, To whom? ....In whose name is the receiver's phone registered. I understand, I want to know of all incoming and outgoing calls at the receiver's number. I want a tap on all lines in that household. Record all conversations made, both incoming and outgoing.' Dudayev hung up.

'They made a call to Ivan Usov at Odessa.' Dudayev made a statement.

'The call was quite short. I also understand that Usov was out of Odessa on the day the call was made. Find out the members in Usov's household. 'As an afterthought he added,' Why did they call Usov?'

Yevgany called his aide.

'I want information on everyone in the Usov household. Their friends, who they sleep with, boyfriends, their banks, what they eat, drink, where they hang out everything and anything. I want it by tomorrow morning.'

The aide nodded and left.

Chapter 58

Date: 28th October 2007, Place: Kiev,
Time: 4.30 pm

Markes and Zonta travelled separately as planned.

It was early evening when they arrived in Kiev, the sun was low on the horizon. They had travelled in different coaches. Markes was closest to the exit. He went on ahead. Zonta saw him move on and followed with the rest of the passengers making for the exit.

Markes saw her, the blue scarf partially around her head. She was looking towards him, but saw no sign of recognition. She wore an ankle length denim skirt, with boots, and a white top. She had dressed casually, which was good since it did not draw too much attention.

Markes continued to walk towards her. He saw her face change from curiosity to concern as he made directly for her.

Markes grinned. 'Hi Zoya.'

She looked surprised then ran to him, her arms outstretched.

He took her in his arms, kissing her, she hugged him and buried her face in his shoulder.

'It's been so long. I was scared that something had happened to you.'

'Shh, it's alright now.' Markes replied, holding her tightly. He realised that he had missed her too.

Zonta saw the reunion and smiled, as he made his way to them.

'Lets get in the car,' Markes told Zoya getting in the front passenger seat. 'My friend will join us shortly.'

Zonta came to the car in a few minutes and slid into the rear seat, behind Markes.

Markes introduced Zoya and Zonta to each other. They shook hands.

'He does not normally look like this. 'He pointed to Zonta's paunch.

'Have we got a booking?' Markes asked.

'I've booked two rooms, one for a Mr and Mrs Usov, and the other for a Mr Grishin.'

Zonta grinned, Zoya had planned it well. She was a clever girl and he liked working with women who thought things out.

They made their way to the Spola. They arrived at the hotel, parked their car in the underground parking lot and made their way to the reception desk. Zoya checked for their reservations. Zoya explained that they had a guest with them, and she checked in for all of them. They were travelling light so they carried their bags to their rooms.

They ordered a meal from room service consisting of roast beef and potatoes, a green salad, two bottles of red wine, and pancakes for dessert.

Zoya was in no mood for any discussions. She had other plans for Markes and no sooner had they finished she hinted broadly to Zonta that she wanted to turn in. Zonta took the hint, winked at Markes, and left. They agreed to meet after breakfast.

The next morning, Zonta dressed in denim jeans, a checked shirt, sneakers and a denim jacket, walked across the hallway to Markes's room and knocked.

'Come in,' he heard Zoya say.

He walked and sat down on the settee.

'Did you two get any sleep?' he asked grinning.

'Plenty,' Markes replied, sheepishly.

'We did get some sleep,' Zoya laughed.

'OK lets get down to business,' Markes got serious.

He made Zoya sit down and then proceeded to explain everything that had happened since the beginning. He did not mention his connection to NATBAL, only that he had received a lead and had gone off to investigate.

'The crucial thing now is to get it to the authorities. It has to be from an authentic source. There are too many hoaxes around, for the Americans or the Russians to believe a story like this.'

'I can tell my father, he will be able to go to the government. Based on his story the government can investigate.' Zoya volunteered.

Markes nodded. 'I looked for some other solution, I couldn't find one. You will have to tell your father that he must be careful. He must tell someone whom he knows really well and the person should be pro government. I have put you in danger by telling you all of this, and the moment you tell your father, he will be a target. The controllers of Intrasyn are ruthless and will stop at nothing.'

Markes and Zoya decided that they would make the call from a public booth, away from the Spola. They made their way to the rail station where they selected a booth away from the public address systems.

She heard her father announce himself. 'Hello, Usov.'

'Hello daddy, when did you get back?'

'Zoya, Where are you?' her father asked.

'Daddy, listen to me very carefully.' Zoya related everything to her father. Even though she had made it short and concise the call had taken her a good twenty minutes.

'Mein Gott,' Usov exhaled. 'Are you sure that this is true?'

'I'm very sure father.'

'But how do you know it's really true?' He is a journalist, and these fellows always add a little spice to the news.'

'I'm absolutely sure father,' she said. He knew Zoya, she was not fooled easily. He had always relied on her judgement.

'OK Zoya I believe you. I'll go to the minister himself. Where can I call you?'

'I'll call you, I can't tell you where I am just now, but be very careful. These people have eyes and ears everywhere.'

'OK Zoya, you be careful too.'

Bye Daddy,' she hung up.

The aide knocked on the door.

Yevgany said,' Enter.'

The aide walked in.

'Have you any news?' Yevgany asked.

'Yes sir, I have information on the entire Usov household. Information here shows that Zoya the daughter of Usov and one of the men we are looking for, Markes have known each other for many years. They both studied in the University of Kiev, though not at the same time. They are known to be close. Markes was a frequent visitor to the Usov home. He worked as a free lance journalist with the Demokratichna Ukraine, and is quite popular in social circles. He is also known to be a computer specialist.'

'Where is this daughter, what's her name..Zoya?'

'She left a couple of days ago, no one knows where?' The aide replied.

'No doubt after the phone call she received.' Yevgany said.

Dudayev turned from the map on the wall. 'Get a photograph of hers, send it to our operatives in Kiev. If they spot her, they are to take no action but notify us immediately. Continue the taps on the Usov phone, and keep us informed.'

The aide left.

'What would you do if you knew the plan and had to stop it?' Dudayev asked.

'I'll try and have the treaty scuttled, no treaty means no meeting of the Presidents, no assassination, which means our personnel are not in position for the next phase.'

'Exactly, have the chopper readied, we'll leave for Kiev immediately.'

Just then the aide rushed in, checked himself at the door, and cleared his throat.

'Yes, let's have it,' Dudayev said, recognising that the aide had something important.

'It's the Usov household sir. We have recorded a long conversation between Ivan Usov and his daughter.'

'Play the transcript,' Dudayev instructed the aide.

The aide had come well prepared, he inserted the tape into the player and switched it on.

The tape ended with Zoya wishing her father goodbye. There was pin drop silence except for the steady hum from the player. Dudayev, Yevgany and the aide had heard the entire plan being spelt out by Zoya to her father.

Dudayev went to the red phone on his desk, picked it up and spoke to Pushkin.

'OK, lets make it to Kiev.' He said leading the way out of the door to the chopper.

Usov dressed for the meeting with the minister. He had briefly explained the findings to him on the phone trying to sound convincing.

'Bring both Zoya and Markes along'. The minister told Usov on the phone.

'Zoya and Markes are not with me, minister,' Usov replied.

'What do you mean, not with you?' the minister asked, his tone clearly showing his irritation.

'I mean, I don't know where they are? Usov replied. 'I got this call from Zoya, telling me this on the phone.'

'And you believed her?' The minister asked.

'She's my daughter, and I know how she thinks. This is true, you must believe me.'

'OK, you come along then, do not say a word to anyone on this. If what you say is true, you and your daughter are in great danger. Have you spoken of this to anyone else?'

'No minister.'

Usov dressed, thinking of what the minister had said. It was good to have the minister as his friend, he was grateful. He worried about Zoya, he kicked himself for not insisting on knowing from where she was calling.

He walked to his car, the driver held the door open for him. 'Usov was surprised, 'Where is Soloyov,' he asked.

'He fell ill, and asked me to drive. 'The new man said.

'But he was fine this morning.'

'Yes sir, but he took ill about an hour ago, said it was something he ate or drank.'

Usov knew this fellow, he had stood in for Soloyov a few times in the past.

He turned to his butler, 'I won't be back for dinner tonight, if Zoya calls tell her I'm at the minister's place.'

It was early evening as the car made its way to the suburbs where the minister had his official residence. The house was built in a large compound with plenty of trees and a high wall. The house could not be seen from the street.

The guard recognising the car and driver opened the gates. The car drove to the porch. The driver got out and held the passenger door open for Usov. The minister appeared at the top of the stairs leading into the house. Usov got out, straightened his jacket and came around the car. He came to the foot of the stairs and looked up. He noticed that the minister was not looking at him, but beyond him. He saw the nod from the minister and felt the presence of a man near him. He half turned and saw a well-built man with a wire held stretched in both hands, close to him. As if on que, the man looped the wire around Usov's neck from behind. Usov grabbed the man's wrists, as he felt the garrotte tightening. Usov was a large man and was very strong. His grip on the man's arms behind him tightened as he tried to twist himself around. He kicked hard as he felt another man grab his ankles, and heard him grunt in pain. He felt a tightness in his chest as his lungs fought for air. His fingers dug into his attacker's arms, ripping flesh. The last thing he saw was the face of the driver who stood in for Soloyov, the man who had grabbed his ankles.

The minister turned to his aide.

'Put his body back into the car, drive to the Central Hospital, and wheel him directly to emergency. The doctor there is one of ours I'll speak to him. He'll see that Usov is admitted and put in an intensive care unit. Inform his household, and tell them to specially tell his daughter if she phones, that her father has had an accident and is in intensive care.' He paused,' I want to know if she calls.'

Chapter 59

Date: 28th October 2007, Place: Kiev,
Time 5.30 pm

Zoya and Markes decided to take a walk around the venue of the treaty. Markes had changed Zoya's appearance from a striking blond to a plain looking brunette. He was still in the disguise that he and Zonta had adopted after leaving the boat at Viljandi.

The hotel staff were discreet and did not question patrons or their companions. The doorman at the hotel, wished Markes and Zola as they left the hotel. Markes had seen his puzzled look, when he saw Zoya in her disguise

Zonta had elected to stay in his room. He had laid out his equipment and set about making devices they could use as a diversion. They were miniature bombs and incidenary devices.

The town was filling up with military personnel from various corps of the Russian, Ukrainian, Estonian, and Belarusian armed forces.

Markes and Zoya had spent the day near the open ground where the treaty was to be signed. The ground was situated in a large park. The actual area a huge open lawn the size of four football fields was cordoned off, with barricades. It was an unusual event and crowds of townspeople were hanging around. Hawkers selling popcorn and candy were doing brisk business. Markes bought two popcorns and handed one to Zoya. They mingled with the crowd.

The corps of engineers of the Ukraine army were building a platform at one end of the grounds. Scores of army and security personnel from the United States, Estonia, Belarus and Russia were checking every item that was brought in. They had various detection devices. Markes looked around, there were no high rise buildings around the ground. No opportunity for a sharpshooter with a high velocity rifle. The approach to the ground was by the paved roads that led into the park. Road blocks had been set up and each approach manned. The perimeter of the cordoned off area had signboards.

Approach to the ground by foot was possible, but to enter the venue of the treaty a pass or an entry permit was required.

Markes saw them erecting two large glass panes one in front of the platform and one behind. These were obviously bulletproof glass. A number of potted plants were placed around the dais and the VIP enclosures adjacent to the dais. A truck bearing the Ukraine security symbol pulled up. Four men took off the canopy of the truck revealing four very large potted plants. The security men brought a small crane and started the process of unloading the pots. Before the pots could be moved, one of the security men at the site stopped them. His uniform was that of a major in the United States Marines. He beckoned to some of his men who brought detection devices. They spent the next twenty minutes checking the pots. He seemed satisfied and waved them through. The pots were placed at the rear of the platform, between the platform and the glass pane.

Markes and Zoya went to one of the signboards, which showed the layout of the area. On either side of the dais were areas for VIPs. Twenty yards from the bulletproof glass in front of the dais was the enclosure reserved for the press. Behind the press enclosure were the seats for the public. Look out posts were being erected around the enclosure. Each of which would be manned by a mixed security team.

They walked back to the room. On the way, Markes saw a kiosk selling books and newspapers. He bought three international newspapers.

They returned to the hotel. Markes and Zoya helped themselves to a cold drink from the mini bar, and sat down to watch Zonta at his work.

'Find anything about the venue?' Zonta asked.

Markes explained the layout to Zonta.

'What are they planning? 'Markes thought aloud.

'With the infiltration that has taken place, it could be an inside job.' Zonta remarked.

Markes was leafing through the newspapers. He picked up the News de Internacionale and looked at the front page. All the newspapers had the same news, the news of the treaty. He flicked the pages to the editorial section.

'Hey, this is the guy I saw or rather the photograph of the guy at Cerkessk.' He said aloud, to Zonta.

Zonta and Zola looked at the picture in the photograph.

'Who is he?' Zonta asked. 'I haven't seen him before.'

'This is one of the three from Cerkessk, the ones who survived the massacre. I saw his photograph with that of the other two.' Markes explained briefly.

'What massacre?' Zoya asked.

'It happened a long time ago, we don't have time to go into that now.' Markes explained to her.

'Where is he now?' Zonta asked.

'He's the editor of the News de Internacionale.' Zoya said.

'How do you know?' Markes asked.

Zoya smiled. 'Its written here,' she said pointing to the article.

Markes looked at Zonta, Zoya did not know the entire story and his involvement with NATBAL.

Markes looked at the name, it was Boris. So Boris was the Yuri from Cerkessk.

'Lets go,' He grabbed Zoya.

'Where to?' Zonta and Zoya asked simultaneously.

'To the library, I need to check a few things.'

The doorman at the Spola, hailed them a cab. Markes and Zoya directed him to the Central Library of Kiev.

Markes explained to Zoya that they needed to obtain some information on Boris of the News de Internacionale. They asked for and were directed to the reference section of the library. Markes went to the back issues, dating back to the massacre.

It was about ten months after the incident at Cerkessk that the News de Internacionale announced the opening of the Baltic office with Boris Pugo as its editor in chief. Markes, checked on Boris Pugo, the information that was available showed that he was an excellent free lance war correspondent. Very highly rated both for his photography as well as for his journalistic abilities. The signing on by the News de Internacionale of Boris was considered a coup in international magazine circles. On the origins of Boris there was no information at all. Markes was sure that Boris's identity had been painstakingly built up, but that would have to wait. There were more urgent matters at hand.

They returned to the Spola.

'Would it be possible to send an email to NATBAL, even if we cannot directly speak to them.' Markes asked Zonta.

'No way, all email messages are through a server, and all messages will be monitored, especially now. A time delay is built in the transmission protocol that routes messages through a special folder that enables checking of messages, prior to onward transmission. A trace can be put on the message that will lead back to us.'

'We must disrupt the meeting. If they succeed, we will have a situation where Intrasyn will have legitimate control over governments with nuclear arsenals.' Markes clearly agitated, paced the room.

'We can set up explosions around the periphery, the explosions could disrupt the meeting.' Zonta thought aloud.

'I don't think we can get within a mile of the venue with explosives. The American security agents are everywhere and they check everything very thoroughly.'

'This Boris is a photographer. He is known to be very hands on, his style is to be where the action is. I think he will be among the press.'

'He is a photographer, isn't he?' Markes stopped.' That could explain the "Framed in Eternity". What does eternity mean, it could mean after death…..to be framed in eternity?'

'What does a photographer carry with him? Cameras, film, a battery pack. Spare lens.' Markes looked serious.

'I think you are right. Boris is the one to carry out the assassinations, but how?' Zonta asked.

'I don't know, but if we have to stop him, we must get close to him.'

'He will be in the press enclosure. Every member allowed to enter the enclosure will need to have top security clearance.' Zonta added.

Zonta having worked at the Third Chief Directorate, knew the policy and the detail of security arrangements for VVIPs.

'With four presidents attending, security personnel from all the participating states will be present. There will be more security personnel than non-security personnel.' Zonta explained.

'This can work to our advantage since there will be so many new faces that entry and exit can only be controlled by papers issued to these personnel.'

'Can we get into the press enclosure?' Markes asked.

'Not as a member of the press.' Zonta replied.

'Then how?'

'As a member of security.' Zonta said.

Markes asked,' And how will we do that?'

'I don't know yet, but we'll find a way.' Zonta walked to the window. He could see the lights of the bars and the restaurants all lit up as the town filled up with people who had come to witness the signing of the treaty.

Markes and Zonta decided to leave Zoya behind at the hotel.

It was early evening and the bars were filling up mostly with security personnel who were being imported from the surrounding states.

Markes and Zonta decided to make a round of the bigger bars in town. The four bars that they had visited were filled with young soldiers. There were groups assigned to the entry and exit points, car parks, perimeter and other areas. Zonta learnt that groups had been assigned to the VIP enclosure, press enclosure, and the front and side enclosures.

The fifth bar was large and had a girl gyrating on a table at the centre, The drinks at this bar were expensive.

They walked up to the bar and ordered vodka.

They were groups, from the directorates of the three states.

A group of young soldiers, with insignia denoting that they were from the elite corps of The Fourth Chief Directorate of Belarus came up to the bar beside them.

'Vodka,' they waved to the bartender trying to catch his attention.

He looked at them and nodded,' I'll be with you as soon as I've served these gentlemen.'

The bartender filled four shot glasses of vodka which he placed in front of the soldiers. They picked it up and drank it in one gulp. They were out to get drunk.

The bartender served them two more rounds which they downed.

Zonta turned to look at the group.

'Where are you from?'

'From Minsk, from the ancillary unit of the Fourth Chief Directorate.' The soldier slurred, and pulled himself up with pride.

'What is your role here?' Zonta asked

The soldier's face fell.' We will be responsible for security in various sections. Some of us are assigned to the VIP enclosures, some to the entry points, and others to areas, such as the press enclosure and the lookout towers.' He looked at his empty glass.

'Let me buy you all a round.' Zonta beckoned to the bartender to refill the glasses.'

The face of the soldier brightened up.

'So what is your assigned area?' Zonta asked.

'I've been assigned entry point, six, and my friend here,' he turned to his mate.' He is in the press enclosure.'

Zonta asked for the bottle from the bartender, and placed it on the bar next to the soldiers. He filled the glasses as they were emptied.

'How many are being assigned to these enclosures? 'Zonta asked.

'They are plenty of security personnel at each of the enclosures.' The soldier dug into his trouser pocket, and pulled out a card, which he showed Zonta.

His friend took out his card, which he showed them. The soldier's card was security clearance for entry point six, his friend's card was security clearance for the press enclosure.

Zonta and Markes looked at the cards which had a photograph and was signed by the chief of the fourth chief directorate. The passes were bar coded. The bar was very crowded, they were being constantly jostled. Zonta leaned to the soldier, spoke to him and put the bottle on the bar. He nudged Markes to join him. They left the bar.

Markes was puzzled.' What next?' he asked Zonta.

'We get back to the room, we've some work to do and then we'll return.' He reached into his pocket and pulled out the card the second soldier had shown them. The security clearance to the press enclosure.

'How in hell did you pick his pocket.' Markes exclaimed

'One of the tricks of my trade.'

'Won't the soldier report the loss of his card?' Markes asked.

'He will if he does not find it in the morning.'

Markes and Zonta made their way back to the hotel.

Zonta set about making identity cards for both of them for access to the press enclosure. He took out a mini Polaroid camera with which he took photographs of Markes and himself. Made two cards with some paperboard, plastic film and the photographs. He cut a potato in half and engraved it with his penknife. He then took a stamp pad and pressed the engraved portion of the potato and tried it on a piece of white paper. The stamp was passable. He asked Markes to remain in the room and left. He returned fifteen minutes later.

'Where did you go?' Markes asked.

'To the business centre, to xerox the card.' he showed Markes the A4 sheet of paper with the bar codes. The bar coding was in black which helped, it was easy to xerox.

Within an hour Zonta had two cards which on inspection was identical to the card that he had picked from the soldier. Only the photographs and the names were different.

They made their way back to the bar. The soldiers were still at the place where they left them. The bottle was almost empty. The young soldier and his friend saw him.

'Where have you been?' his friend slurred.

'I had to see a friend at the 'Ryzhkov', Zonta smiled.

The girl on the table did a quick turn, her skirt billowing.

The young soldier swayed as he leant forward to look up her skirt and nearly fell. Zonta grabbed him and steadied him.

'Take it easy, she's not going anywhere.'

'We have to leave, see you around.'

'Thanks for the drink,' the soldiers replied.

'Did you return his pass?' Markes asked impatiently.

'Of course I did, didn't you see me?'

They returned to the hotel, decided to order room service and have an early night.

'I want to call my father and see if he has been able to speak to the minister.' Zoya spoke to Markes.

Markes and Zonta looked at each other.

'Lets phone from a public booth, its easy to trace a call back to the room.' Markes suggested.

Markes and Zoya decided to take a stroll after dinner to make the call.

Zonta left them for his room.

Markes stood outside the booth as Zoya called home. The ring went on a for a bit.

'Hello, Leonid, where is father? she asked.

Markes watching her saw her turn pale. She let the receiver drop and started crying. Markes held her and led her out of the booth.

'What happened Zoya?'

She hugged him holding him tight.

'My father's had an accident. He's in intensive care at the hospital. I must go to him.'

Markes shook his head.' I'm sorry Zoya, so sorry. You can't go, it's a trap.'

Zoya pushed him away.' All you can think of is this assignment, my father is fighting for his life.'

Markes held her close.' I understand,' he stroked her hair,' but you must believe me, Intrasyn has eyes and ears everywhere. Do you have any friends you can call?'

Zoya nodded,' Our neighbours are very close to us, we have known them for years. I'll call them.'

She called and spoke to her friends for a long time. When she had finished, she was distraught.

'I'm sure that something is wrong. Our friends are surprised at the information. Valentina the daughter of our neighbour was on the same route and was behind my father till he turned into the minister's residence. On her return about two hours later she took the same route, there was nothing to indicate that there had been an accident.'

It was a well-known fact that the police would barricade the portion of the road if an accident took place. It usually took three or more hours before the barricade was removed.

Markes was silent, he held Zoya close.' Let's get back to the hotel.'

'What about my father?' Zoya asked.

Markes spoke to her very softly, holding her close. 'The whole thing is a lie, it is a ruse to get you back, and us with you. If your father is in intensive care, he'll be well looked after. You must be careful.'

Zoya nodded, tears streaming down her face.

Chapter 60

Date: 29th October 2007, Place: Kiev,
Time: 4.30 pm

Dudayev and Yevgany landed at Kiev. They were picked up by a limousine on the tarmac and taken to Pavlovsky, who was now the chief of Ukraine security.

Dudayev and Yevgany were ushered into Pavlovsky's office.

'Good morning, Dudayev, Yevgany,' Pavlovsky walked around his desk to shake hands with them.

'How is the search progressing.' Pavlovsky had heard of Markes Trubin, Andreas Komanovsky and the break in at Muhu.

'They are in Kiev now.' Dudayev explained.

'Do you have photographs which I can circulate?' Pavlovsky asked.

'We do, but they have disguised themselves.'

'They have a young woman with them. She's the daughter of Usov.' Yevgany said, holding out a photograph of Zoya.

He looked at the photograph. 'She's attractive, so people will remember her. I'll get some security agents to ask around.'

'Boris is in Kiev' Pavlovsky announced.

'He'll need to be protected. I'm certain that the two have guessed his role. Markes has seen a photograph of Boris at Cerkessk.' Yevgany added.

'They know the entire plan, except perhaps how the assassination is to be carried out.'

'What would you do if you knew the plan and wanted to prevent it?' Dudayev asked.

'Take out Boris, or reach one of the friendly western governments.'

'I'll double the security detail for Boris,' Pavlovsky reached for his buzzer.

An aide walked in.

Pavlovsky gave him instructions.

'How will you be controlling access to the various sections?' Dudayev asked.

'The respective chief directorates have issued passes to authorised personnel. The passes have photographs and are bar coded for identification.'

Dudayev thought about it and seemed satisfied.

'Boris will be in the press enclosure,' he made a statement.

'Yes' answered Pavlovsky. 'He will be directly opposite the dais.'

'What about the explosive devices?'

'In pots, very large pots. They are filled with a mixture of urea and pebbles. The pebbles are half an inch in diameter and serve as shrapnel. There is very little earth in the mixture. On inspection it will show up as any other potted plant. Each pot is a lethal bomb all that is required is a detonator.'

Pavlovsky buzzed. The aide came in.

'Show them their office,' Pavlovsky instructed.

He turned to Dudayev. 'If you need anything let me know.'

Dudayev turned to Yevgany, 'Have a photograph of Zoya Usov circulated to agents at the rail and coach stations.'

'I'm quite sure the two would have come in disguised from Viljandi.'

Yevgany spoke into the phone, giving instructions.

'Lets go have a look at the grounds where the meeting is to take place.' Dudayev picked up his coat as he walked to the door.

Yevgany received a call late that evening.

'Yes, OK put him on the line.' There was a pause, 'Yes this is Yevgany. Did you see the two men she picked up, and the car she was driving. What about the license plates, were you able to get the number.'

Yevgany turned to Dudayev. 'She was at the rail station yesterday, and drove a red Renault. He didn't get the number, must have been busy looking at her. She met two men, both were non-descript, though one was paunchy.'

'OK, circulate the description of the car, check the garages. If she came in a car they might be staying out of town. Have all the nearby villages and boarding houses, hotels checked.'

It was 5 p.m. on the 29th, less than twenty-four hours to the signing of the Treaty.

Yevgany pulled out a small worn black note pad

'All calls, both incoming and outgoing at hotels and boarding houses in Kiev will be monitored.'

'An agent will be assigned to each hotel. We are checking all hotel and boarding house guests who checked in during the last three days. Descriptions and photographs have been given to each field agent. The garages of hotels will be checked.' Yevgany read out his action plan as he ticked each entry.

311

Chapter 61

Date: 29th October 2007, Place: Kiev,
Time: 5.30 pm

Leonid Kototich now pushing forty worked in the MVD the Ministerstvo Vnutrennykh Del, which was earlier the ministry of internal affairs. He had seen better days, but his love for vodka had turned him into an alcoholic and he was demoted. He had been right for recruiting when Intrasyn approached him. He needed the money to send to his family in Bila Cerkva, and to maintain a mistress in Kiev. He received a pay packet regularly from Intrasyn in addition to his normal MVD salary.

He had received a call from his contact in Intrasyn on the morning of the 29th and had been assigned to the Hotel Spola. His contact explained what he had to do.

It was 5.30 p.m. on the 29th. He had just come off duty and had asked his boss for a days leave, but had been refused. He needed a drink and made his way to his favourite bar.

He knew he would be up the whole night. He called his mistress, and told her not to wait up for him. She didn't argue, she knew his line of work.

Leonid settled himself behind the bar, ordered a couple of stiff vodkas, and downed them. He selected some smoked salmon for starters and followed it with roast beef and potatoes. He washed it down with some more vodka then picked up a large mug of coffee and settled down at a far table. The bar was filling with security and army personnel. There was an air of excitement. Kiev had not witnessed such a gathering of world leaders. The whole town was packed, and business was brisk.

He finished his coffee, paid and left. It was 7.30 p.m., the air was distinctly colder. He pulled up the collar of his overcoat and made his way to the Spola.

The Spola was lit up, and decorated, that the hotel was full, was evident from the number of people coming in and going out. There were many men in uniform. A steady stream of cars drove in and out of the front lobby.

He went to the entrance and was stopped by the doorman. Leonid showed him his ID. The man nodded and let him in. Leonid made his way to the reception counter and asked to see the manager. After a short while the manager came out, looked at his ID and asked him into his office.

'What can I do for you?' The manager asked.

'I'd like to see the guest register and the names of all guests who registered over the last two days. I would like to have a look at your underground parking as well.'

He saw the manager hesitate.

'It's a matter of state security, and this is routine procedure. We have the heads of state of four countries, and one of them is the President of The United States of America.'

The manager nodded, he understood. He buzzed for his office assistant.

'See that Mr. Kototich is given the information he requires'.

'There is a desk in the office, you can use.' The manager offered Leonid.

Leonid thanked him and followed the assistant to the adjoining office.

The assistant produced a sheaf of papers.' These are computer print outs of the hotel's guest register for the last two days. It lists dates when guests check in, their current status if they are still in the hotel, and the dates they have checked out, if they have left.' He placed them in front of Leonid and left.

Leonid looked at the sheaf of papers, it was depressing. The papers were arranged in chronological order, so he started with the papers dated the 7th. He went through the list looking for names of all persons who had registered after noon on the 7th. He went through all the papers and made a list. Most of the names were of couples or single men. He thought about it. They could have registered under false names, in which case he wouldn't have a clue. He went through the lists again, running his fingers along the names of all couples. There was something he was missing. He looked at his watch, it was past eleven, and he was feeling drowsy, the effects of the vodka and the heavy meal. He decided that he would go back to the lists later.

He remembered the photograph of Zoya, pulled it out from his pocket and looked at the photograph. She was a good looker, he would show it to the assistant when he returned. He stretched yawning. He decided to have a quick nap and then get back to work. He kicked off his shoes, and slid down in the chair. The chair was comfortable, large and upholstered with leather. In a few minutes he was snoring.

The assistant walked in a short while later, saw Leonid stretched out fast asleep, the papers strewn on the table. He turned off the lights and went back to the front desk.

Loenid woke with a start, the curtains were not drawn and the light had woken him up. He cursed and checked his wrist watch, it was six in the morning. The Intrasyn big bosses who had flown into Kiev would have expected the reports to be in by now. He had to take a piss, his bladder was full, in his hurry he walked into the door, almost breaking his nose. He pulled the door open, his nose hurting and eyes all watery and made his way to the bathroom at the far end of the corridor. The night assistant saw him, wished him good morning. Leonid grunted in reply. He was out of the bathroom fifteen minutes later, his face washed and hair slicked back. His shirt had been tucked in. He looked neat except for the stubble.

He had to check the garage and show the manager the photograph of Zoya. He walked to the manager's office, saw he wasn't there and looked around the lobby. The time was a little past six in the morning. It was an important day and the lobby was full of men in suits and some soldiers in uniform and ladies in all sorts of ensembles. He saw the manager at the far end of the lobby and made his way to him. In his hurry he bumped into a lady, dressed in a traditional Arab dress with a veil over her face. He apologised and waved to the manager.

The manager saw him.' The blundering idiot,' he said under his breath as he saw Leonid bump into the woman.

Leonid reached the manager, pulled him to a side and took out the photograph of Zoya.

'Have you seen this lady?'

The manager looked at the photograph, he instantly recognised her face. 'Of course, that's Mrs Usov.'

Leonid was stunned, Mrs. Usov, the name was on the list that he had made last night. 'Do you know the room she is in?'

'Yes, but its early and they might be asleep.'

'No, no, I don't intend to wake them up, just wanted to be sure that they are in their rooms.'

The manager led the way to the reception desk.

'Are Mr and Mrs Usov still in?'

The clerk checked the pigeon hole and replied.

'Yes, they are still in.'

'Do you know the make and registration of their car?' Leonid asked.

The clerk checked and gave him the information.

The doorman at the Spola saw the two men in uniform accompanied by a lady in an Arab ensemble.

'Good morning ma'am. Good morning Sirs'.

'Good morning,' they replied.

'Can I call a taxi sir?' he asked.

'Yes please.'

They got in and asked the driver to take them to the coach station.

They got off at the coach station, paid off the taxi and walked to the rail station.

'I'll stay', Zoya said. Markes could see the tears through the veil.

Markes turned to her, held her by her arms,' It's not safe here, or even in Odessa. You will be safe only when this is out of the way.'

'When will I see you?' she cried.

'I'll see you in the monastery, as soon as I've finished here. Till then lie low, do not contact anyone. No one, not even your closest friends, or your home.'

They checked the timetable for the train to Vinnycja. Zoya would make her way to the Sisters of St Sebastian. She would be safe there. Markes went to the ticket counter and bought her a ticket.

She kissed Zonta on the cheek, then put her arms around Markes,' Be careful, I want you safe.' She said, choking back her sobs.

'I will, you be careful, don't take the veil off till you are inside the monastery.' Markes cautioned her.

They waited till the train pulled out of the platform. The clock in the station read seven. The countdown had begun. The program would start in four hours.

Leonid went back to the desk where he had left his papers and called the number that he was given to contact, should he find anything.

'Yes?' Yevgany answered.

Leonid explained his findings.

'Stay there, and if you see them in the lobby call me immediately. If they leave the hotel follow them.'

'Yes, sir,' Leonid replied.

In less than five minutes, two unmarked cars pulled up at the Spola. Four men got out of one and spread themselves out around the hotel. Dudayev, Yevgany and another man got out of the second car and made their way into the hotel. The manager and Loenid met them. They made their way into the hotel lift.

They reached the floor stepped into the corridor, and followed the manager to room 309. The time was seven in the morning. He tapped once, then a second time.

Dudayev said under his breath.' Use the master key.'

The manager did as he was told. The door opened, the man accompanying Dudayev and Yevgany stepped into the room, a gun in hand.

'They are not here', Dudayev stated, looking around. The bed had been slept in, but not made and their clothes were in the cupboard.

'They haven't checked out, I, we would have seen them if they did.' Leonid spoke looking at the manager.

'Let's get down to the lobby, check with the doorman and the hotel porters. Ask if they saw Mr and Mrs Usov walking out. Check the restaurants.' Dudayev made for the staircase.

'What about the car?' Dudayev asked. 'Where is the garage?'

The manager led the way down the stairs to the basement parking lot. They checked each bay, and found the Renault parked behind a van almost out of view.

'Have a team sent in. I want this car, the hotel, and the lobby under twenty-four hour surveillance. I want to know of all guests entering and leaving the hotel. He turned to Yevgany,

'Check the hotel's telephone logs, I want to know of any calls made to any embassy, whether Russian or Foreign. And all calls made from the Usov room.'

He turned to the manager. 'Did anyone else check in with Mr and Mrs Usov?'

'Yes another gentleman'.

'His name and room number 'Dudayev asked, his voice taking on an edge.

The manager fumbled with the register.' A Mr. Grishin, he is in Room 312.'

Room 312 was in a similar state, bed slept in but with clothes still in the cupboard.

'We let them slip through our fingers,' Dudayev said. He turned to Leonid. 'When were you assigned to the Spola?'

'Last evening at six thirty', Leonid stammered.

'What did you do between six thirty in the evening and seven this morning? Dudayev asked.

Leonid was silent, his face pale and ashen.

Dudayev's fist lashed out catching Leonid full in the face, knocking him down. 'Take him away,' he told the third man. 'We'll deal with him later'.

Chapter 62

Date: 30th October 2007, Place: Kiev,
Time: 6.00 a.m.

Markes and Zonta made their way to the perimeter fence at the grounds.

The perimeter guards were in place; only security personnel were being allowed into and out of the perimeter. The perimeter fence was a thousand meters from the venue of the meeting and the dais; the dais was not visible from where they stood. The watchtowers were manned by a mixed security team consisting of Russian, Ukrainian, Belarusian and American security agents. The security guards, on the towers, and the bodyguards of the Presidents were armed, all other security agents were unarmed. All security agents carried mobile communication equipment.

'The security detail of each section will be brought by truck from their barracks, three hours in advance.' Zonta said, looking at his watch. 'We have half an hour before we can make our way through the perimeter.'

They walked away from the perimeter fence. Chose a quiet bench behind a clump of trees in the park, next to the stream and sat down. It was early, there were very few people around.

'We will have to neutralise Boris inside the press enclosure,' Markes said.

Zonta nodded. 'I'll create a diversion, you will have to use that opportunity to kill him.'

'Expect to be frisked by the perimeter guards.' Zonta said.

319

Markes nodded, unclipped the baton from his belt, released a hidden catch and turned the handle anti-clockwise, the handle with the blade sprang out. Markes pulled it out fully revealing a nine-inch long stiletto blade.

Zonta checked his baton, the stiletto released neatly.

They each twisted the heel of their right boot, the heels came off, revealing the tags and ring pulls embedded inside of the heel.

'We have the same bar codes, so we will have to enter the perimeter at different points,' Markes said.

Markes checked his watch the time was seven fifteen. A sign board was being erected at the perimeter, where the road entered, they got up and moved towards the signboard for a closer look.

The signboard was a plan of the dais and seating arrangements for VIPs, diplomats and press. The dais was flanked on either side by watch towers and the VIP enclosures. The press enclosures were opposite the VIP enclosures. The area opposite the dais between the two press enclosures was for diplomats. The general seating areas were behind the press enclosures. Arrows indicated the route cars had to take. The parking areas were divided, and carried boards with a letter of the alphabet. Drivers were required to park in the area which corresponded with the letter on their passes.

Zonta grabbed Markes arm, fingers digging into flesh.

'There are two press enclosures,' where will Boris be placed?'

Markes thought about it. He looked at the plan, there was a press enclosure opposite each of the two VIP enclosures. He pointed to the enclosure opposite the VIP enclosure marked 'Russian', 'Ukraine'. 'My guess is, he will be here.'

The enclosure was farther away from the dais than the other VIP enclosure.

The other VIP enclosure read 'American' and 'Belarusian'.

'We cannot take any chances, we will split up and cover both press enclosures'. Markes decided.

They checked their watches, synchronised them.

'We should spot Boris quite easily.' Markes said.

'I'll create a diversion if he is not in my enclosure, or you create one if he is not in yours. Time it for the start of the Russian national anthem.'

They agreed to meet after the event at Vinnycja, at the Sisters of St Sebastian. They shook hands, they had grown close, these last few weeks.

'See you soon,' they said to each other, and moved away in opposite directions.

They made their way to the entrance points at opposite ends of the perimeter.

Markes showed the guard his pass. The guard looked at it, then at Markes and swiped the card. The bleep sounded, recording the entry. The young guard seemed satisfied with his pass, but seemed unsure of whether to let him through.

'Why are you coming in through here?' he asked. 'You have a separate entrance with the rest of the press security.'

Markes looked sheepish, leant close to him,' I couldn't get back to the barracks last night before lights out.' He winked. The guard understood and smiled.' You'd better be careful, officers are making the rounds regularly.'

Markes thanked him, and was about to leave.

'Hold it' the guard said.

Markes froze, his mind racing, wondering at the reason.

'I need to check you for weapons.' The young guard replied.

'Sure,' Markes replied, relaxing and holding his arms out as the guard frisked him.'

'OK, carry on,' the guard turned to the next person in line.

Markes looked across the park, he saw that Zonta had cleared the guard as well.

Markes entered the press enclosure. He had pinned the pass to his jacket as the others had done. He pulled his cap down over his forehead so that his face was not fully visible. He joined the other security guards at the enclosure.

'Hello,' he was startled by a voice behind him.

He turned to see the young man they had met in the bar, the one assigned to the press enclosure.

'Hi There,' he replied.

'Why didn't you tell me you were in the press enclosure too. What is your unit? he asked.

'The third chief directorate of Ukraine,' Markes replied.

'Is your friend here?' the young guard asked.

'He's in the other section.' Markes answered looking at his watch, it was nine.

'I'll see you around,' he said to his young friend.

'The press is at the Palace. Covering the meeting of the Presidents before the public ceremony.' The guard said noticing Markes looking at his watch.

Chapter 63

Date: 30th October 2007, Place: Kiev,
Time: 9.00 a.m.

Dudayev checked his watch, it was nine, 'Lets go,'

A car waiting for them at the hotel entrance drove them to Pavlovsky's office.

They were ushered into Pavlovsky's office.

They could feel the tension in the air. Pushkin, Zhirinovsky and Sakarov were there.

'What is the situation? 'Pushkin asked Dudayev.

'We know he is in Kiev, but don't know exactly where he is, Sir'

'He is a tough and determined man. Will he be able to disrupt the meeting and prevent Boris from carrying out his task?' Pushkin asked.

'We have assigned bodyguards for Boris. They will be with him till he enters the press enclosure.

'What about the security checks for the press and the equipment?' Pushkin asked.

'All press personnel are required to leave their equipment for checking by a team drawn from the security services of the four countries. The team checks each piece of equipment and clears them. 'Pavlovsky explained.

'Has Boris's equipment been cleared?' Pushkin asked

'I've taken care of that' Pavlovsky answered. 'The camera and the battery pack was cleared by me personally.'

Pushkin seemed satisfied.

'What about Markes and Zonta, have they tried communicating?'

'We are sure he has not been able to contact any foreign office, all international calls have been monitored. All hotels and boarding houses have been under surveillance. No calls have been made from any of them.' Dudayev replied.

'What about the data he copied, we know he has a lap top?'

'The lap top was destroyed at Muhu, the piece of ABS plastic with metal which we recovered from the cliff edge was the hard disk of his lap top. I have had the lab check it and it has been confirmed.' Dudayev answered.

Pushkin nodded,'Good,' he knew how Dudayev worked.

'What about the arrangements at the venue?'

Pavlovsky explained the seating arrangements. 'The potted plants are placed between the dais and the bulletproof glass behind the dais. Potted plants have also been placed in all the VIP enclosures.'

'OK, 'Pushkin made a decision. 'Sakarov and Pavlovsky will take our positions in the VIP enclosures. Zhirinovsky and I will leave for Muhu. We need to assess the damage, and make changes as required. We have to assume that the data will be passed on. Just make sure that Boris gets to accomplish his task.'

There was silence as the group digested what he had just told them.

Pushkin went on. 'Markes and Zonta will be at the venue. They know our objective. They might not have guessed how we intend to carry out the assassinations, but my guess is they will do their best to try and stop us. What about the rest of the arrangements?'

'The tower overlooking the VIP section will be staffed entirely by security agents from the three republics. All are Intrasyn men. One side of the watchtower is hidden from sight when viewed from the presidential dais. The tower and its occupants will not be visible to anyone watching from that side. The American security agents have taken position in the area around the presidential dais. Dudayev will be in one of the watchtowers accompanied by Samsonov the markesman from the Ukraine. He will be able to look down into both the press enclosures. We also have our agents in each of the press enclosures and will closely monitor all entrants into the area especially around Boris.' Pavlovsky explained.

'I will be able to spot Markes if he makes an appearance, even if he is disguised.' Dudayev said.

Pushkin seemed satisfied with the arrangements.

'Send us word at Muhu, as soon as it is over,' he turned to Zhirinovsky, 'Lets go.'

Pushkin and Zhirinovsky left with their bodyguards. This was a change in plans. Pushkin was known for that.

Dudayev gave instructions to Yevgany. The motorcade with Pavlovsky, Sakarov, Dudayev and Samsonov left for the venue, the clock tower in the town centre struck ten.

On the way, Dudayev spoke to Pavlovsky. 'You said that the passes issued to all the guards had a bar code?'

'Yes, each security agent within the perimeter will need to carry his pass at all times. The passes are swiped at the entrance.'

'Would it be possible for a card to be swiped twice and the bearers allowed entry?' Dudayev asked.

Pavlovsky frowned, he couldn't quite follow Dudayev's thinking.' Yes as long as the code is correct. The bar code machine will bleep once which will allow the guard to clear the bearer for entry. If it bleeps continuously it means the bar code is incorrect. The control room will be notified automatically, and back up despatched to the location.'

Dudayev turned to Yevgany. 'I want a listing of all cards swiped this morning. Check the computer, sort out entries. I want a list of all cards swiped more than once, with locations.'

He added.' If a card has been swiped more than once I want the guard at the barrier questioned, why was it done and the identity of the person he let through.'

The motorcade screeched to a halt. Yevgany got out and got into one of the accompanying cars and sped off in the opposite direction.

Dudayev and the others reached the venue. Dudayev saw Sakarov to his seat and left for the watchtower. The watchtowers were positioned at the far ends of the VIP enclosures, fifty feet above ground level, situated on both sides of the dais.

Dudayev started up the metal ladder leading to the watchtower, nodding to the guards who saluted him. He noticed that Samsonov had taken his place and was checking his rifle and scope. The rifle had a silencer.

Pavlovsky in the meanwhile left for the Ukrainian President's palace to accompany him and the other Presidents to the venue.

Dudayev could hear the sirens in the distance. He heard his walkie-talkie crackle. He listened.

'Where and how many times?'

'Twice,' Dudayev repeated after Yevgany.

'No, Thrice,' he heard Yevgany say.

'Where?' Dudayev asked his pulse quickening.

'At the perimeter, entrance.' Yevgany replied.

'Was it at one point or more?' Dudayev asked.

'At three different entry points. One was at the checkpoint for the security guards, just after the barracks. The other two were at points at the perimeter entrance.

'Have you checked with the guards at the perimeter?'

'The first one was the guard assigned to the enclosure. I have verified it personally. We have questioned the other two guards. They have given a description of the two men, they are wearing the insignia of the fourth chief directorate.' Yevgany said.

'Are there any others assigned to press security from the fourth chief directorate?' Dudayev asked.

'I've checked, none.'

'How many guards are assigned to the press enclosure?' Dudayev asked.

'Five' he heard Yevgany answer.

'Repeat that,'

'Five' he heard Yevgany.

'OK we know where they are, they are in the two press enclosures.' He told Yevgany.

'Have a detail sent to the press enclosure immediately?' Dudayev instructed, looking down into the enclosure with his binoculars. The press were being ushered into the enclosures, there was a scramble as the photographers set up their tripods and cameras.

The sirens were getting louder. Dudayev could see the motorcade, entering the perimeter. The motorcade slowed to a crawl as the crowds on either side of the road waved flags of the four nations. The motorcade was led by the President of the Ukraine, followed by the President of the United States of America, the Belarusian President and the Russian President.

'We can't send a security detail into the enclosure now, it will draw too much attention. The Americans will call off the whole thing at the slightest hint of danger.' Yevgany replied.

'Contact our agents in the press enclosure, they are to take out Markes and Zonta at the first opportunity.'

'I'll do that right away,' Yevgany replied.

Boris looked up and saw Dudayev in the watchtower. He looked at the VIP enclosure, and was surprised to see that Pushkin and Zhirinovsky were absent. He frowned. He looked around him and saw that the other photographers were busy setting up.

There was a mass of humanity, waiting for the Presidents to arrive. They were dressed in an assortment of colours. The atmosphere was that of a carnival. Vendors were doing brisk business in the crowds lining the driveway, selling ice cream, savouries, popcorn, candyfloss and hot dogs.

The crowds that lined the route in the park cheered and waved as the motorcade drove through. Children from various schools were lined up in front along the barricade with adults lined up behind them. Some in the crowd threw flowers at the motorcade, much to the chagrin of the security guards who tried to stop them. It was impossible, the people had come to celebrate a new era with a promise of peace and prosperity, they simply ignored the guards.

The sirens were turned off as the motorcade with the Presidents arrived, drawing to a halt behind the dais.

Those seated in the VIP enclosures and the other invitees stood as the President of the Ukraine, led the way to the dias followed by the other Presidents.

Dudayev looked through his binoculars, into the press enclosure. He focussed on each of the six security guards, zooming in on the right hand of each one. The first two drew a blank, he moved the binoculars down towards the right palm of the third guard, when he stopped, there was no mistaking the double thumb of Markes. He looked at his shoulder, the insignia of the fourth chief directorate was clearly visibly.

'Got you.' He said to himself. He turned to Samsonov.

'Can you see the third security guy, standing on the far side of the enclosure? He pointed to Markes.

'Samsonov looked through the scope, 'The guy with the insignia of the fourth chief directorate, standing between the two guards with red caps, yes I see him.'

'Take him out at the first opportunity.' Dudayev ordered.

He looked at the second enclosure. Focussed on the six faces there, but could not make out Zonta alias Andreas Komanovsky.

Markes mingled with the rest of the press in the enclosure, looking at each of the faces. They were jostling for a good place. Markes saw a familiar face. It was Boris, or rather Yuri, there was no mistaking the high forehead and the aquiline features. He noticed the way Boris carried the camera, it seemed to be quite heavy, he was using both arms.

Boris did not seem to be in any hurry to set up his camera. Markes watched him as he selected a place at the end of the bunch of photographers. There were a few members of the press between him and Boris. The majority were clustered towards the eastern end of the enclosure.

He saw Boris look up at the watchtower, and saw the glance that he exchanged with a man who held a pair of binoculars. A man with a rifle, a sharpshooter evident from the scope fitted to the rifle stood next to the man. Both were looking in the direction of the press enclosure.

The photographers in the enclosure were busy clicking away, flashes going off at regular intervals. Markes noticed that Boris was setting up the camera, looking through the viewfinder and making adjustments to a dial. He did not seem to be taking any photographs.

Markes edged his way towards Boris. He looked up at the watchtower sensing that he was being watched, He saw the man with the rifle looking down the scope, but the line of sight was not clear, there were many in the press who were taller than Markes. He was about fifteen feet away from Boris, when the crowd fell silent. Markes looked at the dais to see the President of the Ukraine stand up. The band struck up the national anthem of Ukraine. The photographers stopped whatever they were doing with the exception of Boris who continued making adjustments to his camera.

It suddenly struck Markes that the camera Boris was carrying was no camera at all. It had to be some sort of device that Boris would use. He realised with a shock what "Framed in Eternity" meant.

329

Boris saw a movement at the corner of his eye, he turned and saw Markes about ten feet away. They exchanged glances, and at that moment Boris realised that Markes was the agent who was after him.

Boris looked up frantically at Dudayev. Dudayev had seen Markes edging closer to Boris. He had seen too the look on Boris's face.

Dudayev spoke to Samsonov,' We don't have much time, take him out now.'

'I can't get a clear shot at him, there are too many of the others milling around,' Samasonov said exasperated.

'I don't care who else gets it, just take the bastard out, now.'

The Presidents were standing. The Ukraine National Anthem was coming to an end. Markes turned and glanced at the press enclosure at the other end. He saw Zonta and nodded.

Zonta bent down to twist the heel off his shoe. He saw a movement, behind him. He turned and saw the arm with a baton descending on him. He twisted away taking the force of the blow on his left shoulder and neck. His heard a crack as his collarbone broke. His shoulder and arm had gone numb. He saw the guard raise his arm again, and moved his right arm in an arc, his elbow catching the guard in his crotch. The guard's eyes opened wide, he tried to cry out, no sound emanated from his mouth. As he doubled over in agony. Zonta made his fingers rigid, his arm shot out, the blow catching the guard's throat. The guard's head jerked and he slumped forward, towards Zonta. The reporters in the press were shocked.

'Don't worry folks, he had a problem but he'll be fine in an hour or so.' Zonta said as he straightened up, his left arm hanging useless.

Some of the photographers moved their cameras away from the spot.

'He's been taken care of.' Zonta told the others. 'He went berserk, I had to knock him out,'

Zonta, bent, holding his ankle with his good arm, pretending to limp as he moved away.

The others looked bewildered. They didn't quite know what was happening. The band started playing the Russian national anthem. They turned their attention to the dais.

No one was paying him any attention, Zonta bent and twisted the heel off his shoe. He put the heel on the ground, held it with one foot and pulled at the ring pull embedded in the heel. He picked up the heel and tossed it underhand away from him, towards the far corner of the enclosure. It had taken him a less than thirty seconds. He looked around to see if anyone was interested, no one was, they were too engrossed with the dignitaries on the dais.

Markes gripped his baton and moved towards Boris. The band struck up the Russian national anthem. He waited, there was no sign of the diversion that Zonta was to create. Markes looked to the enclosure, but couldn't see anything. Zonta might be having a problem. He decided to go ahead, and moved towards Boris.

Almost instantly he heard the muffled crack and a thick black cloud of smoke billowing from the other press enclosure. The press inside scattered. The photographers in his enclosure heard the explosion, and noticing the commotion, swung their cameras around.

Markes saw Boris bend down and look through a viewfinder his finger on the camera trigger. His was the only camera pointing towards the presidential dais. Boris took no notice of the commotion in the other enclosure, he was engrossed in his task.

Markes was five feet from Boris, when he noticed a movement behind him. He turned and saw one of the security guards moving towards him.

The guard saw Markes turn around, and raised his baton. Markes knew that he had to move fast. Knew too that he would have only one chance to neutralise Boris.

Dudayev saw Markes move towards Boris. Samsonov next to him was looking through the scope on his rifle.

Markes twisted his baton to release the stiletto blade. He was five feet from Boris, who was busy looking through the viewfinder. He lunged at Boris from behind.

The guard behind Markes, left arm outstretched, lunged at Markes at the same moment, the baton in his right hand coming down in an arc. The baton missed Markes's head, caught Markes on his shoulder close to the neck, numbing his shoulder and throwing Markes off balance. Markes' blade missed Boris' back catching him at the top of the right shoulder, the blade tearing through his jacket and flesh.

Samsonov held his breath, he had Markes's head in his cross hairs, and squeezed the trigger the very instance Markes lunged at Boris. The high velocity bullet missed his head and went through the flesh between Markes' left shoulder and neck, and through the heart of a photographer who was standing to Boris's right, knocking him down like a rag doll, his life snuffed out.

Boris finger was on the camera trigger, he pressed it just as Markes's blade caught him behind the right shoulder spinning him around to the left. The camera tipped over, pivoting on one of the legs of the tripod, its lens moving in an arc as it fell. Markes felt his hair stand on end as the high intensity energy beam left the camera and passing over his head.

He saw a white flash as one of the pots in the VIP enclosure exploded. The pebbles inside turning into lethal shrapnel. The occupants in the enclosure lifted and dashed to the ground like rag dolls. Their bodies bloodied and mangled. The bulletproof glass cracked, turned opaque from the blast, then crimson as the splattered blood ran down the pane. Boris's finger was still pressing the trigger of the camera as he and the camera fell to the ground. The beam struck a smaller pot at the foot of the watchtower. The pot exploded, the force ripping apart the legs of the watchtower. The pebbles, lethal shrapnel now ripping through the platform and its occupants. Markes was flat on the ground, his face turned towards the watchtower. He saw the watchtower buckle and come down, heard the whine of the shrapnel as it passed a foot above his head and the screams of the people, as the shrapnel found its victims.

The bulletproof glass around the President's enclosure cracked but held, protecting all those inside. The bodyguards of the Presidents swarmed over their masters, protecting them. Sirens sounded as security agents brought the Presidents' cars to the dais. Their bodyguards bundled the Presidents inside. The cars sped away, with ambulances following, their klaxons wailing.

There was pandemonium with bodies and blood strewn everywhere. There were cries for help. Markes saw the crowd surge forward. Stampeding, trying to get out, not knowing where to go. Some were making for the main dais, others were making for the exits behind the VIP enclosure. He saw the crowd move towards him as they broke through the barricades. He felt a hand grab his arm, and looked up to see Zonta. He caught Zonta's arm and hauled himself up, one arm useless and bleeding. As he and Zonta ran he looked around to where Boris had fallen. He saw that Boris was standing clutching his bloodied shoulder with one arm, making towards the fallen watchtower.

Markes and Zonta ran with the crowd for some distance, making their way to the perimeter. The barricades had been knocked down by the surging crowd. They reached the clump of trees where they had spent the earlier part of the morning. The crowd had thinned out considerably. No one was taking any interest. They stopped running, and slipped into the clump of trees.

Zonta retrieved the bag that he had hidden in the bushes. He took out the first aid kit. His left arm though sore was now less numb, and functioning. His collarbone hurt like hell. He quickly swallowed a painkiller and gave one to Markes. With difficulty he bound Markes' wound as tightly as possible to stop the bleeding. They got rid of their uniforms, changed into jeans, worn out jackets and wigs, their transformation was complete. They moved out from the trees, and made for the exit.

Ambulances with medical teams had arrived at the park and had set up make shift first aid booths for treating the wounded. The doctors and nurses were efficient, those that required hospitalisation were sent away immediately in ambulances, while those with minor injuries were treated as out patients.

They knew that they would have to seek medical attention for Markes at some stage, and decided to join one of the lines treating minor injuries. The doctors examined them in turn, gave some instructions to the nurse who attended to them. Zonta's arm was bound tight against his chest to prevent movement of his collar bone, while Markes had his injuries sutured and bandaged. They were each given a shot of tetanus and a strip of pain killers.

No questions were asked.

They made their way to the rail station, picked up some sandwiches and were on the next train to Vinnycja.

Epilogue

Shortly after the assassination bid the personal physician of the President of Russia fell mysteriously ill and passed away. The autopsy report listed blood poisoning as the cause. The doctor who performed the autopsy was an Intrasyn man.

Druskayev, the politburo member in charge of health and a known hardliner who was close to Pushkin appointed Dr Ruskayev an Intrasyn man as the personal physician of the President.

The President of Russia who was quite healthy was prescribed a tonic by Dr Rskayev, who also saw to it that the tonic was administered daily. The President suffered a stroke seven weeks after Dr Ruskayev appointment.

According to senior politburo members, all Intrasyn men and his personal physician the President had signed a decree that named Zhirinovsky as his successor. The politburo members produced the President's decree to the Kremlin, which they had witnessed and signed.

The President of Russia was now a mere puppet, Zhirinovsky controlled all matters.

Markes, Zonta and Zola, made their way to England, where they met Brian. Markes and Zonta were debriefed by MI6. A special envoy was sent to the Russian President with the findings on Intrasyn and Muhu, urging him to take action. The envoy met the President of Russia and Zhirinovsky. No action was taken.

The assassination bid and the findings on Intrasyn was raised in the UN Security Council by the United States of America and Britain who wanted a world-wide ban on the organisation. Russia promptly vetoed the motion.

Yuri and Irina met at Haapsaalu after the botched bid. Pushkin and Intrasyn had no more use for them. This suited them fine, they went back to Cerkessk and were married by Father Joseph.

It was a sunny day, a couple of months later. Yuri and Irina had returned from the local clinic.

'What will we name our son?' Irina asked leaning against the pillar of the portico.

Yuri went to her, took her in his arms.

'Dimitri,' he answered.

The United States Secretary of Defence, Ronald Dumsfield met NATO allies in January 2008, and presented to them the details of Washington's plan for defence against ballistic missiles. The presentation showed footage of US anti-missiles destroying warheads in flight. NATO raised concerns that the 1972 Anti -Ballistic Missile Treaty (ABM) would be scrapped since it prohibited the introduction of a missile defence system. The US brushed aside these objections.

The United States of America shortly thereafter scrapped the START-II and the ABM treaty amidst opposition from NATO states and China.

It was the summer of 2008, Brian was scanning recent reports from Interior Furnishers, NATBAL's clandestine agency which operated out of Geneva.

'Damn,' he said to himself. He had a photograph in his hand of Pushkin, Zhirinovsky and the profile of a man, who Brian could have sworn was the ex Chinese Defence Minister.

'What the devil is this bloke doing here?' he said aloud.

The End